ENDORSEMENTS FOR *DECEIVED*

If you like to walk with characters through their struggle for survival in an ever-darkening world, you'll have the read of your lifetime.

— K.R. MATTSON, Author

Deceived was an entertaining read, and I'd recommend it to those who enjoy Christian fiction, fantasy, and allegories.

— KRISTINA HALL, Author

I've just given [*DECEIVED*] a place of honor on my favorites shelf, and Madisyn Carlin is officially an auto-buy author. I will read everything she puts out after this incredible, incredible debut!

— JOY C. WOODBURY, Reader

The worldbuilding was fantastic. As someone who has created my own imaginary world and knows how hard it is, I deeply appreciate Madisyn Carlin's work.

— KATJA LABONTÉ, Author

An amazing fantasy. Very impressive worldbuilding and good characters.

— CATHERINE T., Reader

DECEIVED

The Deception Trilogy - Book 1

DECEIVED

The Deception Trilogy - Book 1

MADISYN CARLIN

DECEIVED
The Deception Trilogy – Book One

Copyright @2022 by Madisyn Carlin

Published by Maplebrook Publishing

Cover Design by Lynette Bonner of Indie Cover Design

Proofreading by Angela R. Watts

ISBN: 978-1-957847-90-0
AISN: B09RG325FV

All rights reserved. This book or parts thereof may not be reproduced in any form, stored in any retrieval system, or transmitted in any form by any means—electronic, mechanical, photocopy, recording, or otherwise—without prior written permission of the publisher, except as provided by United States of America copyright law.

This is a work of fiction. Unless otherwise indicated, all the names, characters, businesses, places, events and incidents in this book are either the product of the author's imagination or used in a fictitious manner. Any resemblance to actual persons, living or dead, or actual events is purely coincidental.

Scripture quotations are from the ESV Bible (The Holy Bible, English Standard Version), copyright © 2001 by Crossway, a publishing ministry of Good News Publishers. Used by permission. All rights reserved.

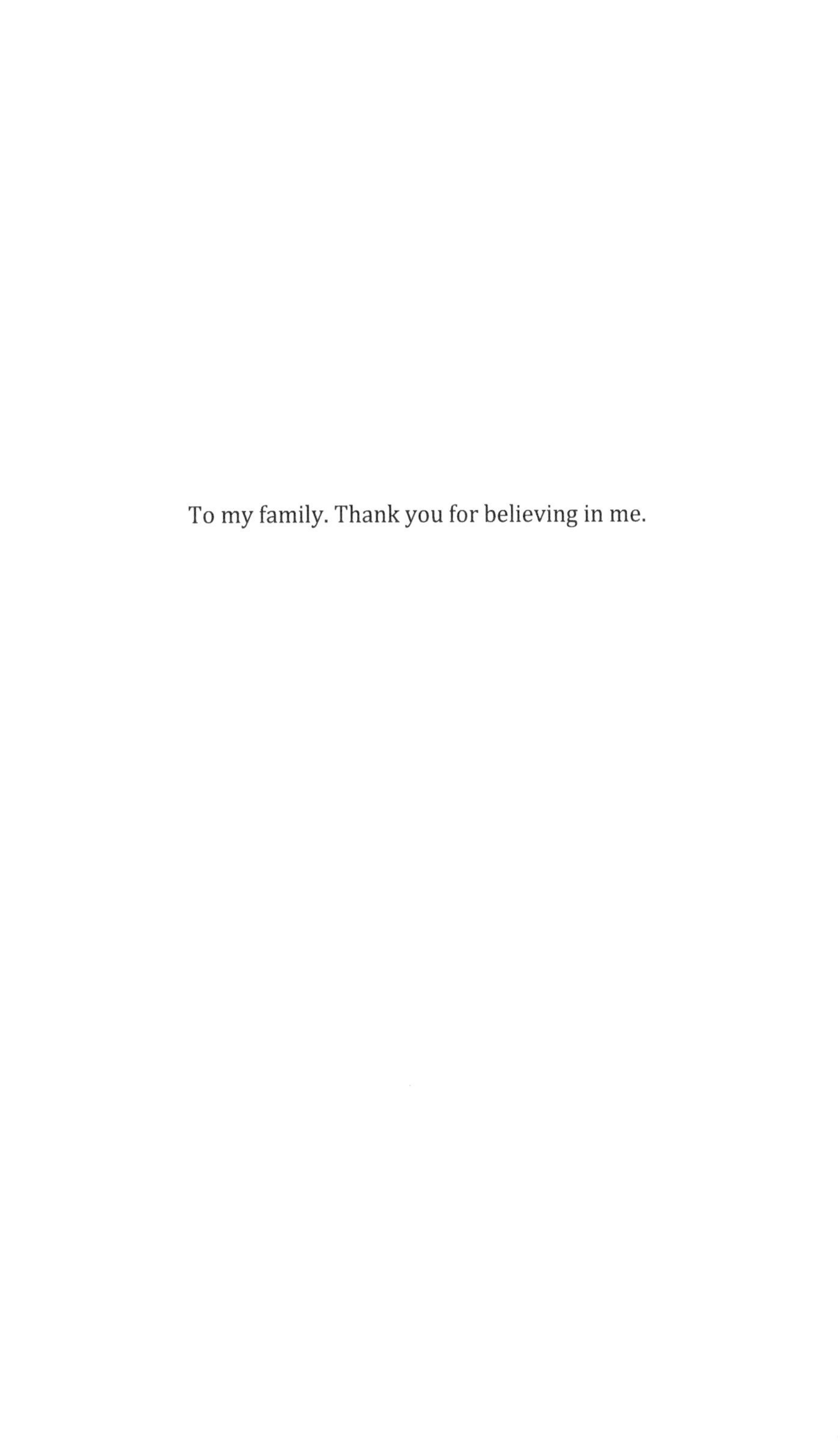

To my family. Thank you for believing in me.

The people dwelling in darkness have seen a great light, and for those dwelling in the region and shadow of death, on them a light has dawned.

Matthew 4:16

CHAPTER ONE

HOLDER

THE SMALL BODY huddling near Holder's leg shuddered as the wailing incantation rose in volume. Cold hands gripped his, fingernails digging into flesh.

If only he could tell her it was almost over.

But it wasn't. Death's sting never truly faded.

A tall figure cloaked in red separated from the mass of mourners and glided toward the two caskets glinting in the dim light. "Today we mourn the loss of two loyal and fair rulers." The voice settled over the crowd, quieting the mourners.

The silence felt unnatural. Almost otherworldly. Nothing moved and no one breathed. If this was how the land mourned Lord Frigdor and Lady Ancelle, how much more would they grieve when the king retired?

King Eligor lowered his cloak's hood and rested a hand on each casket. "Bring forward the princess."

Holder freed his hand from Princess Anastasia's clutch and placed it on her shoulder. She trembled as the crowd before them parted to create a pathway wide enough for one man.

Stars, please give her comfort. No child should have to endure this.

The deep black carpet Princess Anastasia's parents used to walk every sunrise and sunset muffled their approach. Shadow and light mingled to create a chilling combination across stone walls and pillars. Death was eerie enough without the traditional red mourning cloaks, silence, and Rex Dorcha's unsettling interior.

Holder clenched his teeth. He could no more provide adequate comfort for the grieving child than bring back her parents.

King Eligor extended a hand to the princess. If he felt the icy chill radiating from her skin, he gave no indication. With a ghost of a nod, he led Princess Anastasia to the caskets, which lay before the throne. "Would you like to see them one last time?"

"No," Princess Anastasia whispered. Her words trembled like a leaf in an autumn wind.

"Very well. Anastasia, daughter of Lord Frigdor and Lady Ancelle, joint successors of Orm, you are hereby under my protection and named as my sole heir. I promised your parents I would take you as my ward if something ever befell them. Thus I stand on my pledge."

Princess Anastasia's curtsey wobbled. Her miniature frame shook with a sob before she rushed to Holder. Arms the width of twigs encircled his waist.

"She may be taken to her room if she does not wish to witness the burial. Everyone else will travel to the graveyard and complete the funeral." King Eligor's eyes locked with Holder's before shifting over the mass of guards, soldiers, and servants. "King's guards, prepare the caskets for transport."

Holder guided the princess up the stairs. Crimson cloth wound around the railing's handrail. Just another reminder of death, of a young child left parentless.

Princess Anastasia's soft cries accompanied their footsteps. At the top, when they were hidden from prying eyes, Holder shrugged off his mourning cloak and kicked it against the wall. Such an act would be considered disrespectful, but he couldn't move in the thick, heavy garment. And the princess needed comfort. Not yet one more reminder of her loss.

He knelt to her level. Her teary gaze stung his heart. He could relate to the pain in her eyes. Could relate to the desperate hope that this was just a dream.

She sobbed into his shoulder. "I miss them."

"I know."

"Will you find the bad men who killed them?" Her sniff did little to stop the mess draining from her nose.

Holder unclasped the limp mourning cloak bunched haphazardly around her neck. "My job is to keep you safe. Someone like Rogan or Captain Geros will find the bad men."

"I don't like Captain Geros. He scares me."

"I know." Holder stood. "Come on. I think King Eligor sent Svetlana to help."

"She scares me too."

"She scares everyone."

Shoes clacked against the floor as a murky figure appeared. Graying hair pulled into a severe bun drew an already high forehead even further up Svetlana's scalp. "Come along, Princess," she snapped. Her narrowed eyes glared at Holder. "You must clear the room before I help her highness prepare for a nap."

Like a nap would help the poor girl recover.

Holder plucked the candle from Svetlana's hand and pushed the princess' bedroom door open. After clearing the room, he returned the candle and stepped into the hallway. His heart constricted as Princess Anastasia's sobs seeped through the thick stone walls. The king and Svetlana were fools if they thought the princess would cease mourning after her parents' funeral.

They were fools if they thought she'd ever fully recover.

Svetlana exited the bedroom, shutting the door behind her. She bestowed upon Holder a glare that made a kitchen knife look dull. "Stand guard. I will return in an hour to awaken the princess. She will not be mollycoddled simply because her parents passed."

Did no amount of kindness or compassion reach Svetlana's stone heart? Did she not understand Princess Anastasia would be forever changed? Would forever mourn?

"You are competent enough to know what to do, are you not?"

How could a woman whose head didn't even reach his jaw look down her nose at him? "Yes."

Svetlana sniffed. "See that you do. You are expendable if you fail in any way."

"I know what to do, Svetlana."

"How dare you, a mere guard, address me in such a manner?" Her expression curdled. "Your insolent presence is giving me a headache, and now I must abandon my duty to fetch a cure. Such incompetency is abhorrent."

Holder grit his teeth as Svetlana stalked down the stairs. He could only pray the princess hadn't heard her nurse's callous words. It was hard enough losing parents. She didn't need Svetlana's heartlessness on top of everything else.

Holder pushed a hand through his hair as he stared at the spilled barrels of water and scattered candleholders. "This is what you called me down for?"

"Yes, sir." The young private wrung his hands as his gaze darted between Holder and the mess. "I don't know who did it, sir. I was making my rounds when I saw someone run by. They knocked this over."

"You do realize I am the princess' bodyguard, right?" If King Eligor caught wind of Holder leaving his post—and he would—there would be questions to answer and possibly a punishment to endure. A royal bodyguard did not leave his ward at any time unless an emergency occurred or the king declared otherwise.

Not for the first time, he wished Princess Anastasia had her own retinue of guards like the king did. But she hadn't handled it well when an attempt was made, and the constant crying wore everyone's nerves.

"I swear, sir, this isn't a prank or me just horsing around. I promise I saw someone. I called for you because you're the highest-ranking soldier here right now."

Holder couldn't recall the youth's name, but he could recall being just as nervous when told he'd become a specialist, trained to be the princess' bodyguard. Why they chose him, he'd never know. "It's fine. Next time, call for dungeon guards. I can promise you no one purposefully goes down there."

With the lad's thanks echoing behind him, Holder darted back up the stairs. The interruption, while breaking the monotony of standing guard, settled in his stomach like a bite of undercooked bread.

"There you are." Svetlana met him near the princess' door. "Negligence," she sniffed. "Why the king chose you is beyond me. You're neither the brightest, nor strongest, nor fittest."

"Do you have a point, Sveltana?"

Svetlana's mouth twisted into an even deeper moue of displeasure. "The princess will attend the burial."

"What?"

Svetlana's pinched mouth tightened. "Princess Anastasia will attend the funeral. It is befitting she honor her parents in such a way and, if she expects to become King Eligor's successor, she must learn not to take everything to heart. It has been over an hour, enough time for the caskets to reach the cemetery. You will wake her while I fetch a pitcher of water so she can wash her face. She will not arrive looking like a blubbering commoner."

"With all respect, awakening her is your job. That would be improper on my part." Holder tensed to keep from twitching under Svetlana's harsh glare. She stared at him like she could see his deepest, darkest secret.

Sweat dampened his skin at the thought.

"You are a mere guard. You have no say in such matters." Svetlana advanced until her breath, reeking of old milk and spinach, assaulted Holder's nose. "You are not so important that King Eligor will overlook your wrongdoings, of which you have committed many just in the past two hours. By now the caskets will have reached the cemetery, and by the time the graves are dug, we will be well on our way."

Holder gripped his sword, biting back a protest. It did no good arguing with a woman who'd rather see his head on the cutting block than attached to his neck. "I'm going."

He withheld a snort as he unlocked the princess' door. Svetlana should be grateful she dealt with him and not Rogan. She'd receive a blistering response if she'd spouted such things to the prickly guard.

Holder rapped on the door. "Princess, I'm coming in."

The hair on his arms and back of his neck prickled as he opened the door. Something felt...off. Instead of candle wax and warm brick, a musky, coppery scent touched the cool, still air.

He drew his short sword and stepped inside. One of Rogan's favorite curses jumped to his tongue. The princess curled beneath her coverlet, snoring softly and unaware of the knife plunged into the other pillow gracing her bed.

His stomach turned as he drew a dagger and advanced. Blood dripped down the nearest wall from a spray arcing across at least half the wall's length. Small puddles formed on the floor.

Svetlana's acerbic voice cut the air. "Whatever is wrong now?"

"Stay in the hall."

Mentally cursing himself for leaving his station, Holder searched the armoire, beneath the bed, and behind the curtains and other pieces of furniture. How could this happen? He'd left for only a minute. Had the accident been a ruse? His dagger had been in the lock, just as he left it, and no one could escape through the window.

His stomach curdled as he snatched the knife from the pillow and picked up the letter. It sagged, soaked with blood, but the message, the crisp handwriting slanting and sharp, sent more than chills up his spine.

As the hairs on his arms again rose, Holder once more scanned the room. No sign of forced entry marred the door or furniture. No scuffs blemished the floor. No footprints besides his and Svetlana's marked the rug.

Stars, what do I do?

He placed the letter and knife atop the armoire before waking Princess Anastasia. She stirred, blinking at him with crossed eyes. "You need to get up, Princess."

When she slid from her bed, he snatched a cloak from the armoire and wrapped it around her before ushering her out.

Svetlana squawked. The door shut and he jammed it with a dagger so no one could disturb the evidence. Not like the dagger stopped the intruder the first time, but maybe it'd be a deterrent to anyone else contemplating entering the room. "Come with me."

"Holder?" Princess Anastasia grabbed his hand.

"Princess, I need you to obey everything I say, understand?"

"Like what King Eligor told me to do?"

"Exactly." Holder pulled her along. Manners could wait. Assassins cared not if he followed the rules and let the princess precede him. Now was not the time for something like this to happen.

The great hall was empty, void of the multiple persons who gathered a few hours before. Holder held his sword out as he hauled the princess across the floor. Curse whoever left the lanterns lit. While their light provided him the ability to see his surroundings, they also increased Anastasia's chance of becoming a target.

His heart rate doubled in speed as the doors lining the right wall neared. Which would be safest? The mini armory containing weapons only for show? The storage room with blankets and linens? Or the other storage room with ink and writing supplies and seasonal tapestries?

He spun as something clattered behind him, whipping Princess Anastasia between his back and the wall.

Svetlana stared at him, lips pursed and eyebrows almost meeting her hairline. Long, bony fingers tapped as she tilted her head at the bronze candle holder rolling near her feet. Remnants of candle splattered the floor.

Jumpy. That's what he was. Just as jumpy as a nervous cat. Was he overreacting?

No, whoever wrote the message was serious.

"In," he hissed as he opened the armory door. "If anyone besides myself comes to get you, don't open the door and don't let them know you're in there. I'll be back as soon as I can."

Princess Anastasia whimpered and latched onto his elbow, just above his vambrace. "I'm scared."

"I know. But you need to trust me." *Stars, guide me.* After doing a quick search, he ushered them in and locked the door, Svetlana's crusty glower finally cut from view.

Breathe. He needed to breathe and assess the situation. The culprit could be hiding behind one of the twenty pillars, or behind the thrones, or in one of the other closets. The culprit could have easily seen him hide the princess.

Praying the door would remain locked, he drew his third dagger and skirted the room's right edge. A scuffle of leather upon stone sent him spinning, weapons ready.

No one. Nothing.

Pulse pounding, Holder inched for the front door. Only shadows moved, but shadows could easily disguise an arrow aimed for his heart or throat.

Another of Rogan's favored expletives rose to mind. Where were those guards when he needed them? If only that spill had happened ten minutes later.

He huffed. If the spill hadn't happened, he'd have caught the intruder. Stopped this blasted thing before it occurred.

He fumbled the handle and stumbled into chilly air. Soft snowflakes stung his exposed skin. Each panted breath rose in misty clouds that dissipated in the wind.

"Bodyguard Lygor?" A thin woman with poofy hair snapped to attention. The seven other guards clustering around did the same.

"I want five of you inside. Secure the great room. Let no one in, not even the maids. The other two I want out here. One of you stay at the front door. The other, check the west entrance. Bar the door if it's not already."

"We're to stay in pairs."

"You're to do as I say unless you want the king's wrath upon your heads."

Holder bolted for the stable after the lazy kids scattered to obey. Set upon the higher ridge, his calves burned at the climb. Training hadn't included what to do for threats written in blood. Training hadn't included what to do if a threat occurred and every quality soldier and king's guard was away.

Heart hammering, he shoved the stable door open. More adrenaline coursed through him like fire, bringing with it memories. No matter how many times he entered, he always looked for Father and the old, swayback mare he'd learned to ride on.

But Father had disappeared and the swayback was long dead.

"We're outta horses. Stable master Slowman at your service." A thick, squatty man ambled into the room. "Oh. What're you doing here again? And at this time? Aren't you to be guarding the princess?"

"Is the roan still here?"

"Of course he's still here. No one dares ride the beast except you."

"Where is he?"

Slowman sighed. "Right through that door to your right. But he cain't be safely ridden yet, mark me words. You'll get thrown and bust a bone, I'll reckon. All that trainin' you're trying with him isn't doing a lick 'o good. What're you doing here anyway? You're actin' shifty."

Holder ignored the man's chatter and cracked the door open. The scent of horse sweat and fresh hay threatened to draw him into the past. He shook the pull away and assessed the seven horses shifting in wide stalls.

"They're half wild. More than happy to bite a chunk out of your arm. That pinto broke me best trainer's wrist and the three mares have taken more bites out o' us than I can count. Still, they'd be better than that red devil."

Holder slipped around Slowman into the tack room and snatched a soft, worn leather bridle from a peg. The horses snorted, some stomping and others arching their necks over the stall doors to nip at him.

He swatted them away and dodged and ducked until he and the last stall's occupant stared at each other.

"I still say you're bein' a fool. That one's the fastest an' deadliest. Fly off his back and hit anything hard, you'll be dead."

"I know, Slowman. I've trained him."

No one else wanted to go near the beast. The only reason he was allowed was because he'd managed to mount the horse when no one else could. The temperamental equine became his responsibility to train.

Holder let the gelding whuffle the back of his hand. "You'll behave today, won't you?"

The horse snorted and nodded, nostrils flaring. Its eyes dared Holder to bring the bridle closer.

"Behave." Holder scratched under the gelding's mane, giving it a warning look when a glint sparked in its eyes. The horse was built for speed, but he hadn't tested its endurance. Would it make it to the cemetery and back?

The horse huffed.

"Slowman, would you open the stable doors?"

"You aren't thinking about riding him, are you? That's a death wish, mark me words. No matter how much training you've put that accursed monster through, he'll never be tame."

"Not thinking about it."

The man's sigh gusted from his rotund body.

"I've already made my decision. What I need you to do is open those doors then lock this place up after I leave. Go to the castle and help guard the front door."

"What's going—"

Holder swallowed a snapping retort. He wouldn't gain cooperation by being rude. "Slowman, please. I don't have time to explain." He slipped the bridle on. The gelding pulled back and tossed its head. Ears flattened as teeth bared.

"None of that." Holder tugged the reins and opened the stall door. He didn't have time for a cranky, stubborn horse. With as long as this was taking, it'd be faster if he ran to the cemetery.

The roan twitched and snorted.

Slowman squawked and scurried away. A minute later, he hollered that the doors were open.

"King Eligor would have me neck if he lost his ward's bodyguard from a riding accident."

"Don't know why, seeing as it's my decision and not yours." Holder gathered the reins and threaded his fingers through the gelding's mane to pull himself up. He commanded the roan to a trot. The horse usually either left the stable at a full gallop or refused to leave at all. At least the cantankerous animal wasn't throwing a fit. Yet.

Slowman stayed well out of the way as Holder rode through the doorway. If the man said anything else, the wind whipped away his words.

Holder spared a glance at the castle. Never had he anticipated anyone harming the princess. The king wasn't someone most wanted as an enemy.

The gelding shifted and tugged at the reins.

"Behave."

No time to prepare the horse for a gallop. At his command, the gelding lunged into a ground-eating lope. Cold wind whipped the air from his lungs as iron-shod hooves clattered against stone and dirt.

Holder lost count of time as he rode. It'd be a miracle if his skin ever unthawed, and he could only pray the stars felt mercy toward the princess and concealed her hiding spot from any lingering threat.

As the gelding neared the last stretch of the plain between Rex Dorcha and the cemetery, Holder shifted his weight and tried to speak over the wind's push. Every second counted. "Let's see how fast you are."

CHAPTER TWO

THERESE

MORE DEATH. IT was never-ending. Unstoppable.

Therese rubbed her frozen fingers as wind cut through her cloak. If only there was a way to cease death. A way to keep loved ones from dying.

But then, she wouldn't have a job.

"Poor little princess," Jolie murmured as a mix of scarlet and blue cloaks covered the far-off path between Rex Dorcha and the cemetery. "To have her parents stripped from her at such a young age and in such a manner."

Oh, the irony. Therese eyed her friend. "It happens to more children than you think."

"I know. Unfortunate, but 'tis the way of the world." Jolie gripped Therese's shoulder. "Smile, sweetie. Their deaths don't change our lives."

Perhaps not, but it altered the life of an innocent little girl.

"Lucian should be back soon. Maybe after Scholl drills him about his mission we can discuss making you a permanent part of the team. Business has spiked this past month and people are jittery with King's Day approaching. Amazing how many turn on friends and family when they think they're in danger."

Therese stared at the line of soldiers and guards decked in the traditional mourning color before tensing as the wind carried a faint patter of hooves on earth. "Lucian is here."

Jolie's laugh pitched high as a familiar gray mare trotted into view. "Thank the stars." She jumped to her feet and almost ran to the approaching rider. When would she learn everyone knew of her feelings for Lucian? Not that she did the best concealing them, and not like Lucian didn't already know.

Lucian dismounted and caught Jolie in a hug. They shared a whisper and laugh before returning to the porch.

"Therese Westa, you're a sight for sore eyes. How'd your mission go? How are your sisters? Oh...here." Lucian dug through a saddlebag and tossed her a parcel. "Figured they'd like these. A farmhand's wife makes them. They reminded me of the younger Westas."

Therese peeled back the cloth wrapper. Two pairs of navy mittens embroidered with tiny white goats rested inside. Her breath snagged and her eyes stung. One less thing she had to buy with limited funds. "Lucian..."

"Got them after I rescued a kid—a goat kid—from a coyote. Lady was so grateful she asked me how old my children are. Since I don't have any, I thought of your sisters."

Fighting back the lump in her throat, Therese blinked away the threatening tears and moved her hands under her cloak so Jolie and Lucian couldn't see them trembling. When was the last time something like this happened? "Thank you. They'll love these."

"That was so sweet of you." Jolie grinned as red tinged Lucian's ears. "How was your mission?"

"I never want to see another goat again." He swiped animal hair from the front of his tunic. Drying flakes of a reddish-brown substance smeared across his hands.

Therese's stomach turned. *Blood.*

Jolie poked him. "Messy, much?"

"Hey. This isn't exactly a clean job."

"Can be if you take a distance shot."

"Nah." Lucian patted the knife at his hip. "I prefer up close and personal. That way I can make sure I've completed the mission."

Therese slipped away. The lovebirds could flirt all they wanted, but if she heard any more of Lucian's mission, she'd lose her last meal and then some.

She took the mare's reins and led her to the wooden building off to the house's left. Warmth and the scent of horses soothed the edge in her spirit. Wind whistled through the thatched roof and wooden walls, a welcome call to any who entered.

Therese stroked the mare's nose. "Happy to be home? You're lucky to not have to worry about anything."

Hay crunched underfoot as she tethered the mare to the rail running the right wall's length. The two other horses ambled forward and greeted their friend.

Therese removed the tack and set it on the empty sawhorse in the narrow corner boxed off from the horses' reach. The smallest saddle still bore chew marks from when the curious animals were allowed free reign of the stable.

The mare nickered as Therese poured fresh water into the trough and grabbed a rag and pick from the cupboard hanging near the doorway. If only life could be as calm and sure as caring for horses was.

"Hey."

She jumped at the voice.

Lucian leaned against the wall, arms crossed and blond hair ruffled. A slight grin lifted the corner of his lip. "Jolie told me you did well."

Too well. After the extensive training Jolie put her through, it'd been all too easy posing as a waitress and slipping hemlock into the targets' ale. Just as it'd been all too easy posing as a maid and serving the target tea laced with autumn crocus.

She squirmed as Lucian's gaze turned penetrating. "It's already costing you, isn't it?"

"Cost doesn't matter." She switched sides and felt the mare's leg. If horses weren't so scarce, she'd take a job caring for or even training them. But everything good was in short supply.

"Jolie tells me you want to become part of the team. You know what that means. No more simple jobs. A client might request you use a blade to dispose of a target, and you'll not have the ability to refuse. Not unless you want Scholl's wrath."

"I need a real job, Lucian." Four bits a week were not enough to support a family.

Lucian winced. "I know. I just don't want to see you become jaded. You're so young. Scholl might agree since business has increased. People are on edge since the lord's and lady's deaths. Couple that with the general mistrust and skirmishes constantly going on, and I think we could find you something. But you know Scholl is hesitant."

"Why? I thought my landing a few real missions would bring him more money." And help eliminate the overwhelming debt her parents accrued. Death claimed them before they could pay it off, leaving their twenty-year-old daughter to face the burden.

"Physically, you are more than capable. Mentally and emotionally? Stars above, I've seen grown men with pasts darker than those in Rex Dorcha's dungeons unable to carry out jobs like what you're asking for."

Weight grew in Therese's chest as she cleaned the supplies and put them away. It wasn't like she could leave, find a better job. No, Scholl made it clear the debt must be paid within two years. And the only jobs paying enough to accomplish that were being an assassin or a prostitute.

Difficult as it was taking lives, at least the job only required her conscience and not her body and soul.

Lucian's hand weighed like a brick on her shoulder. "You'll make it eventually, Therese. Something this job requires is patience. You think I wanted to spend two months caring for smelly, stinky goats and pigs?"

"The hair suits you well."

He scoffed. "You'd lose such optimism if you had to muck out stalls and slop noisy animals that look better in a frying pan. My point is, every job requires something you won't want to do. Be patient and you'll get what you want. Act with haste and you'll ruin your shot."

Patience did not always get one where they needed to be. What if, due to Scholl's hesitation, she missed the two-year mark to pay the debt? She still had a year to go, and she'd never make it with her current pay.

"Go inside and get something to eat. I'll finish up here." Lucian grimaced as he eyed the horses. "Looks like the straw needs mucking."

Therese drew up her hood and stepped outside. The wind exterminated the stable's warmth. She hunched as her stomach churned with guilt. Only one of three in her family would be adequately fed that day if she couldn't squirrel away some leftovers, and only one of three would survive the winter if things didn't change for the better.

She shivered. No matter what it took, she had to secure a true spot on the team.

Stars, please. For my sisters' sakes.

Scholl's coal black eyes met hers as she stepped inside. His graying beard protruded from an angular face, complete with an out-jutting brow and cheekbones. Clothes as dark as his eyes and skin covered a thin body.

"You want a spot."

Not want, *need.* "Yes."

"Do you think you are ready?"

"Yes."

"Do you think you are capable?"

"Yes."

He scrutinized her with eyes as cold as ice. "You've done a decent job so far, but you're behind on payments."

How? Scholl took over three quarters of her pay.

Therese released a breath that did little to ease the pressure in her lungs. She must be strong for her sisters. "I have successfully completed my missions. The clients have not complained."

"Those were easy." Scholl tapped his fingers on his elbow. "Being on the team means you have your own client with no supervision. Do you think you are prepared for that?"

If she didn't pay off the debt, her sisters would become indentured servants at best or executed at worst. Those in charge made it clear they wanted no more "infestations" of orphans and homeless children. She wasn't blind. She knew of the times when innocent little lives had been exterminated for the sake of clearing the streets.

"Yes, I do." She had to do this. She *must* do this.

Her sisters' survival depended on it.

CHAPTER THREE

ROGAN

FUNERALS HAD AN odd way of happening on the worst days.

Rogan fisted his hands. The thin leather gloves did little to deter the wind's bite and his fingers were almost numb. Thank the stars this was a private funeral. If someone or something attacked, he'd be incapable of drawing his sword.

He snapped his attention back to the fresh mounds of earth rising above frost-laced grass. King Eligor stood between the graves, hands upheld and voice joining in the mourning chant. Three down, four to go.

A cold gaze caught Rogan's. Eyes narrowed in silent warning.

Even if he stood still as a statue, Father would find something wrong. Chances were he already had.

Rogan reset his stance, his left upper arm tingling with the remembrance of painful grips and harsh words. He stared at the line of guards opposite him. Their faces matched their scarlet cloaks and most wore expressions of icy fury, like they wanted to depart without consent and find the royal couple's murderers.

He stiffened as a red roan burst into view, rider crouched low over its neck. Framed by towering trees

20

stripped bare and the dull brown of winter, the horse resembled a spark from an errant fire.

"Cetrin," Captain Geros snapped. The inflecting chants muffled his voice. "See what's wrong."

Rogan slipped from his spot and skirted the impeccable outer row of soldiers gathered before the gravesites. He fingered a dagger strapped to his chest. If there wasn't a good explanation, he wasn't getting blamed for stupid incompetence. Everyone in Orm knew not to interrupt a royal anything, much less a funeral when the chants were still being intoned.

"By the stars, what are you doing?" he hissed.

Holder stalked toward Rogan. Wind-blown hair plastered to his forehead, and the tattoo on his cheek of a serpent surrounded by a circle twitched as his fingers clenched and released. "The princess has been threatened."

"Where? How?"

"Her room." Holder waved a hand in Rex Dorcha's direction. "Look, interrogate me on the ride there. I need you *now*, and I think whoever did it still lurks around the castle."

"Where is the princess?"

"Locked in the mini armory attached to the main hall."

Not the best location in the castle, but it'd do for an impromptu hiding place. "How bad is the situation?"

"Bad enough that I need backup."

"The horses are tethered to the trees in the copse across the path. Grab mine. I'll report the situation." Rogan about-faced. Sparks of adrenaline coursed through his blood, warming his muscles and preparing every instinct beaten into him.

He'd need a shield. A spear wouldn't hurt either. A short sword could only prod so far and still be within easy reach of a longsword, or even a broadsword or claymore.

"Report." Captain Geros met him at the edge. The man's steely demeanor hardened even more as Rogan relayed the news.

"Juan will lend you his shield. Ride ahead with Bodyguard Lygor and assess the situation. Proceed to the scene of the threat and establish control. The second king's guard and I will meet you there."

Holder met Rogan with his horse, Juan's shield already attached. The horses shifted as they mounted before breaking into a ground-eating trot.

Rogan leaned into the wind. It bit through his clothes and, if a threat really was loose in Rex Dorcha, he needed to be as limber as possible. "Tell me what happened."

"I was awakening the princess from her nap and doing a check of her room." Holder raised his voice over the drumming of hooves. "There was a note pinned to her pillow. It was coated in blood."

"What did it say?"

"That Princess Anastasia is next."

"That is the precise wording?"

"'*You're next*' is exactly what it said. Stars above, Rogan. Does it matter? We need to track down whoever did this, not inspect the grammar."

"I wouldn't ask it if it didn't matter." Rogan ran a hand over his four daggers. Each one represented a test, an accomplishment. Perhaps soon he would wear the fifth dagger, the one hardest to obtain; perhaps soon he would bear the coveted title of *captain*. Then he could show his parents he was worth more than they believed.

He shook the thoughts aside. Now was not the time to dwell on the future. He needed to plan, to strategize. His sword would be beneficial for close combat, but with no bow and quiver, he'd have to throw a dagger if the traitor tried anything from a distance.

Rogan scanned what he could see of the castle's exterior. Father's rough voice blasted through his mind in reproach. There would be nothing to see and, even if there was, what could Rogan do from such a distance?

Rex Dorcha loomed over the valley. Carved from the very ridge it sat on, the castle looked like its ruler. Impenetrable, invincible. A black flag waved, making the red serpent on it ripple. A warning. A threat.

"The front doors are locked. I exited through the side door attached to the main hall."

"And did you think to lock the side door so the intruder couldn't escape?"

Holder didn't answer.

Rogan sighed. Locking the princess in a mini armory was understandable. So was interrupting the funeral for the king's successors. But forgetting to lock the door to trap the intruder? Did Holder even think?

The red roan surged ahead of Blackie as Holder reined it up the slope leading to the stable.

The stable master waddled out. "You're back alive and in one piece. How'd you do it? That beast is a monster."

Rogan didn't want to know. If he tried keeping count of every one of Holder's harebrained ideas, he'd have time for nothing else.

He dismounted and handed the reins over. Energy surged through him at the prospect of catching a criminal, but it would be at least another fifteen minutes before Captain Geros and the second king's guard arrived. What would happen in that time?

Rogan looped his left arm through the shield and inched inside as he nudged the side door. It whispered open, revealing the same gloomy atmosphere from the first part of the funeral. Lanterns still hung from their hooks inset high on the pillars and ledges, swathing the room in ever-shifting shadows. The intruder could be hiding anywhere. Behind the pillars, along the room's edge, or even next to or beside the staircase.

He kept his steps light and soundless. Any scuff could expose their tenuous position.

If they weren't already targets.

Holder nudged his arm and pointed to the stairs.

Rogan nodded and led the advance. A quick sweep of each stone slab revealed no leather scuffs or candle wax droplets. Either the intruder had been in no hurry or he wore cloth shoes.

Holder pried away the dagger jamming the princess' door shut and entered, weapons ready.

Rogan shouldered ahead of him. Juan's shield was standard circle and size, but he would live if shot in the leg. A hit to the torso or neck was a death sentence.

A search under the bed and in the armoire revealed nothing and no one. "Where is the threat?"

Holder grunted as he double-checked under the bed. "On top of the armoire. And there is blood sprayed across the wall."

"I don't see anything."

"What? This isn't funny, Rogan."

"I'm not being *funny*. I. Don't. See. Anything."

Holder felt on top of the armoire before looking past Rogan. His shoulders slacked and his eyes rounded. "It's all gone."

Rogan rubbed his forehead. The funeral chants had set a dull pounding in the back of his skull. Holder's antics brought it to the forefront. "What do you mean?"

"They were here. I saw them." Holder's eyes narrowed. "Just before I left to get you, I heard someone slinking around. It would make sense if they snuck up here and cleaned up the mess."

Stars above. Rogan rolled his shoulders as the headache worsened. "Was it even real in the first place? Think about it, Holder. It was dark, there were shadows. You could have imagined it."

"Like I would put my job in jeopardy."

"Which is exactly what you've done. Something like this could get you stripped from your rank." Rogan unhooked the shield. "Go release the princess. I'll find Captain Geros and try to keep you from losing your position."

"Rogan—"

"I know you don't make things up, Holder, but I do know people can hallucinate due to strain or fatigue. Hopefully that's the conclusion Captain Geros and the king will draw as well." Rogan left the room gritting his teeth. The fuss wasn't his doing, but that would matter little once he arrived home. Then there would be some reason it was his fault.

Holder was smart and he did his job well—most of the time. Rogan refused to take even a sliver of blame for the fiasco. Too much rested on his success. Defending Holder in any way could ruin everything he strove for.

He fingered the dagger at his right hip. Of the eighteen king's guards, why must he be the one drawn into chaos?

Rogan paced the length of the hallway until the clamor of armor, shouts, and swords being drawn echoed through the hall. He met Captain Geros and the second king's guard halfway down the stairs. His stomach churned as he explained the situation. At least Father was stationed elsewhere. That was one tongue-lashing avoided until later.

Captain Geros cursed. The captain's insignia on his cheek convulsed. "Have Bodyguard Lygor ensure she is safely in bed before reporting to me in the staff room."

"Yes, sir." Rogan saluted and waited at the bottom of the stairs until Holder joined him. The bodyguard's face lacked color, but his hazel eyes held steely will. Whatever was about to go down, Holder would fight until the end.

Something that would either save or destroy him.

"I didn't imagine it, Rogan."

"Whether you imagined it or not, Captain Geros orders you to meet him after Princess Anastasia is in bed."

Holder muttered as he unlocked the mini armory door. Princess Anastasia and the pinched-faced nurse staggered out. The scent of metal and copper wafted from them like onions and garlic clung to the cooks.

"Here to release us permanently, I hope," Svetlana snapped. She patted at her hair and straightened her rumpled apron. "I heard what was said beyond that dastardly room's door. I hope you are immediately removed from your position and we get a new and more competent bodyguard. The princess deserves only the best."

Holder glowered at Svetlana before eyeing the princess. "Are you okay?"

She nodded before flinging her arms around Holder's waist. "That was scarier than the mourning chants."

Rogan removed himself from the scene. Holder was a good bodyguard, but he forgot one of the top rules: his job was to protect, not form a relationship.

His throat tightened as he reported the end of his shift and walked home. He faltered as he neared the cabin. Did he really want to face what awaited him?

Don't be a coward, Cetrin. It'll be no worse than usual.

Dark silence greeted him as he entered, closing the door as quickly as he could. A few enraged kicks could destroy it, but for a few minutes, it offered protection.

He exhaled as the mourning cloak dropped from his shoulders, freeing them of a burden replaced all too soon as the door opened.

"Where is your mother?"

"I don't know." Rogan hung up the cloak and unbuckled the leather belt diagonally crossing his chest. The muscles in his lower back tensed as he inched away from the looming figure. Why wouldn't King Eligor make an exception and let him live in the barracks? Anything was better than living in the Cetrin cabin.

Curse that "families lodge together" rule.

"Captain Geros told me what happened." Father's slight accent grated Rogan's ears. "You handled that inappropriately."

"I handled it according to my training."

"Geros trained you incorrectly," Father growled. The cabin's murky light masked his eyes, but not the growing fury in his voice. "How many times must I tell you? You go by what I say, not the rubbish he's filled your mind with."

Rogan backed away until the loft's ladder bumped his shoulder. His skin tingled as he rubbed his forearm. Would Father mete out another set of bruises? "I have explicitly been instructed to only incorporate Captain Geros' training." A captain's words were law. A first lieutenant's weren't.

"Want to say that again?" Father's voice coiled like a rattlesnake preparing to strike.

The ice coating Rogan's fingers moved to his throat. How often had he paid for speaking his thoughts aloud? "I'm on duty tomorrow," he warned.

In the past, that threat did little good. Father certainly cared not if others saw his handiwork. Handiwork he was all too pleased to give.

"Good. It will keep your stupidity away from me for a few hours." Father flexed his fingers.

"What are you doing here? Today is the first guard's turn for overnight protection." Rogan gripped the ladder. Rules kept him from using the crown-given weapons against another in the king's service, but a royal hadn't issued him the wooden training sword waiting in the loft above.

Mother shuffled into the cabin, candle in hand. "Maximo?"

Father's teeth bared. "I'm going back to the castle. Don't expect me home until tomorrow." He spun and strode away. The door banged shut behind him.

Mother's thin shoulders drooped, but her expression held a warning. "Go change, Rogan. You smell like that awful incense they burn at funerals. And not a word about whatever just happened. What matters is there will be no questions tomorrow. Now go."

Rogan's arms shook as he climbed the ladder. The small loft marked as his room provided the only barrier between himself and Mother's gaze, but it did nothing to quell the sudden and unwanted internal storm.

He removed the rest of his weapons and hung them up. His skin prickled with cold. Father's time as an overnight king's guard never improved his mood.

Holder once told him he was lucky to still have his parents.

Yeah. Real lucky.

CHAPTER FOUR

"BY THE STARS! Are you trying to kill me?" Alvin writhed beneath Ivelle's grip as Claudine stitched the gash spanning from his knee to his ankle. "Hand me the whiskey, woman."

"And have you be a drunken fool by the time I'm finished? No. And stars, be quiet. You'll alert all of Varway to your stupidity. Hold him still, darling."

"Rather be a drunken fool than one in pain," Alvin muttered. He hissed his most colorful curse yet as Ivelle pressed on his wrists.

Claudine rethreaded her needle. "It is not my fault you played a clumsy buffoon and almost got caught."

"Woman, it was for you!"

"Me?" Claudine inserted the needle. "I was not the one who told you to go raid the old castle ruins. I was not the one who told you to be spotted by soldiers, work yourself into a frenzy, and step in an old bear trap. Use what little of your mind you have left, Alvin."

Alvin howled as she continued to stitch. "What I meant was I was looking for items for your little store."

"It is an emporium."

"The only difference is a fancy name."

"Ivelle, tie his wrists down. If he is not man enough to stay still, we shall have to secure him to the operating table. I am going to fetch some salve."

Ivelle met Alvin's stare, his eyes wide with panic. "Would you prefer rope or cloth?"

"You're nothing more than a younger version of Claudine."

Rope it was. Ivelle opened the tallest cabinet along the left wall and withdrew a coil of thin hemp rope. She could have retrieved the salve, seeing how she made it two days ago and knew where it was, but Claudine was up to something, and far be it from Ivelle to interrupt the woman's fun.

Alvin stayed still as she tied down his arms and torso. His legs were already secured to the thick wooden table, ensuring the vocal patient went nowhere.

"Ivelle?"

"Yes?" She'd heard of a thing called puppy dog eyes when people, youngsters especially, wanted their own way. Alvin's attempt made him look like a crazed raccoon.

"Could I have a small cup of whiskey?"

"No."

Alvin whined. "Why?"

"Because you smell bad enough without stinking like that nasty brew." She gestured at his sweat-stained shirt and smudged pants. "Besides, it addles your brain and is bad for you."

"You're a healer, aren't you? Isn't that what Claudine is training you for?"

If only learning to heal could lessen the scars and pain inflicted so long ago.

Ivelle forced aside the thought as Alvin continued muttering and cursing. "Yes, which is why you get no whiskey."

The operating room reeked of Alvin's body odor, blood, and the alcohol Claudine used to clean the wound. Cupboards hung from wooden walls lined with lower cabinets. Thin, old bearskins stretched across the floor, nailed in place to keep passers-through from tripping.

An odd place, Claudine's, but it was home nonetheless.

Claudine bustled through the doorway. Her bright yellow dress clashed with the room's orange curtains, just as the devious grin revealing perfect teeth clashed with Alvin's sudden frenzy of fresh begging.

"Hush, you old goat. This won't hurt a bit."

"That's what you said about cleanin' and stitchin' my leg. That hurt." Alvin ended with a curse as Claudine swatted the top of his head.

"Language. Tender ears are present."

Ivelle bit back a grin and turned away. She trailed her fingers along wooden jars capped with soft flannel. The gibberish scrawled on the labels saved their necks many a time when soldiers came to visit, poking their noses around and sniffing for illegal activities.

Like they could find anything better than a blind and deaf hound with a broken nose.

And a good thing they can't, too. She tugged her sleeves over the thick, raised scars. Derision for the murderers who claimed to protect Orm's people swelled as commotion sounded beyond the wall.

"Ivelle, please see who that is. And keep them away from here."

"Yes, ma'am." Ivelle settled the cloth that served as a door and held her breath as she crept into the main room. The worry eased from her lungs. "What are you doing?"

A mustache streaked with gray lifted in what Ivelle knew was a smile, but what others saw as a sneer. "I need your help."

"Borros?" Claudine's voice carried from the operation room. "What trouble have you gotten yourself into this time?"

"Nothing to concern yourself with, Claudine." Borros parted his coat to reveal a red cloth belt.

Safe. Ivelle sighed. "I'll tell Claudine."

"I'll do that. Go change into something you can dirty."

Borros was munching on a biscuit while leaning against Claudine's counter when Ivelle emerged in pants and a long-sleeved shirt. Her thick boots clunked as she stumbled over cracks in the floor. How did the soldiers walk so quietly? Or was that another way they were taught to catch innocent lives off guard?

A haywire eyebrow lifted. "Let's be off. I promised to have you back in three hours."

Three hours? Just what did Borros have planned?

Ivelle kept quiet as Varway's commotion faded to the sounds of hooves against dirt and rustling leaves and branches. She closed her eyes. Claudine mentioned something called peace once, though she had no solid explanation for how to find it. Just that it was the deepest type of calm.

Perhaps this feeling when in the woods was peace.

"We're here," Borros said after a lengthy silence.

Ivelle forced her eyes open. The calm her heart longed for vanished. Tall trees towered over them. Thick trunks spoke of the forest's age. "Where are we?"

"Near one of Argbil Forest's abandoned areas." Borros dismounted and tethered his horse to a tree. "Come."

Ivelle followed. Her legs ached from the ride. How long had it been since she last rode?

She willed her complaining muscles to cease complaining and followed Borros through a maze of trees. Pine needles crunched under their feet.

"There."

Ivelle followed his thick finger. The remains of an old cabin slouched in the middle of a clearing. Her mouth dried as her chest tightened. This wasn't her former home, but it looked very much like it. She forced the memories away. This was neither the time nor place to remember. That was behind her. No use dwelling on the past.

Borros untethered the packages attached to the packhorse. "Grab the shovel, would you?"

Ivelle fetched the tool. "What happened here? That cabin looks ready to collapse."

"Probably is. This was the first base for our work. Claudine's grandfather built it when he was around your age. It was the base of operations until we had to flee when one of our scouts saw soldiers approaching."

"It has secret areas, then?"

"A few." Borros kept silent until a sizeable hole was dug. He peered over his shoulder, scanning the area. "Hand me the crates, please."

Soon, crates, boxes, and waterproofed bags filled the hole. Ivelle pressed a hand to her stomach as Borros again peered around. She shouldn't be nervous. This was simple protocol. Borros did this at least once a month, provided the ground wasn't frozen or buried beneath feet of snow. At his directive, she brought him the remaining bundles. "What's in these?"

Borros answered with a whisper. "Open the top box."

Ivelle unwrapped the tarpaulin to find metal boxes as long as her arm and twice as wide. She flicked the clasps open. Daggers with coiled serpents for hilts and slightly wavy blades glittered against black velvet cloth. "What are they?"

"Eligor blades. Legend has it King Eligor fashioned the first of them when forced to protect the people. That's why they're named after him. You have heard of them, yes?"

"Yes," she breathed. "They are deadly. They must not be very old."

"They age like their creator."

Ivelle traced a hilt. It felt cold and smooth against her fingertip. "There is no way these can be over fifty years old, much less made centuries ago."

"Believe it. The legend goes on to say he fashioned these blades to never lose their sharpness. They are not normal blades, just as he is not a normal human. How else would they remain in perfect condition and be so deadly?"

"Excellent upkeep? I don't know." Ivelle jerked her attention to the trees as a murder of crows burst from the treetops.

Borros cursed. "Hand me the boxes. We've been here too long."

Ivelle helped fill the hole with dirt and scatter pine needles over the area. Hopefully the storm clouds gathering above the horizon would bring snow. "What are you saving them for? And why did you need me for this?"

"What we save everything else for. The market. I brought you because you never know what can happen. Something may occur when you need a weapon and these are the only ones accessible. Claudine and I want you to know where an extra stash is in case trouble arises. Now let's go."

Claudine met them near the storefront, arms folded over a smudged apron and hairs escaping her wimple. "It is about time."

"I told you three hours."

"And it has been longer than that. A shipment arrived half an hour ago. I need you to take care of it before my customers demand to know what is inside. Ivelle, help him, would you? Be on the lookout for snoops and soldiers."

Ivelle's pulse thrummed. Soldiers rarely entered the market district unless there was a complaint, but snoops abounded. She retrieved the crate from the counter and slipped through the glass doors to the left, where rooms and doors led to a hidden space.

The narrow room, accessible only by those who knew of its existence, smelled of clay and paint. Borros balanced on the ladder, peering through the false picture overlooking one of Claudine's warerooms. "Be quick."

"I always am." Ivelle drew a knife from her belt and sliced the crate's lid off. The pungent scent of herbs filled her lungs.

"What is it?"

"Medicinal herbs." Ivelle loaded the wax cloth packets into a basket.

"Claudine should be careful. I can smell those from the other side of the room."

"These are quite rare. Some are said to cure any ailment and some to stop bleeding almost immediately." Others could kill, but never reveal all the facts, as Claudine would say.

"Will they make money?"

Ivelle sniffed a packet and grimaced. This would make the operating table smell like cayenne pepper for days. Claudine would have to burn more incense candles to mask the smell. "Yes."

"Why would anyone need these? Who even knows of their existence?"

Ivelle draped cloth over the basket and filled the other. "There are rumors and any healer knows they exist, just not their location. If you survived an assassination attempt and lived long enough to get help, or had internal bleeding or a fatal illness, you would pay anything to get your hands on an herb that would cure you."

Borros kept quiet as she finished transferring the packets and filling the crate with satchels of incense. To the untrained nose, the herbs and incense smelled similar.

Ivelle grabbed the baskets and slipped into the other room after an all-clear from Borros. She inched along the hallway's wall before pausing at the main room's entrance.

The easy part was over. Now to get them to the back room without being seen.

Claudine provided cover as she gushed over two visiting noblewomen and ushered them into her clothing room. "Surely you have no use of weapons," she laughed, sweeping a hand at the various daggers, axes, and shields covering the walls in the main room. "I just received a new shipment of silk. Why don't you come see it?"

Ivelle darted to the room. She placed the packets in jars, and covered and labeled them before fingering the lone leaf she set aside. A muted, fruity scent rose from the leaf, smelling much like the plant it was harvested from.

A kettle whistle later, she cupped a saucer of tea and maneuvered down a narrow hallway to a pair of folding doors.

"Come in," a weak voice called.

"Emmi? I have tea." Ivelle stepped inside. Faint candlelight illuminated a thin face shining with a smile.

"I missed you." Emmi's youthful voice didn't match the age dulling her eyes. Though the child was nine-years-old, the weariness and pain in her eyes gave her countenance an aged appearance.

"I missed you too. Once you feel better, you can sit in the shop and help me sell wares. You'll like meeting the customers." Ivelle knelt by the trundle bed and offered the saucer of tea.

Emmi's hands trembled as she sipped the concoction. "And find my family?" Her voice pitched with hope.

Ivelle's heart sank. How could she tell Emmi there would be little chance of that ever happening? How could she tell such a sweet, innocent child that even if she absolutely knew for certain where her family was, she could do nothing about it? "And we'll see if we can find your family."

A gnarled hand reached for Ivelle's. "Can you help me tell them about home? I think our kitten ran away and the curtains were torn. Mother won't be happy about those."

Ivelle swallowed the lump in her throat. Emmi was too frail, too ill to worry about breaking such shattering news. Or hearing the truth about it. "Yes. I'll help you tell them about your home."

If only she could tell Emmi the truth. There was no hope for her family.

CHAPTER FIVE

HOLDER

HOLDER GROUND HIS teeth as King Eligor stared at the grouped guards and soldiers. The king's eyes passed over each man and woman, as though he had to assure himself no one sent imposters.

He stood near the two squads of king's guards, alone, like a target. Would the king publicly issue his punishment or would he wait and have Holder dragged before him in private before delivering the edict? Captain Geros hadn't alluded to Holder's fate during the report.

The threat had to have been there. The coppery scent of fresh blood, the way it dripped down the stone, the knife pinning the note to the pillow, so close to the princess' face...no one could imagine that.

Right?

A sharp pang in his side snapped his gaze to the right. He rubbed where Rogan elbowed him.

Rogan stared back. "Relax. The morning meeting is over."

Over? How? The cursed thing lasted half an hour, longer if a problem arose. Holder rubbed his eyes. King Eligor's throne sat empty and the low murmur of voices hummed in the background.

The tension in his neck and shoulders tripled. When would he be dragged to meet his fate?

"Holder." Rogan's voice held the same lack of emotion as his expression. "You need to continue your job until otherwise notified. If the king sees you continuing to ensure his ward's safety, his opinion of your mistake could be softened."

How reassuring. Instead of ordering his death by hanging, the king would order his death by beheading. Faster, no pain, no waiting period to die.

"Holder…"

"I'm going." Holder passed a hand over his sword to check its position and started up the stairs. Each step felt weighted, like the thickest chain was fastened around his ankle. Lack of sleep burned his eyes. Would he still have a job after this? What would he do if he lost his position? His hands knew no type of trade other than wielding the sword and his mind was conditioned only for the work of a king's guard and bodyguard.

Escape, a distant voice whispered. *Leave. Listen to the letter.*

Holder shoved the thoughts away. He could think treasonous thoughts later.

Svetlana met him with the same pursed-lip frown. "The princess is ready for her daily duties and activities, of which you will not be present for."

First Lieutenant Cetrin materialized behind Svetlana. Arms crossed, he pierced Holder with the same gaze he would bestow upon a criminal.

Holder's heart relocated to his throat. Was he being replaced? Why had no one said anything? Was he in worse trouble than he imagined? But what else could he have done? He followed protocol the best he could—training hadn't included what to do when one discovered the princess' chambers drenched in blood.

Prickles surged up the back of his neck as, behind him, leather scuffed upon stone and someone cleared their throat. He fisted his hand to keep from grasping his sword as he turned.

Juan and Captain Geros blocked his path to the stairs. Something akin to sympathy, as much sympathy as a king's guard could possess, furrowed Juan's brow, but cold light glinted in Captain Geros' eyes.

"Bodyguard Lygor, His Majesty, King Eligor, commands your presence."

⋄⋅⋅⋅⋅⋄

Stars, help me.

Holder wiped the sweat off his palms before again clasping them behind his back. He hadn't taken to the sword like Rogan, but the loss of its familiar weight left him bare and vulnerable.

The plentitude of mounted maps did little to lessen the stone walls' unforgiving chill. The floor matched the walls, and the wide rectangular table bore more scars and nicks than the armory's. This was not a room meant to relax those within it.

Wood whispered over stone. He straightened his posture. His back ached and his head throbbed from the tension tightening the lower muscles in his back. The inability to grab some water before being locked in the room and commanded to wait made his mouth as dry as the desert rumored to cover the land beyond the High Mountains.

Orange, blue, and deep brown moved in his peripheral before King Eligor took his place at the head of the table. Captain Geros flanked his right while Officer Torgord stood on the left.

Sweat cooled Holder's skin as he bowed to the king. *Stars, help me.*

Not his first prayer and, if things went south, not his last.

"Sit down, Specialist Lygor."

Specialist. Not bodyguard.

Holder fumbled the plain wooden chair before managing to pull it out and sit. His heart thumped with such ferocity his chest ached. Every muscle begged to run, to escape.

Officer Torgord meandered around the table, hands loosely clasped behind his back, like he ambled along an afternoon stroll rather than looking like he intended to live up to his reputation as Orm's most feared interrogator.

"Recount what happened yesterday, Specialist."

Struggling to form words, Holder complied. His voice felt thick, unwieldy as he reported, once again, what occurred.

No emotion crossed Officer Torgord's mustached face as he continued asking questions. With every demanded answer, more fog filled Holder's mind. The questions had nothing to do with the incident.

Chills climbed his spine. It was almost as if...as if they were examining his loyalty.

A snippet of Mother's letter invaded his thoughts.

"I wish I could explain, my dear son, but I am unable to adequately put my thoughts into words. Be wary, Holder. Evil is often cloaked in a guise of good."

Cold blue eyes catalogued Holder's every breath. "How old are you, Specialist?"

"Twenty, sir."

"How long have you been in his lordship's army?"

"For as long as I can remember, sir." Holder's swallow stuck in his throat. What was the reason for such an interrogation? Would one of his answers incriminate him?

"When did you aspire to be a personal bodyguard?"

Silence highlighted Holder's shortened breaths. "I never aspired, sir. My training overseer recommended me for the job at age sixteen. I was given the required training before beginning at age seventeen."

"What about your parents? Our records show your father being the stable master."

"Never speak of us to the king or Officer Torgord." Mother's caution burned his conscience. Whatever the reason his silence was needed, it could place him in even greater trouble if his silence appeared as disrespect.

"That's what I've been told, sir." Holder stuffed away the upswell of pain and stab of guilt at disobeying his parents.

"And your mother helped mend the armor and clothing." Officer Torgord's graying mustache twitched. "An admirable profession. Clearly they believed in you since they enrolled you at age five. How do you like being the princess' bodyguard?"

"It is an honor, sir."

"And never in your time of being a bodyguard have you ever been accused of or experienced hallucinations until now."

"Correct, sir." Holder fisted his hands under the table. Where would this go? *Stars, please have mercy.*

"Preliminary reports indicate your mental state may be faulty. Even Specialist Cetrin expressed doubt regarding your mental clarity."

Rogan. Pain stabbed Holder's heart. His best friend—a man he almost considered a brother—betrayed him?

His breath rasped as Officer Torgord's arm shot out and thick fingers gripped Holder's hair, yanking back his head. "What did you really see?"

"I already provided my report, sir." Holder managed to inhale despite the awkward angle. He *couldn't* be wrong. One couldn't imagine such gruesomeness. Couldn't dream up the sheer amount of blood soaking the pillow, note, and wall.

"Speak truth and you will only lose your job."

"I am, sir." Was he, though? He *thought* he spoke truth, but was Rogan right? Holder couldn't recall anything placing him under more strain than normal. He acquired enough sleep and didn't have an overactive imagination. Surely the threat was real.

"At ease, Torgord." King Eligor's smooth voice did nothing to diminish the cold glint in the officer's eyes.

Holder fisted his hands to refrain from rubbing his neck as Officer Torgord resumed his place beside King Eligor. His heart threatened to burst from his chest. Would he leave the room dead and bled out from a slit throat?

"Specialist."

"My king."

Black eyes searched Holder's face. Slight wrinkles bracketed King Eligor's mouth and eyes, and traces of gray showed against dark hair. *Ageless.* King Eligor had witnessed centuries, but his lack of aging made the king look to be in the mid-fifties.

"Specialist, do you know how many hours have passed since you were brought to this room?"

"No, sir."

"Five."

Holder schooled his expression. *Five* cursed hours? While it'd felt like a day, he hadn't expected them to leave him to stew in the possibility of losing his job and life for five hours.

"During those five hours, my ward continued with her schedule. On her ride, an assassin targeted her."

Holder choked on his inhale. "Is she okay? Was she struck? Did they catch the assassin?"

"She is shaken, but fine. The stars be thanked the assassin's poor aim placed the arrow in the turf and not in her or her pony."

Thank the stars.

King Eligor's calm mien remained, but something about him hardened. "Specialist, today's events have convinced me that what happened yesterday was not a hallucination. Someone is out to get my ward. Thus, a new protection plan will be implemented. Beginning tomorrow, you will be the only one of a few keeping my ward safe in an obscure location until I deem it safe for her to return. The less who know her whereabouts, the safer she will be.

"Yes, my king." A surge of panic swallowed the wave of relief at being found innocent. How could only a few protect the princess without available backup? What if they were outnumbered? What if he was rendered useless and the princess suffered because of it?

The princess would be left to her lonesome, with only a finicky, snappish nurse and a cold guardian who showed her little of the love she needed.

"You will resume your duties tomorrow. For the rest of the day, I want you to brush up on your training." King Eligor's gaze burned. "She is my ward and successor, Specialist. Failure to ensure her safety will be costly."

Holder pulled in another lungful of crisp air as he made his way to the training grounds. Walls hewn from the same stone as Rex Dorcha created a maze for those unfamiliar with the layout. A mixture of sand and slushy snow squished beneath his boots as he located the training grounds' entrance.

An occasional shout broke the clang of blades. Patches of soldiers and guards practiced under the stern eyes of instructors. Skirting the edge, Holder scanned the areas. Lower half walls created smaller areas within the overall training square. Locking in on his target, he arrived at the other side just as Rogan knocked Juan to the ground and rested his sword's tip at Juan's throat.

"I yield, I yield." Juan scrambled to his feet when Rogan sheathed his sword. "Stars, man. I'm never sparring with you again. I thought you wanted to take my head off."

"Too messy."

"That's comforting." Juan rolled his eyes. "Hey, Holder. Did you hear what happened to the princess?"

"I heard."

Rogan barely spared Holder a glance. Silence settled until Juan coughed. "Well, I should get going before someone thinks I'm loitering and assigns me latrine-cleaning duty." He scurried away like an irate mother bear chased him.

Holder stuffed down his irritation. Rogan's tense shoulders and fisted hands indicated a less-than-amiable mood. The last thing he needed was to be the brunt of Rogan's irritation. "You told Officer Torgord you don't think I'm mentally stable."

"I said nothing about your mental stability."

Another pang. "But you told him I'm incompetent."

Rogan huffed and stalked to the weapons rack pushed against the nearby wall. He selected a sword and tossed it at Holder. "I only told him you could have imagined the severity of the situation due to your desire to protect the princess."

"Was that all you said?"

"You're getting nosy, Holder."

"I have a right to be nosy when my life could be on the line."

"Your life is safe."

Holder clenched his teeth. His knuckles cracked as his grip on the sword tightened. Rogan wouldn't understand. Captain Geros welcomed him with open arms due to First Lieutenant Cetrin's status and infamy as one of Orm's greatest swordsmen.

"Look. Just do the best you can, don't imagine anything else, and you'll be fine."

"I didn't imagine that."

Rogan shrugged a shoulder. "As long as the king thinks you're capable, I don't know why you're worrying."

Holder scoffed. Rogan was the closest thing to family he had, but sometimes he wondered if Rogan saw him as a friend or brainless nuisance. "You don't understand. He straight out told me the price of failure is my life. I didn't need you casting doubt on my competency."

"I didn't cast doubt. I told the truth." Rogan met Holder's gaze, no sign of friendliness in his eyes. "Loyalty to the king above all else, Holder. You know that. You've grown up with it same as I have."

Yes, but the difference was Holder knew how to think for himself.

He forced his jaw to relax. Shifting his grip on the sword, he fell into position. "Might as well practice while I'm here."

Maybe then he could bury the premonition Rogan's loyalty might someday cause even greater problems.

CHAPTER SIX

THERESE

"I NEED YOU to go to the merchant's quarter and purchase some supplies." Scholl placed a silver on the desk's scarred top. "That is yours after you return with the purchases. If you find everything, I'll deduct the silver from your debt."

The uncharacteristic display of kindness settled in Therese's stomach like an iron block, but she wasn't stupid enough to pass up the offer. She willed her voice to remain steady. "I understand."

No emotion touched Scholl's squinty eyes or mustache-framed mouth. "Part of having your own client and target is knowing how you will eliminate your target per the client's specifications. If you were prohibited from using poison, and the target was nearby and unassuming, what method would you employ?"

A test. Stars, guide me.

Therese stiffened to keep from shuddering. What was she turning into that discussing ways to murder someone became easier every time? "Slip a blade between their ribs or slice their throat."

Scholl's gaze again pierced her. He pulled out a drawer and removed a slip of parchment, giving no indication if

Therese's answer satisfied him. "These are the herbs I need. You know where we purchase them?"

"Yes." Jolie and Lucian had discussed the place before, mentioning the owner was as eccentric as the wares she carried.

"You'll need to get something to make the transaction appear legal to any onlookers. Ask Jolie and Lucian if they need anything. If they don't, buy a bolt of dark cloth. Preferably from the south. Their dye withstands stains and liquid the best."

"I   will."

Scholl handed Therese a navy reticule. "There is enough in there for the purchases. Bring back a receipt. You do know how to stay inconspicuous, don't you?"

"Yes." Remaining inconspicuous had saved her life more than once when evening fell and taverns released their inebriated hostages. Slipping through throngs of people in daylight was nothing compared to skirting ominous buildings in the dark.

"Good. I expect you back in two hours. And walk. Don't take a horse. It draws too much attention."

"Yes, sir."

Therese's stomach knotted as she traveled the narrow dirt path leading into Varway. The town radiated the hum of life—shouting, braying, and noise from the nearby mill. People moving like ants, their dark shapes filling the streets.

She kept her eyes down as she entered. Soldiers lingered about the entrance, though their presence did little to discourage pickpocketing and other minor crimes. She clenched the edges of her cloak. The reticule hung at her hip, jangling with each step.

Varway stank with the intermingled smells of taverns, smoke, and unwashed bodies. Wood and brick buildings loomed over dirt streets. Signs indicating businesses' purposes hung over doorways. Somewhat charming in the daylight, but at night the place turned into a nightmare.

Therese's nerves were as frayed as a threadbare garment by the time Claudine DeGrim's Emporium appeared. A tall brick building, the emporium nestled amongst other stores and merchant stalls with bright awnings, and featured large glass windows filled with doodads from every corner of Orm. Mannequins dressed in peculiar fashions joined the novelty items.

She exhaled and entered. The sweet scent of incense filled the air.

"Welcome to Claudine DeGrim's Emporium. I will be with you in a moment. Feel free to look around." A short, slender woman in a fancy, light blue dress smiled at Therese as she bustled by. Two women in elegant gowns trailed her, chattering about rare jewels and combs.

Therese grimaced. What was there to look at in this odd room besides the assortment of shields, swords, and axes lining the walls? She traced a simple design etched into a wooden shield near two double doors. This curious place, with its rich clientele and extravagant proprietress, was more suited for Jolie's expertise.

"Can I help you?" A young woman in a simple navy dress emerged from an arched entryway on the back wall.

"I, uh, need to buy some herbs."

The girl neared. Sharp gray eyes pierced Therese. "We don't sell herbs."

"Oh. I was, um, told to get them here."

"By whom?"

"Scholl."

The girl's shoulders retained their stiff set. "Do you have a list?"

"Yes." Therese fumbled through the reticle. Her fingers trembled as she handed the list over. Was Scholl wrong? Why the suspicion? He conducted regular business with the emporium.

No questions. Just think of the debt.

The young woman scanned the list. "I will be right back. Feel free to look around. In here we showcase the best weapons. Through those two doors on the left wall you will find fabrics, premade clothing, and a fitting and measuring room. The door to the incense and jewelry room is on the right wall."

Therese hugged herself as she stared about the room. A large counter sat before the door. 'Twould be easy for someone to rob the place if an employee wasn't in the room. She moistened her lips. The incense made her throat raw and her head pound. But it was worth the silver waiting on Scholl's desk.

She perused the daggers beside the door. Mounted on wooden ledges, leather sheaths protected the blades. But no sheath could protect or hide the design of a certain hilt. Therese's breath caught and she reached out to touch the coiled serpent.

"An eligor blade." The young woman's voice was no louder than a sweep of fabric against the floor. "Named after our king."

"I know what it is." Therese traced the hilt. "How did you get it? I thought these were rare."

"They are. Though it is uncommon, the Emporium sometimes acts as a pawn shop. That dagger was brought in yesterday."

A chill shot up Therese's spine. The emporium's patrons had no clue they were in the same vicinity as the most dangerous weapon ever created.

"That will be eight bits." The girl placed a flat package on the counter. "Is there anything else I can help you find?"

"Oleander."

"Excuse me?"

"I...I don't think oleander was on the list. I need ten petals." Lucian had mentioned extra ways to worm into Scholl's good graces and convince him Therese was competent enough to join the team.

"Ten?" She scrutinized Therese like she could see through her and uncover the reason for such a lethal purchase.

"Ten. Yes."

"Very well. I'll be right back." She returned seconds later with another small package. "That will be two bits, so ten bits total. Anything else?"

"Do you have a bolt of black cloth from the south?"

"You want an entire bolt?" Her eyebrows rose. Skepticism invaded her expression.

"Yes, if you have it."

The young woman shrugged and disappeared through the doors on the left, reemerging with a bundle wrapped in oilcloth. "That will be two silvers or forty bits."

"But the herbs and oleander—"

"Are ten bits. The cloth is thirty. Do you want it or not?"

Therese fingered the coins in the reticule until she found two silvers. She plunked them on the countertop.

The girl pushed the bundles her way before leaning forward. "Look." Her voice was a harsh whisper. "I don't know what you're doing with these purchases. Nor do I care. But here's some advice. Don't be so obvious. Your expressions give away everything. Anyone paying you half a bit of attention would know you're up to something."

Therese clutched the bundles. Her heart hammered. Had anyone guessed the purpose for purchasing the herbs and cloth? "Thank you for your help."

The young woman's response faded as Therese stepped onto the street. Scholl would be more than displeased if Therese ruined his plans in some way. Then again, that had been her first foray to the Emporium. Surely no one knew her identity.

Scholl met her in his office. His black clothes almost blended with his skin. "You were successful?"

"Yes." Therese set the parcels on the desk and handed him the reticule. Would Scholl hold his end of the promise? *Stars, please grant mercy.*

"Who helped you?"

"A girl. Dark hair and gray eyes. Rather brusque attitude."

Scholl grunted as he procured the silver and handed it over. "Did you see anything of interest?"

The silver warmed in Therese's hand like the sliver of hope warming her soul. "There was an eligor blade."

Graying eyebrows shot up. "A true, honest-to-goodness eligor blade?"

"Yes."

Scholl rubbed his hands. "I may have to investigate further. That would make missions so much easier."

Therese cringed. Easier, yes, but the thought of leaving someone to bleed out made her stomach roil.

Scholl waved a hand. "Go home for the rest of the week. That will give me time to make my decision."

Relief flooded Therese as she traveled a path few remembered existed. With the silver she could purchase some necessary staples for her sisters. The few bits of each day's pay would also contribute nicely. They would have to ration, but that was better than starving again.

She wrinkled her nose at the stench of mud and pigs radiating from the collection of rundown cabins and shacks. The dwellings curved around a short, squatty well. Towering pine trees cast the area in shade. One of Varway's poorest areas filled what could be a scenic setting and tainted the air with the desperate smell of survival.

Despite the odors, Therese drew a deep breath as she stood before one of the humblest huts. Those single or with few family members were given the smaller huts. Despite the cramped quarters, Therese refused to complain. Yes, the wattle-and-daub building trapped in dampness from last night's rain, but it provided shelter for only two bits a month.

She opened the door. Light from a lone log in the fireplace illuminated the table and three chairs, a three-cabinet kitchen, clothing hooks, a battered dresser, and three pallets. The entire building could fit inside Scholl's office, but it was home. "Girls?"

"Therese." Nora launched herself from a chair. "Delli, Therese is here."

Therese caught Nora's hug. Delli inched from her spot in the corner, clutching a ratty cloth doll. "Therese?"

"Hi, Delli."

"Therese!" Delli joined Nora and wrapped thin arms around Therese's waist.

Therese blinked back tears as she ran her hand over lopsided braids. Since their parents' deaths, Delli had difficulty believing Therese would return each evening.

Whatever it took, even if it meant becoming a soulless, heartless murderer, she would provide and care for the two dear ones clinging to her.

"How long are you home for?" Nora peered at Therese, arms crossed.

"Scholl gave me three days. Are you two okay?"

Nora rolled her eyes. "You know we are. You've only been gone a few hours."

"Wabbit." Delli tugged Therese's sleeve and pointed at the shadowy corner. "Wabbit."

"We just caught a rabbit." Nora puffed with pride. "He's a little fatter too. I reset the snares. The river looks full. Maybe we can fish tomorrow."

"It depends on the river." Therese inspected the rabbit. It would provide two days' meat if she ate even less than usual. "I'll get some water. Nora, would you get the pot out? Delli, I need you to put this in our savings jar."

"A silver?" Nora ran her finger over the shiny surface. "Where did you get a silver?"

"I work, Nora. You and Delli stay inside. I'll be right back." Therese grabbed the bucket and stepped back into the chilly air. Stars be thanked for the rabbit. And if they caught plenty of fish tomorrow, she could dry and salt the meat. Not the best tasting, but edible and filling.

She lowered the bucket into the well's dark surface. She had to convince Scholl to let her join the team. Her sisters' survival depended on it.

CHAPTER SEVEN

ROGAN

SINCE WHEN WAS the second king's guard demoted to conducting raids and inspections?

Rogan squinted at the order fluttering in Captain Geros' gloved hand. In all his years, he never would have imagined being regulated to such insignificant tasks. Not that hunting smugglers and law breakers wasn't important, but he was a second king's guard. He should be at Rex Dorcha preparing for his shift.

"You four, guard the back entrance. Miller, Konst, see if there's a side entrance. Arrest anyone who attempts escape. The rest of you are with me. Remember, we're looking for anything illegal. The informant claims they specialize in herbs, weapons, artifacts, and contraband. If we do find anything, be prepared to arrest the smuggling scum."

"And how are we supposed to know who did it?" Juan muttered. He shifted in his designated spot beside Rogan. "They won't be wearing a sign announcing their illegal activities."

Captain Geros nailed Juan with a glower. "The owner of this store is a sly one. Watch her for any sign of lying."

Rogan trailed after Juan and the other two guards, common guards and not king's guards, as they followed Captain Geros through Varway. The town smelled nothing like Rex Dorcha or the forest, and the sheer number of people bustling about grated on his nerves. Cursed thieves and black market operatives.

He cringed as they passed by the store's large front glass window, which displayed an eyesore of a dress and some simple weapons and knickknacks. The sheer frippery and ridiculousness alluded to the store's primary clientele.

Rogan huffed. If that was all this emporium sold, the search was a waste of time.

Shocked gasps and whispers rose over the thumping of their boots on the boardwalk. Even if they discovered nothing, the owner's reputation would be tarnished. Ruined, even. People were odd when they believed certain ideas, and if anyone thought Claudine DeGrim's Emporium was involved in scandalous, illegal activities…

Rogan almost felt sorry for whoever owned the hideous store.

Captain Geros shoved the door open and entered.

By the stars. An overwhelming smell of incense burned Rogan's nose. If the smugglers did indeed have anything to do with this place, perhaps they could be identified by the respiratory disorders they contracted after breathing such awful stuff.

"What is the meaning of this?" A short woman with dark hair stomped into the room. Her ferocious scowl made her look like she would seize one of the many weapons hanging on the walls and use it on them. Effectively. "What do you want?"

"Captain Geros of the second king's guard. DeGrim, you and your store are under suspicion of King Eligor to be involved in the black market. Surrender to being searched."

"*Miss* DeGrim, thank you very much, and I shan't fuss about a search, although I am certain your boys care little for rummaging through bolts of taffeta and bags of spices. Whatever your intent, do try to be civilized. You'll frighten my more delicate customers."

"Taffeta and spices are not all you sell. Bring out your other employees."

Miss DeGrim shook her head before disappearing through the back door. She reemerged with a young woman and a bear of a man. "Darlings, this is the terribly esteemed Captain Geros of the second guard. He usually protects the king."

Captain Geros' fingers flexed near his sword at the veiled insult. "Alvaraz, Smit, guard the front door. Cetrin, Benito, assist in inspection. Miss DeGrim, I will remind you once, and only once, that disrespect will land you in the dungeons. Each of your employees will escort a soldier around this place. Any damage sustained will not be recompensed. If your employees attempt to harm my men in any way, their heads will be had."

"Quite the threat for a simple emporium," the woman remarked drily. She sighed as though bored. "Borros will escort you, Captain. I will deal with the skinny lad, and Ivelle will suffer the tall, blond, and grumpy one." She flapped her hands at them. "Well? Let's get going. I have more to do than babysit a youth too young to grow facial hair."

Rogan eyed the female employee. Taller and stockier for a woman, she moved with dangerous ease. Dark hair and cutting gray eyes assessed him, her glare as cold as the High Mountains during wintertime.

"Well? You did not come here to stand around."

Words sharp as Miss DeGrim's spurred Rogan into action. What luck that he had to be assigned the rudest, snobbiest woman alive. He'd take Miss DeGrim with her snide remarks over this sharp-tongued nag-in-the-making.

Ivelle moved through two curtained, skinny glass doors along the left wall. "We will begin here."

Indignant squawks bombarded Rogan the second he passed the threshold. He recoiled as three women, two as plump as hens meant for market, glared at him. One wore a dress held together only by pins, dark skin turning darker with displeasure. The other two held various amounts of fabric.

Heat crept up his neck and invaded his face. Lowering his gaze, he inspected the overstuffed settee, boxes, cabinets, and the floor and walls. "Next room." His voice emerged an undignified rasp. Father would be most displeased at his less-than-soldierly response.

Ivelle led him through a wooden door directly across from the two glass ones after watching him search what she called the *spice room*. "This is our break room. Don't keep the ice box open for too long. Claudine just received her ice order. She will be most cross if you cause it to melt."

Rogan searched through the cupboards and under the counter. The room was bigger than his family's cabin and reeked of the same incense permeating the rest of the building. How did it not taint the food?

Ivelle's gaze turned haughty when he faced her. "Disappointed at your results? Hopefully your job doesn't depend on you finding anything illegal in here." A mountain accent brushed her voice, hinting at a heritage beyond Varway's borders.

"Next room," he snapped through gritted teeth. Had King Eligor commanded this search on purpose? Was Claudine DeGrim in on the scheme? Was he purposefully set up with an uppity brat to test his patience and obedience?

Ivelle gestured about. "This is the only other room on this side of the building."

"Really?" Rogan moved beyond the last cabinet and fingered the red velvet curtain hiding the wall. "I'm not stupid. This building is far too large for just three puny side rooms. What does this cover?"

"A portrait of Claudine's family. She doesn't like it on display. Something about it featuring the black sheep of the family."

Rogan yanked the curtain aside. A large painting with a white sheep among several black ones covered the space from top to bottom. He trailed his fingers along the edges. "Do Miss DeGrim and her family believe themselves sheep? This doesn't look like a portrait. Who painted this?"

"I've no clue and I don't question Claudine's tastes in art. Look in the bottom corners. That's usually where artists place their signatures. Not that I'd expect you to know that. The only thing your type does is destroy."

Rogan inserted his finger into an indent and pushed. The picture slid to the left, until the right side caught on the edge of the two wooden rails keeping the frame upright and secure.

He couldn't help a smirk at the revealed door. "Since when did a door become a portrait?"

Ivelle paled.

Rogan tried the door latch. "Where's the key?"

"I don't know."

Sure she didn't. "I'm trying to be courteous and not do this the hard way, but I'll have no choice if you don't provide the key."

More like he just didn't want to deal with fighting what looked to be an old-style latch and lock. The last time he'd seen one destroyed, it'd taken both Captain Geros and Father five tries each.

"Like I said, I don't know." She crossed her arms. Almost his height, she didn't have to tip her head too far up to meet his eyes. "If you break something that's not yours, that's destruction of property. I doubt the king will be pleased to receive the bill. This is an antique door, and quite expensive."

"Then it shouldn't be too hard to break down."

Rogan backed away and delivered the first kick. The wood splintered.

"Stop. Stop right *now*."

"You had your chance, lady." Three more kicks saw the door hanging on hinges and down a lock and latch. Stars be thanked the hinges hadn't been old-style.

Rogan pushed the door's remnants open. A narrow hallway swathed in shadows stretched before him. "Get a candle."

"There's nothing—"

"Get a candle before I call in Captain Geros. You won't find him nearly as patient."

Her lips pursed and fire flashed in those intriguing eyes before she retrieved a candle and thrust it at him.

"It's useless without a flame."

"You never specified."

"You look more intelligent than you actually are, it seems."

She lit the candle while serving him the greatest heap of scorn he'd been subjected to in a long time.

Rogan snatched it and scanned the hallway. One door to each wall. He started for the right.

"No." Ivelle's fingers latched around his bicep. "You can't go in there."

"What are you hiding?"

"My sister is ill. You cannot enter." She pulled at his arm.

Rogan drew a dagger. He didn't want to hurt her, but orders were orders. Any resistance would be met with arrest. "I already told you I'm not stupid. Lying will get you nowhere. Keep this up and this entire place will be burned to the ground."

"I just told you—"

"Orders are orders. And if you keep yanking on my arm, I can't guarantee I can keep a grip on the candle."

Ivelle dropped her hands, fisting them at her sides. "Please don't go in there." Her accent thickened, slightly warping her vowels.

Rogan ignored her and entered. Mixed scents of strawberry and lavender soothed the incense's roughness on his aching throat. It didn't smell like illness.

The room was no more than seven paces long and nine wide. A small desk filled the right corner, bearing nothing but bundles and a candle bathing the room in golden-orange glow. To the left, a narrow bed covered in rumpled blankets was flush to the wall.

A pale face peeked from under the blankets, the movement disturbing a book resting on the covers. "Who are you?"

"Don't talk to him." Ivelle's voice shook before strengthening. "He's just doing a routine check. He'll be on his way now."

A lump filled Rogan's throat until a small satchel caught his eye. He snatched it and tugged the drawstring open. The satchel bulged with green leaves.

Rogan grabbed Ivelle's wrist and forced her into the hallway. If this turned violent, the child didn't need to be a witness.

He dangled the satchel before her face as anger burned within. How dare she subject a little girl to outlawed goods? "These don't grow around here. What is this?"

CHAPTER EIGHT

IVELLE

IN ALL HER days, she'd never met a more vexatious man.

"They're strawberry leaves." Ivelle yanked the satchel from the soldier's grasp. "They help Emmi with her illness." She grit her teeth and stared at the despicable being before her. How dare he grab her wrist and corner and interrogate her like she was some common criminal?

A criminal she may be, but common she was not.

Ivelle stomped into Emmi's room and slapped the satchel onto the desk. *Brute. Barbarian. Wretch.* "You could have just asked in a more humane way."

"Ivelle? What's wrong?" Emmi's sweet voice collided with the soldier's animosity. "Did someone get hurt?"

"No, sweetie. Nothing's wrong."

The soldier sheathed his dagger. No emotion touched his face or eyes. "I apologize for disturbing you, miss," he murmured to Emmi.

"Yes, you should be terribly sorry," Ivelle snapped. Her heart hammered. The soldier was close, so close, to discovering their secrets. Where would that leave Emmi? "Now get out. You've seen all there is to see."

He backed from the room, eyes flickering once more to Emmi. Once the door closed, he faced Ivelle. "Why is she trapped in a room? There are several qualified physicians in Varway.”

Ivelle fought back memories of fire, blood, and pain. His blue cloak and threatening, strong build dredged up the past when it needed to stay buried. She fisted her hands to keep from rubbing the scars on the underside of her forearms. “Claudine and I are more than capable, thank you.”

He ignored her and opened the other door. “Your dusting skills are as deficient as your overall level of intelligence.”

Took one to know one. Ivelle swept past him and entered the room. Arms wide, she turned a slow circle. “Just a guest room. Will you be fine with me fluffing the pillow or do you prefer to stab it with your glorified knife so you can claim a thorough search?”

“Hand me the pillow.” His eyes flickered with warning as he accepted the cloth stuffed with goose feathers. Heedless to the hours of work put into cleaning the item, he mangled its shape before shaking it out.

Not only did his social skills require assistance, but his pillow-fluffing ability as well.

After he inspected the dresser drawers and beneath the bed, Ivelle crossed her arms and did nothing to quiet her sigh. Are you finished?”

“Depends. Any other *portraits* I need to know about?”

“No. Now, if you will kindly exit the building…”

He scoffed but followed her back into the break room. The dark tattoo on his cheek jumped as he stared at the cabinets.

“You already scoured those, you know. Unless you believe things can appear out of nowhere, you’re wasting your time.”

The soldier—specialist from the tattoo—returned her glare. Deep blue eyes narrowed. "Are there any other rooms?"

Ivelle bit her tongue before she spit out a sharp comment. Her brother had made that mistake all those years ago, and the soldier facing him down had been less than amused. This soldier, with his stony countenance and arrogant attitude, was likely the same.

Her breath felt lodged in her chest until the blue-caped menaces left. If they discovered what Claudine hid, a fate worse than being reminded of the past would meet those who operated the Emporium.

After the soldiers disappeared down the street, Borros muttered what had to be curses as he tugged his sleeve up to reveal a slender knife. "That egotistical idiot thinks he's so mighty just because he's been the captain over the king's guard for years. Thinks that gives him a right to come in here spouting off ridiculous nonsense."

Claudine placed a hand on Borrors' shoulder. "Hush. We will discuss this later. Let's get business going again."

"If it goes at all. That worm probably scared off our customers."

"Hush. Go. Ivelle and I will reassure our patrons."

Ivelle's curiosity piqued as Borros glanced her way. "When will you talk with her?"

"Not at this moment, I can tell you that." Claudine flapped her hands at Borros. "Go."

The mountain of a man mumbled as he disappeared into the back room.

Claudine faced Ivelle, rings flashing as she rubbed her hands. A devious glint sparkled in her eyes. "Well? How did our plan work?"

Ivelle grinned. "I've never seen a soldier blush like that."

"Those ladies have a sly side that supersedes my own. How did it go?"

The tempest returned in vengeance and full force. "He found Emmi."

"*What?*"

"He looked under the red curtain and followed the hallway to Emmi's room."

Color drained from Claudine's face. "What did he do?"

"He demanded to know what strawberry leaves were. I thought he was going to arrest me."

"Did he frighten Emmi?"

Ivelle thanked the stars as she replayed the scene in her mind. "No. He showed surprisingly decent manners toward her. Even apologized."

Claudine harrumphed. "Decent manners or not, he is a soldier." Her tone softened, similar to how Ma's had. "How are you doing?"

For more than one reason, Ivelle fought against the moisture gathering in her eyes. She'd not shed a tear since that day ten years ago, and she refused to start now. "Aside from wanting to stab him, I'm fine."

"You did admirably. Now let's get this place back up and running. I need to speak with you later."

The gold of dusk streamed through the emporium's windows when Claudine gestured to the break room. "Join me for tea, won't you?"

Ivelle drew a breath. This was nothing bad. The worst Claudine could do was tell her Emmi was being sent away.

Liar.

The worst Claudine could do was tell her she was no longer needed.

No longer wanted.

Ivelle shook her head. No, that would not happen. Why would Claudine say that after ten years? Besides, Ivelle knew too many secrets. Hiding places, codes, escape routes...

She stiffly sat at the table, lacing and unlacing her fingers as her stomach churned and bile stung her throat. Where was the girl who had insulted and dealt with a king's guard only hours ago? Where was the girl who knew the locations of illegal and antique goods by heart?

A chair scraped across wooden flooring. Claudine took a sip of what smelled like peppermint tea before smiling. "How do you like Varway?"

"It's fine." The old fears swept in like a summer thunderstorm. She clenched her fists, struggling not to fall prey to the whispers in the back of her mind.

"How would you like to go on a trip with me to the High Mountains?"

"The High Mountains?" Chills climbed Ivelle's spine. The last time she'd been in the rocky range, blood had flowed about her like water after a pounding rainfall.

"Yes. I need to resupply certain wares that can only be found there. I'd like you to come with me."

"Why me? Who will watch the emporium?"

"Because it's high time you get a break from Varway. You can't expect to stay sequestered in the Emporium forever. A trusted friend will come and stay with Emmi and Borros will take over the Emporium, hopefully without burning the place down. I've also asked the seamstress to oversee clothing orders while I am away. I adore Borros, but I don't trust him anywhere near my cloth. If you accept, we leave tomorrow."

⋄⟡┄•┄┄┄╌┄┄•┄⟡⋄

Ivelle glowered as she stumbled from her room. Sleep still clung to her eyes and she wasn't entirely certain her clothes weren't on backwards. The pack hanging from her shoulders weighed like a wheelbarrow of bricks.

What part of Claudine's brain forgot Ivelle was not an early riser?

"Good morning, sleepyhead." Borros' deep chuckle drifted by as he dangled a cloth bag before her face. "Breakfast. A biscuit and jerky."

"There you are." Claudine sailed past, a dark green cloak swirling about her. "You'll have to eat on the road. We are starting later than I wanted."

Later? By the stars, how could they leave any earlier?

Ivelle followed Borros outside. Icy air nipped her skin, scented with the smell of snow. Buildings were mere outlines in the darkness. Not one pinpoint of light pierced the black.

"Mount up. Claudine will be out in a moment." Borros pointed to the dim shapes of two horses tethered in front of the emporium.

Claudine emerged minutes later. "Let us be off."

Ivelle waited until a crooked wooden mile marker indicated a league between them and Varway. "Where are we going?" Her stomach twisted into a knot.

"DorFord. It is a small village at the foothills of the mountains and is the prime trading center in this region."

"Why a place so far away? Wouldn't Varway be a better option with being so close to Rex Dorcha?"

Claudine chuckled. "Not when half the items are illegal. King Eligor keeps a close eye on imported goods. You saw how those king's guards hounded the store."

How could she forget? Their arrogant stances, tattoos, blue cloaks, and easily-accessible weapons refused to leave her memory. Especially the upstart Claudine forced her to deal with.

She rolled her eyes. If she never saw the stoic, rude, blond-haired young man again, it would be too soon.

After five days of travel, the High Mountains blocked the horizon from view. Tall, colossal, and covered in snow, the mountains offered escape from the punishment for crimes and granted opportunities for death at the jaws of wild beasts. Beyond them lay a land touched only by the banished—those both lucky and cursed enough to escape death.

DorFord looked like any other small mountain village, with log buildings, wide stone chimneys, and rutted dirt streets. Caravans covered the field just outside DorFord's natural stone walls. Flags of every color and design flapped in the brisk mountain breeze blowing rifts of snow off housetops.

"Stay close," Claudine instructed "DorFord has its own law enforcement, but the taverns can get rowdy at times."

Ivelle tugged her cloak about her. The mountainous foothills were colder than she remembered. "You're not concerned about muggings or thefts?" Those roaming the streets looked like rogues and scoundrels with their swords and dirty clothes.

"Not really. Most here just want to do business. No questions asked. That means they'll avoid activities which risk exposing their identities." Claudine drew up her hood and dismounted before a simple building. "This place sells the finest cloth you can find in Orm."

Warmth and the pungent scent of dyes rushed over Ivelle as she entered. The place looked like Varway's mercantile with the rows of shelves and the short counter near the room's other end. The only difference was the bolt upon bolt of stacked fabric creating an array of vibrant colors more suitable for summer than the leaving winter.

"Halloo?" A short woman with dark hair and darker skin rounded the corner. Her dress, the same material as the bolts on the right, swished across the floor.

"I need to place an order." Claudine nudged Ivelle. "Peruse the cloths. See if there is something we can take back with us."

Ivelle wandered between the aisles. Dust and the smell of sweat clung to her clothes and skin. If she touched one of the shimmery fabrics, she'd ruin it. Not to mention the cost. How could Claudine afford so much material?

She stared at a vibrant smoky-blue bolt. Her linen blouse suddenly felt scratchy. What would it be like to wear such fabric all day every day without worrying about mussing it up?

"Thank you." Claudine's voice drifted down the aisle as coins clinked. "I will expect the order's remainder in a fortnight." Boots clomped against wooden boards. "Ivelle, did you find anything? I was thinking of cloth for spring wear."

Ivelle backed away from the delicate cloth. "Nothing here would keep a spring's chill away." Linen and flannel were what Claudine needed, not silk, satin, and organza.

Claudine hummed. "Well, then, off to another shop."

Three purchases and one armful later, Ivelle wrapped the material in oilcloth and secured it on the back of her saddle. Hopefully it would survive the five-day return to Varway. If not, Claudine was eight silvers out.

"I'm famished." Claudine peered around the village square. "For something other than biscuits and jerky. What about you?"

"As long as it's warm." Ivelle tucked her fingers into her sleeves. Was it her imagination, or had it grown colder?

"Come along, then. I know of a place that serves decent food if you stay away from the vegetable dishes. I don't know where they get their produce, but they are sorely lacking. Tastes like slime. We'll drop the horses off at the livery first."

The diner Claudine led Ivelle to was small. A wooden sign bearing a slice of pie swung above a wood-and-glass door, which opened to an eating room filled with patrons sitting at wooden tables.

"We can sit here." Claudine almost plopped into the squatty chair. After their order was taken and two cups of something called *coffee* placed before them, she laced her fingers and leaned forward. "How do you like it here?"

Ivelle grimaced at the drink's taste. How was it considered a delicacy? "I like Varway better. It's noisier and I don't like the guards swarming about, but it's familiar."

"I'm with you."

"What?" A knot began in Ivelle's gut at the hesitant expression adding more wrinkles to Claudine face. "What's wrong?"

"Nothing is wrong, dear. I just remember having this conversation with my aunt when I was your age, a few years after I lost my parents. We are not so unlike each other, you and I." Claudine stared at the table before starting and shaking her head. "None of that. Tell me, how have you been? We haven't had much time to really have a nice chat without interruption."

CHAPTER NINE

HOLDER

"THIS PLACE IS about a league into the forest and has been abandoned for a few years, but is still in decent condition."

Holder grimaced at the sloping roof and crumbled porch. Decent? More like decrepit. The old cabin slouched against some of the largest trees Holder had ever seen. Sparse grass quivered in the stiff wind, and pine needles crunched under the horses' hooves.

This was where he'd spend the next few months?

"No one will think to find you here." Officer Torgord dismounted. "Supplies will be brought every week by either Captain Geros or myself. One of us will always be in the general vicinity should you require assistance."

Holder joined him at the cabin's door. A musty smell leaked from the gaping crevice between the door and frame. How could this building be safe to live in?

"A stream is just beyond that line of trees." Officer Torgord's mustache shifted upward with his smirk. "I don't envy you hauling water for the princess' bath."

"Bath?"

"Yes, Specialist. Bath. You think just because she'll be living in a dump of a place for a few months means she will abandon hygiene?"

Pressure built in Holder's chest as Officer Torgord continued showing him around. Would he be a bodyguard if his family still lived? Or would his life have taken a different path? Would Father be proud?

No. No, he wouldn't be. Not if the letter's contents were anything to go by.

"First Lieutenant Cetrin is on his way with the princess, Svetlana, and enough supplies to last you the first two weeks. Only leave this place if there is immediate danger and you have no other choice. Svetlana will travel to the castle every few weeks to provide a report."

"What about the horses?"

"Build a lean-to for them." Officer Torgord eyed the roan like it would spit fire. "I'd trade that wild thing for another horse, though. You can't go chasing after it if it breaks loose."

Why did everyone assume he was inept?

Holder stuffed aside the rising aggravation. Officer Torgord only wanted Princess Anastasia to be safe. "Why this place?"

"It was a smuggler's hangout at one point." Officer Torgord's thin smile chilled Holder. "That ring is taken care of. No one else knows of this cabin. Smugglers keep their hiding places secret."

The sounds of horses tramping on pine needles drew Holder's hand to his sword. Safe this place might be, but he couldn't shake the feeling of unease.

He relaxed his grip as familiar faces entered the clearing. First Lieutenant Cetrin and Svetlana rode their own horses, while Princess Anastasia rode behind Captain Geros. Two overburdened pack horses staggered behind.

"No one else knows your location," Officer Torgord uttered. "Not even Cetrin's boy."

That could go one of two ways. Either the lack of knowledge would secure the princess' safety or, if they were attacked, they'd be left with no hope of reinforcement.

The warning in the back of Holder's mind told him it'd be the latter.

"Holder?" Princess Anastasia latched onto his hand after dismounting. She clung to him as the official, captain, and lieutenant disappeared into the trees, leaving the princess with only a twenty-year-old soldier as her sole means of protection and a nurse who possessed no ability to smile as her caregiver. "Why are we here?"

Svetlana scoffed. "Asking so many questions is unladylike, Princess. Just accept your lot in life and keep silent."

Was that what Svetlana had done? Holder studied the woman's narrow face. Gray streaked her hair and wrinkles formed canyons around her eyes and mouth, which was twisted in a permanent scowl of distaste. Was that what caused her to be so miserable to be around?

"Holder?" Princess Anastasia's voice cracked.

He knelt to her level. Something within ached. If history traveled an alternate path, would he have siblings? "We're here to keep you safe, Princess. King Eligor wants only the best for you and, right now, this is where you need to be."

Right?

If the king truly cared, wouldn't he allow his ward time to mourn? Wouldn't he assign her better protection? Holder was young and, while above average in his skill with the sword, was no Captain Geros or First Lieutenant Cetrin.

She blinked teary eyes. "How long will we be here? I miss my pony. Why couldn't we bring my pony?"

"Just for a few months." As for the stubby, overweight equine, it'd only be a hindrance if they needed a quick getaway and the princess refused to leave without her pony.

Holder offered what he hoped was a reassuring smile. "Think of it as an adventure. You'll get to learn all about the forest. Maybe even a bit about some of the animals living in it."

"Will you learn things too?"

"Yeah."

"Like what?"

"Like how to build a lean-to." Holder ushered her and Svetlana inside the cabin. The wooden planks stretching from wall to wall creaked beneath his weight, like one wrong step would cause them to cave in.

Dust coated the old, rickety pieces of furniture left from past inhabitants. A table shoved against the far wall sagged in the middle, rot visible even under the dust. Two three-legged stools were pushed under it. A river-rock fireplace and one single cabinet graced the room's right side.

By the stars, how much work would he need to do? He was a bodyguard, not a craftsman.

⬦⸱⸱⸱⬦

"I'm tired."

Holder closed his eyes and rubbed his forehead. A headache lingered, the result of a prime combination of stress, strain, and frustration. Cutting down and hauling logs wasn't in his military contract.

"You are a princess." Svetlana's words dripped with derision. "You are not meant to traipse through the wild like a hooligan."

Holder tugged a log. The axe, provided by Officer Torgord, made his muscles scream after a day of chopping, but it did the job. Sweat tickled his back, likely causing his shirt to look like the coat of the fabled leopard.

The forest swayed around them. Frost melted off branches in icy drips that somehow found his exposed skin without fail. One hundred steps until the cabin was in view. Maybe after this log he could take a break.

"I do not see why we must accompany you through this uncivilized forest. It is unbefitting for women of our stations."

"Mud won't kill you," Holder grunted. His shoulders ached in a way sword training couldn't dream to emulate. If nothing else, he would surely win a log-hauling contest on a muddy trail with little space to maneuver.

The lean-to entered his view first. A hodgepodge of logs and clay chinking, it looked like a mini forest lost a fight with a tornado.

Svetlana snatched Princess Anastasia's hand and pulled the little girl to the cabin. Only slightly less pitiful, the leaking roof had been fixed, the rotting table supplied parts of the lean-to, and the place had been gifted a thorough scrubbing under Svetlana's unblinking scrutiny.

Holder never wanted to see a rag and bucket of warm, sudsy water again.

"This is an outrage. I am a princess' nurse, not a scullery maid or cook." Svetlana gestured to her stained apron as she began her daily rant. "Surely there is one competent maid who could do the cleaning. And this hovel is an eyesore. Why the king would allow such an ugly thing in Orm is a mystery."

"I think it is charming." Princess Anastasia grinned at Holder. Her frilly green dress dragged with pine needles and splats of mud. "It's not scary like Rex Dorcha."

Svetlana peered down her thin nose at the princess. "Rex Dorcha is the highest architectural achievement in the world. You should appreciate the four hundred years' worth of work King Eligor poured into it. You should feel honored to live in such a place."

The Ageless King. King Eligor's nickname scraped across Holder's mind. How could one man live so long while everyone else died? How did the title of kinghood grant him what seemed to be immortality?

"What do you know of the king?" His words strained as he positioned the axe behind his shoulder and braced a foot on the log to keep it in place.

"Why?" Svetlana eyed him like he would concoct a devious scheme if she offered information.

"I don't know much about him. The history lessons didn't say much."

"He saved everyone in Orm from a despotic, greedy ruler. In return for his kindness and bravery, the stars granted him immortality."

"Why did he choose Lord Frigdor and Lady Ancelle to be his successors if he'll never die?"

Svetlana's gaze sharpened. "Mind your tongue. You are just a soldier and it would be but a headache for the king to have you silenced if you stick your nose where it does not belong." She called to the princess before disappearing into the cabin.

Holder shut his mouth and swung the axe. The reverberation of contact sent a tremor through his arms and shoulders. His stomach twisted like a tornado formed within. It was a simple question, one asked without malice or ill intent. Why the suspicion? Why the secrecy? Why the warning?

Or was it a threat?

What would the king have to hide? If he had saved the people of Orm, those who lived before Holder and those who would live after, why would he not have praises sung and stories told and his honor commemorated?

Even if the king was not one to seek accolades, such bravery and courage would not go unnoticed by others. Surely there were bards and scribes when the event took place. Someone would have recorded it.

If it even happened in the first place.

Holder stilled before mentally berating himself. *Stupid, foolish idiot.* Such thoughts would get him hanged for treason. The king would not lie about such an event.

Right?

The contents of his parents' letter flashed in his memory. According to them, the king wasn't who he said he was. So who—what—was he?

"Holder!" The princess skipped from the cabin, blonde braids bouncing. "Nurse says to go wash up unless you want to sleep in the lean-to."

Holder stowed away the tools and gathered clean clothing before once more traipsing through the forest. The stream lapped around his hands, gentle yet frigid. Splashing water onto his face, he scrubbed away the day's sweat and grime. His mind whirled from the conversation with Svetlana. Was he misreading the entire situation?

He stood and pulled off his dirtied shirt. The brigandine had proved impossible to work in, and it wasn't like someone was going to shoot him or try to place a knife in between his ribs as he hauled tree trunks.

His heart jumped when Princess Anastasia's voice belted through the forest, calling his name. He yanked on the clean shirt and bolted for the cabin. Blood rushed through him as adrenaline mounted, and he unsheathed his knife. Trees blurred in his peripheral.

Princess Anastasia met him at the clearing's edge. Her bright smile eased his thundering heart. She looked unharmed and unworried.

Thank you, stars.

"Come see what I found." She latched on to Holder's hand and tugged him toward the cabin. "Nurse says 'tis nothing of importance and only holds spiders and snakes. I think it is a secret cove."

"A secret cove?"

"Yes. You were right. This is an adventure! Do you think pirates lived here? Do you think they left their buried treasure?"

Svetlana met them in the doorway, a glare deepening her engraved frown lines. "Do not be preposterous, Princess. It is just a hiding spot. Nothing exciting and certainly not something to act like a commoner over."

"Nonetheless, I need to inspect it." Holder lit a candle and stared at the square hole beneath the table. If Officer Torgord was right and this had been a den for smugglers and those with the black market, then the hiding place might not be empty.

He lowered himself onto his stomach and held the candle in the opening. The dim light illuminated packed dirt below. "I'm going to check it out. If I can't climb back up, there's a ladder behind the cabin." It was as rotted as the table had been, and likely wouldn't hold his weight, but something was better than nothing.

Holder's body lurched from the jolt of landing. In every weapons and combat class given to guards and soldiers, they'd forgotten how to instruct landing without injuring the knees.

He turned in a slow circle. The dry scent of earth and mustiness spoke of the hiding place's secure build. Stone walls kept out moisture, but did little to deter the creepy crawlers that made the multiple spider webs stretching across the corners.

Light glinted off metal.

Holder advanced. The glint morphed into locks attached to three oblong boxes and a small chest lodged in the left corner. Splinters embedded themselves in his fingertips as he opened the first box.

By the stars. Three swords, untouched and untarnished, glimmered in the candlelight. Pale hilts decorated with golden ribbons spiraling around the pommels and onto the cross guard marked the weapons not from Orm. A peek into the other two boxes revealed the same.

Where had the swords come from? Who crafted them? Who wielded them? *Who smuggled them?*

Holder shook away the dazed wonderment and closed the lid, moving to the chest. Dust dimmed the wood's rich color, which looked to be a deep brown or even black. He traced the leather strap running widthwise over the arched lid. Where had such wood come from?

"Well?" Svetlana's sharp voice sliced through the silence. "What did you find?"

Something restrained him from speaking of the swords. "A chest."

"Is it filled with pretty jewels and flowers?" Princess Anastasia's clap echoed in the small dirt chamber.

"No." Holder tried the lid. "It's stuck. Empty, I think. Whoever was here before us cleared everything out. They just forgot this chest."

The lie tasted bitter, but no matter his attempts, he couldn't speak of the swords. If the weapons and chest belonged to smugglers, why forget such valuable swords and something made from a type of wood not found in Orm?

He glanced in the chest's direction as he hauled himself from the hiding place. It wasn't empty. He didn't know how he knew it, but that chest held something important.

CHAPTER TEN

THERESE

"SCHOLL WANTS YOU." Jolie's words rang through the Westa cabin like a mourning bell.

Therese shivered and tucked her hands into her sleeves. "He has decided?"

"He has, though he's not told me the verdict."

Therese's legs trembled as she bade her sisters farewell and traversed the path to Scholl's. Her heartbeat tripled in speed as she neared the office. No matter how many clients entered the office—and there were many, ranging from greedy kinfolk to rival gangs—it always smelled the same. Wood, tallow, and the mixed scents of autumn crocus and oleander leaves mingled to create a scent Therese associated with death.

Scholl sat straight as a sword's blade behind his desk. Another man lounged in the only other chair. A snake pin secured a blue cape over a leather breastplate. Vambraces encircled thick forearms. A military rank tattooed his cheek.

Scholl waved a hand in Therese's direction. "This assassin has been under my tutelage for a little over three years. She exhibits great skill with the bow and arrow, good comprehension of the knife and short sword, and is learned in herbal lore."

Weight grew in Therese's chest. Just what went on? And under Scholl's personal tutelage? Never once had the man personally trained her.

She stared at the shelves lining the back wall as the man perused her like one would a weapon for sale. Light from the old lantern illuminated the stacks of parchments on the farthest shelf. Her heartbeat quickened. Did this mean Scholl allowed her to be part of the team?

Please, stars, let it be so. She'd heard the stars controlled peoples' lives and often responded to prayers. Though she'd only seen evidence to the contrary, Therese grasped any thread of hope, no matter how random and unlikely.

"How many missions have you been on?" The man's voice twanged with the slight drawl of those from the High Mountains.

"Four, sir."

The man turned a lethal glare toward Scholl. "That is hardly enough experience to carry out one of the most important missions of the century."

"Look at her. Look at her face and eyes. Does she look like what you'd expect? No one will suspect her true intent under the guise of innocence and youth."

Therese bit her lip. Most missions required them to be stealthy and out of sight. Just who did this man want dead?

The man scrutinized her again before withdrawing a cloth pouch. Coins jangled as he tossed it on Scholl's desk. "Half now. You'll receive the rest when the job is completed."

"You accept her, then?"

"She will do. The target will be too busy to suspect a thing and, if she is seen, her average appearance will lessen suspicion."

Scholl snatched the pouch like he was afraid the client would change his mind. "Very well. I will let you two discuss the details while I draw up the contract."

The man stood. Tall and broad, he dwarfed the short and lean Scholl. Whatever rank he held, he likely intimidated those beneath him. "I require the girl to come with me. The necessary information cannot be discussed here."

Scholl's eyes almost disappeared from his scowl. "You know that is not how I conduct my business."

"I can go to another. Your type are not in short supply."

Scholl cursed. "Fine, but give us a minute."

The man grunted before eyeing Therese with a look that surely struck fear in the hearts of his fellow soldiers. Shivers traveled down Therese's spine. His eyes were cold, harsh. Cruelty hid in the dull green depths.

"You have five minutes."

Once he left, Scholl slammed shut the door. He whipped around. "I am giving you a chance. Mess this up and I'll send you to a brothel, understand? That debt will be paid one way or the other."

"I won't fail." Therese resisted the urge to tremble. She had to be strong for her sisters.

Whatever the cost.

Therese adjusted her hood as her client led her through a sylvan maze. The gelding beneath her startled as a rabbit hopped from behind a tree. The furry, potential meal stared her way before darting into the underbrush.

She drew a breath of crisp air. Butterflies bumbled in her stomach, producing an almost giddy feeling. She had her first client. At least a quarter of the coins given to Scholl in payment were hers. She could stock up on stores, maybe purchase fabric to replace Nora's and Delli's worn clothing.

The slight bubble of elation shattered as Rex Dorcha's black spires punctured the pale blue sky. Was this a trap? Rumors mentioned the king cracking down on the invisible black market and smugglers. Was he also implementing measures to catch Therese and fellow assassins?

Her client reined his horse onto a long black bridge spanning the chasm between the land and the five ridges on which the castle and its surrounding buildings were constructed. Hooves clattered against the stone.

Therese whispered her sisters' names to keep from turning around and running the other way. *This* was for them. *This* was so they could rise from where life brutally dumped them. *This* was so Therese didn't have to go with the only other option of repaying their debt.

The bridge ended at a large bailey. Two soldiers stood on either side of two massive wooden doors. Brick walls framed the bailey's left and right sides. Sounds of weapons clanging and shouts filled the air, rising beyond the right wall. On a higher ridge, past the first level of clay soil and sedimentary stone, sat a long, narrow building. The dim, shadowy shapes of horses grazed nearby, shuffling through that morning's skiff of snow.

"This way." Her client's gruff voice tempted Therese's heart to cease beating.

The soldiers saluted and opened the doors.

Lukewarm air carried the faint scents of smoke, oil, and wet stone. Therese gnawed at her lip to keep from gawking at the thick, high pillars, arched ceiling, and intricate red-and-black tapestries. So this was what the interior of a castle looked like.

Her client led her past the throne and into a slender hallway. "In here." He flicked a hand at the door.

For Nora and Delli. This is for Nora and Delli. Therese fisted her hands as she entered. A large, rectangular table surrounded by chairs filled the room. Maps hung from every wall, illuminated by candles held in intricate sconces. Deep scarlet rugs covered the stone floor.

Her client spread a map onto the table and jabbed a thick finger at it. "I will give you this map so you won't fail the mission by getting lost."

Therese wet her lips. Confidence, Jolie said, was one-third of the job. "Sir, what is my mission?"

Her client's harsh eyes met hers. "What do you know of spying?"

Therese squinted as the young man called another command to the feisty steed. The horse tossed its head but, after a moment, obeyed and shifted from walking to a trot. The man could be an ordinary citizen if not for the daggers strapped across his chest, the sword at his hip, and the military tattoo marking his cheek.

A king's guard.

Her stomach turned. Her client wanted her to kill one of his own.

Her breath caught as the horse halted without warning, flicking its ears and lifting its nose to snuffle the air. Did it smell her? Hear her? Silence was key to accurately beginning the mission, or so Scholl once told her.

She secured the light linen cloth over her nose and mouth, adjusted her hood, and traced the dark line drawn by her client on the map before he escorted her back to Scholl's.

At least one league into the forest, the cabin—and her target—was well hidden.

Smoke drifted from the sturdy stone chimney, which looked to be the strongest thing about the structure. The remnants of a porch lingered along the front and black rot spread along the roof's wooden shingles. One other horse grazed nearby.

Something within twisted. Though the cabin could soon be short an inhabitant, right then, the scene represented peace and tranquility.

If only such things truly existed in this dark, hopeless land.

Therese startled as the cabin door opened. "May we go exploring?" A child's voice bubbled with hope. "These trees are ever so pretty. Please, may we?"

A thin woman with graying hair and a young girl exited the cabin, the girl skipping and squealing. Was that the princess?

The man—bodyguard—secured the horse in the lean-to before scanning the area. His posture tensed before his shoulders slumped as the princess tugged at his sleeve, an action the older woman reprimanded in a harsh tone.

Therese held her breath. If the bodyguard spotted her, things could turn nasty. She conducted a mental scan. The map and the knife Lucian gifted her hung from her belt, as did a vial of sleeping powder she could use if the bodyguard caught and overpowered her. Other than that, she possessed no weapons, nothing else to ensure her survival.

For Nora and Delli.

She exhaled the breath trapped in her lungs. *Patience*, Lucian said. But how could she be patient when her sisters' lives were at stake?

Patience. If all this job required was stalking and investigating, she could do it. This was easy compared to some of Lucian's and Jolie's tales.

The princess clapped her hands as she jumped up and down. "Please?"

Therese's heart pinched. When was the last time Nora or Delli faced the day with such excitement? Had she done enough to keep them safe from the burdening cares of life?

She strained to hear the woman's answer. If they left, she could sneak into the cabin and investigate.

"Please?"

The bodyguard glanced at the horses before nodding. The princess squealed and clapped her hands despite the woman's fearsome glower.

Heart thumping, Therese crept across the clearing after they disappeared from view. What if they found her horse? What if they returned when she was still in the cabin? She was too clean to claim being lost, too equipped with her knife and the oleander in her pouch to claim total helplessness.

If they returned and found her, she could take on the woman. She could even take on the bodyguard, knock him out with the sleeping powder. But the princess? How could she subject a child to such a thing?

Stars, please keep them away.

Therese inhaled a steadying breath. *Brave.* She had to be brave for her sisters. The second half of the money promised could see them through a year if she properly rationed the funds between supplies and paying toward the debt.

The door creaked as she slipped into the cabin. Did her target know nothing of safety? Why had he not installed a lock? Then again, the sagging wood likely wouldn't support the weight of a lock.

The cabin was simple and twice the size of the Westa hut. A table and two stools stood nearest the door. A miniature cooking area and large fireplace covered the room's left wall. Pinecones and stones decorated the simple, half-rotten mantle. Three bedrolls took up the remaining area, along with crates, a pile of canvas bags, and one wooden trunk piled in the corner.

She crossed to the bedrolls. All three were neatly made. Her fingers trembled as she reached out to touch the nearest blanket. Lucian's training echoed in her mind. It smelled of soap and pine. The other two smelled like the floral soap Jolie was so fond of.

Therese eased a hand beneath her target's pillow. Nothing but rough wool scratched her fingers. No bumps or lumps indicated a hidden item.

She moved to the pile of sacks. Three opened to reveal a woman's and a child's clothing while blankets filled the other. Underneath the sacks lay a pair of leather saddlebags. The flaps and snake clasps lifted to reveal a miniature dagger and a folded shirt the same color as the one her target wore.

Therese bit her lip as she eased the saddlebags from the pile and removed the shirt. The material felt like linen, soft and easy to move in. More clothes and a folded piece of parchment followed. Her breath caught as she unfolded the yellowed material. Delicate writing flowed across the page, creating a letter from a mother to her son.

She traced the worn edges and faded ink. Had he also lost his parents?

No! It was imperative she stayed on task. Though tears gathered in her eyes after reading the letter, its contents were nothing short of treasonous. She searched until she found the princess' sketchbook and pencil. Holding her breath, she copied the letter's contents before tearing out the page and stuffing it in her belt.

Therese thanked the stars as silence greeted her when she tiptoed back to her horse. The stars must be granting her favor, for never had she heard of a mission being resolved so quickly and easily.

⋄

"This is what you uncovered?"

Therese nodded. Energy coursed through her, making her hands shake and her breaths tremble. She did it. She had completed a mission in less than a day. Perhaps her success would convince Scholl he hadn't made a mistake.

Her client stared at the copy, like doing so would summon the bodyguard. "You read the original thoroughly, I assume."

"Yes, sir."

"Excellent." Her client placed it on the table. "I commend your promptness. Now for the second part. This is where your sneaking skills come in."

A haze settled in Therese's mind as her client—a captain, she'd heard—detailed the next step in his plan. Usually, clients were eager to see the target killed. Why drag it out?

"If your hand if forced, remember the princess is delicate. Nothing more than a child who knows little of Orm's dangers. The nurse is an asset to us. No harm is to come to her or the princess. When you dispose of the bodyguard, do it quietly. If blood is spilled, clean it up before the princess sees. If you accomplish this task by other methods, and there is no blood and no sign of injury or trauma, just leave the body."

91

"Yes, sir. How would you like the target disposed of if there is blood?" The word tasted foul. Was she really discussing someone's death in the same manner she discussed stealth techniques with Jolie?

But that was better than the alternative. Revolting as it was, at least it only cost her conscience and heart.

"Drag the body away and leave it somewhere we can easily find and retrieve it. If you don't employ a blade or arrow, leave the body. The princess' nurse knows what to do."

CHAPTER ELEVEN

ROGAN

ROGAN STARED AT the horde of bodies, colors, and objects cluttering Varway's south entrance. Travelers, merchants, and townsfolk scuffed, scolded, and screamed at each other as more collisions occurred.

Chaos. Pure, noisy chaos.

What a mess.

He grumbled and fingered a dagger's hilt. He couldn't find his sanity in the bedlam, much less some artifact meant for the black market.

Common soldiers scrambled toward the mess, their shouts adding to the tumult.

Rogan rolled his shoulders. Captain Geros would march straight into the fray and command the attention and obedience of all involved. Father would bellow out an order to gain notice, hew down those who disobeyed even a fraction, and arrest all involved, whether it was their fault or not.

The back of his neck prickled. He steeled himself and glared ahead. His wrist throbbed, no doubt more swollen and bruised than it'd been that morning. Just another incentive to obtain his fifth dagger. The sooner he could escape Father and his wrath, the better his life would be.

Rogan straightened and locked away the emotions threatening to nudge their way into his day. Messy things, and wholly unnecessary. Besides, they were distracting, and he needed to focus on the task at hand. Best to ignore what happened last night. Best to act like First Lieutenant Maximo Cetrin wasn't watching. Best to act like he wasn't thinking about his father's anger instead of his temporary job.

Which made no sense. Why send king's guards to accomplish what normal soldiers could easily achieve?

Rogan stalked toward the mess. Wagons turned on their sides, their contents spilling out, created a hazardous maze. Just how was he to wade through so much junk? He grit his teeth. He had to do this. This could be a test, could be one step closer to getting that fifth dagger. One step closer to captaincy. One step closer to escaping Father.

The nearest townsfolk eyed him like they would a beast of unknown origin. Maybe that meant they would listen to him. The stars certainly knew he needed their cooperation.

"What happened?" The question was barely formed before harsh voices pelted him from every side. Rogan held up a hand, meeting the scowls with a glare. "Go stand by your wagon, or cart, or horse, or whatever you were traveling with. And keep quiet."

Please, keep quiet. The pounding in his skull worsened with every aggravated shout.

"Reporting in, sir." A soldier with a private's tattoo skidded to a halt next to Rogan. Stiff as a sword blade, he stared at the line of people stretching farther than sight. Round eyes, chubby cheeks, and an equally chubby build marked his youth.

Rogan felt like an octogenarian next to him.

"I am here as well." A tall, thin man with a reedy voice and graying hair took his place next to the private. He set down a bulging satchel before withdrawing a slim piece of wood topped with vellum. Brandishing a quill pen from a hidden pocket in his faded orange robe, he nodded to Rogan. "I am Secretary Lanso. We may begin now that I am prepared."

Irritating little mole-rat.

Rogan grimaced and gripped his sword's hilt. All he had to do was survive. Survive the people and survive babysitting an overly enthusiastic youth and a secretary with an ego too large for his stick-thin build.

He sighed at the line of people stretching around the small copse of trees half a league away. How many yammering voices and irate merchants must he deal with?

Curse the fools who caused the wreck.

He moved toward the first person in line, an elderly gent with a small, two-wheeled cart hauled by an ox. After taking the man's testimony and searching through crates of wool, Rogan sent the grizzled fellow on his way. As soon as the cart cleared the space, another replaced it.

Time passed until sweat gathered on his neck, defying the air's chill. His hand cramped from gripping the unforgiving hilt, and his ears rang from the noise. Rogan braced himself and met the gaze of the next couple. Swathed in bearskin, they stood near a droopy-eared donkey hitched to a cart. "How were you involved or affected by the crash?"

The man ran fingers through a dark, bushy beard. "Just stopped by it. It didn't hurt us or our cart."

"But it spooked Dandy." The woman patted the donkey's neck. Her braid swung as she shook her head. "Poor thing."

"Where are you from?"

"A village in the High Mountains." The man shifted his weight. Sweat sparkled on his brow.

Lanso scratched down the answer.

"What wares do you bring?"

"Skins, furs, and pelts." The woman leaned into the man. Her eyes looked too wide for her oval face. "We trap bears, cougars, wolves, hares...anything with good fur."

"I need to inspect the cart's contents." Rogan stared, waiting for them to remove the tarp stretched across the top. It took everything he had not to give into impatience. The king himself had given him this job, and he needed to complete it.

"If you mess up the merchandise, it won't sell."

"Sir, you need to remove the tarp."

With movements slower than a frozen slug, the woman untied the tarp and folded it back to reveal gray, black, and brown pelts.

Rogan lifted the furs. "How many are you carting?"

"We didn't count. Some village members added some of theirs in as well."

Rogan withdrew a thick brown fur. "What animal was this?"

"A bear." The woman's words rushed. "'Tis massive. Took us a good while to figure out how to fold it without taking up too much space."

"I bet."

"Specialist?" The private shifted. "I grew up in the mountains and I've never seen a pelt that thick."

"It was a grizzly, boy. They're huge." The man pinned the private with a deadly glare.

"I concur with the private. Such a pelt is unnaturally large, even for such a gargantuan ursine." Lanso's pen never ceased. Was the man recording the entire conversation?

Rogan's breathing quickened as he unfolded the fur. If the private was right, this could be a promotion for both of them.

A packet fell to the ground.

"What's this?" Rogan brushed dirt from the leather material and opened the pouch. His throat tightened. He may not be a healer, but he recognized water hemlock when he saw it. "Private, please hand me the rope."

Lanso inserted himself into Rogan's space, peering down a nose as thin as the rest of him. "Indeed. Water hemlock is considered contraband. Smuggling it is a death offense."

A dry, barked laugh shook the man's dense frame. "You think you and some twig of a boy can take us on?" One massive hand moved toward the wide leather belt.

A shard of fear embedded in Rogan's mind. His heart jumped a beat. What a fool he was, that he did not check them for weapons, did not act on the whisper of intuition which told him something was off.

He drew his sword and leveled it at the man's throat. "Private, secure the woman."

"You have no grounds to arrest us," the woman spat.

"You two are under arrest for conspiring treason and harm against the kingdom. You will be escorted to the dungeons where you will await further investigation and trial." When the man snatched at the slight bulge in his sleeve, Rogan pricked him with the sword. "I wouldn't. Now yield or be subdued the hard way."

As a squad of soldiers escorted the couple and evidence away, Rogan clapped the private's shoulder. "Good work."

"You think so?" The boy's face brightened. "My pa was a tanner. I know a thing or two about skins and stuff."

Lanso sniffed. Still in Rogan's space. "Yes, well, let us resume." He backed away. "I am prepared."

Heaviness invaded the swell of pride from saving innocent lives from the hemlock's poison. If only Father would be proud of his son's actions, of how he'd kept the vile substance from entering Varway.

He couldn't remember the last time Father was proud of him.

"I thought they looked suspicious. They were sweating and shifty."

"Right." It wouldn't do to question what could be. His job was to check for dangerous, smuggled items, not dwell on the life he would never have. Rogan blinked away the unsettling feelings. The only way to get through life was to focus on the present and plan for the future.

"I think the next person is hiding something as well." The private nodded as a hunched old woman shuffled forward with a humble, splintery cart. "She's acting awfully suspicious by never looking anyone in the eye."

"We'll see." Rogan waited to address the woman until she drew even with him. Red hung from thin shoulders, wisps of white hair escaping the hood. "Ma'am?"

"Specialist." Her voice croaked. Bloodshot, weary eyes dimmed with age searched his face. "I'm bringing my late husband's things from my home in the foothills."

Rogan moved toward the cart. "I'm sorry for your loss." He cringed at the grief lining her weathered face. The same heartache had clung to Holder for months after he lost his parents. Would this woman recover as Holder had?

"You will find his carpentry tools and some of the things he crafted." Her voice quavered.

Rogan eyed the carving of a fish. He knew genuine grief when he saw it. The only thing this woman hid was the depth of her shattered heart. "Private," he barked. If only he could cease experiencing such deep emotions. "Escort this woman to her destination. Secure her a horse or mule so she can ride."

"What?" the private gaped at him. "But she—"

"Is trying to make a living. Go. Now. She's done nothing wrong."

"All due respect, Specialist—"

Rogan grabbed the kid's shoulder and hauled him close. "Don't let one time of being right get to your head. We have a job to do, one we can't mess up. Am I understood, Private?"

The boy nodded and stumbled away when Rogan released him. Paleness erased his usual ruddy complexion. He scrambled toward the old woman who watched with little change in countenance.

Rogan sighed. *This was his job.* It was his job to do what the king needed him to do. Simple as that. He couldn't complain about it. Wouldn't complain about it. "Next," he growled as the old woman's cart squeaked away.

"That was most unprofessional, Specialist."

"No one asked you, scribbler."

"It's *secretary*." The man huffed. "Youth these days. No ounce of respect. None!" Another huff. "Do not proceed until I am prepared."

Horses clopped forward. Without looking up, he could feel the fiery gaze. Few said anything about his rank and position, either cowed by the blue cape or the emblem painted on his cheek, but he saw the peeks of fear. Heard the muffled whispers.

He groaned internally as his gaze met glaring gray. By the stars, it was just his luck that he would deal with the smart-mouthed spitfire from that ridiculous emporium.

"Did you have anything to do with the crash?" Rogan forced the words through gritted teeth. Those sharp eyes wouldn't draw a reaction from him.

Claudine DeGrim shook her head. "No. We are merely hindered by it. Was anyone injured?"

"Nothing serious. Names, please." He already knew the proprietress', but he'd done everything he could to scrub the girl from his memory.

"You didn't ask the widow her name."

"That is none of your concern. Names, please, unless you want to be fined for hindering an investigation." Wasn't that how these things went? He'd heard Officer Torgord mentioning something of the sort.

"Claudine DeGrim."

"Ivelle Quade."

Lanso muttered as he scribbled.

"Where are you returning from?"

"You act like we're criminals," Ivelle snapped. With her dark hair, unique eye color, and fiery spirit, she reminded him of the statue of the female warrior standing in Rex Dorcha's main bailey. All she needed was a sword and armor.

Of course, she'd probably stab him if she had a weapon.

"Are you?" Rogan locked gazes with her. No flicker of panic or fear, no light sweat on her brow or upper lip, and no shifting. Either she was an exceptional liar or truly innocent.

"What do you think?"

Claudine sighed. "Ivelle, mind yourself. I raised you to be a lady, not a ruffian who engages in useless arguments."

"Ma'am, you failed at raising a lady." More like an untamed brat with a sword for a tongue. Rogan eyed their horses and the lumpy packs hanging behind the saddles. "Where are you returning from?"

"The foothills."

He marked it down. "You traveled unescorted?"

"As you can see, we are fine. There are not so many ne'er-do-wells abroad as there are here."

"I need to examine your belongings."

Ivelle cursed him with a look that likely sent men cowering. "Why?"

"By orders of the king." Stars help him, this was more dangerous than being the king's bodyguard. If he wasn't going to perish from a hidden weapon, it'd be from Ivelle's glare.

CHAPTER TWELVE

IVELLE

MUSCLES ACHING AND mind dulled from lack of sleep, courtesy of the thin mattresses offered at the two inns between Varway and DorFord, Ivelle flopped onto her bed and groaned. The run-in with that infuriating, smug, and arrogant soldier hadn't helped her souring mood.

She cringed at the fatigue brought about from keeping the memories at bay. Why now? Why, after ten years of safety and semi-reprieve from the monsters who upended her life, did the stars think she needed to deal with soldiers? All the encounters did were revive old feelings and remembrances about what had been.

What had almost been.

"Are you okay?" Borros' deep voice filled the small room. "Claudine said you had an encounter with a king's guard."

"I'm fine." Her voice cracked in betrayal.

"I know I'm an old man in your opinion, but that doesn't mean my hearing is gone."

Ivelle flipped onto her back. She'd hate herself later for getting her bed dusty, but at the moment, her emotions had control.

She drew a deep breath. This emotional tumult must go away. She hadn't survived by giving into feelings.

"Ivelle? You need to talk?"

"Why now? After ten years, why *now*? It's like the stars conspire against me."

"I'll take that as a yes," Borros mumbled. He drew the chair from her desk and plopped down. His thick, sturdy frame dwarfed the delicate design. "Spill, kiddo."

"I don't get it. Alright, they arrived and were ungentlemanly and rude while searching the emporium. I thought that would be the last time I had to suffer their presence. But no. What do we find while riding back? A long line of people being interrogated by some fresh-faced, uppity, rude, sarcastic man who thinks we're smugglers."

Borros' weathered face twisted into a smirk. "We are, in a way."

"That's irrelevant. Point is I can't get away from them."

"So you feel like it ruined your day."

"Yes."

A low chuckle rumbled from Borros. "I can tell Claudine raised you. You have her feisty spirit." He turned serious. "Listen. One bad thing does not make your entire day horrible. You had a good trip with Claudine, and I know it was productive. She enjoyed it. Didn't you?"

"Yes." Ivelle groaned and toyed with the ties to her cloak. The aggravation bled away, leaving a space of emptiness. She felt drained, void of anything and everything.

This wasn't right. She wasn't some ninny who caved under ridiculous feelings. She was stronger than that. Smarter than that.

"I wish I could tell you life will be smooth going, but I can't. This place ain't perfect. All you can do is your best, and you'll get on alright."

Wasn't that what she'd been doing? What did the stars call learning secrets that could land her a death sentence if she was caught? What did they call aiding in the black market? What did they call patching up those wanted by the king for nothing more than being unable to pay their taxes?

"Well." Borros slapped his knees and stood. "You know you can talk to me and Claudine, right? About anything?"

Ivelle hummed an answer. As true as that was, she could not voice the pain in her heart.

In her soul.

For so long she had been strong. For so long she had repressed the memories.

Why couldn't she continue to do so? What made it so difficult?

That cursed king's guard.

"Ivelle?" Claudine called from the main area of their living quarters. "We've an influx of customers. Can I get your help?"

"I'll tell her you'll be right in after you change and wash up." Borros left, closing the door behind him.

"Oh, thank the stars. There you are." Claudine bustled toward Ivelle. Three women in bright silk followed. Perhaps wives of King Eligor's advisors, or maybe of the higher soldiers. "Borros is trying to sell some weapons. Can you man the counter?"

"Of course." Ivelle threaded her way around person after person. What was with the crowd? A wave of exhaustion washed over her at the long line of customers curling around the counter. At least the transactions were typically expedient, though some of the grumpier individuals required more patience than she feared she possessed.

"How was your shopping experience?" Ivelle sent a bright smile at the burly man. Calloused hands cleaner than his clothes. The smells of earth and animal drifted from him. A farmer.

"Fine." He placed a square of leather on the counter. "Who is your supplier?"

"I do not know." One of the few truths she told customers about the emporium's supply sources. "That will be six bits."

The line of customers dwindled until the last, a man of average height and dressed in village homespun, shuffled forward. Cropped brown hair matched thick eyebrows hanging over piercing eyes. A yellow bit of fabric draped from a belt. Tendoned hands gripped a crate.

Ivelle stiffened, her smile cracking. Her fingers traced the countertop's lip as she felt for the bump. Ah, there it was. She loosened the clasp, and a similar yellow cloth dangled from a hook. *Stars, please let Borros or Claudine be in here.*

Surely they would see the yellow cloth and realize she needed assistance.

"Hello." Claudine's voice carried none of the wariness infusing Ivelle's muscles. "How can we help you?"

"I have things for your shop." The unique accent marked the man an outsider to Varway. He hefted the crate onto the counter.

"If you are interested in a trade, I will have to give the items a thorough inspection."

"No trade. Just clearing out the barn." His accent thickened the vowels. "Whatever you don't want, give away."

Claudine's mouth thinned. "Sir, this is very unusual. What are you up to?"

"Nothing, ma'am. Your fancy store sells things like this. Rather them here than somewhere that doesn't appreciate their value. They...fit in better."

Ivelle toyed with the knife strapped to the counter's underside. Who was this man? What did he really want? Was he undercover for the king?

Borros had taught her to trust her gut, her instinct.

Instinct told her he hid something.

Claudine lifted the first item from the box. Her forehead wrinkled. "Sir, this could bring you in a good bit of money. Are you certain you don't want to sell?"

"Ma'am, I just want it out of my life."

"I cannot accept this without some form of payment. This dagger alone is worth more than this emporium makes in a year."

"Ma'am, that dagger costs more than your store makes in a decade. It's the highest quality. Made by the best blacksmith in existence." The man nodded at them before striding away. The door banged shut behind him.

"No dagger is worth what we make in a year, let alone a decade." Borros emerged from the back and glowered at the man's form through the window. "I ain't buying that line about it being from the best blacksmith, either. Everyone knows the only quality ones are here in Varway or the south, and that's not of southern make. If it's from anywhere else, it's not worth a grain of dirt. He's pulling your leg, Claudine."

Claudine withdrew a dagger from the crate and unsheathed it. "Ivelle, would you lock the front door and close the display windows' curtains?"

Ivelle snapped the velvet curtains shut and flipped the *open* sign to *closed.* Her fingers twitched as she eyed the crate. What did it hold? How had the man known their signal?

"Look," Claudine breathed. She displayed the dagger.

Ivelle's breath caught. Thin gold bands wrapped around an ivory hilt. One melded into a simple, waved fuller on the short, pale blade. "It looks like light."

Borros grunted and took the weapon. He weighed it, staring at the blade like rays of sunlight would spring from the hilt. "I'll be. Maybe that loon was right."

"Who crafted it, do you think?"

"A master craftsman. No one else could construct such a delicate design." Borros traced the blade. "I don't even think it was made in Orm," he muttered.

Ivelle tore her gaze from the weapon and dug into the crate. Vials of liquid, pouches of what smelled like spices and herbs, fabric wrapped in oilcloth, and a book.

Cracked leather covered the yellowed pages. Tiny letters in slanted, crisp penmanship filled every inch, slightly blurred from water damage. A faded purple ribbon marked the last page with writing.

"What is it?" Claudine peered at Ivelle from her inspection of the fabrics.

"I think it's a diary."

"Why would he think we want a diary?" Borros scoffed. "Who cares to read about someone else's life?"

"I would." Ivelle tucked the book to her chest. "I'll look through it. If there's nothing of interest, we can just dispose of it."

Ivelle stretched her arms before snuggling under the duvet and grabbing the diary. Claudine had warned her it was nothing important—merely the ramblings from someone long ago, but the book's cover alone promised her wrong.

A rectangle was impressed into the once soft and supple leather, framing the slight indent of a name. Ivelle traced it.

The letters were impossible to read in the dull light. Whose was it? Where was the person now?

She opened to the first page.

"'It is as we feared. Mariline and I must leave. Our son, our precious, little son, will be left with his best friend's family. To take a child on such an escape is unfathomable, especially as winter nears. Our survival is far from guaranteed, much less that of our son's. I dare not trust the father, for I've seen the darkness in his eyes, but I know at least he will have a roof over his head and food in his belly. He will be happy with his friend.

"We hope the journey will be easy, but nothing ever is in this painful life. It will be good for Mariline to be away from our precious daughter's grave. A fortnight old is too young to die, but at least she is freed from this world, if there is any sort of afterlife. I pray the stars will show us the foolishness of our idea, but everything I've seen speaks against it. Something is wrong with King Eligor. The darkness in Maximo's eyes is nothing compared to the utter evil I see in the king's. This is not the life of peace my father spoke of. A monster rules us, though few know it."

CHAPTER THIRTEEN

DULL LIGHT SEEPED into the cellar as Holder lowered himself down. Svetlana insisted he make himself scarce during the princess' bath, so scarce he became.

He grunted as he landed. Curiosity made his fingers twitch. That chest couldn't be empty. It alone looked costly. Why would it be left behind?

Grime coated the lock. Holder inserted a dagger and wiggled the tip. The lid unlocked with a soft click.

He held his breath as he peered inside. Yellowed parchments and faded ink lined the bottom. He tipped the chest upside-down. The pages fluttered to the dirt floor.

"By the stars," he whispered. The pages felt delicate between his fingers, as brittle as dried leaves. The scant light did little to illuminate the thin, almost spidery handwriting. Elegant illustrations decorated the margins.

"Holder," Princess Anastasia called. "I'm done. You can come kill this spider now."

"Hang on." Holder eased the parchments into his belt and hauled himself up. He'd retrieve the chest another time.

Svetlana's disapproving scowl stared him down. "I thought you said the chest was empty."

"Thought it was."

"What are those?" Her avian-like eyes trained on the parchments. "What do they say?"

"I don't know." Holder drew a breath to keep the suspicion away. Svetlana posed questions anyone would ask.

But the king trusted her. And his parents hadn't trusted the king. Making those the king trusted untrustworthy.

His pulse drummed. The parchments had to be special or else they wouldn't be in a chest once belonging to a smuggler or hunter for the black market. If only he could read them without the nurse glaring over his shoulder.

If Svetlana was this curious about parchment scraps, how would she react if she knew of the weapons?

"Holder, the spider." Princess Anastasia pointed to a spot near the tub. That awful, cursed tub weighing more than twenty draft horses and that put a permanent twinge in Holder's lower back.

He disposed of the spider and emptied the tub. At Svetlana's insistence, Princess Anastasia began her lessons. When a quick perimeter search assured him the area was safe, Holder snatched his book and settled in the corner, doing his best to tune out Svetlana's annoying voice and Princess Anastasia's whining.

⬦⋯⋯⬦

"I'm bored."

"I know."

"Like, really, really bored."

Holder sighed and set his book down. He'd already tended the horses and chopped enough wood to last them five winters. Without his book, he'd be bored too. At least

Svetlana was at the castle, providing her biweekly report and unable to put him to work doing some tedious task like scrubbing the walls. Again. "Did Svetlana give you any embroidery to do? Or something to sketch?"

Princess Anastasia pouted. "Yes, but that's boring." She grinned and pointed at him. "Read me the story."

"It's a history book, Princess. I doubt you'd be interested."

"But I'm bored. What's it about?"

"Orm's far southern and western areas."

"Aren't they the ones who bring Grandfather those pretty jewels and cloth?"

"Yes." Not for the first time, Holder questioned why King Eligor selected Varway. The nondescript town offered little compared to the cities, and with wood and stone its main exports, it possessed none of the shine and polish either.

"Then read me the parchments you found." She crossed her arms and lifted her chin. "I'm the princess. I command it."

She was a spoiled brat. Still, Holder couldn't deny her. He never thought about starting a family, and it'd likely be best if he didn't. He'd be unable to refuse his children anything.

The thought jolted him. A *family*? That would never happen. That simple knowledge, however, did nothing to ease the yearning he had long buried.

"I don't know if it's a story and, if it is, it looks like parts are missing."

"How do you know?"

Stars help him, she was in a bratty mood. But he'd take this any day over being alone.

Holder showed her the small number on each right bottom corner. "These are pages two, three, and five. One and four are missing. You still want me to read it?" It could be text unsuitable for little girls, but the stunning aqua and purple lines spiraling down the margins and the bright, golden sun in each upper left corner hinted to no frightening words.

At her nod, he motioned her over and pointed to each word read. As Holder neared the middle of the page, tension clenched his gut. The next word…no, that was a coincidence. The name had to be common in the era this was written, yet he'd never heard of another called it.

"This is a weird story."

"Yeah, it is." Holder folded up the parchments. Cold infiltrated his body. If this was the same man who ruled Orm, the parchments were treason.

He would be tried and killed for sedition if King Eligor knew.

Weight filled his chest. The right thing would be to burn the parchments. The right thing would be to tell the princess it was a story written by some deluded, deranged criminal desiring revenge.

Holder's hands shook. This wasn't dangerous.

This was deadly.

"Why are there horses outside the cabin?" Princess Anastasia peeked through a hole of missing chinking. "Were we expecting visitors? Are we having tea?"

The cold in Holder's blood turned to ice, and he took the princess' spot. "No," he whispered. If only this were tea. If only they had the wrong location. But, judging from the knife in one's hand and the loaded crossbow in the other's, the men weren't there for a midday snack.

His breathing quickened as a fine sheen of sweat beaded on his forehead and neck. This was his job, to protect the princess. He just never expected to actually defend her from anything.

"Holder?" Princess Anastasia tugged his sleeve. "What's going on?"

Holder met her eyes. Bright, lively, and sweet. How could he allow harm to come to her? He silently turned the table to its side, top facing the door. No time to lower her into the cellar, not since the ladder broke after Svetlana tripped over the princess' pencil and pitched into it. "Put on something warm. When I open the door, get behind the table until I call. And close your eyes."

"Are they here for tea?"

He knelt to her level and gently gripped her shoulders. Her *life* was in his hands. The life of the king's heir, of Orm's *princess.* An innocent child. The realization hit him like a punch to the chest. He was the only one standing between her and a kidnapping.

"No, they're not here for tea. Take the parchments. And here's a dagger. Do what I told you. Now."

He drew his sword and balanced a dagger in his left hand. He had no shield, no armor other than his brigandine and bracers, which would take too long to get on.

If an arrow hit him in a vital area, getting the princess to safety would be impossible.

He slipped outside, yanking the door shut behind him. The two men stared. Confusion wrinkled their brows before the stockier one pointed the crossbow at Holder.

"So the princess' bodyguard is a mere pup. Drop the sword, boy."

"Who are you? Sweat formed a slick film between Holder's hand and the hilt.

"I want you to drop the sword."

Holder grit his teeth. He'd trained for this scenario, practiced it many times, but never against a loaded crossbow. Instead of someone truly intending harm behind the weapons, it had been Rogan or Captain Geros. He always knew the worst he'd walk away with were a few bruises and minor scrapes.

Now he might not walk away at all.

The sword slipped in his grasp.

The swordsman advanced, sword in hand. "Just cooperate and you'll be fine."

Not really. It wasn't like failure to protect the princess would cost him his life.

Holder lunged. Swords collided before a bolt whistled past, grazing his cheek. With a quick move, the man blasted Holder's sword from his grip. Holder dodged the swipe and snatched the man's wrist, using his bodyweight to turn the man's hand inward. A satisfying crack rewarded him as the man's sword fell and the attacker screamed.

Another bolt flew. He tackled the man and wrestled him into the line of fire. He hated using a human shield, but he had to protect the princess at all costs, even if that meant at another's expense.

The man slammed the heel of his boot into Holder's shin before wrenching away. Holder lurched for balance as pain spread to his knee and ankle. He threw himself down as a brown blur caught the edge of his sight.

A bolt whined overhead and slammed into the cabin's wall.

Inhaling dirt and sweat, Holder drew another dagger while grabbing for the swordsman. He held the edge to the man's neck, keeping enough distance away to protect his shins. "Walk forward."

Uttering oath after oath, the man obeyed. His companion cursed as they neared.

Keeping the blade to the man's neck, Holder drew another. His sword was preferable, but attempting to grab it would result in placing himself in the line of fire. "Drop the crossbow."

The man obeyed. Slicked-back brown hair and a dark complexion marked him from the deep south.

Holder met his glare. The tables were turned, but that could change in a blink. "Who sent you?"

The swordsman's shoulders shook as he chortled. "Your last question, and that's what you ask? You're all the same. 'Who sent you?'" he mimicked in a high-pitched voice.

Holder again formed the question when a dull pain throbbed through his nose as his head snapped back. Blinking away tears, he hurled the dagger in the swordsman's direction. A muffled curse accompanied the sound of a body hitting the ground.

He leapt forward as the other man raised the crossbow, a bolt loaded. The projectile whined through the air as it zipped past Holder's ear. He latched onto the man's arm, yanking him away from the horse.

If he didn't disable the crossbow, he had zero hope of survival.

The man kicked him in the knee. A knife glanced off Holder's shoulder before lodging into the dirt.

Holder staggered backwards before regaining his balance and lunging. The man fumbled the crossbow before lifting it.

The impact tripped Holder. He grunted as he hit the ground. A shadow fell across him.

"You put up a good fight, boy, just like they said you would."

Holder regained his breath and fingered a dagger as the crossbow aligned with his head. When the man shifted his grip, he drew the dagger and stabbed it into the man's foot.

The man howled.

Pushing to his feet, Holder wrestled the crossbow away and threw it toward the trees. He blocked the man's punch and returned one of his own.

The man dropped.

So much for Officer Torgord's promised assistance.

Holder grunted as fire filled his leg. The surrounding trees revealed no movement, no sign that backup was near, but his instinct warned somewhere close there were more kidnappers. And they knew Holder won.

He staggered toward the cabin. "Princess, come out." His voice cracked as though it gave way to the strain of staying upright.

Princess Anastasia raced from the cabin. She stumbled to a stop and screamed.

Holder grimaced. A dead body was nothing she should see at this age, but it couldn't be helped. He gasped as the fire intensified. Dull agony spread through the rest of his body. "Can you grab my horse's halter and reins?"

She nodded, mouth moving like a fish that was out of water, and sprinted back into the cabin.

Holder grit his teeth and lurched toward the lean-to. The gelding snorted and sent him a look promising trouble. "Not now." *Stars, please not now.*

Princess Anastasia soon returned and thrust the leather tack at Holder. He willed his hands to steady as they trembled during his attempts to bridle the gelding. Once he secured the last clasp, he managed to lead the gelding outside. The horse jerked back and shook its head. Holder tugged the reins. So help him, he'd work this horse into submission. Now was not the time for equine antics.

Everything again blurred. They weren't safe yet. Far from it. Where was the securest place? Rex Dorcha was almost two leagues away, and they'd have to pass through a valley and unwooded slopes before reaching it.

Varway. Varway was closer at just under a league, and it would be easy to be lost amidst the throngs of people.

Holder limped to the tree stump near the cabin. There was no way he could mount without assistance, not with the near inability to walk. He forced himself to stand on the stump and sling his right leg over. "Princess, do the same."

Once Princess Anastasia situated herself in front of him, Holder reined the horse into a canter. Fuzzy darkness framed his peripheral as the distance passed in excruciating slowness.

'Stay on, Son'. Father's voice echoed in his mind, dredged up from some long-ago memory. *'Stay on no matter what.'*

Holder pulled a gasp of air into his lungs. His limbs felt heavy, leaden, and something warm and wet covered his right thigh.

Stay on no matter what.

Branches whipped at his skin. Sweat darkened the gelding's coat.

Stay on no matter what.

Varway's outer buildings entered into view.

Stay on no matter what.

The gate. He needed the gate.

Stay on no matter what.

The darkness thickened. He struggled to breathe. The princess. She needed safety.

Stay on no matter what.

Dim sounds of voices and commotion rose over the thumping of hooves. His body moved with the horse's gait. Princess Anastasia clung to his arm.

Stay on no matter what.

Holder recoiled as the horse slowed. One voice, a man's, spoke louder than the rest. Another kidnapper? He fought the haze of dimming colors and urged the horse to go.

Stay on no matter what.

Stay on. He needed to stay on.

Hands grasped at him. Voices muttered. Princess Anastasia squalled.

Holder dug his heels into the horse's flanks. Safety. They needed safety.

Stay on no matter what.

CHAPTER FOURTEEN

BY THE STARS.

Therese stared at the two men in black as they crept toward the cabin. Had another agency been hired? Had something transpired at Scholl's in the hour she'd been away? Had she failed in less than a fortnight?

The door opened and her target emerged, sword in hand.

Her breath caught as a scuffle commenced. Her target knew how to defend himself, but he was a fool. Did he not know such men brought backup?

Chills climbed her arms as the hairs on the back of her neck rose in premonition. Someone else watched. Did they see her? Did they guess what she was? Her mission?

Therese startled as her target and the princess thundered from the clearing on a massive red roan gelding. She ceased inching toward the clearing's edge as dirt scuffled and humans growled.

Four men in boiled leather armor and blue capes converged, first gathering around the fallen men before the tallest barked out orders. Curses littered the quiet as they inspected the bodies. After removing the knife from the crossbowman's foot and bandaging him up, they loaded the bodies, one dead, one alive, onto horses and all but one trotted away.

The remaining man studied the ground before walking his horse onto the path taken by the target and princess.

Only king's guards wore blue capes, but why would they be at the slumping excuse of a cabin? Why not follow the bodyguard and princess with haste?

She pushed aside the questions. Her job was to fulfill her contract, not ponder the curious actions of soldiers.

Therese crept across the clearing. Her heart drummed against her chest as though it fought to break free. Blood dotted the ground, making a trail to the path. If her target intended to leave no evidence, he failed.

She inched into the cabin. Was there a clue to where her target fled? Or a note of some sort telling where the older woman was? She stepped around the overturned table. Three parchment pages were tucked under the table's edge.

Therese eased the pages away and traced the intricate artwork lining the edges. This was no letter, for no one went to such lengths to create beauty on a note simply telling another their location or plans.

Sharp cold filled her as she read the first few lines. Where had these parchments come from? How did the princess possess something that read like treason?

A shout sent her heart racing, and she slunk from the cabin. She had to track her target so she could eventually finish the job a crossbow bolt began.

Her sisters depended on it.

Therese's heart sank as she stared at where the blood led. With Varway's hubbub, there was no way she could find the target. Her stomach turned and nausea rose. Had she condemned her sisters to death and herself to a job that would destroy her?

Think. Jolie always said half the job was accomplished by the mind.

Therese mounted and reined the horse in Rex Dorcha's direction. The castle's dark outline tightened her chest. If the king knew about the papers tucked in her pocket, she would be tried for treason.

The thought pounded through her brain in time with her heartbeat as the mare's hoofs clattered along the dirt road. If the papers were found on her, she could claim she was bringing them to the king, that she had found them in the cabin where his ward, her nurse, and the bodyguard lived.

Yes, that was what she would say. They had no reason to disbelieve her.

She bit her bottom lip as the castle loomed. The man said she could obtain information there, provided there was a soldier escort. Though cruelty hid in the eyes of him who hired her, he gave her no reason to mistrust his word.

Therese dismounted and drew a trembling intake of air. This was no time to quail, no time to turn and run to safety.

"Halt." The two soldiers guarding the front door blocked her entrance. "Who are you and what do you want?"

Therese relayed her intent and described the man who hired her. Her fingernails dug into her palms as their skeptical expressions remained. She didn't look dangerous, let alone threatening enough to harm a mosquito.

"Wait here." The man disappeared into the castle.

The female guard eyed Therese. "What information do you want?" Armor disguised her lithe stature. Calculating brown eyes bored into Therese.

"I am unable to say."

"Yet you claim Captain Geros authorized you?"

Was that what the symbol on his cheek meant? Therese compared it to the woman's. The man's consisted of a circle bisected by a line, with five snakes in the middle. The woman bore a tattoo of a circle bisected by a line with one snake.

She hugged herself. The lightweight cotton cloak dampened the cold, but not the butterflies infesting her stomach. Why hadn't she foreseen the problems this could cause? Why hadn't she thought this through?

"Here she is," the male guard said as he reentered the courtyard. A tall, blond soldier followed.

Therese forced her head to remain high. The butterflies quadrupled. His blue cloak matched his intense, but emotionless, eyes. A king's guard.

"He told us about her." The soldier's mouth pinched, like the sight of Therese made him ill. "You want access to the archives?"

"Yes." Thank the stars her voice remained steady.

The male guard toyed with his sword. "This is Specialist Rogan Cetrin."

Specialist Cetrin transferred his glower to the guard before facing Therese. "I will be your escort. You have one hour to complete your search once we reach the archives."

The female guard snorted. "Hope you like the dark."

"Enough." Specialist Cetrin inclined his head toward the castle. "Follow me."

Therese interlaced her fingers as she followed him through the castle hallways and passages. *For Nora and Delli. You cannot fail.*

Specialist Cetrin grabbed a torch and led Therese down a long, narrow stairway. A door at the bottom restricted entry. He opened it and stepped through, walking to the third door on the left.

Goosebumps littered Therese's arms at the almost sinister shadows gathering around the torch's light. This place felt not one bit like an archive, but more like a dungeon with the air's chill, the glint of light off metal, and the torches set between each door. Musty air swirled around her, indicating few accessed the archives.

"Here." Specialist Cetrin opened a door to the left and motioned her inside. "One hour, then you're out of here. Any resistance will see you in Varway's jail."

Therese forced a weak smile onto her face. One of life's rules was to never anger one stronger than yourself. To never agitate a predator.

And this Specialist Cetrin, with his height and build and sharp eyes, was a predator.

Her mouth dried as she stared at the shelves of tomes lining the walls. The room wasn't large, and no amount of wall showed beneath the shelving. A small table, hardly a step's length long and paired with a wooden chair, stood in the middle.

Therese scanned the books' labels until she found what she wanted. The *Record of Soldiers* was thick as a loaf of bread and long and heavy as a brick. Dust poofed from the table when she set it down.

Specialist Cetrin stiffened, gaze glued to the book. Likely he'd been told to report everything she looked at.

Swallowing the lump building in her throat, Therese searched for the name. She peeked at the soldier before daring to read the information scrawled on a yellowed page. She'd overheard the target's name when her client spoke with Scholl behind a closed door. A surprise they hadn't heard her, but the information provided opportunity to investigate the man doomed to death.

She traced the names. Two men with the surname *Lygor* were listed. Brall and her target, both somehow connected to a woman named Mariline.

Her finger stilled over her target's favorite weapons. If she was to effectively complete her mission, she needed a way to keep him from drawing his sword. A heavy whiff of citronella should keep him coughing long enough for her to administer the poison.

Therese stared at the words listed beside the names of her targets' parents. *Treason.* How could the king allow the son of traitors to be his ward's protector? The lump in her throat returned as she read on. There was a caution warning, whatever it was, at the bottom. *Keep an eye on him*, the minuscule words said.

A lump grew in her throat. How long had her target's demise been plotted? Did the king know? Was this man a danger or were they eliminating a potential threat?

Her skin tingled under Specialist Cetrin's glower. He couldn't see whom she investigated, she knew that much, but he could easily take her in for interrogation.

Therese flipped the book shut and placed it back. "I am done."

He pinned her under a scowl, but stepped aside.

Breathe. She was an assassin. This was nothing more than gathering information. It wasn't like she planned to end the guard watching her or plotted evil against the king.

Therese's heart ceased beating at the mountain of a soldier waiting at the staircase's top. His eyes were the same blue as Specialist Cetrin's, but they were hard, angry, and his jaw twitched, like he ground his teeth.

"Rogan, Captain Geros is sending you to find Specialist Lygor. Word is he and the princess were attacked."

CHAPTER FIFTEEN

ROGAN

ROGAN GLOWERED AT the small cabin. If one ignored the blood-darkened dirt and deep gouges marring the earth, it could be cute, in a homey way.

If.

As if he could ignore the fact someone had been dealt a grave, if not mortal, injury not too long ago. As if he could ignore the lack of life in the clearing. As if he could ignore the overturned table inside.

What had Holder done this time?

Rogan groaned and kicked the cabin's base. Stars above, how had his friend landed himself in a top-secret location guarding Orm's princess to begin with?

And why hadn't Rogan been told?

Snatching Blackie's reins, Rogan followed the dots of blood leading from the clearing. From the bolt embedded in the cabin's exterior wall, one of the assailants had a crossbow. And with Holder's luck, he'd been grazed, if not shot.

Fool.

He cursed when the trail led into Varway. How was he to find Holder in a town of more than four thousand people?

After reaching the town's outskirts, Rogan dismounted and approached the small group of men sitting by the gate. Five bearded faces scanned him from head to foot, lingering on his cape and weapons.

He resisted the urge to roll his eyes. Typical. The one time he needed there to be soldiers on duty, none were in sight.

The farthest man stood, using a crutch to hobble to the front. Short and balding, the only pudgy part on him was the paunch straining the plain, tan shirt. "What can we do for you?" His voice rasped, like he'd swallowed sand.

"I am looking for a king's guard and a young girl. The guard is injured. They may have been riding a red roan gelding."

"Why are you looking?"

Rogan studied the men. Their faces held less color than before, and none dared meet his gaze. What did they know? Had they part in the attack?

He neutralized his voice and expression. "The king requires his presence."

"Why?"

"I don't ask questions." Rogan leaned forward, allowing his daggers to come to full view. "And neither should you. If you know where they are, tell me. If you saw them, I need their last-known whereabouts."

"How do we know this ain't a trap?"

"Are you hiding something?"

The man muttered before jerking his head at the gate. "Follow me."

Rogan gripped his sword's hilt as he trailed the man. Townspeople gathered in clumps before buildings or trotted about, baskets full or arms laden with supplies. Tradesmen hawked their wares, voices adding to the noisy confusion.

His stomach sank. Any one of these people could wish harm to the king. Any one of them could have taken Holder and the princess.

Why, Holder? Why must you always get into trouble?

"Here." The man stopped before a storefront window filled with dresses and knickknacks. "If this is a trap, you'll get skewered before backup arrives."

"Just lead on," Rogan snarled. His muscles begged for action, his mind for the knowledge Holder lived. He clenched his hands before tethering Blackie as the man entered the store. Why this place? Was this so-called mission not enough of an irritant without mixing in suspected criminals?

"Alvin!" Claudine DeGrim swept forward. Her smile flattened when she saw Rogan. "What are you doing?"

"He's lookin' for the other one."

The woman's mouth pinched, but she nodded. "Follow me."

Rogan locked his expression to keep the worry within from leaking out. Holder's blood had led him along a trail over a league long. Was he weak? Was he alright?

Reckless.

Who went against a crossbow? Surely Holder had time to prepare, had seen them coming.

The woman led him into a back hallway. She paused before a simple wooden door. "He passed out from blood loss and exhaustion. A friend of mine found him almost falling off his horse. We removed the bolt and stitched him up, but he should stay off his leg for a few weeks."

"And the girl?" Holder was more important, but the king didn't see it that way. "How is she?"

A soft smile wrinkled her face. "She is making close friends with one of my wards. A sweet little thing, she is."

Rogan held his breath as she opened the door. The room was small, fitting only a narrow bed, a dresser, and a chair. Lantern light coated the room in orange-gold.

"What are you doing here?"

As if twice meeting the sharp-tongued, gray-eyed, black-haired young woman wasn't enough, now he had to deal with her a third time? Rogan scowled. "What are you doing?"

Ivelle stood from Holder's bedside, cloths in hand. "Ensuring he doesn't get an infection. That bolt went deep and it wasn't immediately tended to."

"What makes you qualified to tend to him? For all I know, you could be some assassin in disguise or have some other plan to harm him."

"Ease up, Rogan." Holder's voice croaked. "This isn't th' training grounds."

Rogan tore his glare away from the impudent woman and shouldered her aside. Politeness was unimportant when it came to keeping Holder out of trouble. "You sound awful." Holder looked it, too, with pale skin, glazed eyes, and sweat gathering on his brow.

"Thanks." Holder grimaced. His hand trembled as he shifted. "Why're you here?"

Behind Rogan, Ivelle snorted.

"Captain Geros sent me to find you. Everyone is concerned."

"They should be. Someone is after..." Dazed as they looked, Holder's eyes flitted beyond Rogan. "Something's not right."

Rogan could only thank the stars no one would recognize Princess Anastasia. The child hadn't been visually introduced to the public yet, and for good reason. "You think? You were attacked, became a bolt's pincushion, and provided a bloody trail to Varway. What were you thinking, taking on a crossbowman?”

Holder grimaced after a slight chortle. The gray sheet held barely less color than his face. “Returned the favor. Left a knife in his foot.”

“Real smart, Holder. Real smart.” What possessed him to act so dimwitted? Leaving the enemy with a weapon told not only Holder’s rank, but made it easier to find him again.

Skirts rustled before Ivelle stared down at him, arms crossed and eyes narrowed. “Excuse me, but I wasn’t finished.”

Rogan searched Holder’s face. His friend could keep a stony expression in some circumstances, but surely he’d alert him if something was amiss. “What was she doing?”

Holder winced. “Preparing to change the bandage.”

“Why? You’ve been here for what, three hours?” At least, that was how long it felt like. Babysitting miss detective-wannabe had thrown his sense of time off.

“Clearly you know nothing about tending wounds.” Ivelle shoved Rogan away and drew up the chair.

“Ivelle…” Claudine DeGrim’s voice carried warning. She stood in the doorway, her bell-shaped skirt threatening to take up the entire space.

Rogan gripped a dagger’s hilt to keep his fingers from twitching. He needed to remove Holder from this odd, hostile place. “What is the damage?”

Ivelle pulled the blanket aside.

Rogan’s stomach lurched at the thick bandage wrapped around the middle of Holder’s right thigh. Faint red marred white cloth. Was Holder’s wound worse than they thought?

“Well?”

“The bolt partially embedded in his leg and damaged the muscle. I’ve stitched the wound and applied frankincense to aid healing, but there is nothing I can do for the muscle. He needs to keep weight off his leg for at least six weeks, and thereafter limit activity to slow walking on a flat surface for another three."

Holder scowled. "I can't do that. My job depends on my mobility."

Rogan sighed. Aggravating as Ivelle was, it appeared she knew her stuff. "Holder, you'll do as she says. I'll help you with whatever, but that leg is going to fully recover."

Ivelle propped a stack of pillows under Holder's knee and calf and undid the bandage. "We will send crutches and a sack of herbs with you. When will you take him?"

"I planned today. Can he be moved?" His pride prickled at having to ask, but he'd risk nothing.

Claudine DeGrim's voice came from behind. "He needs to stay the night so we can watch for infection. Return at noon tomorrow and we will have him prepared for travel."

"This is most unfortunate." King Eligor reclined in his throne, chin propped on a fisted hand. "How did my ward act?"

Rogan kept his gaze on the king. His skin prickled under his father's glare. "She was skittish, my king, but otherwise calm. There was a little girl there who befriended her."

"Very well." King Eligor straightened. Despite the severity of the situation, his actions lacked the urgency thrumming through Rogan. "Since Specialist Lygor will be incapacitated for several weeks, you will assist him in protecting the princess."

Rogan choked. How? He was no bodyguard. He possessed neither the patience nor the personality required for such a job. "My king, may I speak?"

"You are free to do so, Specialist."

"My king, I am unsuitable for the job. I can assist Holder—Specialist Lygor—in other ways, but I am not bodyguard material."

King Eligor's gaze burned, but with wrath, disappointment, or something else, Rogan did not know. "Specialist Lygor will assist and instruct you on the skills required. I have full confidence you can do this, Specialist Cetrin. You are capable with weaponry and have a tactical mind. Officer Torgord will escort you to the new location since the last was compromised. End of discussion."

Rogan offered a half-bow. His mind filled with protests, but he bit his tongue. King Eligor knew best on the matter, and it would not do to question him.

"Specialist." Officer Torgord inclined his head to Rogan. "We best be off. We have quite a ride ahead of us."

Captain Geros strode forward. His bulk made Officer Torgord look like a sapling in an oak's shadow. "Gather your things, Specialist, and bid your family farewell. This stint will last a few months, and it is doubtful you will see them until its completion."

Rogan felt Father's glare burn into his back as he left the throne room. He inhaled brisk midday air as he exited the castle. Bid his family farewell? Only if Mother were at the cabin. Thank the stars he would be free of Father's disapproval for a few months. Perhaps then he could regain his sanity and the latest round of bruises would heal.

His legs felt leaden as he walked the stone path between rows of cabins. His fingers refused to open the door's latch.

Get a grip, Cetrin. You've faced worse coming home.

He inhaled a deep breath that tasted like smoke, and entered. Mother sat in the rocking chair near the fireplace, a mess of yarn in her hands. The rocking chair's steady creaking drew Rogan back to a simpler time, when home was not equated with fear and was a refuge instead of a trap. Once Holder was old enough to live at the barracks, Rogan got his loft back to himself, but Holder's absence, and thus the lack of witness, also invited Father to begin using his fists.

An invitation Father hadn't refused.

"Rogan?" Mother set aside the yarn and stood. "What are you doing home so early? It is not your day off."

He accepted her hand brushing his shoulder, brisk as it was. "I'm temporarily reassigned and will be leaving the area for a few months."

"Oh." Her expression conveyed neither disappointment nor concern. "I will see you when you return, then."

"Yes." *Maybe.* Maybe he should again petition the king to let him join Holder in the barracks. "I need to pack."

Rogan stuffed changes of clothing into a pack with as much force as he tried stuffing logic into the cold, lingering hole in his heart. It was blood, not love, which made a family a family. It was heritage, not an emotion, that made people related and care for each other.

He could do this. It would be nice getting away from the cabin which had housed him from birth. Away from the constant disappointment and unworthiness seen in him by his father.

Away from being unwanted and never good enough.

Yes, it would be nice getting away.

CHAPTER SIXTEEN

"NO SIGNS OF infection yet." Ivelle smeared another drop of frankincense oil onto the soldier's wound. "I meant it when I said you needed to stay off your leg for six weeks. If you don't let the muscle heal, you can kiss your job farewell."

He winced. Dark circles under weary hazel eyes created quite the contrast to his pallor. "Will it be healed after that?"

"Fully? Only you will know. You can return after six weeks and we will look at it, but without a way to see the muscle—aside from cutting you open—you have to go by observation. Whether or not it hurts, if there are abnormal bumps or discolorations, or similar symptoms." Ivelle wrapped the bandage. It was so much easier answering this soldier's questions than his friend's. Where one was quiet and did not strike her as heartless, the other was arrogant and the perfect definition of the brutes called soldiers.

Why did she not dislike this soldier like she did all the others? Why did he seem innocent and helpless and lost?

"My name is Holder." He grimaced as she tightened the bandage. "Please, just call me that."

"Holder it is, and I am Ivelle. You are much easier to be around than your friend."

He chuckled. "You have to get used to Rogan. He's an acquired taste."

"I will take your word for it." When his gaze moved beyond her, she turned. "Emmi?"

Dark, kinky hair framed Emmi's pale face. Cradled to her chest was the journal. "Is my friend coming back? We wanted you to read this to us."

Oh, no. The writing quickly moved into what could be considered treason. How had they gotten hold of it? What if the princess told the king? "Emmi, I need you to put that on this dresser and forget about it, okay? It's too old for you." Too sad, too dark.

"Okay." Emmi padded over and obeyed. "Will my friend come back?"

"I don't know, sweetie." Ivelle kept her eyes on the child as Holder's gaze burned into the back of her head. How could she tell the little girl her new best friend was Orm's princess?

Emmi's forehead furrowed. "I liked her. She was nice. She can read better than me."

"I'll practice more with you."

"And I liked the story. I like the name Mariline."

Holder stiffened in the corner of Ivelle's peripheral. "Mariline?"

"Yes." Ivelle's heart hammered. This soldier seemed kinder than the rest, but he was still loyal to a man who would happily end Ivelle and Claudine if he heard of the journal. "It must be a common name."

Holder kept silent, but unnamed emotion glimmered in his eyes.

"Here is the tea." Claudine swept in, cup in hand. "It is peppermint, so it should taste fine without honey or sugar."

Ivelle stared at Holder as he downed the liquid. Her hand trembled as she took the cup. "That will help you sleep, which is vital to the healing process. I'll return in a bit to see how you are."

"Well?" Claudine asked after Ivelle shut the door. "How is he?"

"I think he will heal if he stays off his leg."

Claudine's hands framed Ivelle's face. Brown eyes searched, as though looking for an answer only found written on skin or in hair. "You are pale."

Ivelle released pent-up breath from her lungs as she traced a scar. "I don't think he's like the rest, but it's still hard."

"I know, but you have to remember not every soldier is the same as the ones who..." Claudine paused and bit her lip.

"The same as the ones who ruined my life? Who murdered innocents? Maybe they are not the same people, but they all obey the same man who ordered it." The same man who would order it again if it suited his cruel whims.

Claudine sighed. "He will be gone tomorrow, Ivelle. Until then, I think it would be good for you to continue helping him. The king is already suspicious of the emporium. We don't need anyone saying we are hostile to soldiers, especially after you smarted off to his friend."

With his arrogant attitude, he deserved it.

"Understood?"

"Yes." Ivelle bit back a grumble. Claudine was right, but that didn't make it any easier.

She put the remaining supplies away and wandered to the front. Women assembled around the counter, their high-pitched chatters making the room sound like an aviary. Plumed hats bobbed and fancy material rustled.

"Can I help you?"

The tallest one turned. Her gaze swept Ivelle before she smiled. "We are here to be fitted for new gowns for King's Day."

King's Day. *King's Day.* Why would they want to celebrate a murderer? Ivelle's smile felt stiff. "That is a month away."

The woman laughed. Her friends joined. "Darling, that is why we are coming in now. It will take that time for us to be measured, fitted, and the dresses made." She waved gloved hands. "I was thinking of red taffeta with black velvet trim and a black veil attached to a ruby headband."

Ivelle pursed her lips. Did Claudine even have taffeta? "I will fetch Claudine for you. As for your other ideas, you will have to consort with the milliner two buildings down."

She found Claudine in the back room, sorting herbs. "There are women here who want to be fitted for King's Day."

Claudine paused, brow scrunched. "By the stars, why would they begin thirty days in advance?"

Ivelle shrugged. "That's their issue. They're waiting for you."

"Oh, so you dumped them all on me, did you? I suppose, out of the kindness of your heart, you're pushing me into a den of twittering ninnies in exchange for completing the herbs?"

"Precisely." Ivelle nudged Claudine to the doorway. "Off you go. Best not keep our customers waiting."

<hr>

Another floorboard creaked.

A shadow flitted past the doorway.

Ivelle crept forward. She had no true weapon, and a wooden cup did little to deter evil or someone with ill intent. She scowled at the dark mass creeping toward the soldier's room. How had this person infiltrated the emporium without anyone noticing the sound of the lock being compromised? Had they heard of the journal and come to claim it as evidence against Ivelle and Claudine?

She choked at the thought. Oh dear. How could she have forgotten the journal in Holder's room?

Ivelle counted her breaths to reorient herself. The intruder stood not far from the room where she'd been munching on a late-night snack while perusing the herbal inventory.

Of all the times to be interrupted, it had to be while enjoying a few of Claudine's sugar cookies.

When the intruder paused, Ivelle launched. Breath whooshed from her lungs as she tackled them. She caught flailing wrists, twisted them behind the trespasser's back, and yanked the intruder to their feet, pushing them into the room. "Who are you?"

Hopefully the ruckus wouldn't awaken Emmi.

"Let go."

"I said, who are you?"

"I can't tell you." The girl's voice faltered. "Please, let go."

Ivelle tightened her grip as she felt along the girl's sides the way she'd seen Borros pat down a suspected spy for weapons. She withdrew a dagger and pressed the tip into the girl's back. "To the chair."

The girl made no effort to resist as Ivelle pushed her into the chair and secured her hands before once more placing blade to throat. The candle's dim light highlighted escaped strands of dark auburn hair and a slenderer figure. Fear glinted in wide eyes.

"What is your name?"

The girl stared at Ivelle. "First, promise you will say nothing of this to any guards or soldiers."

Ivelle pressed the knife in a tad harder. "That depends on what you intended to do."

"I mean no harm to you."

"Name. Now. Or I will alert the first guard I see." On an afterthought, she added, "And there is a soldier here. He can come arrest you if I deem it necessary."

"Therese." The girl's breath shuddered. "My name is Therese."

Therese dressed for danger, but she more resembled a frightened kitten with her pale face and trembling hands. A hooded, dark gray dress fell to her knees, topping dark leggings and boots. A black leather belt held a small pouch and sheath. Strands of hair escaped a braid to frame a pale face.

"Therese." Ivelle ground the name out. The girl flinched. "What are you doing here?"

"I need to speak with the soldier."

Ivelle nodded at the pouch. So help her, she wasn't allowing any type of danger in the emporium. She'd give her life before allowing harm near Emmi, and business was threatened already with the soldiers sniffing about. "What's in there?"

Not waiting for the girl to answer, she fished out soft, almost velvety, yellow petals. A warning bell rang in a distant recess of her mind. "Oleander? You don't just want to *talk* to him, do you."

"I don't...I don't know." Therese slumped against the chair before her expression hardened. "I just need to see him. Please?"

"About what?"

"Confidential."

Ivelle snorted. Confidential, her foot. "Listen, Miss I-can't-tell-you-anything-because-I'm-hiding-something.   I don't know who you are, or where you come from, or who you're working for. The only thing I can reasonably discern is that you mean him harm. If you purposefully have oleander petals, you know what they are and what they do."

"Look," Therese snapped. "Part of my job is speaking to him."

"Why should I care about your job?"

"I need to speak with him."

"About what?" Ivelle rolled an oleander petal between her fingers. So pretty. So deadly.

Therese hesitated. "Could you untie me? Please?"

"Fine, but I will have no qualms hurting you if you try anything."

After Ivelle untied her, Therese rubbed her wrists before removing a square of parchment from the pouch. "I need to speak with him about these. I...I have a question."

Ivelle studied the young woman. Should she trust her? What was her story? Why did she avoid answering questions? Doing so told she hid something, but was that really Ivelle's business? *And why am I so protective of this soldier, anyway? Just because he looks innocent doesn't mean he is.*

"Fine. But if he's sleeping, I'm not waking him up." She beckoned Therese to follow. "How did you know he was here?"

Therese's footsteps were a mere scrape of leather against wood. "I saw the end of his attack. He rode off before I could do anything. I trailed him here."

"And you waited all this time?"

Therese shrugged.

"What made you sneak in? Why not come through the front? Everyone saw Borros carry him in."

Therese's sigh, quiet as it was, reeked of impatience. "I didn't know what you had done to him. Now that I know he is safe, I thought it best to continue."

Ivelle knocked on the door before opening it. Holder lay still and silent save for his breathing. "He's asleep."

Therese entered the room and stared at the injured soldier. Her expression tightened, the emotion on her face as mysterious as her answers.

"Well, you've seen him. Now you leave." Ivelle tugged her from the room. "How do you know him?"

"Confidential."

Of course.

"Ivelle?" Claudine appeared in the doorway. "A shipment came in. I need you to unpack it in the back room."

"Right now?"

"Yes, right now. This fabric was expensive. I'll not have it ruined." Claudine stared at Ivelle with pressed lips and crossed arms. A red-and-yellow scarf looped around her neck.

Use caution, but all looks safe.

Ivelle set the piece of toast down. By the time she returned, it would be cold and hard. She nodded at Claudine and slipped through small groups of people and into the back room. Hopefully they would dissipate before Holder was removed. Gossip already spread like illness and it only caused suspicion about the emporium.

A large, flat cargo crate sat on the table. Iron bands and a bronze lock secured it, but criminals and ne'er-do-well smugglers had ways of breaking in and altering the contents without others' knowledge.

Ivelle traced the engraved words. *DorFord.* What had Claudine ordered from the small town that required such care?

She unlocked it and peered inside. Red and black bolts of fabric peeked from under a layer of cheesecloth. A normal way to ship material, and one that garnered little suspicion. She placed bolt after bolt in another crate before gold glinted.

"By the stars," she breathed. Two daggers lay at the bottom. Deep brown leather sheaths molded to the blades' shapes. Delicate, black leather braids crisscrossed the sheaths in a diamond pattern. Iron capped the ends.

Ivelle loosed the smallest weapon. The edges were honed to a dangerously sharp edge and sliced through the leather bindings surrounding a packet of herbs without problem. Beautiful. Deadly. Elegant.

"Who sent you?" she murmured. "And why?"

"Weapons are always good to have in stock." Borros stood in the doorway, thick frame silhouetted by the blanket. "We are in the black market, Ivelle. It makes sense we would have items that are black-marketable."

"But why weapons like this?" Ivelle held the dagger for him to see. "Borros, these are like the one from that man and are from a land no one in Orm has ever traveled to, let alone purchased anything from. How were these obtained? How much are they worth?"

"How much do you think an object from another land is worth? If Claudine really wanted to price these for their worth, she'd be rich and the purchaser poorer than those in the poorest sector in Varway."

"How can she obtain them, then?"

Borros snorted and shook his head. "She's Claudine DeGrim. She can obtain anything she wants. Come on, now.

Another shipment has arrived. Fool brought it to the front door. I need your help carrying the items to the back."

Ivelle brushed limp strands of hair from her forehead as she followed Borros into the main area. Handling—knowing about—black market items was dangerous and could potentially land her a death sentence if anyone found out, but this life was simple, perfect compared to where she could be had Claudine not rescued her.

She held her arms out for the bundle Borros handed her. Heavy and thick. Tomes or manuscripts from the feel of it.

Ivelle stumbled back as she turned the corner and crashed into hard leather. Metal bit at her arms through her sleeves. The bundle slipped, thudding to the floor.

Panic pulsed through her as she dropped to her knees. The cloth had flipped aside, revealing *Verum* burned into a book's leather cover. She flipped the cloth over the dangerous title. Whoever decided to send it so poorly wrapped had pebbles for brains.

She met narrowed blue eyes as she stood.

Holder leaned against his taller friend, who glared at Ivelle like he just caught her committing a crime.

Her heart plummeted like a rock in a lake.

Ivelle clamped her teeth together to silence the ragged breaths tightening her chest. What price would she pay for her stupidity?

CHAPTER SEVENTEEN

HOLDER

"HOW FAR AWAY is this place?" Holder blinked the world to rights. His leg throbbed, what felt like a bonfire's heat radiated from his body, and he was cold and miserable. Riding intensified everything.

"Two leagues." Rogan's voice clipped.

Holder glanced to his left. Rogan stared straight ahead, mouth compressed and posture rigid. His blue cape, the status he lived by, fluttered in the slight breeze.

"We saw nothing, Rogan."

"We saw something that could possibly end the filthy black market ring," Rogan snapped. "You saw the book's title. I looked it up and it's listed as treasonous and not allowed in Orm. I know guilty when I see it, and Ivelle was guilty—she knew what she was doing. Captain Geros was right. That place is a haven for smugglers and the black market."

Holder placed his palm atop the bandage winding around his thigh. "They saved my life. The princess' too. They didn't have to do that."

"They hide and sell contraband. And it is their duty to help."

Holder inhaled a deep breath of crisp wintry air. Dark gray clouds bunched over the horizon, promising snow in the next day. "To help the princess, yes. Me? No. They not only kept us from an interaction with those who could profit from the princess' kidnapping, but they pulled a bolt from my leg and ensured it wouldn't become infected. I know what Ivelle carried was illegal, but one book can't do that much damage. If anything, it's been blown out of proportion. Please? Forget about it?"

"That book is on every watch list. You know they broke the law."

"Rogan…"

Rogan's shoulders slumped and he forced a gloved hand through his hair. "Why didn't you tell me?"

"Tell you what?" Holder rubbed his eyes. Despite sleeping most of the time at the emporium, his eyes threatened to close.

"That you were in danger."

"What?"

"I found out yesterday, from my father of all people, that the princess had gone into hiding and you were guarding her. One kid can't defend a princess from those who mean harm."

Holder grit his teeth. Just who did Rogan think he was? A weakling who knew nothing about weapons? Someone who hadn't had fourteen years of training? Someone who hadn't made it to the elite king's guard? Besides. He'd seen the king's guard's blue cloaks flitting about ever so often. He hadn't truly been alone in protecting the princess. Their absence during the attack was coincidental. There was no other explanation.

"Look at your leg. You could have died from blood loss. And, if not that, then they could have skewered you. I don't know how you did it, but the odds of you taking on a crossbowman and surviving were slim."

And yet, I still survived. Holder cleared his throat. "Must have been the stars."

Rogan huffed.

"You don't believe they guide and help us?"

"What I believe is irrelevant. What matters is the truth, and the truth is you almost died. You should have told me. Should have asked for help."

Holder ducked under a branch. Sharp pine needles scraped his cheek. "Well, something helped me. And it was a *secret* for a reason. What matters is I'm alive and the princess is safe."

"You're alive no thanks to your careless and reckless ways."

Holder bit the inside of his cheek. What made Rogan so bitter? So sharp tongued? He and First Lieutenant Cetrin didn't get along well, that Holder knew, but why would that cause Rogan to be so embittered?

He released a breath, watching as it turned to a visible vapor as a chill infiltrated the forest. Best to appear untouched, unbothered by the harsh words, and move the conversation onward. "What is this place? I've never heard of it."

Rogan shrugged. "Neither had I until Officer Torgord showed me. I researched it in the archive before I came and retrieved you. Records tell it as one of King Eligor's original attempts at building Rex Dorcha."

"What place could be worse than the ridges? Do you have any idea how many men lost their lives building the castle and surrounding buildings?"

"That's why they call that gap the bridge crosses over Dead Man's Drop. Anyway, we won't be relying on supplies being brought in. Officer Torgord thinks that is how the assailants discovered your location."

"Then what will we do?" Holder rubbed the aching muscle in his thigh. He could hardly stay upright on a horse, let alone traipse through the woods to hunt. Maybe he could fish, but if there was a stream nearby, would there be fish in it?

"I'll hunt and lay snares. Stock up on whatever deer and rabbits we can catch. Every other week I'll probably ride into Varway and get supplies. Do you think Svetlana can cook?"

Why must Svetlana be the princess' nurse? Holder grimaced. Being cooped up with the sour-faced woman would do nothing for Rogan's disposition. "She did fine enough at the cabin, I guess. Nothing like the cooks at Rex Dorcha."

Though he wouldn't put it past the old hag to poison someone if they were on her bad side.

"Here we are." Rogan pointed at a gray structure shielded by tree trunks. "It's stone. Officer Torgord had fresh hay for the horses brought here this morning, so they're taken care of."

The horses moved into what could barely be called a clearing. Trees crowded two-story turrets partially hidden by a stone wall. A gap in the wall allowed entrance where a portcullis or iron door would have kept intruders out. More trees grew in the small bailey, littering the ground with pine needles. Vines and moss grew on the stones and the keep looked a hair bigger than two cabins put together.

"We're expected to stay here?" How could this place be safe?

"It's old but solid." Rogan dismounted. "There is plenty of dry wood for the fireplace lying about and a river is nearby.

The princess will arrive tomorrow, so I'll stock up on firewood and meat before then."

Holder rubbed his gelding's neck, like feeling the coat would dissipate the disquiet in his gut. This wasn't Rogan's job, yet here he was doing what Holder should be doing. Surely Ivelle was incorrect and he could be on his feet in a week.

He grunted. Pain throbbed through his leg as Rogan helped him down and inside the keep. The cool, dry interior sported more spider webs and bird nests than lichen and ivy.

"This is the entrance. The fireplace is through that door. A stone counter juts from the wall, so I figured Svetlana could use that to prepare meals. Maybe we can hang a tarp or blanket between those two half-finished pillars so the princess and Svetlana can have some privacy."

Sweat chilled on Holder's forehead. His leg and lungs burned from the exertion of hopping into the room. "You've thought of everything, haven't you?"

"I try. Here." Rogan eased Holder onto one of two bedrolls spread before the fireplace. "This place is filthy, but we'll get it cleaned. The criminal said you need rest, so you better get some sleep. I'm going hunting."

Holder forced his breathing to regulate. By the stars, his leg throbbed. "Since when do you know how to hunt?"

Rogan undid his cape and grabbed a recurve bow and quiver of arrows hiding in a corner. "Since I asked Captain Geros."

Soft breaths. The creak and groans of an old building.

Holder strained for something, anything. The sounds were normal for nighttime in the keep, but something felt *off*.

No, not just felt.

Was.

He forced his eyes open. Sleep clung to his senses.

Darkness filled the keep. Rogan slept in the entryway and a tarp shielded Princess Anastasia and Svetlana from view. Only vague shapes were visible, visual clarity hindered by the lack of moonlight.

Holder blinked the sleepiness away. His breath caught and his heart faltered. A dull human figure, just visible if he squinted, crouched near where he placed his saddlebags.

Curse his injury. He grit his teeth as he slid his hand to the pillow. Cold metal met his fingers and he prepared to draw the dagger.

The figure straightened, stilled like a deer sensing for danger.

"Don't." The female voice sounded like a whisper of a breeze. Leather rustled. "I'm not here to hurt you."

"Who are you?" Holder freed the blade's tip. "What are you doing?"

"I'm not here to hurt anyone." Cloth rustled as the woman inched backward.

"Answer me." If he could nail her with the blade, Rogan could catch and bind her and she could be taken in for questioning.

"Holder?" Rogan's groggy voice accompanied a shift of leather on stone. "Something wrong?" The sound of a match against flint preceded a burst of light that illuminated Rogan's face and spilled into the darkness.

Holder flung the dagger. The woman scrambled out of the way like the stars blessed her with extra grace and physical coordination. She stumbled over nothing at the sound of steel clearing a sheath. In her hand she clutched a rectangular package.

"Who are you?" Rogan pointed the sword at the woman. "Lower the hood and cloth and keep your hands where I can see them."

"Holder?" Princess Anastasia's voice quivered. "Who's that?"

"Stay back," Holder warned. He tried pushing to his feet. Sharp flames of pain erupted when he lurched and placed weight on his injured leg.

"You need to stay down," the woman said. She was slightly shorter than Holder, dressed in dark clothes and bearing no visible weapons. A small pouch hung from her belt.

"Like you care," Rogan sneered. He advanced. "Hands where I can see them. You don't care if he's injured. You came here to kill him and the princess."

"No—no I didn't." She darted away, one gloved hand clenching her hood's edge. She glanced Holder's way before bolting to the entry, slipping past Rogan and ignoring his shouted curse as he chased her. The door slammed.

Holder let himself collapse. Fatigue encased him from the strain of standing. He stared at the princess, who stared back. This place, this wannabe castle, was supposed to be secure.

He forced breath into his lungs. *Stars.* He couldn't be so careless. What if the woman had been successful in slaying him and the princess? Or had she intended to take Princess Anastasia? Despite what his mother's letter warned, Holder didn't wish the stress and grief on King Eligor.

He clenched his teeth as pain seared through his leg. His senses clouded and, as the darkness moved in, only one thought echoed through his mind. He couldn't let this happen again.

CHAPTER EIGHTEEN

THERESE

THE DOOR CREAKED as Therese slipped inside. Her heart still hammered from the near-failure. What if the soldier had wounded her? What if her target had been successful with his dagger? What if she hadn't escaped?

"Therese?" Delli peered from her place beside Nora. A wool blanket draped over their small bodies. "You're back?"

"I'm back." Therese peeled off her dirty clothes and threw on a simple dress. "Go to sleep, sweetie." Exhaustion swept over her. The first rays of daylight would touch the sky in a few hours, and there was so much to do.

Her limbs ached as she stoked the fire's embers. Begin the meal Nora and Delli would survive on for the day, check her supplies, clean her clothes, struggle to repay her parents' debt… *By the stars*, it was too much.

She filled the pot with water and tore strips of jerky into bits. She'd have to purchase more supplies soon and maybe go fishing. Dried fish tasted nasty, but it was better than Nora and Delli starving.

Therese added carrot chunks before sitting back. The parchments in her pouch had scorched through the material and seared her skin. Treason was what they were. Who wrote them? Illustrated them? Brought them into Orm? Near Varway?

Are they true? She unfolded one and scanned it. Who was this King? Even fabled characters possessed names, but he had none save his title.

No, no, the stories could not be true. No one could create the world, and no one ruled over a vast, countless army, not even King Eligor.

'So he was cast out for his arrogance,' the parchment's first sentence read.

Therese traced the illuminated first letter. How could the parchment's writer say such a thing about the king? Why spread such lies?

And why had one of King Eligor's most trusted soldiers possessed it?

She startled at a rattling cough. "Delli? Nora?"

Delli's eyes glowed in the firelight. "Nora's coughing."

Therese scrambled to her sisters' bed and cupped Nora's face. Heat burned her hands. "How are you feeling?"

"Like I was run over by a freight wagon and my throat's filled with sand," Nora rasped.

"Delli, how long has she been like this?"

Delli shrugged. "Coughing after you weft. Her throat and arms hurt."

Therese's heart sank when her attention returned to Nora. Her middle sister had curled up, burrowed beneath the blanket despite her fever. Sweaty strands of dark hair clung to her forehead.

"Nora?" When her sister remained silent, Therese shook her shoulders. "Nora Westa, you answer right now."

Nora only whimpered.

"No, no, no." Therese threw on her other work outfit and wrapped Nora in her cloak. She had no herbs to heal, no knowledge of what Nora's illness was or the complications it could cause. *Stars, if you can hear me, please help her. Help me. Please don't take her from us.*

Therese's fingers turned cold as she fumbled the savings jar. Three silvers and ten coppers clattered at its bottom. Maybe enough for a healer if she worked off the remaining debt, but what would Delli and Nora eat in the meantime? She could only trap and catch so many fish and rabbits, and those were scarcer due to winter.

Think, Therese Westa. Think.

No healer would be open before the seventh hour, and if she woke any up, they would charge double.

Therese gripped her hair. Her breath emerged in short, quick gasps. What could she do for two to three hours that could increase Nora's chance of survival?

Water. Water was good for fever, though it hadn't helped their parents.

"Nora? Wake up, sweetie." Therese eased her sister into a sitting position and dabbed her forehead with cool water. When Nora stirred and blinked at her, she asked, "How do you feel?"

Nora's frame rattled with a cough. "Throat hurts," she whispered in a rough, ragged voice.

"Anything else?"

"Cold."

Therese spooned a dipper's worth of stew into a bowl. "I need you to eat. You'll feel better after."

Stars, I have tried keeping my prayers at a minimum. I don't care if you don't help me with my mission, but please, I beg you, help my sister. Keep her alive. Don't let Delli be next.

⬥ ⬦ • • • • • ⬦ ⬥

The seventh hour came too slow. Therese cradled Nora as Delli followed her through the streets. Townsfolk brushed by on their way to work or opening up shop. Therese stumbled into the street. Who could she trust not to poison her sister?

She sucked in a breath and headed eastward. Delli's grip on Therese's skirt kept her mind from bolting into pure panic. Nora. She needed to focus on Nora.

Cold air tinged with the sound of a town already at work crashed into her senses as she stepped into Varway's busiest business sector. Where was it? She honed in on the ugly storefront. "Delli, stay close."

"I'm tired."

"I know, sweetie. Just a few more minutes."

Therese found the alley and kicked at a familiar door. *Answer. You have to answer.*

The door swung open. Sharp gray eyes widened, then narrowed. "What are you doing here?"

"You're a healer?"

"Depends."

"I can pay." Desperation hoarsened Therese. Even if she had to break Scholl's demands and take on a second job, she would do anything she could to get Nora proper care.

The young woman's gaze swept to Nora and Delli. Her lips pursed before she stepped to the side and beckoned with her hand. "Come in."

A strong mixture of herbal scents cleared Therese's mind. Her arms ached from Nora's weight and her sister's fever burned her, but it was a heat she welcomed, for it meant her sister still lived.

"This way." The young woman led them down the same hall Therese had crept down to plant the condemning book. Sounds of shopping customers sounded from the front. "In here."

Therese placed Nora on the same bed used by her target. The young girl groaned.

"What's wrong?" The young woman nudged Therese out of the way and unwrapped the cloak.

"She's sick. She has a terrible fever, is coughing, and could barely eat."

"When did this come about?"

Therese knelt beside Delli and took her hands. "Did you hear her question, sweetie? Can you answer?"

Delli clung to her. "Befwore Therese came home."

"When was that?"

"I arrived a few hours before sunrise."

The young woman speared Therese with a scathing glare, like she was a terrible sister and human for leaving such small girls alone at such hours.

"Can you help her?"

Therese prayed yet again. Perhaps the stars did care, for they had led her to the emporium.

"I think so. I've seen this before. It is called grippe and has symptoms of headache, fever, sore throat, coughing, and severe aching. Nausea and throwing up sometimes occur, but I'll do my best to keep that from happening."

"Her name is Nora." Delli's thin voice carried none of the fear she usually exhibited around strangers. "And I'm Delli Westa."

"Delli, I am Ivelle Quade." She again felt Nora's forehead. "I will give her some elderberry tea and bone broth, but it will take me a few minutes to prepare. Stay here."

Therese dared to move once Ivelle sailed from the room. Tears stung her eyes. Whatever the price this care would cost, it was worth it. *Thank you, stars.*

She knelt by Nora's bedside and clasped her hand. "I promise, Nora. You will get better."

"You look exhausted." Ivelle lifted Nora's head and held a cup of water to her lips. "Go home and get some rest."

"I cannot leave her." And Delli would be terrified if she wasn't near Nora.

Ivelle sighed and leaned against the dresser, arms crossed. "She's in capable hands. You know that." She studied Therese. "What brought you here? Why the emporium?"

Therese gripped the hems of her sleeves. "I've heard this place houses a healer—a reputable healer."

"True." Ivelle lifted the small book from the dresser and toyed with it. She waved it at Therese when she saw her watching. "It's a journal. Have you ever heard of the name Mariline?"

A whisper of memory stirred before dissipating. "No."

"The only other person who has was the wounded soldier."

"Does it tell whom the journal belongs to?"

"No." Ivelle traced the edge, a guarded expression lining her face. "Few names are mentioned." She set the journal aside and stroked Nora's hair. "It usually takes a week for those with grippe to feel better. I assume Delli will want to stay?"

"If it's no trouble."

"I would never separate siblings. If you need to go home and gather supplies, feel free to do so. Emmi is thrilled to have another girl around, and she's keeping Delli occupied."

Therese dragged a hand over her face. Her entirety felt aged, worn out and old before her time. "I suppose I will return in the morning, then. What time do you open?"

"The seventh hour."

"I'll be here, then."

After hugging Delli farewell, Therese returned home and retrieved her knife. Her fingers hovered above the vial and cloth Jolie gave her when she first received the mission. Best take it. Specialist Cetrin proved a light sleeper, and it wouldn't do to have the princess or her servant wailing and screaming.

Therese crept into the forest. Two leagues was a long way to walk, but she could not risk injuring a horse on the rutted path. Sweat dampened her clothes by the time the moonlight highlighted the ruins.

She took a deep breath and blew out her candle, placing it on the step outside the keep before tiptoeing in. The cloth dampened as she moistened it with the liquid.

Specialist Cetrin's breathing pattern faltered as she neared. Material rustled. He grunted, sounding half-coherent. Steel slid. "What—"

Therese slapped the cloth over his nose and mouth, pressing her fingers into the sides of his neck. He jerked, but his sleepy state combined with the liquid and pressure, and soon he went limp. She pushed his sword into its sheath and moved into the main area. Weak moonlight streamed in through a barred window, illuminating her target's body.

This is for the girls, she mentally chanted as she slipped behind the curtain and repeated the action with the princess and servant.

Get in, plant the "evidence", and leave. Don't be seen.

Before she could drug her target, he stirred and sighed. "Rogan?" His voice slurred before he growled. Material shifted and Therese stumbled back a step. "What do you want now?"

To save my sisters. She fingered the cloth. Trying to apply it now would result in him overwhelming her. He may have a bum leg, but he wasn't weak. The tendons in his forearms when he had trained his horse attested to that.

"I asked you a question," her target ground out. "Answer or you'll be arrested."

"The manuscripts." The words blurted from her mouth before her brain knew they were on her tongue. "Where did you find them?"

His voice strengthened as he fully awakened. "Seriously? Did King Eligor send you?"

"No. Did you read them?"

"No."

She allowed a slight smile to touch her face. He couldn't see her, not with the hood obscuring her face. "You lie. I want to know where you found them. Such things would not be allowed in Orm if the king knew."

He paused. "I read half of the first page. It's treason."

"So you think it is a fable?"

Another pause. "Yes."

Not a lie, but not the full truth.

Stop procrastinating. You need to complete this job. Think about Nora and Delli.

Therese wet her lips. "Did you wonder why the other king went unnamed? Or who would make such accusations against King Eligor?"

He sat. "You're awfully bold to speak so freely with the princess nearby and one of the king's most loyal guards in the next room. Do assassins always chat it up with their victims before they strike?"

Therese ignored the sting of his words and studied what little of his features could be seen, her mind supplying the details. Darker hair, what looked like a straight nose, and a strong jaw in the position of one gritting their teeth. In a quick move, Therese uncapped the bottle, poured a fresh layer of liquid, and pressed it over his nose and mouth.

His fingers dug into her arm, but when she wrenched his head back and applied pressure to the sides of his neck, his head lolled to the side and his body fell slack. She lowered him and stuffed the scrap of paper into his saddlebag before bolting. Jolts shot up her legs from the packed, frozen dirt, and cold air stung her throat and lungs.

She did it. She accomplished the second part.

She was well on her way to repaying the debt.

CHAPTER NINETEEN

ROGAN

STUPID WOOD. ROGAN glowered at the knotted pine log. Dents fractured its splintery top, going no deeper than half a thumb's length.

He growled and massaged his forehead. Stupid wood and stupid headache. He went to bed feeling fine. How had he awakened with the worst headache he'd ever experienced?

Rogan tossed the axe aside and stomped over to sit by Holder. His friend glanced at him before returning his attention to his book.

"How's the leg?"

"Fine."

Rogan scanned the wall encompassing the building. Aside from the unsettling woman a few nights ago, everything was quiet. Almost peaceful, if there was such a thing.

He snorted at the thought. Peaceful wouldn't earn him his captaincy or get him that fifth dagger. Peaceful hadn't kept Holder from getting injured, or the princess from almost being kidnapped.

Peaceful didn't keep his father from using his fists against his own flesh and blood.

"Why do you think King Eligor created Orm?" Holder's voice was low, his gaze unseeing.

"Why are you asking that? Does it matter why? It's built. Nothing can be done about it."

Holder shrugged. "I was just wondering. We've heard a few details about Orm's origins, but nothing much."

"Does it matter?"

"I'd like to know. Don't tell me you haven't thought about it."

"I haven't." What was the point? The past could not be undone nor history rewritten. Personal opinions would not change the who and why. Rogan shifted. Holder's thoughts could lead him down a dangerous trail, one that could result in his friend being punished, if not killed.

"It's just...weird, I guess. I mean, we know King Eligor created Orm as a refuge for him and his followers, but beyond that we've been told nothing."

Rogan leaned against the building's exterior wall. It was slightly less comfortable than lying atop his thin bedroll. Why did this matter? The past was in the past. The only thing that could be changed was the future. "Anything else you've been wondering about?" He switched topics to keep Holder from potentially endangering himself.

"My parents." Dark circles shaded the areas under Holder's eyes and his shoulders sagged. "I'd like to know what happened to them."

"For closure."

"Yeah." Holder slowly stretched his leg out. Dirt had turned the bandage brown. "You're lucky you have yours, even if you don't get along."

Rogan huffed. He wouldn't call the memories of wearing long sleeves in the summertime to hide dark bruises *lucky*. He wouldn't call the emptiness within his chest *lucky*. He wouldn't call the inability to remember the last time he was good enough for the Cetrin surname *lucky*.

"Holder." Princess Anastasia scuffled from the building's area designated for the horses. "My head still hurts."

"Everyone's heads hurt," Svetlana snapped. She followed the princess, her frown more pronounced than usual. How had such a rude, sour-faced woman been allowed as the princess' nurse?

Rogan closed his eyes as his own headache throbbed. "I'm going hunting." He stood and retrieved the bow and arrows. His arms, back, and shoulders still ached from the first try, but fresh meat was better than riding two leagues to Varway, dealing with questions, and keeping supplies from spoiling.

"Be careful," Holder called.

"You be careful. Get away if anyone shows." Blast Holder and his injury. It made protecting the princess twice as aggravating and difficult.

Svetlana muttered something before pinning Rogan with a sneer he'd only seen on the daughters of nobles. "Don't return if the only thing you've managed to kill is a deer. The princess requires a variety in her diet, something you've not adhered to. The king shall certainly hear about this."

"Lady, if the king wanted me to be concerned about the princess' diet, he'd have told me." A twinge of fear shot through Rogan's gut despite his reply. Had the king assumed he would take Princess Anastasia's diet into consideration? Was he supposed to think of things like that on top of safety, supplies, and caring for the horses?

Rogan adjusted his grip on the bow. A skiff of snow covered the ground, blown through the gaps between branches and pine needles. He shivered as a gust of wind blew snow in his face. Spring was a few days away. Hunting would resume for Varway, and then what? How could he protect Holder and the princess with nosy townsfolk sniffing around?

Impossible.

Life was just impossible.

He scowled at the snow. Bleak knowledge that this was all there was, all there would ever be, only worsened things. If this life was terrible, tough luck. It was all you got.

Curse you, stars.

Adjusting his grip on the deer slung around his shoulders, Rogan drew breath into his burning lungs and prepared for the remaining distance between him and the keep. No amount of training readied one for the cramping in the back from carrying their next meal for what felt like ten leagues.

"Hi."

Rogan dropped the deer and spun at the girlish voice. "Where are Holder and Svetlana?"

Princess Anastasia shrugged and played with her skirt. "Holder's hurt and Nurse is no fun. I asked her if she wanted to play something, but she said it is unladylike for princesses to play."

Playtime. While sparse throughout Rogan's childhood, he remembered relishing the times he and Holder could escape into the forest and mock-sword fight, search for legendary monsters, or just explore. Those times turned into sparring as he grew older and more expectations piled upon his shoulders. "So you just...wandered off?"

"No," she chirped. Wide brown eyes stared at him like he was second only to Holder. "I found you. You can't get lost."

"And what makes you think that, Princess?" Rogan retrieved the deer. Great. He'd smell like damp fur after this little excursion.

"'Cause you're a king's guard. Do you want to play?"

"Don't you have a doll to play dress-up with or something like that?"

She shook her head before latching onto his shirt and skipping along. "I had to leave my dollies home. They were sad, but Uncle made me pack in a hurry. And they'd get scared if the men in black came back. I don't want that."

Rogan grunted. *By the stars*, Holder's injury created more problems that he'd planned. "Just because you're bored doesn't mean you can wander off. What if you found a man in black instead of me? I can guarantee you wouldn't be so happy right now."

She sighed. "Mother used to play with me a little before bedtime. Nurse didn't like it."

The ache in her voice triggered one similar in Rogan's heart. He shoved it away. Feelings would only get him in trouble, distract him from the mission. "You miss them."

"Yes. Nurse said I shouldn't cry, but it's hard not to."

By the stars, Holder was much better at this. "I think you can cry." Was that the right thing to say? Or was crying against some royal manners code?

"I hope I'll see them again. Do you think I'll see them again?"

If the death of her parents hadn't broken her heart, the truth she asked for surely would. Rogan swallowed. His throat felt tight. "I don't know."

"Maybe Holder will know. I'm pretty sure he will. He knows everything."

Rogan kept quiet until the old stone walls broke into view. The forest's solitude was nice, and it certainly smelled better than the training area, but he missed the drills. The routine. The simplicity of it all.

"There you are." Svetlana bustled through the opening. The scowl scrunching her already pointed features promised more than one scolding for the princess. "Good princesses do not wander off."

Rogan deposited the deer onto the steps and rolled his shoulders. That woman may intimidate Holder, but to him she was nothing more than a biting horsefly. He stationed himself between Svetlana and Princess Anastasia. "You have no call lecturing her when you refused to give her something constructive to do."

Svetlana's wrinkles, permanent from her constant glaring, deepened as she turned her thunderous expression his way. "What right do you have to speak in such a manner to me? I am the princess' nurse."

"I have every right as one of her bodyguards."

"You are only here because that scrawny boy was stupid enough to get himself shot by fools who didn't think their plan out. Why the king couldn't have sent Captain Geros or First Lieutenant Maximo Cetrin is beyond me."

"That was a mistake," Holder muttered from the doorway. He leaned against the doorframe, balancing on one leg.

The sparks of irritation turned into an inferno of anger. Rogan fisted his hands. His teeth ground together. Chances were she didn't know who his father was. Chances were she threw out that name due to Father's knowledge of weapons. Chances were she was just irritated and saying whatever names came to mind.

"Princess, why don't you go visit with the horses? I think they miss you." Holder grinned at the princess, who complied with a squeal. When she disappeared, his gaze shifted to

Svetlana and hardened. "Rogan, this deer needs preparing before it spoils. I'll help."

Rogan brushed past Svetlana and hauled the deer to the side near a turret. If he had brought a practice dummy and sword, he could beat out the trapped fury by hacking at a straw-stuffed sack. Instead, the final preparations of harvesting a deer would take the brunt.

Holder eased to the ground with a grunt. "Life would be easier if we were born with three legs."

"Maybe." A twinge of guilt lessened the anger. Sweat glistened on Holder's pale forehead and rolled down his neck, darkening his tunic's neckline. His breathing was heavy and erratic and his hands shook as he withdrew a knife.

You should have helped him, a silent voice accused. *He's in pain because of you.*

Rogan shook the voice away. "Your leg. How is it?"

"It's attached."

"When was the last time the bandage was changed?" At Holder's silence, Rogan looked up. "Well? Yesterday? This morning? I need to know."

Holder shrugged. "The store. The place you found me."

Rogan stilled. "What?"

"Yeah. As long as there's no blood, it's fine."

"How is that fine? I'm no healer, but I know a wound needs constant tending to. Do you have supplies for it?"

Holder shook his head. He looked exhausted, like the previous night had been rough. "Let's get this deer taken care of, else your hunting trip will be for naught."

As soon as the deer was adequately prepared and the organs disposed of, Rogan saddled up. His black mare shifted as he walked her into the clearing and mounted. The sun would set in less than four hours, and it would take him a bit over an hour each way, not to mention however long it would take while in Varway.

"Come on, Blackie," he urged. The mare ambled onto the trail. At sixteen hands tall, Blackie put Rogan at the perfect height to be smacked by branches. He ducked a thicker bough and nudged her into a trot.

Rogan's skin felt frozen by the time Varway's clamor met his ears. He grumbled as he dismounted and led Blackie through the crowds of people. Why were they not still at work?

A growl rose in his throat at the sight of the criminal store. It rankled to have to go in and ask for advice. Holder had pleaded for Ivelle and her treasonous literature to be kept a secret. Rogan would keep it only because they had saved Holder's life.

He tied Blackie to the rod out front before entering. A gaggle of middle-aged women giggled as they gathered around that accursed fitting room. His neck prickled as they eyed him. Dirt from hunting caked his boots and he could guarantee he didn't smell fresh and clean, not after hauling that deer around.

The traitorous young woman emerged from the back room, eyes lowered as she stared at a paper in her hands. "Welcome to Claudine DeGrim's Emporium. How can I—" Her rote greeting died when she looked up. Her posture straightened and her arms crossed. "What do you want?"

Rogan clenched and released his hands. What possessed the stars to keep testing him like this? Of the emporium's three employees, why couldn't he deal with the man? He'd even settle for Claudine DeGrim. But not Ivelle. Anyone but her.

"You catch more flies with honey than vinegar, darling," one of the old women sang. She continued, seemingly encouraged by the other women's twittering. "You two would make an adorable couple."

By the stars, this woman needed to shut her mouth.

Rogan bristled. He couldn't determine which insult was worse: being referred to as a fly or the woman thinking he and the traitorous, sharp-tongued, ill-tempered Ivelle would be cute together.

"Wise words for any other situation," Ivelle answered. Her stiff smile more resembled a snarl as she turned to Rogan.

"Holder's injury. How often does the bandage need changing?" Oh, it grated to ask. His pride cringed at the humiliating circumstance.

She sighed and approached the counter. "Really? You couldn't have asked this when you were here and whisked him away without warning?"

"Just answer the question."

"The poultice should be changed once a day. Same with the bandage if he's in a clean environment. How does the wound look?"

"I don't know. What poultice are you talking about?" And what was a poultice?

"Goldenseal poultice. You know, to encourage healing?"

What was goldenseal? Rogan returned her sneer. "You didn't think to tell him that? What kind of healer are you?"

"A smarter one than you." Her smug expression made his skin crawl. "Anyone with a touch of sense would know to change the bandage."

"I know to change the bandage. Is that all there is to it?"

She stared at Rogan like he was an odd item on display before answering. "You really know nothing about this, do you?"

"Just answer the question."

"What are you doing?" Rogan crossed his arms and watched Holder hobble toward him. Despite the crutch and bandage, Holder sported a grin too wide for Rogan's comfort. Whatever his friend planned, he had a feeling he wouldn't like it.

"I need your help."

"With what?" Rogan barely caught the coil of braided material thrust at him. "I recognize this." Which meant only one thing. "No. Absolutely not. I refuse to help you tame that monster. If you want to risk your life trying to control that beast, be my guest, but unlike you, I'm not suicidal."

Holder laughed, truly laughed, for the first time since they'd been exiled to the stars-forsaken hideaway. "It's not suicide, and he's calmed down quite a bit."

"Oh, so he'll only think about murdering me instead of actually trying to?"

"You're being a baby."

"And you're being an idiot."

"Oh, I'm sorry. I forgot you're afraid of a horse."

Holder's sly grin did nothing to quell Rogan's queasiness at the thought of facing the man-eating fiend Holder insisted upon riding. The living nightmare should have been put down at the beginning. "I refuse to be another name on his casualty list."

"You'll be fine."

Ha. Easy for Holder to say. The king of inflicting broken bones and bite marks behaved for him.

"I'll owe you a sparring session."

Rogan snorted. "I'll be waiting a long time for that. If that *thing* bites me, that's an additional session. For every bite."

Really, it should be for every tooth mark. Double if the teeth broke skin.

"Agreed."

"I'll probably die doing this, and I don't even have a partial epitaph in mind."

Holder rolled his eyes. "If you die, I'll ensure your epitaph waxes poetic about your unflinching valor and courage while facing down a horse."

"Making fun of me, are you? I wouldn't expect you to understand. You're the only human that cursed animal doesn't want dead."

"Maybe you hurt his feelings."

"Feelings are overrated." Rogan undid the first loop and flicked it at Holder. "Go get that wild beast."

Holder whistled and the roan whinnied from where it grazed nearby, lead rope tethered to a stake. "Come with me. You can attach the rope before I unhook him."

Rogan managed to attach the rope to the gelding's halter with his fingertips. The roan's ears swiveled, but Holder distracted the homicidal equine with soft praises and promises of a good grooming after the training.

Hopefully Holder didn't think Rogan would be the one spoiling the wretched horse.

After Holder removed the lead, Rogan led the roan to the area Holder designated for training. "Now what?"

"You put him through his paces." Holder explained what to do, then settled back on a large stump, bearing an aggravatingly smug expression.

Rogan grumbled as he took his place in the middle and obeyed Holder's instruction. The gelding tossed its head before beginning a lazy amble.

"Now a trot."

Time passed, until Rogan worked the roan to a gallop. After just a few turns, he slowed the horse and rubbed his eyes, stomach turning at his dizziness. "If I throw up, it's your fault."

"You have a weak stomach."

Rogan's retort died at the feeling of teeth sinking into his shoulder. "*Ow.*" He shoved the biting nuisance's head away and put distance between himself and the equine intent on bestowing harm.

He tugged his shirt to reveal his shoulder. The first discolorations of a bruise already discolored the skin and a pinprick of blood rose from one of the deeper impressions. "You owe me two more sparring sessions."

At Holder's heartless insistence, another round commenced. Rogan armed himself with a stick, placing it between himself and the slavering beast whenever it moved too close for comfort. Finally, after muddy slush soaked his clothing and another bite decorated his right arm, he called it quits.

"I'm done, Holder. If you want this monster to be trained any more today, you'll have to do it yourself." Rogan waved a hand as Holder rose and limped toward him. "Go inside and warm up. Read or do whatever. I'll clean this beast up."

"You sure?"

"Yes, but if I disappear, you'll know it's because it turned me into a snack."

Holder shook his head. "He won't eat you."

"Says the one who's never been turned into its chew toy." Rogan motioned to the remains. "Go."

Once Holder disappeared, Rogan jerked the rope. The gelding huffed its annoyance.

He met the surly beast's glower with one of his own. "Listen, horse. Try that again, and I'll feed you to the bears.

Understand?" He'd heard of bears inhabiting Argbil Forest, but had never seen one. The horse didn't need to know that. "You behave for Holder. He's already injured and doesn't need you misbehaving. If you can manage to do that, you might be worth all this hassle—" and pain— "and I *won't* feed you to the bears. Understand?"

The gelding snorted.

Rogan led the horse to the lean-to and began grooming the cantankerous equine. As he turned to grab the hoof pick, pain erupted as horse teeth sank into his left upper arm.

The things he did for Holder.

CHAPTER TWENTY

IVELLE

"GOODNIGHT." THERESE KISSED Nora on the forehead before standing and leaving the room. Her movements were sluggish and she covered yet another yawn.

"Don't tell me you're getting sick." Ivelle pushed up from leaning against the wall.

"No." Something flickered in Therese's eyes, something often appearing without warning and vanishing equally fast. "Thank you so much for yours and Claudine's help. I don't know if she would be alive if you hadn't..." She shook her head and looked away.

Ivelle studied Therese. The girl always wore dark clothes that accentuated how thin she was, like she didn't eat enough. Her boots often bore mud and pine needles made almost permanent residence in her dark auburn hair. What was her story? Where had she come from? What was her job?

"Where are your parents?"

"They died in the plague that tore through here a few years ago."

Ivelle winced. "I remember that. It took a quarter of Varway's townsfolk and almost that much of Orm." Claudine had run out of herbs, and even the water supply was suspected to carry the illness.

Therese huffed a laugh. "For all his power, King Eligor could do nothing." Her eyes lost focus before she blinked and stared at Ivelle. "What do I owe you?"

"Not the two silvers a week-long care session would usually cost."

Therese blanched.

"I've seen some sort of parchment in your pouch. Let me see those. They might even everything out."

A battle showed in Therese's wide eyes and the lines furrowing her forehead. Her fingers twitched like they fought a battle of their own regarding whether or not to hand the parchments over. She grimaced before fishing them from the thin, black pouch.

Ivelle unfolded the top parchment. Illustrations in faded colors decorated what had to be a centuries-old tale. The writing also was faded, though still legible, and the number two indicating it was the second page of something, a tome perhaps, was written in the old writing used on ancient items. She whistled. "This could be worth a lot. Where did you find it?"

"An abandoned cabin."

Ivelle squared the parchment and smoothed it. The better condition it was in, the higher the price it would garner. "Be safe on your way home. Do you need to borrow a sword?"

"No." Therese touched the knife at her hip. "I will see you tomorrow."

Ivelle waited until the girl disappeared into the night's darkness before slipping to her room. Once changed, she snuggled under the blanket and opened the journal. It was not smooth reading. Rather, the writer had jotted his thoughts down at random times. The full plot was known only to the man who had written on the weathered pages.

"'Mariline and I dislike not bringing our son, but what else can we do? This travel is not safe for a young child, and the dangers we have already encountered are enough to test any with a sliver of strength. Yet we press on. There is a void in my heart, like darkness has corroded something within and only light can heal the wound left behind. Light. I search for a light not like what the sun and stars emit, but a pure light. The Light. There is another ruler as mighty or mightier than our king out there in the world. I can feel it.'"

Treason. Yet the words were written with neither malice nor ill intent. Ivelle traced the woman's name. What she would give to know who this couple was. Were they successful in their search? Was the man who brought the crate in the writer of this journal?

"'We will stop at an old friend's before continuing to Mort. A village as odd as its name, I've been told, but nonetheless that is where we think our answers are. I would pray to the stars for protection, but how can an inanimate object provide safety, much less craft our future? No, my soul tells me there is something—or someone—more powerful than even King Eligor. We just have to find him.'"

Ivelle ignored the knot in her stomach telling her once again it was a bad idea reading the journal. How could someone be mightier than King Eligor, a man who created Orm and saved himself and his followers from an evil usurper intent on destruction?

Yet, the king also was destruction.

Images of soldiers in blue capes and bearing flashing shortswords crowded her mind. They would only attack if ordered by the king.

Mort. An innocent village struggling for survival by fishing and trapping. Once her home. Now the graveyard of innocents.

Ivelle extinguished the candle and stared into the darkness. The writer was right that the stars did nothing, but it was easier to claim faith in pale, twinkling objects hanging in the sky than to accept no deity controlled life and fate.

She cocooned herself in the blanket as chills crawled up her arms. How was it possible that some random man could voice the very roots of doubt scarred into her own heart since ten years ago? And why had they thought their answers were in Mort?

<hr>

"You are friends with Holder, right?" Ivelle watched Therese's expression. Something about the girl screamed *off*, like she hid a dark part of herself, but she acted nice enough. Vague and quiet, but nice.

A pause, then, "Yes."

"So he would let you access the archives if you asked?"

Therese snapped to her full height. A wild glint rounded her dull eyes. "What are you doing?"

"Consider this and the parchments as payment for anything and everything your sisters will ever need." There was nothing wrong with extracting such a price. At least, that was what Ivelle had convinced herself of during the night's sleepless hours. Children tended to fall ill, and surely the girls would bear some sort of injury or illness again.

If not, she'd make it up to Therese some other way.

Therese's fists balled. "What do you want? Why the archives?"

Ivelle glanced at the back room's entrance. Shadows of people, Claudine and shoppers, flitted about. "King's guards destroyed my home village, Mort, ten years ago." She lifted her left sleeve to reveal part of the myriad of twisted scars. "I want to know why."

"When do you want the information?"

"When can you get it?" A thrill shot through Ivelle, a concoction of mixed feelings. Fear that she asked too much, that Therese would get in trouble. Trepidation about what would be found. Excitement that she could finally have the truth and put the past to rest.

Therese answered with a wry, almost sneaky smile. "Whenever I want."

"Ivelle?" Claudine appeared in the entryway. "Oh, hello, Therese. Ivelle, another shipment has arrived. I need you to take care of it. This whole King's Day business is making me insane."

"I will return later." Therese nodded at Ivelle before slipping out the door.

"An odd girl," Claudine muttered. She groaned and pressed both hands against her back. "I'm too old for all this sewing. I've already hired an extra seamstress. Too bad you aren't qualified enough to sew gowns. I could use you."

"I'll mend and sew small things. Not dresses, and not silk and whatever impossible material they want to wear." Ivelle followed Claudine to the caravan wagon outside.

Alvin and Borros hauled in crates, cursing at the weight and amount. "What are you doing, Claudine? Clothing Varway's entire female population?"

"Close to it. What, is it too much for you? Are you so old that you need to take breathers between thinking about working?"

Borros scowled. "I could carry two of these if I wanted, woman. I just don't want you harping on me not to break anything."

Ivelle choked back a laugh and joined Alvin in the break room. "How many crates are there?"

"Enough to build a new Rex Dorcha." He swiped sweat from his face. "Have fun, girlie, 'cause this ain't gonna be enjoyable."

Ten crates later, Ivelle stared at the numerous bolts of material awaiting assortment. By the stars, how was she to finish this before King's Day?

"Ivelle?" Emmi and Delli emerged from behind the red velvet curtain. "Can we see the cloth? Borros told us it's the same as what Lady Ancelle used to wear."

"Close to it." Ivelle ushered the girls to the table. "You may help on the condition that you sit and tell me if it becomes too much for you."

Emmi's gnarled fingers pushed back wayward strands of black hair. "Okay. What will Delli do?"

"What I do?" The slight girl tugged Ivelle's skirt. She and Nora shared the same hair and eye color. If not for their similar, delicate facial structures to Therese, there would be no resemblance to their older sister.

Ivelle knelt and turned Delli around, braiding her hair. A burst of warmth filled her chest. Was this what it would be like having a little sister? "You are going to be my assistant. I will hand you a bolt of cloth, and you will place it in the appropriate pile."

"What abwout Nora?"

"Nora isn't feeling well enough to join us, sweetie. When her tummy doesn't feel so yucky, then she can." For as brave as Delli thought she was, she couldn't handle the truth that Nora struggled to shake the grippe. Lack of quality food put a strain on the young girl, and her body toiled to fight the illness.

Emmi gave Delli a sympathetic smile. "It's okay, Delli. I like being around you. It's like having sisters around my age."

Ivelle unpacked the first crate as Delli peppered Emmi with questions. "You have sisters?"

"Just one. She's older than me." Emmi went silent before her voice quavered with tears. "I haven't seen my family in a few months. I came home from the healer's and they were gone. That's when Claudine and Ivelle found me."

Ivelle forced a smile as pain replaced the warmth. It had been luck she and Claudine intercepted the limping child before she saw the full destruction rendered to her home. "We love having you, Emmi. And don't tell Claudine you know this, but you're her favorite. She loves finding outfits for you."

The pure happiness in Emmi's replying smile pricked Ivelle. If only withholding the truth wasn't so painful.

Therese returned after the sun set and the girls went to bed. Ivelle led her into the break room. "Please ignore all the fabric. Orders triple as King's Day approaches." Pushing aside the growing anxiety, she laced her fingers and bit her tongue. Therese did not look like someone who would use information against her, but appearances could be deceiving.

Therese eyed the fabric like it was poison before fully facing Ivelle. "I found the information you wanted. Mort was a village located in the middle regions of the High Mountains. That explains the slight accent you let slip every now and then."

"What?" Cold swept Ivelle. How could she be so careless? And her accent should have mellowed.

Therese's gaze filled with what could only be pity. "Ivelle, you should sit."

No. No, no. What did she find? "I'll stand."

Therese gnawed her lip before inhaling. "King Eligor ordered Mort's destruction after word revealed two traitors lived there. According to the archives, the village refused to hand them over. He sent his most elite soldiers to complete the task with the order for no survivors." Her eyes filled with sympathy. "The traitors were Brall and Mariline Lygor."

CHAPTER TWENTY-ONE

HOLDER

THE MUFFLED WHUMP silenced even the crows in the nearby trees. For a long moment, nothing moved or made a sound.

The gelding snuffled and turned, meandering toward a patch of dead grass poking through an area where hoofprints had swept the snow away. Unconcerned, it began snacking.

"Is Rogan okay?" Princess Anastasia jumped from the boulder she'd been standing on and tugged Holder's sleeve. "He's not dead, is he?"

Holder grabbed his crutches and rose, sloshing his way through the churned mess of slush and mud. "Rogan?"

Rogan didn't answer. Eyes wide, he stared at the sky, chest expanding with movements as jerky as his short, shallow breaths, which sounded more akin to a noise a landed trout would make.

"Rogan?"

"I'm not meant to go airborne."

"Is he dead, Holder?"

"Almost." Rogan groaned as he lifted his head. "That horse is a devil."

Holder fought for balance as Princess Anastasia joined him and tugged again on his sleeve.

"He's not dead, is he? Nurse wouldn't like having a dead person so close."

"I'm alive. Barely." Rogan muttered a list of curses as he rose. Mud squelched with his every movement and he staggered when he finally found his balance. Hand to his back, he hobbled to the stump and sat. "Your bandage needs changing."

"It's fine for now."

"It'd be fine if blood wasn't seeping through and if you'd actually rest and stay off it."

Holder made his way to the roan and rested his forearms on its back. The horse nickered and continued grazing. Rogan wouldn't—couldn't—understand, and Holder didn't possess the energy to explain it once again.

Rogan sighed and stood, a hand again pressed to his lower back. "I feel like I'm eighty."

"You sound like it with your joints popping like that."

Princess Anastasia skipped to Rogan and tugged on his shirt. "How old are you? Aren't you close to eighty?"

"Princess, I am nowhere near eighty."

"But you are old, and eighty is an old number, so you must be close to it."

"How old do you think Svetlana is?"

"Two hundred."

Holder grimaced. Stars forbid Svetlana hear *that*. The woman was cross enough. Such an incorrect guess regarding her age wouldn't sweeten her disposition.

"You tell her that, Princess, okay?"

Holder sent Rogan a scolding look before shaking his head at the princess' questioning expression. "Don't tell her that, Princess. She won't like it."

"But it's true."

"What is true?" Svetlana's sharp voice cut the air. She picked her way toward them, holding her skirts as she tiptoed around the worst areas. "Well, Princess? Do not be daft like your brainless bodyguards. Answer the question. It is unladylike to ignore those speaking to you."

"You look like you're two hundred-years-old."

Svetlana's face purpled.

"Rogan agrees." The picture of innocence, Princess Anastasia tilted her head and kept her hands clasped as she waited.

If looks could kill, Rogan wouldn't only be dead, he'd be tied to a wagonload of bricks and sinking to the bottom of Orm's deepest lake.

"Princess, Rogan is an uncouth, ill-mannered individual who was raised by cockroaches. You are never to listen to a word he says." She then pointed a long, bony finger at Rogan. "Your father will hear of this."

After another selection of choice insults, Svetlana swept Princess Anastasia inside.

Holder rubbed the back of his neck. "You shouldn't antagonize her."

"Getting offended won't kill her." Rogan twisted, grimacing and again touching his back. "I'm going to clean up. After I'm done, we're changing that bandage. No arguments."

"Too tight?" Rogan's hands paused above the bandage. "I can loosen it."

"You might need to." Holder held his breath as Rogan redid the wrapping. "This will have to be the last time or the poultice will be everywhere but the injury."

"You understand that healing jargon?" Rogan retied the bandage and helped Holder stand. "It sounds like insanity to me."

"Then it's a good thing your skills fall in other areas."

"Funny. How's this? We have to go now if we want to be on time."

Holder rubbed his leg. Though persistent, the pain was a dull throb. Uncomfortable, but manageable. He tested his weight and grunted as his leg buckled.

Rogan caught him. "Are you mad? What part of 'keep off for six weeks' don't you understand?"

"I understand every word."

"Then what's your deal?"

No anger laced Rogan's tone, but the words still stung. Holder grabbed his saddlebags and used the crutch Rogan had fashioned to hobble forward. "Are the horses saddled?"

"Stay here. I'll get them." Rogan brushed past and disappeared outside.

"Is he always so jolly?"

Holder peered over his shoulder at his replacement for the day. "He's just a little cranky."

"If that's just a little, I'd hate to see a lot." Juan rotated his torso to stretch. "So, what do you do in this fun-filled joint? Chase blowing pine needles? Count the clouds? Play tea with the princess?"

"Tea?" Princess Anastasia emerged from behind the blanket. "We do not have tea, sir, but if we mix a pinch of dirt with a cup of water, we can have a tea party."

Juan paled and stared at Holder, eyes bugging out and mouth silently pleading for rescue.

Holder shrugged. There was nothing wrong in playing tea if one didn't drink the concoction. "Welcome to my world."

"Yeah, well, it's gonna be a different world until you return. First Lieutenant Cetrin makes Rogan look like the brightest ray of sunshine." He paused at the sound of raised voices. "Like father like son. I ain't getting in the way. Good luck, Lygor, and may things turn in your favor. Stars know you need it."

Holder hobbled into the bailey. Dread filled him. Would this come to blows? Rogan never specified what happened at the Cetrin cabin, but his angry silence and the obvious hatred in his eyes whenever he saw his father were evidence his home life was anything but loving.

Rogan wouldn't attack an officer, would he? Even though they were related, he could be dishonorably discharged or even hung if the attack caused enough damage.

Rogan and his father stood little more than arm's length apart. Though Rogan was tall, First Lieutenant Cetrin dwarfed his son in height and width. Red filled the man's face and his accent thickened.

"You do whatever it takes to get back in the king's guard, understand? This is a demotion, boy. It doesn't take two to guard the princess. Don't know why the king chose you—you're too incapable to even find contraband in a stupid store. Even if you have to grovel, do what you can to get back to your original position. No Cetrin will fail."

Rogan dodged his father's hand. "We're being watched," he spat. "Wouldn't want to soil the pristine Cetrin surname, would you?"

"Are you disrespecting an officer?"

"No disrespect, *sir*." Rogan snarled the title. "We have to go. Juan has his instructions."

"I give the instructions, boy. Not you." First Lieutenant Cetrin threw Rogan a scalding scowl. "Now shut your mouth, else I'll give you something to remember."

Holder whistled. His gelding's ears pricked and the horse wandered over. "Good boy." Holder attached the saddlebags and drew himself into the saddle. His muscles protested, stiff from disuse. He looked up to find Rogan mounted and blatantly avoiding looking at his father.

First Lieutenant Cetrin glared at Holder as they passed. Chills pricked his spine. The man did more damage with his tongue than he ever could with his sword. How much destruction did Rogan bear?

At least half a league passed before Rogan spoke. "Did you tell Juan everything he needs to know?"

Holder grimaced at his friend's brittle tone. Like the thin layer of ice on a lake, it deceived viewers by looking strong, but would crack under the slightest bit of pressure. "I did." He exhaled and fingered the reins. "You okay?"

"Yes."

Holder paused. Just how should he ask his next question? Rogan *looked* strong. *Acted* strong. He *was* strong. Which made it hard to believe anything could happen to him. "Has he ever…hurt you? Physically?"

"Really, Holder?" The stiffness in Rogan's jaw and posture answered what his words did not.

"I mean, I never saw it when I lived with you, but he looked pretty violent back there." Come to think of it, Holder never saw any type of affection between any of the Cetrins.

"Holder?"

"Yeah?"

"Just ride, alright? Just enjoy the silence. I have a feeling it won't last."

"How is your leg?"

Holder stared at King Eligor. The man sat on his throne, legs wide, elbows on the armrests, and fingers steepled. Sharp eyes peered from under thick eyebrows. The man was the definition of a ruler with his regal bearing and crown and robes.

Did he know the near abuse his first lieutenant put his son through? Did he know how his ward mourned her parents' passing almost every day? Did he know how she cried quietly at night or in the makeshift stable?

Did he know of the treasonous letter tucked away in Holder's saddlebag?

If he was the all-powerful leader he proclaimed himself to be, then he would know.

But he didn't.

Rogan cleared his throat. Holder startled. "It is healing, my king."

"Excellent." King Eligor leaned forward. Captain Geros flanked him on the right while Officer Torgord stood to the left. "You have been through a lot, Specialist Lygor, and you have my gratitude for putting your life in danger to save my ward. I commanded your presence because I am sending you two on a mission. Do you remember about a decade ago when that hardened criminal escaped from the dungeons the day before his execution? Word has arrived that he lives in a small village called Weedcrag. I want you to travel there and retrieve something he stole from the castle. A sword with a white blade and a golden hilt. Don't take him on—you're not ready for that—but get that sword."

A flare of panic swelled in Holder's chest. What if they permanently replaced him while he was away? What would he do then? Being a king's guard was doable, but there was something fulfilling about carrying the mantle of the princess' bodyguard, even if he dealt with an evil king.

"You will leave immediately after King's Day, of which everyone else has already been notified and briefed regarding the setup and procedure. Specialist Lygor, you will remain with the princess at all times. The first king's guard and half of the second will form a protective circle around the stage. Specialist Cetrin, you are included in the other half, which will assist Specialist Lygor in protecting the princess. Afterward, you two will bring the princess back here by way of back trail. She will be fatigued from all the events, but I will need every available sword with me in case rabble-rousers try something again. Am I understood?"

"Yes, my king."

"You are dismissed. Specialist Cetrin, please accompany Specialist Lygor to the healer's so his injury may be assessed."

Holder and Rogan bowed and left the throne room. His crutch clacked against the stone floor, threatening to slip from under him.

He stared at the long, narrow hallway stretching before him. His back ached, his leg screamed, and his lungs fought for breath as sweat dampened his skin. How could he endure such a distance? It was a struggle making it the few steps into the throne room.

"You okay?"

"Yeah." Holder filled his lungs. He had to be. There was no choice, and it wasn't like there was a chair with wheels he could maneuver around in.

Rogan nodded at the hall. "Do I need to throw you over my shoulder and haul you there?"

"You couldn't do that."

"I could." No ounce of teasing marked Rogan's countenance. Only his usual, intense expression. "Do you need another way of getting there?"

"A new leg?"

"None to spare at the moment. Here." Rogan draped Holder's free arm over his shoulder. "Does that help?"

Holder adjusted his weight. "It does."

His mind whirled as they shuffled along. King's guards were just what their title implied: the king's and only the king's. They protected the king day and night, every heartbeat, every breath. Why wasn't Officer Torgord sent? Why not two soldiers not specifically trained for the king's protection?

Something is off, his mind nudged. *Something's wrong.*

But what? And how? King Eligor was intelligent. He'd likely thought over every aspect of the plan before commanding its completion. And it wasn't like Holder could just say something. Mentioning his instinct's warning was akin to asking for a death penalty. He might as well march up the king himself and list how the king really wasn't all-knowing and all-powerful.

"You're thinking."

"Why us, Rogan?"

Rogan's shrug threatened to topple Holder. "I don't know. But the king commanded it, so there must be a reason."

Just because the king commanded it doesn't make it right.

The thought stormed Holder's brain without warning. He faltered, his breath hitching. By the stars, what was wrong with him? Why did he think such things?

Because I know they're true, just like my parents did.

"We're here." Rogan opened the door to the healing chambers and assisted Holder inside. The place smelled of the herbs lining the walls and the clay pots filling three slender bookcases.

The castle healer emerged from a door on the right wall. Lanternlight glinted off his bald head and his boots thumped against the floor as he wove around the operation table in the middle of the room. "What happened?"

Holder settled on the table as Rogan explained. The healer hummed and grunted until he undid the bandage and whistled, his mustache ruffling with the motion. "Whoever stitched you up did a superb job. What else did they say and do?"

Holder relayed Ivelle's instructions. "You'll have to ask Rogan what type of poultice she used."

Rogan scowled. His disdain for Ivelle was evident in everything, from his facial expressions, to his crossed arms, to his contemptuous tone. It wasn't just that she was a criminal. Holder withheld a chortle. Rogan genuinely disliked something about her.

What a show it would be to pit them against each other.

"Well, she's right." The healer adjusted the new bandage. "Stay off it, Specialist. You can't risk the permanent harm it would cause to use the muscle in its current healing stage. Not only would you hinder and complicate the healing process, but you could end up crippled."

A pang of fear filled Holder. What would he do if he was no longer fit and able for his job?

"I am going to make a poultice. Stay here, and don't move." The healer disappeared into the room he first emerged from.

"You're worried." Rogan stretched out in the stuffed chair.

Holder grimaced at his friend. "How can I not be? For all I know, we could die on this *mission*. For all I know, I might not have my job when we return. Or, stars forbid, something else could go wrong."

Stars forbid.

CHAPTER TWENTY-TWO

"HOW IS THE mission going? I haven't seen you much. Everything alright?"

Therese paused her preparation. "It's fine." It had to be. For her sisters.

"Are you excited about the new clients now that you're part of the team?" Jolie beamed at Lucian as he entered, also dressed for work. His dark clothes clashed with his pale skin. Was he nervous? Or did he always lack color?

Therese choked as Lucian kissed Jolie on the cheek. What had she missed?

"You ready for today? Lots of orders to fill. We'll be busy."

"Yes. Do you have the supplies you'll need?"

Lucian patted the pouch hanging at his waist. "Twelve oleander petals and some water hemlock should do it. I always have the blade if I need it."

Therese pulled on a pair of gloves. There was no way to trace fingerprints, but one could never be too careful. She flipped her hood up and slipped out the back to where the horses waited. The simple sorrel mare was fast, not fast enough to outrun Specialist Cetrin's mare or her target's red gelding, but fast enough to make a quick getaway.

A shiver shook her as she mounted and rode toward Varway. Half a league away, she could see the red-and-black banners waving in the breeze, see the throngs of people, and hear a dim chattering noise.

Was she really doing this?

Yes. She was. *For Nora and Delli.*

Therese dismounted in a small cove obscured by Argbil Forest. Her mouth felt as dry as Scholl's biscuits and her fingers as cold as the ice that still coated the ground despite spring's arrival. While this wouldn't come close to eradicating the debt, it'd make a dent.

Her mind jumped to her other mission. She would fulfill the contract, but her target deserved to know the last words his father wrote, if the author was truly his father.

Therese weaved her way through a mass of women in black and red gowns with poofy skirts. They waved miniature banners on slender sticks as though the king already stood before them.

Her stomach heaved. After reading the order against Ivelle's home village, how could she celebrate a man who commanded the deaths of innocents? Did King Eligor's valiant past cancel his mounting atrocities?

She entered the emporium which had become like a second home. Claudine bustled about in a black gown edged in scarlet. Hair escaped intricate braiding and the latest fashion of high-heeled, buttoned-up shoes decked with curlicues tapped the floor. Borros stood in the corner, tugging at a stiff collar trapped by a scarlet tie.

"Ironic that we're celebrating a man we disobey." His low statement filtered through Claudine's ruckus to Therese's ears.

Claudine smacked his head. "Keep your tongue, you oversized buffoon," she hissed before turning to Therese. Behind Claudine, Borros crossed his arms, expression grim.

Therese knew unspoken threats when she saw them.

"I won't tell anyone." She didn't disagree, but that was none of their business. Everyone had their own opinion. Although, for being a smuggler, Borros wasn't too observant. "Is Ivelle here?"

"Aye. She's in the back with the girls. Nora's doing better. Ivelle thinks she can participate in King's Day."

Therese's stomach soured. Did she want her sisters joining in a celebration honoring a murderer of innocents? Would it be seen as treason if they didn't? "What about Emmi?"

"Borros will carry her. Poor dear tires so easily and this way she can nap if she needs to." Claudine gave Borros a look that resembled how Jolie looked at Lucian.

Therese coughed. "May I go back?"

"Certainly, dear."

Floorboards creaked beneath Therese's weight as she walked the now-familiar hallway. Longing filled her. When would their lives return to normal?

Giggles eased the tempest of worry wreaking havoc within. Delli and Emmi chortled as Nora squirmed and protested Ivelle tying a ribbon in her hair. "It's ugly!"

"It's black, a color that goes with anything. Would you rather I give you pink?" Ivelle planted hands on hips and raised a brow when Nora peered over her shoulder. "You should be grateful you aren't forced to wear the latest fashions."

Therese accepted Delli's hug and shook her head at Nora. "Behave. Use your manners."

"But you're dressed for work. Why must I dress up?"

"Because Ivelle is obviously putting time into making you look presentable, which is no easy feat. Don't be rude, be polite, and speak to no one besides Ivelle, Miss DeGrim, and Borros." The last thing she needed was someone trying to take away the girls because they thought she was a terrible guardian.

Nora pouted but held still until Ivelle finished tying the ribbon. She slowly scampered off with Delli, half tugging Emmi along.

Ivelle sighed and brushed hair from her face. "I almost preferred her sick."

Therese allowed herself to laugh. It felt good to ignore the heaviness weighing on her soul for a bit. She sobered at the sight of the cruel, raised burn scars marking the underside of Ivelle's forearms. "How are you?"

Ivelle shrugged. Though she acted like usual with the girls, fatigue showed in her eyes and sluggish movements. "Angry. Like I want to take up a sword and…" She swallowed. "But what can I do about it? Nothing. Even saying this to you has the potential to get me arrested or killed."

"I will tell no one." Therese relaxed when Ivelle said nothing about the journal. It probably wasn't right to swipe the book, but what was done was done. He needed to know.

No one could read that journal and remain the same.

Ivelle sighed as trumpets sounded. She smoothed the front of her ebony dress. "Ready?"

"Yes." Therese hesitated. She wasn't certain what Ivelle knew about her employment, but was it safe to ask another favor that could draw suspicion? "I might have to leave early. Could you keep an eye on the girls for me? It shouldn't take long."

Ivelle's gaze hardened, but she nodded.

Therese followed the others from the store. People crowded the street, waving small pennants and cheering. She scanned the throng for a familiar face. Jolie caught her eye and waved.

"I must go," Therese murmured to Ivelle. She eased into the crowd, not waiting for a reply.

Jolie caught her hand. "Over there," she whispered. "The short one holding a pint. Red robes. Bald."

Therese nodded and bit her bottom lip. Her heart pulverized her chest. Could she do this?

It's not like you haven't done it before.

She kept an eye on her target as King Eligor stepped onto the makeshift podium. King's guards in their pristine leather armor and stunning blue capes surrounded the podium in perfect precision. More surrounded the princess' small figure to the left.

"People of Orm!" King Eligor raised his hands in preparation of the usual speech. They protruded from the multiple layers of large, draping sleeves. "Once again, we gather to celebrate victory against tyranny."

The crowd roared, as though they hadn't heard this story multiple times.

"Centuries ago, I was good friends with a powerful man. We were like brothers and I swore fealty to him, an oath I never thought I would break. Unfortunately, greed captured his heart, and he refused sound advice, endangering the innocent people he governed. In a move of desperation, I was forced to end him."

Silence permeated the area after King Eligor's powerful voice faded.

Therese shivered. Why did it feel like danger and evil infused the air?

"His followers rose up, refusing to acknowledge what their master had done, and endangered our lives. We were forced to make a desperate escape and found ourselves here. From this untouched, pure earth, I built Orm."

King Eligor unsheathed the sword at his hip. It glinted pale gold, like a ray of pure sunlight. "This is a sword forged by the man I once revered. I wear it to always remind me what it means to be a quality leader."

The crowd clapped and cheered their assurances he was the best ruler to ever live.

"Red is the color of mourning and black is the color of power. The red snake against a black background is a personal reminder of the hardships my men and I endured while beginning this prosperous, incredible kingdom."

Therese crept through the crowd. Her fingers sifted through her pouch. Her bald target remained entranced by the story, occasionally sipping from his drink.

"It is unfortunate that some of you, my dear people, forget what makes this kingdom so prosperous and incredible. Some of you are sneaking dangerous contraband and illegal goods into Orm, objects that could harm innocent lives."

Ironic words falling from the lips of one who cared naught for the innocent lives he'd ordered destroyed in Mort.

"I set these rules for the safety of my people. The rules are to keep Orm safe. They must be obeyed. Which leads me to the next part of this celebration."

Therese' heart sank at the dangerous edge lining King Eligor's words. She slipped a petal into another target's drink along the way. Why did her instinct scream for her to escape? To grab Delli and Nora and run for their lives?

No. Focus.

She sidled next to her bald target.

"A few months ago, an innocent girl lost her parents in a brutal, bloody attack. My soldiers found her parents' mangled bodies, identifiable only by their clothes and crowns." King Eligor swept his hand, and Princess Anastasia inched forward. Therese's original target stuck to her side like their clothes were sewn together.

The princess almost leaned into the young soldier, like she needed support amidst standing before curious, unrelenting eyes. Just behind her stood Specialist Cetrin, as impassable as a stone wall.

"Anastasia, my ward, has mourned her parents. My men and I despaired ever bringing her justice, but justice we are finally able to bring."

Therese's bald target roared. She slipped the shredded pieces of two oleander petals into his drink and backed away, starting for her next target.

"We caught the heartless criminals who so gruesomely murdered my ward's parents. Bring them onto the stage."

Therese snuck hemlock and oleander into the drinks of three more targets before making her way to Jolie. The woman looked pale despite her dark skin. "The crowd will grow violent with the promise of public execution. Find your final victims and hurry. Then get out of here. There are few things worse than public hangings."

"They will punish them publicly?" Therese's last meal threatened to revisit. What the murderers did was abominable, but didn't King Eligor know about the young children in the crowd? To witness such a grisly event would ruin them.

Stars, please let Ivelle get my sisters in the emporium before this happens.

If only she could take them home. If only she could protect them.

But survival trumped everything else.

Therese crouched behind the trees as her target, the princess, and Specialist Cetrin rode into view. Specialist Cetrin would be difficult to work around, but at least the other soldiers were removing the three lifeless bodies from the makeshift gallows.

Therese ignored the sense of unease. It wasn't normal for the princess to be escorted by only two guards, not when they rode a path where an ambush could easily take place.

When the horses passed, she held her breath. Sobbing reached her ears.

Her target reined in his horse and waved Specialist Cetrin ahead. "We'll be right there."

"Stupid move, Holder."

"Please, Rogan? This is the only chance she'll have to cry like she should be able to. You know once we reach Rex Dorcha she'll be expected to go on like nothing's happened."

Specialist Cetrin grunted before nudging his horse to a trot.

Therese's target aided the princess down, his leg almost buckling. "Hey, it's okay. The bad people who killed your parents are gone."

"I miss them."

"I know, Princess, but they would want you to keep your chin up and become the best princess you can be."

"I don't think I make a very good princess. Nurse says real princesses don't cry." Princess Anastasia leaned into him, small arms wrapping around his waist.

"What does Svetlana know? She's never been a princess."

"Can I still miss them?"

"Every day of your life." Therese's target awkwardly knelt to the princess' level. His leg clearly still pained him from the way he limped and favored it. "I lost my parents when I was five. I still miss them."

"Did you cry?"

"I did."

A sign. Therese gripped the journal. The stars were giving her a sign. She ghosted forward. Her knife brushed his throat.

He stiffened. "Princess, back away. Slowly. Go for your horse."

"No." Therese stopped his hand reaching for a dagger. "I mean no harm." She wasn't authorized to yet. "I merely want to give you this." She shoved the book at him. "I suggest you read it."

"Who are you?"

She angled the knife along his jugular when he tried turning his head. Thank the stars for her hood and the cloth covering her mouth. "My identity is unimportant. Please, take this. Read it."

"Tell me who you are or I will arrest you on the charges of endangering the princess."

"A threat you would carry out well if you were on the other side of the blade." She studied his thick brown hair and strong profile. What secrets did he hide? What questions did he ask in the silence of his heart?

Her mind registered the pounding of hooves coming up from behind just before pain sliced through her shoulder.

Her target took advantage and grabbed her wrist, twisted it, and spun away from the blade.

Therese forced clarity into her mind and vision. Warmth spread along her back. She grunted and dodged Specialist Cetrin's blade. *Stars, help me.*

She met her target's eyes for the briefest of heartbeats before panic settled in. They would catch her. Reveal her identity. Interrogate and kill her for putting the princess in the slightest of danger. Her sisters would be left at the mercy of a woman with no reason to claim them as her own. No reason to offer assistance.

Run! Adrenaline burned a painful, fiery path through her veins. She sprinted the ten steps to the trees. Horses could not enter and the soldiers would be forced to approach on foot.

Her breath sounded like the clarion ringing of bells, alerting her pursuers of her location. Colors blended into an array as her boots pounded loose earth.

Sweat stung her eyes by the time she reached the mare. Therese gasped as she mounted. Did they still chase her? Had she just endangered her sisters' only means of support and chance at survival? Was pitying her target a mistake?

Stars, help me.

CHAPTER TWENTY-THREE

ROGAN

ORM'S PRAIRIE WAS bland, boring, and ugly as winter faded and spring emerged. Dead grass and barren trees made the stretching land and low hills look like a floristic graveyard.

Rogan pulled his cloak tighter about his shoulders as cold wind cut through the thick wool cloth. By the stars, he hated traveling. Though he was no fan of large crowds, he found himself preferring Varway's clutter to the prairie's eerie openness.

Holder's red gelding plodded along, its rider immersed in a faded, tattered book.

"Holder."

No response.

"Holder?"

Holder turned the page.

"Holder!"

Holder jerked, almost losing his grip on the book. His shoulders relaxed as annoyance brushed his expression. "What?"

"You're supposed to be talking." Rogan smirked at his friend's blatant irritation. "How's your throat?"

Holder traced the scabbed cut. "I don't remember it's there unless you bring it up. Honestly, Rogan, my answers won't change. You've interrogated me five times, and all five times I've answered the same."

"So you remember nothing else about the assassin?"

Holder's tone held the exasperation in his sigh. "Like I've said, she wasn't an assassin. She wasn't trying to kill me or the princess. True, her clothing was odd and she knows how to handle a knife, but she could have slit my throat where I knelt. She didn't."

"How kind. You sure she had no distinguishing facial mark?"

"Unless you want to search all of Orm for a woman with vibrant blue eyes, no."

Rogan scowled at the space between Blackie's ears. The attack made no sense. His plan for the ride back to Rex Dorcha had been destroyed when Holder's attachment to Princess Anastasia made him enact yet another foolish plan. If he'd allowed Rogan to be present, nothing would have happened. The simple plan of riding from Varway to Rex Dorcha as the celebrations continued simply hadn't allowed for any hiccups.

Like Holder cared about the plan.

Then came Officer Torgord's interrogations, though the man acted unconcerned as he leaned back in his chair and asked questions in a voice dripping with false care.

Captain Geros had been no better.

"Rogan?"

"Yes?"

"Do you think I'll still be the princess' bodyguard when we return?"

Rogan shifted at the open display of raw vulnerability on Holder's face. There was no reason for Holder to be demoted or moved, but who was he to guess the king's mind?

He cleared his throat. "I think Princess Anastasia will pitch a royal fuss if King Eligor tries replacing you."

"You really think so?"

"If I didn't, I wouldn't have said it."

Holder again immersed himself in the book.

"What's it about?"

"Huh?"

"The book, Holder. What is it about? What's so important about it that some wannabe assassin had to give it to you while holding a knife to your throat?"

Holder's brow furrowed. "I think it's about my parents."

"How did she get it?"

"By the stars if I know, Rogan. Just...let me read, please?"

Rogan stared at the waving prairie grasses. If someone gave him a book about his parents, would he read it? Would he care enough?

Unlikely.

He stuffed logic into that gaping hole slowly enlarging in his heart and spirit. No one was important enough to want to read about, and that most definitely included his parents.

Although...some wee part of him wanted to go back in time and discover when Maximo Cetrin first felt the vestiges of hate against his only child. Though Rogan remembered the first time Father bruised him, he couldn't discern when Father's revulsion took root.

He shivered and tightened his hold on his cloak. Oh well. It was for the best that he didn't remember when the pain, the emptiness, and the knowledge that he would never be good enough or wanted began.

He had enough pain to deal with now without living in the unchangeable past.

◇◦─·····•───◦◇

Rogan snatched his sword as another coyote howled. His pulse throbbed in his neck. How could people live on the prairie where predators roamed unchecked? At least it was still early spring and rattlers were in hiding.

He leaned back and sighed. Give him Argbil Forest with its obnoxious crows or Varway with its human varmints he could catch.

An arm's length away, Holder burrowed in his bedroll. The campfire flickered light over his friend's relaxed expression. When was the last time he'd seen Holder so at peace?

Rogan sighed. His arm stung from where that blasted gelding bit him earlier; his bones ached from riding all day; his head throbbed from trying to plan how to find a man whom he'd never heard of before eight days ago; and his soul hurt from the lack of care Mother showed when he told her about the mission.

Why are you surprised? When has she ever cared about anything you do?

Holder's book caught his eye. It's lined, faded, leather cover showed signs of wear, tear, and hard times. He eased it from Holder's saddlebag and flipped open the page Holder bookmarked before they set up camp for the night.

The chomping of horses eating grass lulled Rogan into an uneasy calm. If the horses showed no nervousness, then he had no need to. He fingered a weathered page before reading.

"'Mariline and I left Mort yesterday. We could not bring ourselves to stay longer, knowing we already put them in danger by accepting their gracious hospitality. It is hard to believe three years have passed. Is our son alright? Does he thrive under the evil choking Orm? I trust Maximo and Monica little, but they were the only ones who will keep our son safe. I

worry also for their son, that he will grow into a man like his father.'"

Rogan ground his teeth. Paper crinkled under his grip. Even then all those years ago, he showed potential for becoming another Maximo Cetrin.

Stars, I don't care if that's what you planned for me. I refuse to be like him. I refuse to be him.

He drew a breath and shook his right hand free of the coming ache. Nothing moved in the darkness and the horses stayed calm. He forced himself to read the next entry.

"'This little village is a mystery. The people live much like the ones in Mort, with their log cabins, homespun clothes, and jobs, but I see a freedom, a light in their eyes I've never before witnessed. Mariline has also commented on it. These villagers are nice people, kind and generous, but they have the propensity to say unusual things. The other day they were reading from a thin collection of parchments. 'Greater love has no one than this, that someone lay down his life for his friends', the old patriarch read. I suppose it is true, but what great scholar or philanthropist told such a small, high mountain village this? These people are a curiosity. I must investigate deeper.'"

Holder's groan yanked Rogan from the bizarre writing. Brall Lygor must have been suffering from insanity, for no one in their right mind wrote treason or traveled to the high mountain villages.

Holder groaned again. Sweat shone on his forehead and his head whipped from side to side. "No," he gasped. "No, don't. Where are you?"

"Holder!" Rogan shook his friend. Fine time for him to have a nightmare. Predators would attack if they perceived any weakness. "Holder, wake up!"

"What?" Holder braced himself on his elbows. Hair clung to his forehead. His eyes were wide, almost panicked in the way they scanned his surroundings. "What's wrong?"

"You were having a nightmare."

"Oh." Holder sat and reached for his canteen. His shoulders heaved with thick, heavy breaths. "Was that it?"

"Was that it? By the stars, Holder. You were almost shouting. Keep it down. We don't know what's out there."

Holder stared at Rogan for a long while before swallowing and nodding. "I'll try." He paused. "Anything else you need to tell me?"

What made Holder so snappy? "No, go back to sleep. Just keep quiet."

"Right." Holder almost glared at Rogan before turning to his side and lying down.

Rogan ran a hand through his hair and shoved the journal back into Holder's saddlebag. Wherever Holder's attitude came from, he needed to lose it. The mission would be difficult enough without having a grumpy partner.

Morning arrived in a blend of pink and purple. Rogan cracked his eyes open and forced himself to rise. Holder had been so cranky he hadn't dared wake him up again for the shift change. The fire had dwindled to a smoldering pile of coals, and the horses lounged in the coming daylight.

He pushed to his feet and stretched away the kinks and stiffness. "Holder, get up."

"M'up." Holder yawned. "Since when were you an early riser? I almost had to drown you in snow when we were guarding the princess."

"Since we decided to ride into the middle of nowhere." Rogan doused the fire with water from his canteen. He'd have to refill it at the small stream before they left. He pulled a strip of jerky from a saddlebag and gnawed on it. Deer was much better fresh.

"You read the journal?"

"One page. Doesn't make for an interesting read. Happy for you, though, that you have it. Something to remember them by."

"Yeah." Holder's voice lacked enthusiasm. "If you want to read it, feel free."

Rogan swallowed to dissipate the lump in his throat. Did he really want to read something written by a man who thought he could become as wretched as his father? "Time is precious. I don't want to waste it reading that."

Yet, despite the pain Brall Lygor's words inflicted, his mind kept replaying a certain phrase over and over. *'Greater love has no one than this, that someone lay down his life for his friends'.*

Wasn't the greatest type of love when one gave their life for their king? That was what Father and Captain Geros pounded into his mind from the first day of training. Dying in the line of duty for King Eligor was the greatest honor. The greatest type of loyalty.

Who was right?

He shook the question away. Captain Geros had to be, for a man who spouted treason could never be right.

Right?

Rogan cleared his throat and rolled up his bedroll. Thinking such things would get him in trouble. It was clear who was right, and it wasn't Brall Lygor. "Holder, we need to get going."

"You need a name."

Rogan stayed the whetstone and glanced Holder's way. Just beyond Blackie stood the man-eating monster. Holder placed a hand on the beast's muzzle while stroking its neck, keeping up a muttered stream of nonsense.

"Yes, you need a name. Maybe then people won't be so mean to you."

"Are you baby-talking to a horse?"

"No." Answer clipped, Holder kept his attention on the devil.

"Sounds like you are. That thing is a freak of horseflesh, Holder. It could eat you where you stand and not be one bit remorseful. It'd probably chew your bones up too and leave them mangled messes."

Holder did look his way then, an eyebrow quirked and something almost...distrustful lining his expression. "You're seriously afraid of him."

"Not afraid. Just wary."

"You're afraid of a horse."

"He's a monster."

"He's a horse."

"No regular horse's favorite pastime is seeing how many chunks they can take from you."

What might be fond exasperation quirked Holder's mouth into a half-smile. He resumed stroking the roan's neck. "You only do that when you dislike someone, don't you?"

Rogan snorted. "You're baby-talking again." Still, the conversation was worth it if he could draw Holder from this uncharacteristic melancholy.

"He needs a name."

"How about Biter? Or Mauler? Murderer? Brat?"

"You just dislike him because he bit you."

"Yeah. Three times."

Silence settled. Rogan returned to sharpening his daggers. He'd done the same last night, but with nothing to do as he awaited the final rays of dimming sunlight to disappear, picking up the whetstone had been a natural inclination.

The fire snapped and crackled. On the prairie, only dustings of snow topped the dead grass and weeds. A blessing since Rogan didn't fancy traveling during snowstorms and definitely didn't care to meet his death through hypothermia.

His fingers twitched, muscles begging to pick up his sword and find a sparring partner. It'd been too long since he'd crossed swords, and the growing turmoil and emotions needed to be worked off before he fell beneath their influence and did something stupid.

"Redwing."

"What?"

"I'll name him Redwing." Holder limped to the fire and sat across from Rogan. "He's fast like a red-winged blackbird and he's almost as vibrant as one."

"If that's what you want to name him. I still say Mauler is better."

Another barely-there smile. Something withheld Holder, kept him from being himself. And Rogan was too exhausted to figure out what.

When Holder didn't respond, Rogan replaced the dagger with another. The silence wasn't heavy like at the Cetrin cabin, but it wasn't amicable either. Oh well. Holder was twenty, old enough to work out his problems without Rogan's assistance.

Hopefully, after Holder dealt with whatever bothered him, things would return to normal.

Rogan repressed a shudder at the thought of returning to his parents. Actually, some things were better never returning to normalcy.

CHAPTER TWENTY-FOUR

IVELLE

NUMB. COLD. HOT. NUMB.

Ivelle stared at her pale reflection in the mirror. Dark circles marked the skin under her eyes, testifying to the nightmarish night. She sighed and splashed cold water on her face. Her hands trembled. Why did it affect her so? She'd witnessed death before—the death of her family and friends, which had been much more gruesome than the three she struggled to remove from her mind.

"Hey." Claudine knocked. Her smile was sympathetic, but it only drew tears to Ivelle's fatigued eyes. "Decided not to try to sleep?"

"What's the point?" Her voice rasped, hoarse from the screams torn from her during what should have been hours of rest.

"Oh, sweet girl." Claudine entered and turned Ivelle from the mirror to engulf her in a hug.

It felt so similar to how she remembered Mama's that the gathering tears over spilled with vengeance.

"What's wrong?"

Ivelle shuddered. They had gotten the girls inside in time, but the sight of King Eligor's blue-caped soldiers leading out Emmi's family seared her mind. "Yesterday...it melded with Mort. I couldn't stop them then. I couldn't stop them yesterday." Flames and blood and rope combined into a grisly mixture of pain, horror, and death.

Watching one's family being cut down was horrific. Watching innocent adults and a teen girl be hung was equally dreadful.

"Why?" she whispered. Her voice cracked. "Why?"

"Oh, sweet girl." Claudine rubbed Ivelle's back and smoothed her hair. "Honey, I don't know why life turned against you like it did, but I know you are a fighter. You wouldn't have made it this far if you weren't. You survived the destruction of your home village, and now you will help Emmi survive the loss of her parents. It helps that she didn't see their deaths."

"No, but she'll always wonder. And when she asks me, I'll have to lie. I'll have to say I don't know."

"Ivelle Quade, we all lie. You lied when those soldiers came and searched the place. You lied when you told Therese the parchments alone wouldn't square Nora's care. You lie when you walk out onto the street and act like a normal citizen. You aren't normal; you are part of the black market, something the king hates."

"I hate him." Anger and heat filled the aching gap in her soul. "I hate him with everything I am."

"Ivelle!" Claudine's tone cut like a dagger. "You may not agree with everything he does, but he is the king. You must show him some modicum of respect."

Ivelle fumed. The heat grew, flourished until a bonfire the size of Varway consumed her. She would show no respect to the man who ordered the deaths of her family and village.

She would show no respect to the man who ordered the hanging of innocents.

No. If King Eligor wanted her respect, he had long ago destroyed his chance.

She refused to revere a monster. A murderer.

"Ivelle?" Claudine held her at arm's length. Warnings gathered in Claudine's eyes and the lines creasing her forehead. "Promise me you will never say such things again. They could get you killed for treason. I can't lose you." She shook her. "Promise me. Promise me now."

Ivelle forced the word off her tongue. "Promise." It tasted bitter, nasty.

It was a lie. Another lie told. A lie she would not, could not keep. But like Claudine just said, Ivelle lied every day.

"They're playing." Ivelle led Therese down the hall. The shorter woman remained silent. While not overly talkative, she usually asked a question or two. Her pale face and weary eyes reminded Ivelle of her own exhaustion. Despite being four days since King's Day, the nightmares remained.

She gestured to the room.

Therese made to enter. She walked stiffly and the upper back part of her simple black shirt was bumped up and rumpled, like it hid a thick bandage.

Ivelle touched Therese's arm. "You okay?"

"Yes." Therese stared ahead.

"You look like you hurt. Does this have to do with the job you had to disappear off to on King's Day?"

"Maybe."

Therese was nice, but there was just something...not quite right about her. Ever since the day she came and purchased those herbs and the bolt of cloth, something in the back of Ivelle's brain warned her. Then, she caught her sneaking to Holder's room. And Therese always dressed in dark gray.

Ivelle stared, mouth moving before she narrowed her eyes. "Are you an assassin?" She'd heard of the unexpected deaths around the city in the past year, and ten deaths had been reported by the end of King's Day. Seven were from unknown causes. The other three victims bore slit throats.

Therese swallowed. Nerves and what looked like fear drew her expression taut and widened her eyes.

"You weren't coming to visit Holder. You came to kill him. And at King's Day? I bet you had a hand in those deaths." Ivelle grit her teeth. Therese was no better than King Eligor. No better than his minions who gladly inflicted pain and suffering. "Well?"

Therese's thin frame trembled. "I will do whatever it takes to provide for my family. Yes, I was sent to kill Holder. By whom, I don't know. But I couldn't—can't—bring myself to do it."

"Yet you had no issue killing people on King's Day."

"You think I want to kill for a living?" Therese hissed. Her face reddened as her hands fisted. "I had a choice. Either learn a profession that would kill my heart and soul, or work at a place that would kill every part of me. Not everyone has a happy ending like you do."

Therese brushed past and entered the room. Emmi sat on the chair and Nora and Delli perched on the bed. The girls shared a laugh as Nora failed to catch a piece of popcorn in her mouth.

"Nora, Delli, we are going home." Therese held up a hand to ward off their complaints. "Nora, you are fully healed. It would be rude to take advantage of Claudine's hospitality."

Ivelle bristled. It was Claudine who allowed them to stay, but it was Ivelle who convinced her.

"Pack your things."

Emmi was still sobbing ten minutes later as they left.

Ivelle brushed hair from her face and placed an arm around fragile shoulders. "You will see them again, Emmi." A lie, she was certain, but Emmi was doing so well. It would be tragic if her health took another downfall.

The small girl sniffled. A familiar rash covered her arms, and her skin felt too warm. Her tiny hands hung limp. "My fingers hurt."

"Let's get you in bed. Then I'll bring you some strawberry tea."

Emmi snuggled against her shoulder, half asleep by the time Ivelle took the twenty steps to Emmi's room. She pulled a thin blanket over the girl before standing back and watching. Was Emmi in danger? It was unlikely King Eligor knew her parents had another child, but the man, for all his evil, was canny and devious.

Ivelle rubbed her chest. Her heart physically ached. She had never formally met Emmi's parents and sister, only waved and exchanged greetings as she and Claudine passed by after visiting or sniffing out a purchase, but they seemed like a nice family. Happy, loved each other and their daughters, and content in life.

It made no sense. Emmi's father had been a money-changer. He looked unable to lift more than a medium sack of coins, let alone a sword or club or bow.

By the stars, everything feels off.

"There you are." Claudine found Ivelle in the kitchen, staring at the wall as the kettle heated. "I need you to take something to the attic."

"Claudine..."

"You act like there is a body up there, girlie. The only dead things are bugs. I can't convince Borros to go and Alvin is nowhere to be found, so it is up to you."

"It's creepy."

"It's an attic. Filled with junk and extra supplies."

"It's creepy."

"Ivelle." Claudine graced her with the perfected *you-will-obey* look. "The crates are on the counter in the front. Don't forget to be quiet. I don't need questions because customers hear you tromping around."

"Can I at least take a candle?"

Claudine's impish smirk looked out of place with her height-of-fashion orange organza gown. That woman was up to no good.

Ivelle muttered as she lit a candle and gathered the crates. She paused at the room's edge. Claudine could be right that the only dead things in that attic were bugs, but Ivelle refused to take the risk. She snatched a slender sword from its place on the wall and took a breath.

An attic. It was just an attic.

But, by the stars, a spine-chilling attic.

Ivelle slipped into the back room and tugged a cabinet aside to reveal a square opening half her height. She set the crates on the fourth step and squeezed herself into the hole. The wooden stairs creaked under her weight, and the lantern cast flitting shadows.

With no railing, one wrong step would send her plummeting to her death.

Dusty air irritated Ivelle's throat as she staggered to the top. She shivered. Nothing in the attic could hurt her, not unless the dead spiders returned to life, the headless mannequins crashed over, or the piles of crates and trunks fell on her.

She eased the crates down on top of a trunk bearing more dust than wood. What did they hold? How long had they been in the attic? She tiptoed to the furthest stack of flattop trunks and brushed dust and dirt off the locks.

The trunks were old.

What did they hold?

Ivelle jimmied the top trunk's lock with the sword. The pile rose to her shoulders, and she stretched to open the lid. Soft leather met her fingertips as she reached inside and felt around.

Verum, the book's cover read. Claudine must have locked it away.

Dust poofed as she opened the book. Crisp writing in black ink covered the pages in perfectly straight lines. The same book that had almost gotten her in trouble. Thank the stars Holder's friend knew to hold his tongue. Was it about Orm? About King Eligor? The title certainly promised interesting information. Or was it about herbal and medical knowledge?

What if it is something entirely different?

"We'll see," she whispered. Maybe she'd give it a chance. And even if it was the most boring piece of writing in existence, she'd read it. Maybe it could help her sleep at night, since the journal had disappeared.

Therese.

Ivelle would bet anything that lying little assassin had something to do with it. She could only pray that, if Therese did, she told no one where she obtained it.

CHAPTER TWENTY-FIVE

HOLDER

"THAT IS WHERE he's hiding?" Rogan's voice thickened with disgust. "How is this place inhabitable? Even from here the buildings look like they'll collapse."

"Being made of wood does not mean they are unstable." Holder allowed his eyes respite from the bright winter sun for a brief second. Exhaustion pulled at every muscle and tendon, and his leg throbbed in continual spasms.

Rogan huffed. "You sure this is the place?"

"It's the one Captain Geros told me about. The sign bears the same name." He squinted at the scattered buildings. Sheep and horses pawed through the fine layer of snow, looking for grass. Smoke rose from thin stone chimneys. Small, humanoid figures bustled about.

"If you think so. We should begin over there, where those buildings cluster."

Holder grunted. Weariness and cold scraped his nerves thin, and Rogan's brisk and abrupt attitude scraped his patience thinner. He tugged his cloak around his shoulders. Late winters were never this cold in Varway.

His body lurched as Redwing followed Blackie.

Spring hadn't yet arrived to the area. Frozen grass blades crunched under hooves as the low sounds of voices and farm life welcomed them. A ragged wooden sign slouched before a gathering of five buildings. Burned letters spelled the name *Weedcrag* in harsh, abrupt lettering. Deciduous trees lined the farthest buildings, bare and dull brown.

"We have company." Rogan's hand drifted to his chest.

"Don't do anything brash." Holder sighed. By the stars, they'd emerge with no trouble only if Rogan kept his acrid comments to himself. "Let me do the talking."

Two men approached on foot. The sun shone off spears clenched in their hands. A third trailed them at a distance.

Blackie snorted and shifted.

"Remember, I'm doing the talking. You'll manage to insult someone and get us killed."

Rogan rolled his eyes. "Just don't talk us into trouble. I don't want to hurt anyone, but I will if they are a threat."

The shorter man waved his hand as they neared. "Who are you, and what do you want?"

Holder cleared his throat and willed his exhaustion to vanish. The recurring nightmares hadn't helped, and they loomed in the recesses of his mind like rattlesnakes waiting to strike from the shadows. "We're looking for someone."

"Oh? Who?" The taller, thicker man angled his sword toward Rogan. "If that's all you're doing, tell your friend to remove his hand from the dagger."

Leave it to Rogan to ruin a diplomatic attempt. Holder glowered at Rogan. The beginnings of a headache throbbed behind his eyes and all he wanted was to sleep. "We don't know his name. Only that he used to be a king's guard."

"There is no one here like that." The shorter man glanced at the sky before scanning Holder and Rogan. "I don't know what you two are, who you are, or who sent you, but it won't be pretty if you bring harm to Weedcrag." His mustache quivered. "Just be on your way, please. We are a simple village and want no trouble."

"Wait, Barney." The third man covered the remaining distance. His scruffy beard and hair obscured his facial features and he wore regular clothes like the other two, but he walked with the assurance of a man who knew he was dangerous. "Best keep an eye on them—make sure they aren't up to something."

"No one will take them in for the night," the other man sneered. "An' no one will trust them within a league of their animals. These two smell like trouble."

The back of Holder's neck prickled as the man perused him. What was his intent? Rogan could fight, but he could do little more than ride at a trot, and not without effort. He would get his friend killed at worst. At best, injured.

"Which is why I'll keep an eye on them. They don't scare me. I've faced down bigger problems than two kids on a fool's errand. Go home to your families. And raise no fuss about this."

The other two men shot Holder and Rogan one last distrustful glare before starting back to the village.

The man crossed his arms. He looked strong, from his stance, to his easy, almost practiced inspection. "Dismount. You two could do little harm, but I still don't trust you."

"Holder can't walk."

The man blinked, gaze darting to Holder, then Rogan. "What?"

"By the stars. Are you deaf? Holder. Cannot. Walk." Rogan's cheek twitched like he grit his teeth. "He's injured. Took a bolt to the leg a few weeks ago. He's overdone it since then. He rides to wherever you are taking us."

"Prove it."

By the stars. Holder fisted his hand. What was Rogan thinking? There was no way he could decently prove the injury save for cutting away cloth.

The man tromped over. "Show me where. And stars help you, boy, if you pull anything."

Holder traced the bandage's upper edge. His back muscles tensed. The man could cause serious harm if he wanted, and Holder could do nothing but swing his sword and nudge his horse after him.

"It's on his upper right thigh."

"You lose the ability to talk?" The man peered at Holder with hazel eyes situated under dark, bushy eyebrows streaked with gray.

Holder shifted and looked away. Something about the man's eyes unnerved him. They peered through him, to his soul. To the questions, the doubts, lingering within.

"Fine. You can ride until we reach my cabin. Your mouthy friend will walk."

⬦ ⬦

Holder hissed as pain flamed through his leg. For one heartbeat, the small barn's interior spun. He grit his teeth and drew a breath that tasted like hay and dust. He fought away the dizziness. He needed to be alert. Ready. Prepared.

"You look terrible." Rogan looped Blackie's reins around a rod running the wall's length. "Go sit. I'll take care of your demon horse."

Holder hobbled to the stacks of crates in the corner. A large pile of hay sloughed to his left. It looked scratchy but, at that point, he could probably sleep like a baby on it. "Why did you tell him? You put us at risk."

"You can't dismount without almost collapsing, let alone walk half a league across rutted ground. Plus, it makes you look nonthreatening."

"And weak."

"There's nothing wrong with being injured, Holder." Rogan unbuckled Redwing's saddle. "I won't let him do anything."

"Like you stand a chance," Holder scoffed. "He's got a full head on you and possesses more muscle than the two of us combined."

Rogan's fists clenched. An unnamed emotion crossed his features before his shoulders drew back and his stance stiffened. "I still won't let him do anything. You need anything from your saddlebags?"

"I'll just take them." Holder pulled the saddlebags close and searched for the journal. No matter what, it had to stay hidden.

"You boys done yet?" The man stood in the doorway, arms crossed. He nodded toward Rogan. "I know your friend's name, but what is yours?" He waited until Rogan grumbled an answer before stalking over.

Holder struggled to his feet and drew his sword. Every nerve screamed *danger*. Stars help him, he couldn't fight the man and win.

"Put that away. I'm helping you inside."

Firelight warmed the one-room cabin. A bed nestled against the far side, and a table and chair perched before the fireplace. More crates stacked next to a bookcase. Something in Holder pinched. As simple as it was, it felt homey. Cozy. Nothing like the Cetrin cabin, and definitely nothing like the barracks.

"Holder, sit. Rogan, you can haul one of those crates over here. No, not that one. The one I'm pointing to. No. Yes, the top one. Yes, that one. It should be empty."

Rogan brought two crates over, handed one to the man, and sat on the other next to Holder. In the mix of shadows and light, his expression was fierce, determined. Gone were the harsh, almost cruel comments. Here was the Rogan Holder used to know.

"What is your name?"

By the stars, Rogan sounded like Officer Torgord.

The man settled on the crate and laced his fingers together. "Argus."

Holder startled. Hadn't the journal mentioned something about an Argus? But that was probably a common name in his father's generation. No need to think this man was his father's friend. No need to get excited about possibly meeting someone who might know his parents' fate.

"Argus what?" Rogan was back to his snappish tone.

"You didn't provide me with your surnames, so I'm not giving you mine." Argus moved to the fireplace and withdrew three bowls from a small cupboard hanging nearby. "Hungry? It's goat. I will never win an award for my cooking, but I can guarantee this tastes better than the rations in your saddlebags."

Pale, meaty chunks and small, shredded leaves floated in light brown liquid. Holder sniffed the stew. No scent of venom, no visual proof of poisonous leaves, but that meant nothing.

Argus inhaled a bite. "Not poisoned, boys." He raised a brow and sighed when neither responded. "I can see why you two are king's guards. Cautious, quick on your feet, and alert."

"How did you know?" Holder grimaced as he said the words. There his mouth went again, moving faster than his mind. He cringed from Rogan's dirty look. Saying that just caused more issues than they needed.

Than he could handle.

Argus's eyes slitted, calculating. Hands larger than Captain Geros' or First Lieutenant Cetrin's rubbed together. The man could strangle Holder with one hand. "Your weapons. The insignia with the snake in the circle is unique to king's guards. That and your tattoos. Next time you go on a secret mission, remove them."

"Then why didn't the other men know what we are?" Rogan stared at Argus, like doing so would reveal hidden answers and motives.

"They've lived here their entire lives. They know little beyond Weedcrag and the few other villages nearby. Now eat up. We'll discuss your little dilemma in the morning."

⬥⸺⸺⸺⸺⬥

Father knelt over Holder, eyes kind in a face otherwise blurry. "We need to leave, Holder. They're coming."

Holder opened his mouth to respond, but no sound came out. It was like his vocal chords were severed, or silenced in some way.

"They're coming, Holder. We need to leave."

A sense of dread filled Holder's chest like a weight as Father's eyes changed to deep, dark scarlet. Scales covered his face, and his features morphed into those of a snake's.

"Darkness," the snake hissed in King Eligor's voice. "I am darkness."

Holder strained to use his voice. What happened to Father? The rush of fear made him feel like a young child, like he had when his parents never returned.

"Holder." His name echoed.

He tried to move. Pressure bit into his upper arms. Something was off. Something was wrong. *Stars, help me!*

"Holder."

The blurry blue sky dimmed to darkness. The snake receded until faint red flashed in the distance.

"Holder!"

Holder choked and lurched. The snake's red eyes disappeared, replaced by the dim outline of Argus's face.

He panted. Sweat tickled his skin where it gathered on his forehead and neck. Why did Argus lean over him? Why did his hands bite into Holder's flesh?

"Breathe. You had a nightmare."

Nightmare. *Nightmare.*

Holder gulped down the water offered by Argus. The smooth, wooden cup against his fingers and the cool liquid provided tangible proof he was awake. "Sorry," he gasped.

"Don't be sorry for something you cannot control." Argus sat. Wide shoulders heaved with a sigh. "What was it?"

Should he tell him? His and Rogan's carelessness already put them in a potentially difficult spot. Holder snorted a humorless chuckle. Argus would think he was addled.

Maybe he was.

"Does this have to do with your parents?"

Holder glanced at Rogan's still form. How could he sleep on the hard floor amidst the noise Holder was certain he made? And Rogan possessed little patience for things like this—things like discussing feelings beyond anger and mild happiness.

"Your friend is sawing logs, Holder. He's out cold. You may speak freely."

Could he really? *No.* Holder shook the wistfulness away. To speak freely meant telling of his doubts and questions about King Eligor. Meant telling of the parchments found in the old cabin and the treachery written on their delicate surfaces. Meant telling of the journal, and the treachery and hope and promise concealed beneath the leather cover. Meant telling of the letter.

"I apologize for awakening you." Holder laid down and pulled the blanket to his shoulders. An ache took root in his chest, similar to the one in his leg. Would he ever find the answers he craved?

CHAPTER TWENTY-SIX

THERESE

"I DON'T KNOW how or why you received this, but I don't want it happening again." Jolie slathered cold salve over Therese's injury. "We taught you to be prepared. We taught you to be careful. Weren't you paying attention?"

"Yes." *No?* Therese bit back a squawk of pain. She'd heard the hoof beats, but the sound hadn't registered. Only pain and panic.

Jolie huffed. "You said you were ready, Therese." Her voice softened as she came to sit before her. "Lucian and I are worried about you."

"She's right." Lucian ambled in. Arms crossed, he perched beside Jolie. "You don't look good, kiddo."

"I am fine." Therese forced a smile. It might calm Jolie and Lucian, but it did nothing to calm the storm raging through her heart and soul. Ivelle's accusations weighed on her like the heaviest of chains. How had she admitted the one thing she was to keep secret? If Ivelle guessed her profession, who else would? Who else already had? And what would Scholl do when he heard of her injury? The debt was far from settled.

"Of course she doesn't look good, Lucian." Jolie swatted his shoulder, huffing at his whine. "Anyone who receives a slash from their shoulder to the bottom of their ribs and lost the amount of blood she did will not look well."

Lucian rubbed his shoulder. His eyes held sympathy. "Speaking of which, Scholl wants you. Your client is here. Don't forget to cover your face."

Of course. *Rule One* was to never let the client see your face. Therese's swallow heightened the tension in her chest. She eased into her black overdress and smoothed the skirt. Pain burned the right side of her back.

"Here." Jolie tucked the cloth around Therese's nose and mouth. Dark eyes roved her face, like they searched for an answer. "Good luck."

Therese nodded and made her way to Scholl's office. She could feel her pulse in the injury, an ominous *thwump, thwump.*

"Enter."

Scholl and her client stood. Not for the first time, Therese almost swallowed her tongue. Her target had stood on King Eligor's right side during King's Day. And that insignia on his cheek...nearly the same insignia which her target wore.

Cold drenched Therese. What type of man was her client that he would turn against a fellow soldier?

Scholl excused himself. His hand gripped Therese's upper arm before he stepped outside the room. "Don't mess this up," he hissed.

Therese steeled herself as Scholl closed the door. She could do this. Whatever this man wanted her to do, she could do it.

She had to.

"Specialist Lygor is currently in or near a small village several leagues southeast of here called Weedcrag. I want you to hunt him down and put this in his saddlebags."

Her client possessed an odd way of doing things. Therese accepted the object. The first time it'd been a letter, one she hid in an interior tear, sliding it between the lining and leather.

"If you can end him, do so. Make it look like an accident. Poison him then trip his horse, or shoot him and make it look like a rogue job. I don't care. We just need his body. If you can do this, I'll double the pay. If you can't, make sure no one else disposes of him."

The words tumbled through her mind. Travel? Had Scholl not explained the rules? They were not to go more than three leagues out of Varway. And kill her target if she could? But it wasn't mandatory? Just what was going on? Therese wiped her sweaty palms on her skirt. She was paid to carry out orders, not question them. "Anything else?"

The king's guard withdrew a bag of coins. "There are seven silvers in here. Complete the mission in the timeframe you are given and you will receive this plus the down payment. Lygor is accompanied by Specialist Cetrin. He will not be easy to hide from."

"I understand."

"You will leave tomorrow. I have given Scholl the money for your supplies. Remember: stealth is the only way you will accomplish this. Cetrin is sharp of eye, mind, and reflex, and you will be in trouble if he catches you." He stood and left, the edge of his vambrace catching her arm.

Therese clenched her fingers around the parcel. Seven silvers could pay off a decent size of her debt and provide a little extra for supplies. She forced a swallow down her dry throat. Whether or not Holder Lygor was innocent, he was still her target. Her mission. Her sisters' means of survival.

"Well?" Lucian's voice forced her into the present.

"I must leave tomorrow."

"Tomorrow?" Jolie joined and snuggled against Lucian.

A spike of jealousy and longing pricked Therese. With the way the stars were charting her path, it was unlikely she would ever experience what it felt like to lean on someone during the hard times. To share her burden with another.

She cleared her throat. "Yes. Can the girls stay here?" They wouldn't be happy with her decision, but Jolie would see them fed and kept warm.

"They can stay with me." Jolie nodded assent. Her dark skin glowed in the lone candle's light. "I don't think you are physically capable of travel. Your injury is severe and you are pale just from standing."

"Then the stars will have to guide me." That was, if they really cared. It seemed like the Westa family placed lowest on the list.

Lucian rolled his eyes. "You know the stars don't exist, Therese. It's a wonder King Eligor began the worship of them. You'd think with him creating Orm that he'd be the one worshiped."

"Lucian, your commentary does little good. Therese, bring your sisters here. Uncle Scholl will have to deal with children around him for once. Lucian, you will help me keep them occupied."

Therese managed to voice her gratitude before the two meandered away, Lucian still offering his thoughts about the stars. She closed her eyes and inhaled. Tallow, herbs, and the scent of sweat clinging to her client's armor.

Her stomach curdled at the thought of ending her target's life, but she couldn't turn down the extra coin.

"I can do this." Therese stared at the scattering of buildings half a league before her. "I have to do this."

She nudged the mare to a walk. Scholl had fussed and fumed about lending her his best horse, but after being reminded of the percentage he gained from the profit, he shut up.

Therese shuddered as she reined the mare to the nearest grove of trees. Her back throbbed and, despite the snow falling from light gray clouds, sweat gathered on her forehead and upper lip. What she wouldn't give for Jolie's foul-smelling salve and the Westa hut's plain comfort, such as it was.

"Tomorrow we will head home." She patted the mare's neck. Poor horse needed a name, but Scholl being Scholl succinctly declared horses were not pets, and therefore did not need names. "What about Cherry?" Delli and Nora would love to know their suggested name was used.

Her breath puffed in the air before vaporizing. She missed them so, so much. Were they alright? Healthy? Did Jolie remember to feed them? Nora knew how to dish up stew, and she could cut vegetables, but she was in a new place with new rules.

As though knowing she thought about her sisters and food, her stomach grumbled. Therese dug through a saddlebag and withdrew a biscuit and strip of jerky Jolie packed. Her fingers brushed the leather bundle.

What is in it?

Her client had been firm she was not to look at it. But how would he know if she peeked at the cover? It wasn't like she looked last time they had her put something in her target's saddlebag. They had no reason to suspect.

Therese snatched the bundled and unwrapped the cloth. *Verum*, the title read. Inside, the first page noted the book was written by some scribe from Uri's northernmost area.

Where was Uri? *What* was Uri? It sounded like a province or land of some sort, but there was no place in Orm by that name.

Cherry whuffled as she pawed past the snow and nosed the grass. Therese scanned the hedge of trees, praying Cherry would hear anyone or anything approach. Suddenly freezing, she pulled her cloak tight around herself and turned the page.

"'Upon conferring with my brothers regarding Eligor's rebellion and subsequent murder of our Prince, we have decided to recount the truth that snake tried so hard to mire in his lies and deceit. This narrative is penned by myself and contributed to by Mosais, Gabreel, and Mihai. The people are shaken after witnessing the brutal murder, though they helped play part. The atmosphere enveloping Uri threatens to dim the light this beautiful land bears—nay, bore—so proudly.'"

Therese slammed the book shut. Her hands trembled. She held treason. Pure, total, unapologetic treason. Her breath stuttered from her lungs. This was why her client had insisted she place the book in her target's saddlebag. If she failed her mission, he would be found guilty of sedition, a sure death sentence.

She gnawed her lip. By the stars, if *she* was found reading it, Nora and Delli would have no one to protect and provide for them. Why would this scribe and the others listed accuse King Eligor of treason? Though the king was a bloodthirsty, horrid brute, he had saved countless lives.

And condemned many, many more.

Despite the fear eating at her insides, she reopened the book, her hands moving of their own volition.

Feet crunched in the snow. Voices muttered.

Therese shoved the book into a saddlebag and gripped her knife. Her back screamed from the sudden movement and, for a short time, her surroundings spun in a sickening blur of white and brown.

She crept to the trees and peered between two slender trunks. Three men perched on horses rode near the closest tree grove. The two bites of biscuit threatened a comeback as the wind carried their voices.

"They're in Weedcrag. The head villager was all too happy giving information when we told him the puny village will be razed if the king discovered they're hiding a traitor."

"And the target is injured," a deep voice rasped. "Cetrin's brat can't take three at once—it will be easy to find them before our competition does."

A sudden gust concealed Therese's gasp. Her stomach tightened and her heart jumped to her throat. She was a mere girl, a twig, compared to the nearby thick men clad in black. The only way she could complete her mission before them would be to ride out right then.

But they would see her, hunt her down. Stop her and question her.

She swallowed moisture into her mouth and cringed at their words. What had they been told of her? That she was merely twenty? Struggling to feed her family? Fighting against the emotional and physical pain slowly consuming her? Questioning everything she knew with thoughts that could condemn her life?

When the men became mere smudges, she mounted. Cold bit her exposed skin and her fingers trembled as she adjusted the cloth covering her nose and mouth. Could she enact her plan before the men did?

"Come on, Cherry."

The horse twitched before moving in a choppy walk. Fear stabbed Therese. She hadn't thought to ensure Cherry wasn't freezing. What would she do if the horse keeled over and died from her negligence?

An icy dullness settled into Therese's bones as she scanned the village. How long would it take her to locate her target?

Stars, give me strength.

CHAPTER TWENTY-SEVEN

ROGAN

SLEEP. HIS BODY craved sleep.

Rogan dug the palm of his hand into his eyes as Argus rambled about raising sheep. Who cared how much cities paid for the stinking, walking, bleating fluffballs? He sighed and rested his head against the wall. His legs and lower back cramped from sitting for such a long time.

Holder shifted. Pain lined his face and his eyes looked droopy, but he seemed in decent spirts. At least one of them could be polite to Argus's face.

"I'm going to check on the horses." Rogan pushed to his feet and stalked outside. Silence followed him, but when the door closed, Argus's voice started back up.

Rogan closed his eyes and inhaled the biting, fresh air. It smelled like snow—cold, sharp, and pure. Though he tensed from the frigidity, the pressure wreaking havoc on his muscles lessened.

By the stars, he could see why Argus would live in a place like this. Weedcrag was a frumpy little village, filled with nosy people and smelly animals, but Rogan would almost give up Rex Dorcha's safety, security, and promise of a stable future if it meant experiencing the peace washing over him.

The snow sparkled as though embedded with countless diamonds, and tree limbs topped with the cold, powdery stuff created an ambiance of tranquility unheard of in Varway unless one traveled deep enough into Argbil Forest.

No disappointed fathers. No pursed-lipped mothers. No expectations of perfection and ability. No stress. Just…nothing.

When his body locked from the frigid cold, he moved into the barn. A smaller version of Argus's cabin, it boasted copious amounts of hay, a loft, pegs for tack, and a rail to tether the horses to.

Blackie whickered, ears perking upward.

"Hey, girl." Rogan moved his hand over the mare's strong neck. "How're you doing with Holder's horse? He grumpy like his rider?"

Blackie whuffled and nudged Rogan's shoulder.

"Sorry, no apples. It's winter and I don't think Argus stocks up on them." He stared at the strong buckskin gelding lazing at the bar's other end. Like its owner, the horse looked content.

What would that be like? To never have the sharp, unsure feeling of insecurity nagging at his soul?

Rogan sighed, scuffing his boots through the straw as he made his way to the crates and sat. He cringed as he pulled up his sleeve and traced the fading bruise. Father knew how to leave an impression. Rogan's laugh was bitter. Holder said he was lucky to have Father, even if they did not get along.

Holder was wrong. So, so wrong.

Stars, kill me if I become like him.

He started as Blackie shuffled. Guilt nipped him. How could he leave Holder, defenseless and injured, alone with a man who could strangle him with two fingers?

Rogan lurched forward as his boot caught a crate's corner. Tough straw stung his hands as his knees hit the hard floor. The curse died on his tongue as he stared at the crate. Tipped over, glittering hilts spilled from the shallow, wooden box.

His breathing hollowed. How did...why did...what? His teeth ground together and he grasped one of the daggers, pushing to his feet. Snow snapped under his boots as he stomped from the barn to shove the cabin's door open. Argus's raised eyebrows and opened mouth told him what he needed to know.

"Treason," Rogan hissed. He threw the dagger down, drew his own, and stationed himself between Holder and the traitor. If Argus tried anything, he'd taste steel.

"What is going on? Rogan?" Holder's chair scraped.

Rogan snarled. "Stay down."

"Easy, Specialist. He's only concerned."

With an oath, Rogan shoved Argus backward. "I don't care what Holder is. Right now, I care what *you* are. How long have you possessed contraband? How long have you defied our king?"

"You would call him your king after all he has done?"

"Answer me."

"Rogan." Holder's hand latched around Rogan's shoulder. "Breathe. Tell me what's going on."

"Use your eyes, Holder. You know what that dagger is." Rogan glared at Argus. "That sword with the wrapped hilt— I saw it hidden in the barn. You're the one King Eligor sent us to find. You're the escaped criminal and weapons thief."

"No wonder you're so brainwashed."

"I'm not—"

"Shut your mouth, boy. You can rant after I'm done." In a move faster than Rogan could blink, Argus snatched his wrist and twisted it behind his back.

Rogan grunted as pain throbbed through his shoulder and neck. Argus's fingers pressed on the bruise, likely darkening it. At least this time of year was cold and he could wear long-sleeves.

"You gonna be quiet?"

"You wanna die?" Rogan unsheathed another dagger. Heat burst through his free wrist as Argus grabbed and twisted.

Dirt roughed his hands as he slammed into the floor. Fire burned through his veins. It was his duty to bring this traitor in. His duty to protect Holder. His duty to uphold the Cetrin name.

Weight pressed on Rogan's shoulders, resisting his efforts to rise.

"Use your brain," Argus roared. "I could kill you and Holder before you knew what was happening if I wanted. I just want to talk. Will you calm down? I will tie you up if I must. I refuse to let you endanger Holder."

"Why...why do you care?" Rogan choked for breath. "He means nothing to you."

"Hold your tongue on things you know nothing about."

Argus's hold disappeared. Rogan scrambled to his feet. His chest ached, his lungs throbbed, and his nerves felt afire. There was no way he could outmuscle Argus, no way he could outmaneuver or outsmart a hardened criminal.

"Listen, boy." Argus approached, hand raised to shoulder height. "Listen."

Argus's voice melded with Father's. Rogan scrambled back and smacked against the wall. Nowhere to go. No way to fight back. That hand...he'd seen it before, several times before. It never meant anything good. It only brought pain.

"Rogan. Rogan!"

Holder's face blurred into focus. Rogan choked on a breath. If Holder stood before him, where was Father? Had he left?

Behind Holder, Argus cleared his throat. The man's expression allowed no insight to what thoughts filled his mind.

Argus. Holder. No Father.

By the stars. Rogan dug his fingers into the harsh wooden wall. The texture burned away all remnants of confusion.

"Rogan? You okay?" Holder stared at him like doing so would bare Rogan's mind and explain what just happened.

Too bad it was none of his business.

"Rogan, Holder, sit." Argus said nothing more until they complied. He sighed and shook his head. "Holder Lygor. A name I've not heard in a long time."

"How do you know my surname?" Color left Holder's face. His knuckles whitened.

"I knew your father. Your mother too. And I knew you. I even held your baby sister before she died. You look a lot like Brall."

"How did you know them?" Rogan rubbed his forearm. He could do nothing physical against Argus, not yet, but nothing said he couldn't interrogate the man.

"Whoever rules Uri, I did not want it to happen this way." Argus' eyes closed, like he prayed the traditional way. "There's no easy way to say this, so might as well not beat around the bush. Holder, I knew your parents way back when—helped them escape, even, though I couldn't stand your pa."

Stars forbid. Rogan inched closer to Holder. He'd never seen him pass out, but Holder's gaping mouth, wheezing breaths, and round eyes told Rogan he was close. "Do you have proof?"

Argus rolled his eyes. "Twenty years ago, Holder was born on the second day of the thirteenth month. He was this tiny, squalling little raisin with the reddest face I've ever seen outside of Rex Dorcha. Your parents were pretty darn proud. I wasn't happy when they let you two play together, especially with Rogan being a year older and a good deal rougher. I disliked Brall, but I hate First Lieutenant Cetrin."

Rogan's fists clenched. The man smelled phony and anyone could create such a story. It wasn't like he and Holder could verify it. "That means nothing."

"Rogan is right." Holder's voice strained. "You could have fabricated that. Quit lying to us and admit you are the one King Eligor meant to have hunted down."

Argus steepled his fingers. "Well, now. That depends on what you mean by *meant.* Meant to kill? Aye, he tried that. Meant to end your parents? He attempted that too. Meant that I'm a murderer and criminal? Aye. Meant that I'm the one who 'stole' and 'forgot to return' something to him? That's me too, only I didn't forget."

"Whether you forgot or not is irrelevant." Rogan's fingers twitched. The desire to do his duty mixed with the pain from Argus's grip. "You're stalling."

"Do you want the story?" Argus settled in a chair and propped his boots on the tabletop. Mud crusted their soles. "I think we still have a day before the village folk become suspicious."

"Suspicious?" Holder tried standing. His face paled and he dropped back into the chair.

"Aye. Wilfin is an eccentric fellow, but smart. He kept me alive after I passed out on Weedcrag's threshold."

"You collapsed?"

Argus's brows beetled. "Is all you can do make assumptions and echo what I say? You look somewhat smart, Rogan. I think there are some shreds of intelligence somewhere in that brain of yours. Gather your supplies and tend to Holder's wound. I want to know about you before I tell my story. Well, half is Brall's story, but we'll get to that."

Rogan withdrew the supplies from his saddlebag and undid Holder's bandage. Red skin surrounded the wound, the scab half covering the stitches. Heat radiated from the area.

Infection? Stars, please don't let it be so.

"Tell me about yourself, Holder. What's your job?"

"I am Princess Anastasia's bodyguard."

Argus whistled. "Impressive for one so young. Which king's guard are you in?"

"Second. With Rogan."

Not for long. Rogan rubbed the bruise left by Argus. If he had his way, he'd be wearing the fifth dagger and bearing the title of captain by the year's end.

"You two always were joined at the hip despite how different you are." Argus offered Rogan a wooden jar. "It's chamomile salve. It will help with the swelling."

Rogan grunted his thanks and applied a dollop of the goop. Did the wound hurt much? Holder kept quiet, didn't say a lot. In fact, that strained edge to his voice and expression had surfaced at times before his injury.

Did something else bother him?

"Rogan, why haven't you moved to the first king's guard? You and Holder have been in for so long you would automatically qualify unless Eligor changed the rules."

"I have no interest in the first king's guard." Rogan tore a new bandage. Few remained. Perhaps enough for three or four more changings. Would Holder be better by then?

"Why?"

"None of your business."

"Rogan," Holder hissed. "Be nice. He's done nothing."

"Nothing? *Nothing?* He's a traitor. I let the criminal girl off the hook because she saved your life, but this man...it doesn't matter if he claims to have helped your parents commit treason. He's a wanted criminal. King Eligor had him sentenced to death before he escaped."

"Eligor isn't really your king," Argus interjected. He slouched in his chair in the same position, unperturbed at being labeled a criminal. What was wrong with him? How could he not care about how evil he was?

"Your opinion aside, King Eligor is still in charge. He still sets the law. Something you willfully break."

"Something you would understand would you shut up long enough for me to speak."

"Rogan." Holder gripped his shoulder. Strain pulled at his friend's eyes and showed in his jaw's tight set. "Let him speak. If nothing else, it will provide for us evidence and reason to request his arrest."

Rogan tossed the saddlebag next to the other ones and sat back. He trained his gaze on Argus. The man could speak all he wanted, but Rogan would not be swayed. Nothing the criminal did or said would ever change his mind.

Argus only smiled. His teeth peeked from under his fuzzy beard. "It has been a long day. Why don't we resume tomorrow?"

"I don't think so." Rogan stood, hand on a dagger. They had what they came for. He'd throw Holder over that red devil and lead the beast away if it meant leaving this weak excuse of a town with its criminal-harboring inhabitants. "You don't get to change your mind on a whim. We are here on official business and you will comply unless you want me to drag you before the king."

"Wouldn't that be against your king's command? That's not something you'd do, Cetrin. If you're anything like your father, you'd run Holder through before disobeying His So-Called Majesty."

The accusation stung. Burned. Flamed the heat, the anger, the hidden pain buried deep within. "I am not my father," Rogan snarled. "And I will tolerate your treasonous ways no longer."

"What will you do, boy? Become even more like your father by murdering an innocent man?"

A solid grip on Rogan's shoulder cut off his reply.

Holder stood on an unsteady leg, eyes bright with fever. "Please, Rogan? You can interrogate him to your heart's content tomorrow, but let it go for tonight."

Rogan managed to unclench his teeth. His jaw ached. "Fine." For Holder, but only because his friend would topple at any moment if he didn't get the rest he needed. "But this isn't over."

Off.

Rogan's eyes shot open. He willed his body to stay still.

Silence.

Then the soft whisper-crunch of weight on dirt.

His knuckles tightened around the one dagger he kept strapped to him. As much as he distrusted Argus, the man wasn't inclined to harm Holder.

Another shift of weight.

Rogan's muscles coiled. Tensed. Prepared. If only he could turn and see the doorway. What had possessed him to sleep on his right side?

The impression of a breath.

He shifted slightly.

The person paused with a sharper inhale.

Still not enough to reveal their location.

"Aha! Gotcha." Argus's voice almost covered the intruder's soft cry.

Rogan sprang upright and lit a candle. For the first time, he thanked the stars for Argus's bulk and knowledge of weapons. Unless the intruder was inhumanly quick, Argus could keep them down until Rogan fetched rope.

He stilled. Argus forced a feminine figure to her knees. A black cloth hid the woman's nose and mouth. A dark hood the same color as her dress draped over her hair. Deep auburn strands framed her face.

"You again?" Holder limped to Rogan's side. "What do you want this time?"

The girl clawed at Argus's thick forearm around her neck. "I...I..."

"Argus, let go. She's not a danger."

"No? Then what do you think of this?" Argus yanked a knife from her belt and threw her to the ground. "You think she meant no harm? Holder, she meant to kill."

CHAPTER TWENTY-EIGHT

IVELLE

"IVELLE!"

"I'm coming."

"'We noticed Eligor's irregularities at different times. Gabreel first took note when the King created Uri. Uri. Such a glorious land of trees, plains, and the High Mountains. We watched this from the highest peak across the channel, on King's Isle. It was like green blooming from close to far away. We gathered, all the Assistants, to watch the King, Prince, and Counselor create a majestic beauty none can replicate.'"

"Ivelle. I need your help."

"I'm coming!" Ivelle fingered the page and eyed the scrap of cloth used for a bookmark. The words dripped of deadly treason, yet they were so well written, so clear and simple. Whatever this imaginative land of Uri was, she could already picture it. Deciduous trees turning gold and red in the autumn. The pale azure winter sky. A never-ending green stretching to the High Mountains.

Whoever these King and Prince and Counselor were, it was a shame they did not exist. King Eligor was the only one who could create such a thing described in the book, and when he'd had the opportunity, he wasted it and made a land of darkness, of pain. A land that could not be pierced even by starlight.

You're questioning the stars? That inward voice, the same one that nagged and prodded and examined everything she did and thought, whispered in the back of her mind. *Do you think that wise?*

Ivelle snorted. Wise, her foot. Nothing she did lately could be deemed wise. Assisting an assassin—although she hadn't known Therese's profession at the time. Questioning King Eligor, railing against him, and wishing for his death. Reading what could only be described as treason.

The stars were just something past generations had pinned their hope on because they were so used to the thought of an eternal king. The stars weren't really in charge. How could they be? They were just pinpricks of light.

"Ivelle!"

"Coming." Ivelle bolted from her bed and shoved *Verum* into her dresser's top drawer. Nothing would save her from Claudine's wrath and disappointment if she found the treasonous material.

Claudine stood in the front room, hands disappearing into the waist of her voluminous pink gown. Her hair piled up in an ornate bun, and flowers hung haphazardly at all angles from the forced curls. "There you are. How does this look?"

Ivelle bit her lip to keep from cringing at the puffy leg-o-mutton sleeves. "Like you're a walking strawberry?"

"Ivelle Quade."

"I'm sorry. It's just...that dress is unflattering. What is the occasion?" The next national holiday was next year's King's Day. What could make Claudine dress in such a hideous fashion?

Claudine mumbled, cleared her throat, and mumbled again before huffing. "Borros asked me out to lunch."

"At the place down the street?"

"What? No." Flowers tumbled from her hair. "No. A picnic. He thought it would be nice since today is so...nice."

"Yes, the weather is unusually warm for the beginning of spring." Ivelle fisted her hand against her mouth to keep from laughing. "Go throw on that nice wool. It's heavy enough to keep you warm without a cloak or blanket."

Claudine shook a finger at her. "Do not laugh, young lady. You're staying here and watching Emmi and the store with Alvin."

"Why Alvin?" The man was nice enough, but something about him during the past few weeks prickled Ivelle's spine.

"Because he is an adult, and if there is trouble, people will take him seriously."

Ivelle grumbled as Claudine rushed off. "I'm an adult. People will take me seriously if I carry a sword."

Oh, well. Alvin supervising the emporium allowed her to read more of *Verum.*

Claudine returned in her navy wool. Hair free of flowers lay across her shoulders and back in similar style to one Ivelle remembered seeing in DorFord. "How do I look?"

"Much better." Ivelle draped a silken rose shawl over Claudine's shoulders. "Like Borros is properly courting you."

"Don't be silly. Why would he do that?"

"Perhaps because he has eyes only for you? Because the two of you incessantly flirt whenever you are in the same vicinity?"

"Oh, shush. He'll be here at any time. There is a crate in the back I need you to take up to the attic for me. The shorter box you need to go through and put away. The goods should be labeled accordingly."

Five minutes later, Borros arrived. Ivelle bit back a grin until Claudine and Borros settled in a black chaise too miniscule for Borros' shoulders and rode away.

"To think he actually worked up the nerve to ask that woman on a picnic." Alvin sauntered to the counter, hands shoved in pockets and suspenders giving his corpulent belly little flattery. He scratched his scalp through greasy hair. "You doin' something?"

Chills iced Ivelle's arms. "Yes."

"Huh. That's a shame." He leaned on the counter and fixed small eyes on her. "I wanted to talk with you about something you found."

Ivelle's blood froze. Surely he couldn't mean the journal or *Verum*. She'd kept those hidden save for when Holder was under her care, and then, Alvin had been away procuring less-than-legal items. She forced a smile. "I find many things."

"I'm talkin' about the book that almost landed you on the chopping block."

Breathe! Ivelle forced herself to draw air. "I don't know what you're talking about."

"Sure you do. When those soldiers were here. You know, the injured one and the taller one. The son of one of King Eligor's most reliable soldiers. Arrogant lad. Thought he knew everything."

"I know of whom you speak, but I know nothing about whatever item you mean."

"That book. The one that made the boy's eyes almost pop from his skull. The treasonous one. Where is it now?"

Ivelle shrugged. Alvin had her, her heart's frantic hammering could not deny that, but, "I have no idea. I rarely keep track of what happens to the items Claudine brings in."

"Huh." Alvin straightened. "Just be sure if you do know, no one else does. It'd be a shame for Claudine to be titled a traitor. After all, you know they have no mercy on women."

Ivelle slammed her hand against the tabletop. Her limbs shook, though not from the dull pain. Had Alvin threatened her or was he simply concerned? After all, if Claudine was caught, it was the end of the line for him and Borros.

Concern. That had to be it.

Then why did her intuition say otherwise?

Breath and limbs trembling, Ivelle tugged the shelf back into place. The attic never failed to scare a decade off her life, and this time had been no different. What possessed Claudine to keep half of the store's stock up there?

Ivelle undid the second crate's lid. The spicy and fragrant aroma of herbs soothed her spirit. Slender, silken bags in multiple colors filled the crate to the rim. The scents of frankincense, jasmine, anise hyssop, and lavender filled the room.

Footsteps clomped on the floor. She gripped a bag. None of the herbs were illegal, but the last thing she needed was someone snooping around and poking their nose where it did not belong.

"Hello?" a rough voice said.

Ivelle slipped from the room and pasted on a smile. "Welcome to Claudine DeGrim's Emporium. How can I assist you?"

The massive mountain of a man glared down at her. Blond hair topped a red face, the color from the wind or anger, she could not discern. A blue cape hung from boiled leather armor and a marking she'd not seen before covered the man's right whiskered cheek.

"Sir?"

"First Lieutenant Cetrin," he snapped. "The princess is in your front room. She requires your presence."

"Oh." Ivelle's smile wobbled as she followed the brute into the main area. So this was whom Specialist Cetrin was related to. Like father like son.

Princess Anastasia squealed and rushed forward. Her damask gown brushed the floor, too fancy and formal for such a young child. "Ivelle! How are you? Nurse and King Eligor finally let me visit Emmi. Please, may I see her?"

"Ah…" Ivelle reapplied her smile. The soldiers would not recognize Emmi, would they? The girl looked just like her mother. "I, ah…"

Pain burned the back of her head. "Treat the princess with respect," First Lieutenant Cetrin snarled. "Curtsey and address her with her title."

"Please, First Lieutenant. Ivelle is a good friend. She needn't act so proper." Princess Anastasia beamed at Ivelle, like she hadn't just witnessed a man clouting a young woman on the back of her head. "I am so very eager to see Emmi. Is she available?"

"Emmi was not feeling well last I checked, Princess, but I will go see. It may do her some good to visit with you." *And over my dead body—and a lot of theirs—will I allow them to harm her.*

Ivelle slipped down the hall before the skinny, sneering woman or First Lieutenant Cetrin could say or do anything. Her mouth dried at the sound of steps following. Of course they would send someone. Who did they think she hid from their knowledge? A warrior who could successfully take on five king's guards and the skinny woman at the same time?

She stiffened her wrist to keep her hand from shaking as she knocked. "Emmi, can I enter?" At Emmi's small yes, she cracked the door. "Sweetie, Princess Anastasia is here and wishes to see you. You well enough?"

"For a few minutes." Emmi's cough rattled Ivelle like it rattled in the young girl's chest. "Could you bring some strawberry tea?"

"Of course." Ivelle turned and came face-to-face with a scrawny youth a few years younger than her.

He offered a grimace of a smile and scratched his head through thick black hair. "I'm Juan. I've been told to keep an eye on you."

He seemed nice enough like Holder, but after the information Therese had revealed, Ivelle's stomach churned at the prospect of speaking more than necessary with a man who aligned himself with cruel, heartless murderers. "Then, sir, you will be incredibly bored."

She marched to the kitchen. It would not harm Princess Anastasia and her entourage to wait for Emmi's tea to prepare.

"Rogan told me you were a difficult one."

"I'm sure he did." Ivelle measured the water and set it over the fire.

"Not like he said much. It is hard to get him to talk freely. He is nice enough, I guess. Holder handles him better than I, but he's never been harsh or rude to me."

Ivelle cared no more for the conversation's topic than she cared hearing about Eligor's accomplishments. Such as they were. "Oh."

Armor rustled. "You really don't like me. It's okay. I don't like people I meet for the first time, either. Rogan did say you were prickly, though."

"What else did he say about me?" Hopefully that she possessed the medical knowledge to put this boy in a load of misery should she choose. Hopefully that she lived in a place housing near as many weapons as Rex Dorcha's armory.

Sourness coated the inside of her mouth. How could she purposefully engage in conversation with a man who bore a murderer's emblem?

"That's it, miss. Like I said, he doesn't say much." Juan's voice lowered. "Between you and me, he's growly and cranky, but nothing like his father."

Yet. Ivelle glowered at the boy. "Specialist, if you think you can trick me into saying something I should not, think again." She poured the steaming water into a cup, dropped in a strawberry leaf, and sailed from the room.

Princess Anastasia clapped her hands. "Is Emmi ready? I have been dying to speak with her again."

"Princess," the woman hissed. "You are not dying. Do not engage in such frivolous speech. You, girl. What is in the cup?"

"Tea for Emmi." Ivelle nodded to the princess. "You know the way."

"Indeed I do." Heedless of the woman's gasps and scoldings, Princess Anastasia skipped to Emmi's room.

"You stay right there, Princess." First Lieutenant Cetrin brushed the child out of his way and slammed the door open.

Ivelle snarled at Emmi's scream and the man's drawn sword. "If you think you can barge in here and frighten a child half to death, get out! She can do nothing to endanger the princess." Too late did her mind conjure the knowledge that speaking in such a way would generate no good.

First Lieutenant Cetrin slowly turned. "What did you say?"

Stars, help me. Ivelle brushed past him and set the tray on the desk before helping Emmi sit. The girl's hair sprang awry from her nap. "Here is your tea, sweetie. Princess, I am afraid she will not be able to converse long. She is not feeling well."

"Well?" The woman appeared in the doorway, hands flailing and eyes glaring. "Princess, you must vacate this place immediately. We cannot have you catching ill."

"Emmi is not contagious. Let the girls talk if they want."

"You are a simpleton," Svetlana sneered. "Do you know whose presence you stand in? The princess will be protected at all costs, which includes keeping her safe from scrawny, sniffling little ragamuffins like the urchin in this closet of a room."

Ivelle bared her teeth. How dare this bumptious, snobby woman call Emmi a ragamuffin and urchin? "I have knowledge in healing. I think I would know if my charge was contagious."

Princess Anastasia clasped her hands. "Please, Nurse? Holder would let me."

"That orphaned whelp is no better than this…this sickly waif."

Ivelle studied the woman with her aquiline nose, prominent forehead, and graying hair pulled back in a severe bun. What made her dislike Holder so? She spoke of him with more venom than Ivelle could muster about Holder's friend.

Apparently not everyone was as enamored with the young bodyguard as Princess Anastasia.

Ivelle slumped into her bed. Her head throbbed from First Lieutenant's smack and tears stung her eyes. The outrage that had fueled her vanished. Had she really faced down and disrespected a first lieutenant?

Nose stuffed and throat tight, she reached for the book hidden in her drawer. At least the princess' entourage hadn't poked around. They would have surely located the illegal goods.

Inhaling a ragged breath, Ivelle drew the candle closer and opened the book. Claudine would be away for a good while yet, likely until the sun began its descent, so she had time to read and recover from the past hour.

"'For a time, Eligor celebrated like the rest of us. He marveled at the animals and creation the King made, but mostly at the people. Yes, that was what the King called them. Man and woman. To the man was given the task of naming every animal. It took him time. I cannot fathom how he accomplished such a feat, save that the King had part in it.

"'For a time, all was well, or so we thought. Gabreel notes that just shortly after the incredible display of our King's abilities, Eligor showed the first signs of that disease, that evil pride, which proved to be his downfall. He began questioning, Gabreel says. Questions that first sound normal but, once you uncover their true intent, sear the ears like fire burns flesh. Questions and speculations such as surely we, the Assistants, could have aided in such a creation. Saying that surely he, Eligor, could have aided the King.

"'Foolish man. The Prince and Counselor worked with the King. Why would the King need Eligor when He had Them? 'Tis like a worm thinking he can assist a master craftsman in the greatest work he will ever accomplish. Inconceivable. Ridiculous.'"

"Ivelle?"

Ivelle snapped the book shut and flipped it to its back. "Claudine. How did the picnic go?"

"Delightful." Claudine studied her. "Ivelle, what are you reading?"

CHAPTER TWENTY-NINE

HOLDER

METAL RASPED AS Rogan drew his sword and approached the assassin. "Who sent you?"

Holder lurched forward. He didn't know what the things in Argus' hand were. He didn't know who the girl was. He only knew Rogan would end her without remorse if allowed. "Rogan, stop. She won't answer if she doesn't want to."

"She might." Argus shook the girl and smirked at her squeak. "I can feel heat radiating through her clothes. She burns with fever. Let her go long enough and she will be delirious and answer our questions without resistance."

"I've seen delirium make the person out of their mind." Holder ground his teeth as he set weight on his leg. The girl was not the only one with fever, but Rogan knew little about medicine and wounds, and though Argus had thus far shown no hostility or evil intent toward them, Holder did not trust him.

"True. What do you want to do with her?"

"This is the third time she has tried murdering Holder," Rogan snarled. The tip of his sword leveled with her forehead. "I want answers."

"Answers," the girl murmured. "Holder will collapse if you do not soon tend to his injury. If you want answers, ask your king."

Argus hummed. "Bold words for a wounded lass in the presence of two of the king's most trusted soldiers. Tell me, what gives you such nerve?"

"The same thing as what drives you to lie to them." Despite her words, her voice held little fire, and the small amount of her face Holder could see flushed red. "You've not told them who and what you really are."

"And you know?" Argus shoved the girl against the wall. She gasped and crumpled.

Holder hobbled after Rogan, but he was too slow to stop his friend from kneeling before the girl and holding the blade to her throat. "You will tell us who you are, who sent you, and why they are after Holder."

"Hold on there, Rogan." Argus joined the specialist. "I want to know what you think you know about me, girl."

The girl's cough rattled. "You are Argus Ancorit, former friend of Brall Lygor. You were once a specialist in the first king's guard and one of the highest ranked men in Orm. You helped Brall and Mariline escape Orm."

"Continue." Argus's tone promised nothing good.

The girl shuddered. An arm wrapped around her ribs. "You were suspected of treason once Brall defected. Later you were arrested after stealing a prized artifact from Rex Dorcha. You were caught, tried, and sentenced, but you managed to escape."

"And how would you know this?"

The girl again shuddered. The cloth remained concealing her nose and mouth, but the glassiness in her eyes betrayed the worsening fever. "I...I research."

Holder jumped as Rogan jolted. "You! You're the one I escorted to the archives. You...you were there when Father told me about Holder. That's how you found him in the first place. You spied on us."

"They allow commoners in the archives?"

"She was allowed by Captain Geros."

The girl huffed at the captain's name but said nothing. Her gaze flitted about the room, brightening when it landed on the leather-encased book in Holder's hands. "You still have it? Your father's journal?" Her voice dropped, like she found it harder to be articulate.

Holder swallowed moisture into his throat. The odd hope in her gaze shouldn't fill him with pity. "Yes."

"Journal?" Argus pushed Rogan aside and gaped at Holder. "You have Brall's journal? How? Who gave it to you? I thought it was destroyed or lost."

"She did." Holder nodded at the girl, who slumped against the wall.

"How did you get it?"

"From a store." The girl coughed and cringed. "I don't know where they got it. I just recognized the names."

Being tough is overrated. Holder collapsed into the chair as pain spiked through his leg. His entire being felt like it burned hotter than a bonfire.

Rogan's attention jerked Holder's way and, with another glower at the girl, he stood, sheathed his sword, and made for Holder's side. "What's wrong?"

"Nothing." Holder stared at the journal. Rogan couldn't know. "Nothing is wrong. Argus, how do you know about my father's journal?"

"I saw him writing in it when we traveled. Brall had no common sense and couldn't leave well enough alone. He had to know what was on the other side."

"The other side of what?" Rogan knelt beside Holder and prodded the injury.

"The High Mountains. I don't know what changed Brall, just that he discovered something about Eligor that made him go almost berserk. Holder, he was desperate to get you and Mariline out of Varway, out of Orm, but he knew bringing you along for the initial trip would only be detrimental. You were so young and sickly."

Holder grunted as Rogan undid the bandage. Red stained the cloth.

His friend swore and threw down the soiled bandages. "Holder, what did you do?"

"Nothing."

"Right" Rogan's jaw ticked. Holder could almost hear his unspoken desire to slap him upside the head. "This doesn't look this bad just because you've done *nothing.* This is infected and obviously hurting you. Why didn't you tell me?"

Because Rogan snapped at everything Holder said. Because Rogan had a way of making one feel puny and stupid. Because Rogan made it clear there were to be no unnecessary inconveniences.

Holder pushed aside the hidden, lingering whisper of irritation with his friend. Rogan meant well. He just didn't know how to show it. "Because we were busy."

"So busy that you're risking losing your leg? Argus, do you have anything to help this?"

Holder grit his teeth and stared ahead as Rogan and Argus prodded his injury. Movement near the wall snagged his gaze. The girl stumbled to her feet, an arm still protecting her ribs. Even in the dim light Holder could see her trembling. Was it from the wound inflicted by Rogan?

"I don't think so, missy." Argus blocked her attempted escape. "You're going nowhere. Not after what you pulled."

Holder gripped the chair's seat a Rogan spread paste onto his wound. The stuff Ivelle gave him hadn't stung like this.

"Rogan, Holder, I'm taking her to a friend's place. Someone who can get her fever down and maybe withdraw some information."

"That went well," Rogan grumbled after Argus all but dragged the girl away. "He might as well let her go. She'll tell nothing. That too tight?"

"No. Rogan, I don't think she truly meant harm." Holder flipped through the journal. So many pages he'd yet to read. So many words of wisdom his father could never tell him face-to-face.

Not for the first time, a distinct longing pierced his soul.

"This is the third time she's tried to kill you—us, whoever. She intends death."

Holder held his tongue. Rogan's voice deepened with that familiar tone, where his mind was made up and neither word nor action would dissuade him. Beginning an argument did little good.

Holder traced the words with his thumb. The longing deepened. Intensified. If only his father hadn't perished. At least he knew a bit more about what happened, why they left, but that did little to stop the gaping hole in his heart.

"'I don't know where these people get their little tidbits of peculiar wisdom. Some of the writings they use as pithy little sayings. Here is one I overhead this morn: 'We are to love our enemies and pray for those who wrong us'. Why in Orm would a person do a thing like that? It's unnatural. They're your enemy for a reason. I know I would not pray for Eligor and invite him to a meal. Doing so would be like placing a wolf amidst sheep and saying, "Here you go. Have at them". No. Absolutely not.'"

"If I were Argus, I'd tie her up and interrogate her." Rogan stomped around the cabin, sword in hand, like he expected the assassin to barge in at any time.

Holder grunted a response. His father's writing made no sense. If those people said such abnormal, unwise things, why stay?

"'I asked for clarification about the enemies' saying. The patriarch, or that's what I assume he is since he leads everyone in their morning prayers, said it came from their Prince. Apparently, they live in a land called Uri and are not under Eligor's reign. He said it is what the Prince did when he allowed himself to be sacrificed at the hands of Eligor for all who lived, live, and will live. I wanted more information, but his help was needed by a farmer. It is very confusing here and I would think of leaving if Mariline were not so welcomed by the women.'"

"By the stars," Holder muttered. What altered his father's mind? The writing made no sense. Uri was just an imaginary land, King Eligor reigned over all, and why would someone sacrifice themselves for another?

"They wouldn't." Rogan settled near Holder's feet. "No one with a touch of sanity would sacrifice themselves for others. People aren't worth it."

⋄⊱┈┈⊰⋄

"The girl is settled at Barney's place. The man is a mouse but his wife could scare a grizzly to death. She'll wring the info we need from that little assassin." Argus' stomp discarded snow from his boots. "Don't know how she snuck in here like she did. I should have heard the snow crunching under her."

"Forget about the girl." Rogan propped his elbows on his knees. "We need answers."

Argus' sigh sounded heavy. "What do you want to know?"

"Everything."

Holder tugged his cloak around himself. Despite the fire warming the cabin, a chill invaded his bones. He bit his tongue to keep his teeth from chattering. This wasn't normal, all this shivering, not when Rogan and Argus had their sleeves rolled up.

"As I've mentioned, I couldn't stand Brall Lygor. He stuck his nose where it didn't need sticking and was convinced everyone could redeem themselves. Plain foolishness, I told him. People can't change. Brall and I, we go way back. Grew up together like you two.

"I was a lot like you, Holder. Trusting, more mild mannered. Brall, well, he was the fiery one. He questioned things. Demanded answers that I'm surprised didn't get him killed. I knew he had concerns about Eligor, but he never spoke out for fear Mariline and you would get hurt. Then one day he could withhold it no longer. He did some investigating, asked some questions, and next thing we knew, Eligor sent assassins after him."

"That doesn't explain you." Rogan stared at Argus as though the man would cave and give him everything he wanted.

Argus scowled at him. "Patience, boy, or do they not teach that?" He puffed his cheeks out, releasing air. "Your parents left you with Rogan's family. They knew I was unable to raise a child." His chuckle lacked humor. "Did you know I'm your godfather, Holder? Anyway, once Brall's actions came to light, the concern turned toward me. They thought whatever infected Brall infected me."

Holder swallowed to ease the tightness in his throat. This was a dream. It had to be. How often had he imagined discovering what happened to his parents? How often had he dreamed of discovering a relative? Argus wasn't related, but close enough. It felt surreal, like he watched a scene someone created.

"They were wrong. Brall's inability to just accept things drove me up the wall. If not for you and Mariline, I would have let him be captured. You can't just betray your partner like that. We began fighting together and ended fighting each other.

"I couldn't understand how they could leave you, Holder. You were just this cute little tyke who wanted his parents. Didn't matter. They left you. All I can do is thank the stars you didn't turn out like Maximo."

"And?" Holder forced the question when silence descended. His heart thudded, like if he did not uncover the answer it would beat straight from his chest. His wrist popped as he clenched his hands.

Argus's smile was bitter. "Brall should have withheld his opinions and stayed as stable master. He would have saved a lot of lives that way, his and Mariline's included."

CHAPTER THIRTY

THERESE

HURT. THERESE SHIFTED, but no amount of movement could alleviate the pain consuming her back. She bit her lip to keep from crying. Her heart thundered as her body recovered from the aftereffects of being caught and her identity almost exposed.

How could she have been so foolish, so blind to the danger?

How could she have been so stupid?

Her body shuddered as another sharp breath ripped through her. Everything had been still, quiet, when she snuck into the cabin. Only by seeing Specialist Cetrin walk from the other building had she known where her target resided.

The darkness revealed no moving things. When Argus grabbed her, her heart almost beat from her chest. Being thrown against the wall had done nothing for her injury, and her lungs struggled to refill with air.

"Don't even think about trying anything." The short, plump woman's voice grated Therese's ears. "I won't hesitate to use my frying pan or rolling pin if you misbehave." Footsteps scuffled against the dirt floor. "Now, tell me your name."

Therese forced her body to go lax. If the woman thought she slept, she'd leave her alone. By the stars, she hoped the woman would just go. Her coherency slipped with each breath and her mind was already muddled.

The woman sighed. "I'd have Barney tie you up if you weren't in such poor condition. Youngsters these days. The things you do for coin. Why, when I was a young lady, we made money by sewing, raising sheep and chickens, and baking. You look ridiculous in that dress. The lack of decency! It only reaches your knees. That was considered scandalous in my time."

Sleep. Therese begged her body to sleep, if only for a few hours. Completing her mission was out of the question with the snow and Argus alerted to her presence. She needed another plan, a way to slip the book into her target's saddlebags without them seeing.

She couldn't let Nora and Delli down.

Her sisters. How did they fare with Jolie? The woman couldn't cook, but Lucian could. And while Jolie possessed the hardened heart necessary to complete every type of conceivable mission with grace and ease, she showed a soft spot for the girls. Even if she knew nothing about children, Nora was sure to inform her where she went amiss. At least they would be fed, and that was more than a week's worth of food Therese did not have to pay for.

Stars, please grant me mercy. I cannot fail them. Please, do not punish them for my stupidity and incompetency. I am doing all I can. I swear. Please shine down on me with grace and goodwill. I will do anything you want me to.

The woman moved away, muttering and speaking with her husband. Despite her disapproval, and the horror exhibited when Argus told her to watch Therese like an eagle watched its prey, she'd put Therese in a warm room with what smelled like clean bedding. The bed was stiff, but better than sleeping on the ground or even Therese's pallet back home.

Therese groaned as she shifted to her left side. It put her back to the doorway, which kept her from seeing any who entered, but sight was not the only sense she could use. Heaviness pulled at her eyes and she fought to keep from fully relaxing. Sleep was needed, but she couldn't forget to keep her guard up.

Nora and Delli. This is for Nora and Delli.

Pain burned around Therese's injury as she forced herself from the bed and tiptoed across the floor. Darkness filled the cabin, interrupted by snores. Barney's sheepdog whined as Therese inched past him, eyes and damp nose reflecting the moonlight.

"Good boy," she whispered, ruffling his silky fur. "Keep quiet."

The door opened with a crunch as snow tumbled from the hinges. Therese's body screamed when she tried hunching against the sudden gust of cold. How could she forget the snow, ice, and frigid air waiting outside? Jolie would scold and Scholl would declare her unfit for the job. One always kept their surroundings in mind.

Her boots crunched through the snow. Unless the pink-and-gray sky released more snow, they would track her in the morning. And from the pinched expression wrinkling Argus's face, she doubted he'd let her go without fuss.

Stars, what do I do? Sneaking back to finish what she began would not work and she knew not when her target would travel back to Varway. Her tracks could give her away and they would guess to whom who the lone set of hooves belonged.

Cherry. Poor mare, stuck in an abandoned lean-to. At least it provided shelter and, along with Therese's blanket, Cherry's body heat would keep her warm.

Therese shivered as she crept along the space between cabins. Five two-story buildings created the only street. Beyond them cabins and clumps of trees smattered the land. Would anyone see her? It took little to think one heard something and look out a window.

Prayers rattled through her brain.

The trek to Cherry took longer than Therese remembered. By the time she stumbled into the small, abandoned lean-to, every part of her felt frozen. Her fingers and face were numb, her nose was stuffed, and her body ached.

Cherry whickered. The mare's ears flicked as she nosed Therese, huffing what sounded like a welcome in horse.

"Hey, girl." Therese trembled. "I'm going to steal that blanket. You look toasty enough." If only she could light a fire. But smoke was easily seen at night and training never included how to make a smokeless fire.

No, the blanket would have to do.

Tears stung her eyes as she huddled against Cherry. Why must love be so difficult? Her heart ached with a pain she knew she could never verbally express. To know she could fail her sisters, possibly fail so badly she could lose them, sent a knife into her soul.

The tears quickened as memories replaced every thought. Mother handing her Nora swathed in soft blankets. Mother telling her another sister was on the way. Mother and Father dying from the plague, their raspy breaths suddenly ceasing. At least they died near the same time, as though Father knew the love of his life had passed into whatever afterlife awaited them and had planned to go so he could stay near her forever.

Just like they planned leaving Therese with two bits and two sickly sisters, both recovering from the illness. Like they planned leaving their family on the brink of starvation. Like they planned leaving their eldest daughter to pay their debt. A debt created due to Father taking a loan from the master assassin so he could feed his family while searching for a job after losing his previous employment of ten years.

Therese smeared the tears away. Crying did her no good. It never had. Crying at her parents' graveside hadn't brought them back. Hadn't allowed her the funds to purchase a private lot and move her parents from the mass grave dug for the poor folk who hadn't the money for a personal burial. Hadn't given her the skills necessary for survival in a cruel and heartless world. Hadn't done a lick of good helping her face Scholl when he arrived at the Westa doorstep demanding payment or else.

Hadn't repaired her broken heart.

"'The one thing we always thought would last was our unity. We, the Assistants, were brothers. Strong bonds forged betwixt us, bonds I once thought unbreakable. Mihai and Gabreel, especially, thought Eligor a brother. But brothers do not betray the ones closest to them, nor do they take delight in stirring up rebellion.

"'Mihai and Gabreel are unable to describe the feeling that pierced them when it became evident their brotherhood with Eligor was eternally torn asunder. I can understand, for I* *too had brothers who decided to follow that prideful, arrogant, evil one when he spewed his traitorous jargon.'"*

Therese sighed and closed the book. The words reeked of treason, yet they captivated her. How? Why? How could something so false sound so…true? She stuffed the book into a saddlebag as a gust of wind shook the lean-to. The day was crisp, clear, and she could make out Argus's place through the trees if she squinted.

A lump rose to her throat. In her desire to complete the mission, she had forgotten about the three assassins she overheard. Where were they? Did they scout the place as she'd done? The last she'd seen them, they headed for Weedcrag. Where did they stay? Did they rent a place from a villager?

How could she forget the three men intent on killing her target?

Foolish girl.

Therese shivered. Aside from waltzing into Argus's cabin and telling them, not that they'd believe her, she could do little. Her client would be most displeased if the men completed their mission before she did.

She tugged her cloak about her a day later as her target and his friend rode from the cabin in the early sunlight. As she reined Cherry to follow them, chills not from the cold pricked her spine.

She was not the only one tailing them.

Stars, grant me guidance.

Therese reined Cherry to the nearest tree grove and waited until the three men rode past. Dread grew in her stomach. Fully healed and rested, she stood little chance against one man without poison or the element of surprise. Wounded, frozen, hungry, and facing down three dangerous men, she possessed no chance.

She toyed with her pouch. Five oleander petals rested within. Three were preferable for a grown man since the more poison one ingested the quicker they perished, but two could cause sufficient harm as well.

Therese huffed at the irony. Trying to save her target from men wanting to kill him just so she could end him later? Who did a thing like that?

Someone desperate.

Forcing herself to swallow despite her dry mouth, she nudged Cherry to a walk. Snow crunched beneath the mare's hooves. The chirps of robins added to spring's gentle sounds, but those sounds might not mask the noise of her approach.

The effort to stop these men would be difficult, if not impossible. But if it meant double the pay, the effort was worth it. The fact that the awaiting silvers would eliminate one-twentieth of the debt controlled Therese like a bit and reins controlled a horse.

Darkness fell when she allowed herself within less than half a league of the assassins. They gathered in a cave not far from a hunting hut where her target and his friend hunkered down for the night. Tiptoeing, Therese crept near the entrance.

"We'll move before sunrise. Get ahead of them, set up an ambush."

"Can we do that with the snow?"

"They'll think we're villagers or tradesmen. From what he said, those boys ain't too smart. They won't guess. We'll catch them like a rabbit is caught in a snare. Quick and effortless."

CHAPTER THIRTY-ONE

ROGAN

"HOW'S YOUR LEG?" Rogan knelt before the fire. Its heat almost seeped through his frozen clothes. Would he ever be warm again?

Holder shrugged. Ever since just before arriving at Argus', he'd been quieter than usual, more reticent to speak, like something weighed him down.

"Holder, what's going on? You've been different lately." Rogan dug through his saddlebags for the salve and bandages Argus provided before they rode off. His fingers brushed the golden dagger, a smaller version of the sword he'd snuck into the barn to look at. Would King Eligor believe the story Holder insisted on?

"Just tired."

Weren't they both. "I need to see your injury." It was imperative they reach Rex Dorcha in a decent timeframe. Not only due to the cold, but because the sooner Rogan reached the routine security his title and job provided, the sooner the irritating sense of insecurity would leave and the sooner he could again begin working toward captaincy and his fifth dagger.

If only reaching Rex Dorcha didn't mean reaching home, if it could be called that.

"Rogan?"

Rogan shook the fatigue away. Ever since the female assassin's third attempt, sleep eluded him. How could he protect Holder, who could hardly walk, if he slept? The thought of her creeping around made his skin crawl. It was worse when Argus reported she disappeared. How could they not keep a close watch on her? She was a murderer. Someone who wanted to harm his friend.

He undid the bandage and smeared more salve on. Why wasn't Holder's injury healing as it should? Hadn't that lawbreaker, Ivelle, said a month?

"Six weeks." Holder hissed as Rogan wrapped the bandage. "She said six weeks before I should walk without aid."

Which Holder hadn't obeyed. The black-haired brat may be a traitor, but she wasn't incompetent in the medical field. "Does it feel any better?"

"Some."

Yeah, right. If Holder's leg felt any better, Rogan was squatty and had brown hair and eyes. "You know you can tell me, right?"

"Yes."

Really? Did Holder really know? Then why didn't he act on it? It wasn't like he could effectively hide his emotions. Everything played out in his eyes or expression.

"Rogan, just get some rest. We have a long ride tomorrow and it will take time to find the cabin Argus told us about."

"Do you think he told the truth?"

Holder waited before answering. "Yeah, I do. He wouldn't benefit from lying. And how would he know that stuff about us? I just...to be blamed for what my father did had to be hard. I could tell he liked his job. And I read his name in the journal.”

The journal. An important book to Holder, but one that could see him dead. “What will you do about it? You know what King Eligor will do if he discovers you have it.”

Holder’s sigh drifted in the warming air. “I want to keep it. It’s almost the only thing I have to remember them by.”

Understandable, but treasonous. Rogan chewed his lip and traced the tattoo on his cheek. Ever since becoming a king’s guard, the emblem had been a comfort, something real in a home where he questioned everything due to how his parents treated him.

The emblem also was a promise to King Eligor that Rogan would protect and obey at all costs, no matter what.

He sighed. Where did that leave him? Holder was his friend, his best friend, but did the bonds of friendship trump justice, honor, and duty?

Friendship, though a bond, was a feeling, and feelings could not be trusted. But a bond was more than feelings. It was a brotherhood, another name for something forged between them, something that could neither be broken nor shaken.

His four daggers said differently. Determination. Skill. Perseverance. Decisiveness. Determination for pledging himself to the hardest job in the king’s service. Skill for accomplishing everything taught to him, and then some. Perseverance for surviving the intense, almost traumatic trainings. Decisiveness for holding true to what he was taught and for never turning aside.

The fifth, should he earn it—no, *when* he earned it— would symbolize loyalty. It would take him from a mere specialist to a captain of the king’s guard. One of the most honored positions in Orm.

Why, *why* must he face such a test? Keeping Holder's secret meant disobeying King Eligor. Keeping Holder's secret meant helping his friend keep the only remnant of his past and parents.

Why, stars? Why?

Holder coughed, shoulders hunching.

Argus had expressed concern to Rogan in private. Holder should be better, or at least more healed than he was. Infection tried setting in and fever could take over at any time. Holder shouldn't be walking, much less travelling.

What had they been thinking? The thought snuck up on Rogan so quickly he couldn't stop his strangled choke. What was wrong with him, thinking such a treasonous thought? How dare he question the king, his most trusted advisor, and most esteemed soldier?

No, Holder's injury was just bad timing. At least Argus handing over a dagger helped their luck. The man claimed King Eligor did not know the extent of weapons taken, but Rogan doubted that. King Eligor was intelligent and it sounded unlike him to not know the precise amount of weaponry stolen.

Argus's story echoed in his mind. It sounded far-fetched like it'd been crafted by a madman out of desperation. How could Holder believe without question?

Rogan sighed and tugged his cloak tighter. Holder slumped against the wall, already drifting off. So much for him taking first watch.

Oh, well. Holder needed the rest. The hut had been relatively easy to locate once Argus alerted them of its existence, but Rogan's gut warned tomorrow's resting place would not be so easily accessed.

He stared at the flames, hand twitching before he reached for the journal. Might as well occupy himself so he didn't fall asleep while on watch, even if the content reeked of sedition.

"By the stars," Holder hissed. He hunched into the howling wind, nothing more than a dark outline amidst swirling white. "I thought the weather was supposed to clear up."

Rogan fought for breath. How could it be so cold? Such frigidity never hit Varway. "I don't think the weather cares what you think."

A curse filled his mouth as Blackie slowed and jerked at the reins. Danger lurked about them from the cold and the last thing he needed was Blackie misbehaving. Rogan squinted past the horse's ears. Snow coated three black forms slumped on the ground.

"Can you see what it is?" Holder's voice wavered in the wind.

"Faintly. I'll look." Rogan dismounted and inched toward the nearest form, sword drawn. The forms had humanoid shapes. No one would live just lying on the ground like that, and no one could have seen them coming in the blizzard.

When the forms did not respond to the nudge, he knelt, drawing a dagger and cutting away the dark cloth on the closest. Unblinking eyes met his.

Bile rose in Rogan's throat as he uncovered the man's throat and torso. No dried blood, no signs of trauma or attack. The other two revealed the same lack of injuries.

His back muscles tensed. Did whoever murdered them linger in some hidden area, watching, waiting, for their next victim?

"Well?" Holder asked once Rogan mounted. "What was it?"

"I'll tell you once we find shelter."

Doing so proved no easy task. Deep tree groves and sheer, rocky cliffs dotted the land, transitioning from the prairie to more dangerous terrain.

'Second grove to the left,' Argus said. His arms had been crossed, his mouth flattened with disapproval at their decision to travel back. *'If you miss it, don't backtrack to look. You* will *get lost.'*

No pressure. No pressure at all.

Rogan squinted into the whiteness. "Is this the second grove?"

"By my count."

"Then let's go look." Rogan commanded Blackie to a walk. Even if they didn't locate the cabin, the trees could offer some shelter. No one would be out in such weather, so the chance of encountering desperadoes was slim.

Thick tree trunks allowed for little movement and little knowledge of what awaited them beyond the nearest line of wood. Snow crept past the branches and pine needles, swirling and drifting downward.

"There." Rogan pointed at a squatty cabin. It looked like a dogtrot cabin complete with the typical breezeway in the middle.

"Who builds that type of cabin out here?" Holder led his horse toward the breezeway.

"I don't know." Rogan tried the door on the left part of the building. The latch wiggled but the door refused to open. The right door swung open with little issue. "Holder. In here."

Holder lit a candle and passed it to Rogan. "If you start a fire, I'll care for the horses."

"Deal." Rogan grit his teeth at the stinging in his face. Soon his hands would feel the same, followed by the rest of him as he unthawed. He set the candle on the cracked, wooden mantle and fumbled the logs and kindling into the fireplace's small mouth.

"I don't think anyone's stayed here since Argus saw this place." Holder draped the saddles over two three-legged stools. "There's more dust than wall."

Rogan struck flint against a dagger, praying for the sparks to catch. "I know. This wood is dryer than dry."

Once heat warmed the air and he unthawed, Rogan felt every ache and bruise from riding and staying the past night in a hut with a stone floor. Peeling his cloak off and setting it before the fire to dry, he withdrew the salve and bandages. "Sit."

Holder obeyed, stretching out on his bedroll. Darkness smudged under his eyes.

"What are you thinking about?"

"Once we arrive back in Varway. Do you think that dagger will satisfy King Eligor? I know what he said, but I have the feeling he meant something more."

Rogan stiffened to refrain from squirming. Guilt nagged him that the same thought had drifted through his mind. He'd always perceived the king to be an upfront, honest man. The notion that he meant ill affected Rogan's gut like a punch.

No. How dare he question a man who had ruled centuries longer than Rogan had lived?

Pages rustled. Holder flipped through his father's journal until he found the page he wanted.

Silence descended. Rogan settled on his bedroll and tore into a strip of jerky. If only the fire would crackle louder, or the horses would nicker, or the wind would howl. The silence pricked him, uncomfortable and heavy. How often had the Cetrin cabin sounded like this after a beating or yelling?

He sighed and stared at the fire. The pressing memories and the rogue, treasonous thoughts daring to flit through his mind threatened his sanity. If his father knew what Rogan thought of, unintentionally or not, there'd be a beating like none other.

Stars, help me vanquish these thoughts. Such things only brought death and danger and dishonor.

Such things would ruin everything he was working for.

CHAPTER THIRTY-TWO

IVELLE

"WELL, HE CERTAINLY gave you a goose egg." Claudine tsked as she smoothed Ivelle's hair into place. "I've seen him before. A big blond brute with cruelty ingrained in his face. Where were you, Alvin?"

"Behind the counter."

Ivelle growled at his smug tone. The skunk could have stopped First Lieutenant Let's-hit-innocent-girls-on-the-back-of-their-head, but no. Instead he cowered behind the counter.

"I put you in charge." Acrimony sharpened Claudine's words. "Please tell me you did not let him do anything else."

"He terrified Emmi."

"What was I supposed to do? Pull at his arm and beg him to stop? He wouldn't a' listened." Alvin glowered at Ivelle as he toyed with a rare southern scimitar displayed on the far wall. "He's a king's guard and a first lieutenant at that. You don't mess with those people. They'll cut you down just for thinking they're arrogant pigs. I don't need more injuries."

"Not doing anything when you could do something is cowardice," Ivelle muttered. She rubbed the back of her head and grimaced at the tenderness.

A gust of cold air silenced Alvin's reply, though it did nothing to cool the scathing glower on his whiskered face.

Borros trundled in, brushing snow from his clothes and cursing the weather. "It was nice yesterday. By the stars, the weather is temperamental."

"Yes, it is. Perhaps it heard how your brother failed to stop Ivelle from getting whacked on the head." Claudine scowled and withdrew a pin from her hair.

Borros whined as it bounced off his cheek. "That almost hit me in the eye."

"All the better if it had," Claudine retorted. "You are tracking mud onto my clean floor."

"Claudine, mud chunks already litter the floor. It's not clean."

Ivelle grinned. Despite the headache throbbing through her skull, watching the interaction made the pain worth it. "Lovers' quarrel, Claudine?"

"Why, you!"

Ivelle danced away as Claudine reached for another pin. "Perhaps you and Borros should go on a date more often. I rarely see you so carefree. Don't you agree, Borros?"

"Ivelle Quade, you are not too old to get in trouble." Despite the threat, a blush coated Claudine's cheeks. "For that, you can help me clean the attic."

Borros snorted. "You'll need the stars' help with that. That room has more dust than knickknacks, and that's saying something."

"Hush, Borros. I never asked for your opinion. Ivelle, go change into an old dress. I don't want you ruining that one. I'll fetch you when it's time."

Ivelle scurried off. She kept the slight grin pasted on her face to defy the sweat accumulating on her palms. The attic? What possessed Claudine? The attic could be left dirty. It was a creepy, eerie, nasty place that didn't deserve even a quick dusting.

The mess of nerves grew as she waited for Claudine. Why was she such a wimp about a simple attic? It wasn't like an evil entity waited to jump out and destroy her.

With a peek at the door, Ivelle withdrew the book from her dresser's top drawer. Though the writing within could see her killed, the words offered an unexpected sort of comfort.

"'Our hearts ached as we stood on the palace gatehouse's roof. Below, staining and killing the lush green grass with their shadows, stood those who used to be our brothers. Dark armor marked by a red snake contradicted that fashioned for us by the King. Their faces, once so open and kind and humble, now twisted with hatred and arrogance. What hurt even more was the sight behind them. I wanted so badly to unsheathe my sword and cut down those...those traitors. Those Nolemti.

"'I knew my real brothers felt the same way. Gabreel and Mihai gripped their arrows so hard they snapped and Mosais glared at them like he wished they would burst into consuming flames. Anger, hurt, sorrow, and the sense of betrayal contributed to the raw rage, but what made us desire to go against the Prince's commands was He himself.

"'The way He stood there. He was in pain from the beatings those wretched humans rained upon Him, but though He could have summoned us to destroy them, or destroyed them Himself with His power, He did not. Like a lamb led to slaughter was He led to the execution block. I could not bear to look as Geros and Torgord secured him while Frigdor and Maximo trained arrows at the people. I could not bear to turn my gaze away as Eligor raised the sword and brought it down.'"

"Ivelle?"

Ivelle jerked and bit her tongue as her elbow hit the wall. "Ready?"

"Yes." Claudine eyed the book with a taut expression. "Ivelle, I respect your privacy, but please reassure me you are not reading something that could land you in trouble."

"I promise. You have no need to worry." The lie tasted bitter, but it was better than revealing the truth. Ivelle tucked the book under her blanket and joined Claudine.

"Borros has taken the buckets of soapy water up for us, but we'll need to carry the cleaning rags." Claudine deposited an armful of ragged strips of material into Ivelle's arms. "You ready?"

"Can you ever be *ready* to go into the attic?"

"Touché, my dear. Touché."

<hr>

She was never again cleaning this cursed room.

Ivelle dragged her arm over her forehead to remove another layer of sweat. Boxes and crates lined one wall, distasteful objects like that scary mannequin were shoved against the wall near the door, and trunks stacked against the other long wall, each labeled with what they contained.

If Claudine wanted something from here, she could get it herself. If Ivelle never saw the attic again, she would die happy. Her body ached, her hands and knees were bruised from kneeling and scrubbing, and her eyes watered from the stirred dust

"Well." Claudine stood, hands bracing her back. "I think we transferred all the dust and dirt from the room to us."

"Probably. I've never seen your skin so dark. Not even when you're blushing around Borros."

"Ivelle," Claudine hissed. Her slight, girlish smile betrayed her. "Is it that obvious?"

"It's been obvious for some time that you two have feelings for each other. If you would stop skulking around and actually talk about it, I foresee your wedding in the next year. How did the date go?"

Claudine choked with a sound the mixture of a laugh and audible cringe. "It wasn't a date. It was a nice picnic away from everything and everyone."

"Everyone except the man you've had your eye on since I can remember. You are avoiding the question."

"It was wonderful." Claudine giggled. "Oh, why am I tiptoeing around the topic? You'll drag it out of me one way or the other. It was delightful. Simply and utterly dreamy. He was such a gentleman."

Ivelle smirked. "You two are such a cute couple."

"Ivelle!" Claudine flapped her hands. "Take those buckets down. Borros has the bathtub and water prepared, and I set out some supplies and a towel beforehand. Go clean up. I'll have him keep enough water heated in case you need more."

After returning the now-empty buckets and locking herself in the break room, she pulled off her dirty dress and lowered herself into the oblong tub. The warm water soothed her muscles and aches. She sighed and leaned against the wooden side. Reaching for the bar of soap, she grimaced at the darkened water. Good thing Claudine would get fresh bathwater.

After she forced herself out of the tub and into the dress draped over a chair, Ivelle hobbled to her room. The water may have calmed her muscles, but it did nothing for her bruised knees.

Her heart stopped at the sight of Claudine and Borros crowding the small area. "What's wrong?"

Tears created tracks through the grime on Claudine's face when she looked up. "Oh, Ivelle. I thought you promised."

"Promised what?" Ivelle forced her words to remain steady and not jump an octave. There was only one thing Claudine could mean.

Borros held up *Verum*. "How could you, Ivelle? You know what this is."

Ivelle dropped the pile of dirty clothes into the only available corner and sank onto her bed. Fear stole any ability to speak. How foolish she was, thinking she could get away with reading a forbidden book. Her breath hitched. Would Claudine throw her out? If that happened, what would she do? There were few jobs for single women.

"Ivelle, we must have an answer. The store is closed and Alvin has gone home, so you needn't worry about anyone overhearing."

Ivelle pressed her eyes shut. Tears threatened escape. Had she just jeopardized her place in the only home she knew for the past decade? "Someone already knows."

"What?"

She drew a deep breath. If the stars really could help, she would be on her knees begging for assistance. "Do you remember that soldier Borros hauled in? The one with a bolt in his thigh?"

"The princess' bodyguard? Yes." Claudine gasped. "Ivelle, do not tell me he saw this book. He acted like a nice young man, but his duty is to the king."

"He didn't."

Claudine exhaled, relieved.

"His friend did."

Borros choked. "You mean the taller one? The cranky one that never smiled? The second king's guard one?"

"Yes. A shipment had just come in and I was carrying some of the items back. I somehow crashed into him and the bundle slipped, revealing that book."

Claudine clutched Borros' arm, blind to the filth smudging his shirt. "What was his reaction?"

"He glared at me. Said nothing. Helped his friend out. The last time I saw him he came in demanding some herb for Holder's injury. He said nothing about it." The worry Ivelle had stuffed away after the encounter came roaring back. Though multiple weeks separated that event from the current day, she could still be reported.

Borros stroked Claudine's hand. "Several weeks have passed and nothing has happened. My guess is he kept quiet as a way of repaying us for caring for his friend." His eyes hardened. "Even so, that does not explain what you are doing reading it."

Ivelle forced her thick tongue to form words. "I wasn't at first. I found it in the attic. It happened when the nightmares began. None of the teas and fragrances helped. I needed something to help me sleep. I thought..." her voice wavered, hinting at the tears building in her throat and eyes. "I thought reading something mundane would bore me to sleep."

"Did it help?"

"It is anything but mundane."

"Ivelle, you know the dangers of reading this. You know what will happen if you are caught. Do you want to share Emmi's family's fate? By the stars, have you thought of *our* fate if this is discovered? Have you thought of what could happen to Emmi?"

"No," Ivelle whispered. She blinked, but the tears still emerged.

"Oh, Ivelle." Claudine's shoulders slumped. She bore the look of a woman wholly defeated and fatigued. "Why do you keep reading it? What draws you to it?"

Ivelle closed her eyes. It was a solid question. Just what drew her back to the heart-wrenching story? "It is so poignant, so raw and...and it just feels real, like it really happened. I can't stay away from it. It's like the words refuse to let me go."

Borros rubbed his forehead before placing the book on her dresser. "It is not our job to remove this or forbid you to not read it. You are twenty-one. You are mature enough to make the right choice, which I trust you to do." He pulled Claudine close to him and steered her from the room. "Come on, Claudine. You need to clean up."

Ivelle's muscles and bones failed and she slumped against her mattress. They said nothing about her leaving, or even if they wanted her to leave, but would they after her transgression settled into their minds?

Whoever listens, whoever cares, please hear me. Please grant Claudine the mercy to allow me to stay.

"Ivelle?"

Ivelle forced herself to sit. "What are you doing up, Emmi? Is everything alright?"

The petite brunette shuffled forward. A rash covered her small hands and neck and her gait threatened to lurch her to the floor, but an adoring smile crinkled her cheeks. "I heard what happened. What was that about my family?"

"Nothing, sweetie. Borros doesn't know what he speaks of when he is angry."

Emmi nodded and reached out a hand.

A fresh batch of scalding tears built as Ivelle took the gnarled little fingers between her own. "Would you like to sit?"

"No, but thank you." Emmie's smile turned secretive and her voice dropped to a whisper. "It's okay, Ivelle. I believe too."

"You believe what?" That Ivelle was a boneheaded idiot for not considering the consequences?

"I believe what the book says."

"Emmi, don't say that. You don't know what it says."

"Not that book, but I read the journal before it disappeared. I believe what it says about the King and Prince and Counselor."

CHAPTER THIRTY-THREE

HOLDER

SILENCE.

Holder cracked an eye open and scanned the sagging wooden ceiling. His body hurt, especially his leg from his wound and his chest from breathing cold air for multiple hours on end. His head throbbed and his back felt stiffer than stiff from only a thin blanket between him and the floor.

Rogan stirred but didn't move otherwise. The horses stood in a corner, occasionally munching on the oats Holder set out for them.

He sighed, chest and back protesting. Thoughts crammed his brain. He believed Argus, but the thought of actually having a godfather was almost unimaginable. For almost fifteen years he'd thought himself alone.

Why? Why had Argus disappeared? He'd told his story, which sounded absolutely believable considering what Holder observed, but why would he abandon his godson, and a five-year-old boy no less?

Loneliness had haunted Holder's days. Before and after trainings meant wandering around Rex Dorcha's grounds, talking to the horses, and shadowing Mister Slowman, his father's successor as stable master.

Rogan had been fully invested in training, almost to the point of wearing himself to exhaustion. Occasionally, they wandered into the woods during the weekdays, investigating and playing, but it was the weekends when they went riding, exploring, and discovering what it meant to be carefree young boys.

He lit the candle and fingered the journal. It was a source of companionship. Rogan's aloofness and sharp answers inserted a wedge in their relationship. At least he could count on the prickly king's guard to ensure they reached safety.

The thin scrap of material used as a bookmark fluttered onto his chest as the book opened. Learning about his parents and what they went through almost eased the ache in his heart. It helped solidify the fact his parents were *real*. That they weren't just distant figures who disappeared into history with no trace of who they really were.

"'Though some of the villagers' sayings still don't make sense, I understand some of them now. The thought that I ever believed the stars held power over our lives is laughable, and I pray to Uri's ruler my son also sees the foolishness of such a thing. A village elder, Ihon, (though he does not look old enough to be an elder) has offered to answer any questions I may have. Wisdom beyond the normal fills his eyes. Mariline remarked last night he oft surveys the residents of DorChast with a relieved air. Why, we could not discern.

"'Despite his oddities, Ihon has provided clear, simple answers to my questions, though his answers can be peculiar. I asked if he knew of Eligor's origins and whether or not 'tis true he is centuries old. Ihon answered yes, then proceeded to tell me about some rebellion in Uri against the ruler's son. The things they said and called for...Mariline was in tears by the tale's end, and I will admit that I did not walk away dry-eyed.

"'How could the people call for their ruler's son's death? From Ihon's account he sounded like a good ruler, just yet merciful. An odd thing about the tale was that Ihon claimed Eligor stirred the rebellion and eventually was the one who murdered the ruler's son.'"

"How are you?"

Rogan's sleepy voice drew Holder from black ink and yellowed pages to the room's dark interior. Something in him ached from what he read. What was the point of such a tale if it ended that way?

"Holder?"

"I'm fine."

"You sure? It looked like something was bothering you."

Holder closed the journal and managed to stand. His clothes rumpled from sleeping in them and he probably needed a bath. "Just something I was reading."

Rogan's expression tightened, but he kept quiet.

It was a surprise Rogan said as little as he did. His disapproval shone as bright as a full moon against a midnight sky. A lump grew in Holder's throat. If Officer Torgord caught wind of the journal, or Holder's almost-relation to Argus, would they question Rogan? If they did, would Rogan turn against him?

Rogan shuffled toward the door. "I'm checking the weather. If it's not snowing, we can continue riding."

⋄⟡⋯⋯⋯⟡⋄

"Who do you want to answer King Eligor?" Holder knotted the reins around his fingers. His stomach roiled at how the report could go. If not handled carefully, would he lose his job? Princess Anastasia was a brat at times, but a sweeter, more genuine little girl Varway never saw. Holder would never have a sister, but guarding the princess allowed him to act like the older brother he'd dreamed of being.

"I don't know. King Eligor mainly addressed you, didn't he? He sent me along for protection."

"You don't think I am capable of defending myself?"

"With the shape your leg is in? No."

Holder kneaded his forehead. Although it pricked his pride, Rogan had a point. It was a struggle walking. Fighting would be impossible.

"You."

"What?"

"You can talk. Between the two of us, you have more tact."

You think? Did Rogan just now figure that out? The desire to ask Rogan if he would say anything about the journal stuck to Holder's tongue. Could he really ask such a thing?

He shook his head. No, no he could not. Things already felt tenuous with Rogan. The last thing their relationship needed was Holder bringing up a delicate, dangerous subject.

"I think you should have the healer look at your leg first. It shouldn't look the way it does so far into the healing process."

The healing process. Just how far along was he? Protecting Princess Anastasia at the old cabin felt like years ago. Six weeks, Ivelle had said. Had six weeks passed, or were they not yet reached?

Holder reached back and fumbled in his right saddlebag. Several leagues separated them from Varway, and with nothing to look at but melting snow and the beginnings of the Argbil Forest, it would be nice to take his mind off the growing sense of dread building in his chest.

"'DorChast is a delightful village, full of kind, gracious, and hardworking people. I never thought myself one for the mountains, yet watching the sunrise and breathing the sweet, fresh air as I help plow convinces me otherwise. Though Mariline and I do not regret leaving Orm and its darkness, we hold much sorrow over other things, and people, we left behind. She misses the true few friends she had and I miss my job and the horses. Such gentle creatures despite the men they carry. But what we miss most are our children. Our son is safe and our little daughter lies still in her grave. What I would give to hear my boy's multitude of questions. To feel him hug my leg. To watch him ride the old gelding._

"'Despite the good life we could have here, I fear we must leave. Reports have reached DorChast of another village we sheltered in for a time: Mort. Word came from a neighboring village that Mort was attacked and burned to the ground a few weeks ago. There were no survivors.'"

"Holder?"

"Huh?" Holder dragged his gaze from the pages to Rogan. Furrows lined his friend's forehead and something akin to concern narrowed Rogan's eyes.

"You're crying."

"I am?" Holder brushed a hand across his face. His glove came away glimmering with liquid.

"You okay?"

Holder cleared his throat. How had he not noticed the emotion building within? The deep ache that was just made deeper? The intense longing for parents he would never see again? "Yeah."

"Was   it   from   what   you're   reading?"

No man cried. Telling Rogan would solidify his wimpiness and weakness. But Rogan already saw the tears.

Not much more could be incriminating than that. Holder read the brief passage. When he looked up, he glimpsed what looked like deep longing in Rogan's eyes before the king's guard turned and faced forward.

Stars, if at all possible, let me see my parents again.

⸻ ◈ ⸻

Rex Dorcha's turrets loomed dark against the pale blue sky. Holder shielded his eyes and squinted at the black flag hanging from the pole. If red was the color of mourning, why was the serpent emblem scarlet?

He shook aside the random thought. Now was not the time for such frivolous wonderings.

"Did you forget what normal civilization looked like?" A smile tilted Juan's voice.

"You would too, if you were surrounded by prairie for days on end," Rogan growled. The last two days of travelling tripled his normal grumpiness.

Holder knew of one thing Rogan cursed more than travelling. Maximo Cetrin.

Juan sniggered. "Well, it is good to have you back. Lygor, I hope you can soon take over as the princess' bodyguard. I don't know how much more of that Svetlana I can handle."

"Welcome to my world."

Juan outright laughed before waving his hand at the guarded entrance. "Captain Geros ordered me to inform you that you are wanted before the king immediately."

"Juan." Rogan's tone cut the air. "Holder needs his injury seen to. Would you ask Captain Geros if we can do that first? It looks infected."

"Sorry. Direct orders, Rogan. The captain said you were to do *nothing* before obeying orders."

Holder stopped Rogan's protest. He chose the oddest of times to act like a true friend. "It's fine, Rogan. I can make it."

"Yeah, if you want to forever damage your leg."

"Rogan..."

"Fine, fine. Let's go. Juan, would you take our horses to the stable?"

Juan took the reins, inching as far away from Holder's gelding as he could and still effectively lead them. "Sure, but, Lygor, I'm blaming you if this wild creature takes a chunk from my shoulder."

"Here." Rogan slipped Holder's arm around his shoulders. "Where is your crutch?"

"I couldn't bring it with us. It was an inconvenience."

Rogan muttered something about Holder and inconveniences as they approached the main hall.

Nerves attacked Holder full force. More soldiers than normal milled about, standing in small clusters, or watching his and Rogan's every step with almost predatory stares.

He swallowed an upheaval of the jerky eaten for breakfast. No, they had no idea about Father's journal. No idea about his relation to Argus. No idea he was the son of two traitors.

Were they right? The question rose unbidden. Were his parents right to run? To betray? To leave their young son to be choked by the very darkness, the very evil, they fled?

"Royal bodyguard Specialist Holder Lygor and Second king's guard Specialist Rogan Cetrin entering," the announcer said. The thin man held himself like a haughty rooster despite drowning in the robes covering his skinny frame.

"You may approach."

Was it Holder's imagination, or did ice coat Officer Torgord's words?

Holder bit back a grunt as more pain stabbed through his leg. The sooner this passed, the sooner his wound would be looked at, cleaned, and rebandaged.

King Eligor sat on the largest of two thrones. The rubies and onyxes in his crown glittered in the light of multiple lanterns. A brilliant, pale sword rested across his knees. To his left stood Officer Torgord, armed and dressed in leather armor. Captain Geros' usual spot at the king's right was empty.

A few paces away from Officer Torgord stood the first king's guard in a straight, neat row. At the right was the second king's guard. Juan slid into his spot as the king spoke.

"Specialists Lygor and Cetrin. You have returned. I trust your journey was fruitful?"

Holder forced himself to bow. "Yes, my king. We were able to retrieve the item." He forced his tone to remain neutral, respectful.

"First Lieutenant Cetrin, retrieve the object."

Rogan's father lumbered forward, scowl in place and eyes hard and cruel. He plucked the bundle from Holder's grip and transferred it to the king.

"This is all?" King Eligor unwrapped the dagger. "He took much more than this."

"My king, that was the only thing he told us of. We searched the place but found nothing more."

"Indeed. He did not, by chance, have a leather-bound book, did he?"

"No, my king."

King Eligor hummed. "And the man. Was he insane? I remember his sanity slipping."

Perhaps it is your *sanity which slips.*

Sparks of anger flamed. Holder forced himself to remain respectful. "He appeared quite sane, my king, though it is possible he hid his insanity from us."

"My king." Captain Geros walked around Holder and Rogan and knelt before King Eligor, cape draping around his body. "My king, you were right."

King Eligor took the object from Captain Geros and opened it.

Even from the distance away Holder was, the storm cloud gathering upon the king's brow was evident. "Specialist Lygor."

Oh, no. By the stars, no. He found the journal.

"Yes, my king?"

"You claimed you were given no book."

"I was not, my king." Holder's heart drummed mercilessly against his chest. What would happen? Surely he could explain the desire to know more about his father. He could twist the truth. Claim he skipped over every part that read treasonous with the intent to burn the book after reading it.

"Then explain why *Verum* was found in your saddlebag."

"My king, I've never heard of the book."

"Oh? Well, you've certainly been reading it." King Eligor removed a small cloth bookmark. "Captain Geros said he found it in your saddlebag. Tell me, Holder Lygor, why should I believe you? The evidence is clearly against your favor."

Holder's breath lodged in his chest, built up until a burning, almost unbearable pressure ruined his ability to breath. "My king, I have never seen nor heard of the book."

"Enough," King Eligor hissed. "Captain Geros and First Lieutenant Cetrin, take him to the dungeon."

CHAPTER THIRTY-FOUR

THERESE

WISPY DARKNESS FRAMED Therese's vision as Scholl's house came into view. Each breath made her innards feel like an iron hand gripped and twisted them. Her legs buckled as she dismounted.

"Therese!" Jolie's voice echoed in the distance.

Therese shuddered. Hadn't she reached Scholl's? She could have sworn she rode up to the steps.

Hands aided her to her feet. The ground dipped and swayed. Therese bit the inside of her cheek to keep nausea from escaping.

"She's burning with fever. I bet her wound is infected."

Therese struggled to drag herself from the spreading, welcoming darkness. Something nagged the back recesses of her mind. But what? Why couldn't she remember? Why did everything feel and look foggy, like she'd inhaled Jolie's sleeping liquid?

"I'll carry her to the guest room. Jolie, keep the girls occupied. They'll scare if they see her like this."

Time swirled into dark nothingness, broken only by icy liquid dribbling down the side of Therese's face. She jolted, a cry rising in her throat when her back protested.

"Easy, easy." Jolie's dark face moved into focus. Concern thickened her voice and rounded her eyes. "Therese, you need to change. I've laid out one of Lucian's shirts and a pair of your leggings. You'll need something looser for the bandage."

"Right." The word moved from Therese's tongue, thick and unwieldy. She stumbled to her feet when Jolie left the room, managing to peel away her clothes, replacing them with the beige shirt and black leggings draped over a chair.

"Jolie?"

"You done?"

"Yes." *Stars, where are my sisters? What is wrong with me?*

Footsteps tapped against the wooden floors as Jolie entered, nothing more than a blurred figure. "I need to see your injury." She cursed after helping Therese manipulate the shirt to show her back. "This is not okay. Lay down. I'm going to see if we can find a suitable healer.

Darkness drifted across Therese's vision.

"Stay with me, Therese. Stay with me. Think of your sisters."

Nora and Delli...this is for them.

The darkness returned, embedding her in nothingness.

Linen.

Therese inhaled the gentle scent of freshly-washed linens mixed with a pungent herbal odor. Coldness spread across the skin between her right shoulder and ribs.

"Well?"

"She will be fine as long as you keep the fever down and apply this every six hours."

That voice. Therese knew that voice.

"What is it?" Jolie formed her words the way she did when she was on the edge of losing her temper.

The other woman sighed. "Goldenseal salve. One of the best for infection."

"Oh." Floorboards creaked as weight shifted. "Well, you have our thanks. What do we owe you?"

"I'll send you the bill. Right now, you can leave the room. Therese and I need to talk."

"I am not leaving you alone with her."

"Yes, you are. One, you owe it to me after the way you dragged me here. Two, Therese and I know each other."

"Right." Jolie's tone sounded sour. "Nora said something about that." Her words turned menacing. "Don't think about doing anything to her. I'll be outside the door."

"I have no doubt you will be." The woman waited until a door closed before speaking again. "The salve should be dry. You can sit or turn over if you'd like."

Therese adjusted her undershirt and forced herself to sit. She choked at the sight of Ivelle's pursed lips and crossed arms. "What are you doing here?"

Ivelle reached for the pitcher perched on the dresser opposite the bed. "You needed help. Nora apparently mentioned my name and where I live and, next thing I know, that woman places a damp cloth over my nose and mouth. I wake up in a strange house with a strange couple hovering over me like I'm dangerous."

She was, but Therese wouldn't say it. "Thank you." The cool water eased the froggy rasp in her throat.

"Don't thank me yet. Your infection still needs to heal. What were you doing?"

Therese grimaced. "My job."

"Ah, yes. Your assassin job. Mind telling me who needed to be killed so much that you left Varway to your health's detriment?"

A young man who did not deserve death. A young man whose death could secure her sisters' survival. A young man who was likely already convicted due to the "evidence" she planted in his saddlebag at the dogtrot cabin. Her stomach twisted. He wouldn't have noticed, not with the way she concealed the book at the bottom of the saddlebag and covered it with his clothes while the men slept like the dead. "I can't tell you."

A mixture of thoughts and expressions darkened Ivelle's eyes. She glanced at the door before sitting on the edge of the bed. "Therese, was it Holder?"

"I...I can't tell you." Therese's heart raced and adrenaline spiked. Ivelle trod too close to the truth.

"Therese...word has spread that a traitor was arrested this morning at Rex Dorcha." Ivelle's gaze turned calculating, like she could see through Therese's exterior and into her heart, mind, and soul.

Therese stared at the plain gray duvet. She hadn't failed the mission. Not really. She'd planted the book, kept him from dying by another's hand. Why then hadn't she found the courage to end him? She'd had a few clear opportunities. The payment would only reduce the debt. What his death would do to her soul was irrelevant.

"You didn't kill him."

"How could I?" How could she kill an obviously innocent person? Those at King's Day and the other assassins waiting to end the two soldiers were evil, deserving. Nothing her target did merited such a fateful end.

By the stars. How could she pass up such an opportunity to provide for her sisters? Scholl would be furious, seeing it as a sign of failure. How could she pass up such an opportunity to better herself in the master assassin's opinion? Her failure could mean the loss of the only thing keeping her from losing herself to the evils of perverted men and her sisters from losing their lives.

"Therese." A kindness Therese had seen given only to the girls softened the usual edge in Ivelle's countenance. "Why are you an assassin?"

"Survival." Her voice cracked. "Claudine DeGrim took you in. The girls and I were not so fortunate." And it wasn't like they could escape over the mountains. What lay beyond made prostitution and Varway at its worst seem like a pampered, safe life.

Ivelle hummed in acknowledgement before reaching for her bag and digging through it. "This is the calendula salve I used on you. That woman knows what to do. Stay in bed, do nothing strenuous until the infection clears up, and get plenty of water and food. Your body is weakened and you will need strength if you want to fully recover."

⌁

"Therese! You're back."

"Yes. I am back." Therese sank against the pillow as Delli attacked her with a hug. "Did you behave?"

"Yes."

"Delli..."

"The yam is yummy." Delli's toothy grin showcased pink-stained teeth.

"Just how much jam did you eat?"

"All of it." Another grin.

Stars have mercy. Now Delli would have enough energy to sprint to the High Mountains and back—five times.

"Finally." Nora all but stomped through the doorway. "They wouldn't let us see you for the longest time." Her nose wrinkled as she sniffed. "You need a bath."

"Jolie cooks." Delli tugged Therese's hand. "She cooks."

"Not very well," Nora grumbled. "All she knows how to make is butter-and-jelly sandwiches. Lucian is better. His stew is almost as good as yours."

"Then you were fed well?"

"Uh-huh." Nora stared at the floor. "Did you know they eat three times a day?"

Therese bit her tongue to keep tears away. What a failure she was, that her sisters could not have the adequate number of daily meals. What would they do when they returned home? How would their bodies respond to the reduced amount of food?

"Scholl is weird." Nora plopped on the bed. "I don't like him much. He scowls a lot like he's eaten a rotten piece of fish."

"He does, doesn't he?"

"Yeah." Delli snuggled into Therese.

Ignoring the pain in her back, Therese drew Nora into the hug. By the stars, she had missed them. So, so much.

"Jolie said Scholl went on a trip to somewhere called DorFord. I like it when he's gone. I don't think he likes kids."

"I don't think he likes anyone." In fact, the only person Scholl acted kind toward was Jolie. Probably because she was his niece.

Jolie and Lucian replaced Nora and Delli once the girls scampered away. Therese's throat tightened at their serious expressions. "What is wrong?"

"You have some explaining to do. Including how you left with one horse and returned with four."

"I overheard three men speaking about my client. They'd been hired by someone who knew I was employed to handle this particular target." Therese suppressed a cringe at how casually she spoke. "If they reached him before I did, I would lose the money. They planned to ambush him, and I...stopped them."

"How?" Lucian's eyebrows reached his hairline.

Should she feel bad for taking three lives, even if they meant another ill? "I snuck into their camp and poisoned their water with oleander. When they went to prepare their ambush, I followed them, waited until it did its job before taking their horses." She shrugged. "They look like quality animals."

Jolie stared at Therese like she was a puzzle. "You just left the bodies?"

"It was snowing. I wasn't about to haul them."

"Well." Lucian dropped three sets of leather packs onto the dresser. "It's your job then to go through these. Unique way to handle the issue. I'd say you have the makings of an excellent assassin. Good job, kiddo."

"Yes." Jolie leaned against him, trading a look of pure adoration before grinning at Therese. "Scholl will be pleased with the horses."

Therese forced a smile. She retrieved the first saddlebag and withdrew a folded parchment resting on the top. Nausea and bile seared her throat. No official seal, no special mark signified who wrote the message, but the name at the bottom did little for her unsteady stomach. Did this lieutenant know nothing of her client's order?

No matter the answer, one question remained: why would two king's guards separately arrange the death of another?

'Something this job requires is patience.'

Lucian's wisdom rang through Therese's brain as she crept down wide, stone stairs. Cool, damp air drew chills to her arms and a musty scent assaulted her nose.

She fingered the small pouch hanging at her hip. Was she really doing this? Could she do this?

Yes. She had to. There was no other moral choice.

A stone arch and two torches announced the dungeon's entrance. Two cups and a plate of biscuits sat on a square wooden table shoved against the right wall. Hooks with keyrings lined the wall and spears cluttered the corner. A nailed, rectangular parchment hung near the opening.

Just what she needed. Therese squinted at the scraggly writing. *Cell Six.*

"Someone from the kitchen will be down soon with supper," a gravelly voice said.

She darted into the shadows as two bulky guards ambled into the small foyer.

"As long as they're on time," the other grumbled.

"Aye, by the stars, they better be. I'm tired of listening to your stomach growl."

"What can I say? I'm hungry."

"You're always hungry."

Therese held her breath as she crept into the dungeon. Cells lined both sides, separated by thick stone walls that looked carved from the very ground Rex Dorcha was built from. A wooden board hung above each cell, a number burned into it.

Chills crawled up her spine as chains rattled and prisoners shifted to stare at her. Would they alert the guards? Would she end up in a cell?

Cell Six. Therese tightened the cloth covering her nose and mouth before stepping in front of the iron bars. Her target sat in the small cell's corner, arms folded and gaze staring at the floor. Even in the dim light she could see the tears and smudges littering his shirt and jerkin.

They must have convicted him at his arrival.

She withdrew the oleander petals and the key swiped from one of the hooks. A small bit of wood dangled from the top of the key's shaft, marking it the key for her target's cell.

Therese inserted the key. Waves of relief filled her when it unlocked without sound. Her target jerked his head up, eyes widening before he struggled to his feet, fists clenched.

"Come to finish the job?" A near whisper, his voice was ragged. Strained.

Therese winced at the combination of exhaustion and desperation in his eyes. How often had she felt the same way? "You know what they do to traitors." She kept her voice soft. "Do you want to face that?"

"I did nothing wrong. I don't even know how that book got there."

You may not, but I do. "Do you think they will believe that?"

Her target's sharp laugh dripped with derision. "I've done nothing to promote myself as a traitor."

"They will not believe you. Not if Captain Geros or Lieutenant Cetrin speak against you." The men's names tasted foul.

"Why would they speak against me? It's clear I was set up."

Her target spoke truth. He *had* been set up. *By her.*

Therese withheld a groan. Why? *Why?* All she had wanted was a job so she could support her sisters. All she wanted was to keep herself away from a livelihood which would suck the life and soul from her. And all she received were two men looking to set up an innocent boy.

If the circumstances were different, if she could turn back time and find an alternative source of income, she would free Holder Lygor.

But her sisters were highest priority.

Still, something deep within fought the injustice. *Stars, I need your guidance. Please, please. Guide me. Show me what to do.*

CHAPTER THIRTY-FIVE

ROGAN

"' OUR SON IS SAFE.'"

Not now. Not anymore.

Rogan grimaced at the writhing mess of emotions growing by the hour. Had reading his father's journal encouraged Holder toward harboring a treasonous object? Or was Holder right and someone framed him?

The desperation in Holder's voice when Rogan visited him echoed in his memory. If Holder was right, what could Rogan do? It wasn't like he held status or had a special place in the king's heart.

He touched the sore, tender area along his jaw. Father's fist had flown as harshly as his words when he discovered Rogan's visit to the dungeons. Rogan's vision still wavered at times and a deep headache seared beneath his skull.

He ignored the five bruises in the shapes of fingerprints around his wrist as he flipped the journal shut. Holder had a good heart and deeply cared for the princess' safety. What would drive him to the action which saw him arrested?

"Rogan," Mother called from the bottom of the ladder. "Captain Geros is here. He wishes to speak with you."

Rogan shoved the journal beneath his mattress and descended the ladder. He pushed away the thin, inward voice whispering aggression against the captain. It wasn't his job to question. He was to show respect and honor toward his superiors, not contempt and anger.

Mother stood near the table, hands on hips and lips pursed so thin they hardly showed. Her eyes narrowed under a forehead exposed by her tight hairdo. "Here he is, Captain."

Rogan silently cursed. How had he not noticed the captain looming in the doorway? He managed a salute, still squashing the silent whispers of fury that his friend was imprisoned.

"At ease." Captain Geros stepped forward. His eyes lacked their usual amiable glint. "Rogan, Officer Torgord wishes to speak with you."

To interrogate me, you mean.

Rogan answered with a nod and followed the captain outside. The row of cabins belonging to soldiers with families had been alight with gossip last night. Gossip about Holder. Gossip about his best friend.

Friend. Was it right to call Holder a friend? Or was admitting to a bond, an almost-brotherhood, treason?

Captain Geros led Rogan to the room King Eligor and Officer Torgord questioned him in after Holder's supposed sighting of the threat pinned to the princess' pillow. That time, Rogan had been confident, his only aim to assure Orm's ruler and investigator Holder was still fit to be bodyguard.

Now?

Now ice coated his fingertips and banded around his chest.

"Specialist Cetrin."

"My king. Officer Torgord." Rogan bowed to King Eligor, who sat in the largest chair centered at the table's middle. Officer Torgord sat to his left, and Captain Geros slid into the seat to the king's right.

Officer Torgord exchanged a look with the king before steepling his fingers and piercing Rogan with cold blue eyes that seemed to scour his thoughts and soul. "How long have you known Holder Lygor?"

"For as long as I can remember, sir. He came to live with us for a time after his parents disappeared." Or enacted treason, if the journal and Argus were to be believed.

"Has Lygor ever said or acted in a way that pointed to silent treason?"

Besides reading a journal reeking of it and believing a man who assisted two traitors in escaping, "No, sir."

"Are you certain?" If possible, Officer Torgord's eyes narrowed even more.

Rogan's back muscles tensed as he fought to keep from squirming. Why did he lie? "Yes, sir. Holder was, is, dedicated to protecting the princess and has always exhibited loyalty. I've never witnessed anything close to sedition in him."

"I think you know who Argus Ancorit is and the real reason we sent him away." A threatening undercurrent laced Officer Torgord's words. "Did he tell you? Did he say anything to Holder?"

"He said many things, sir, but I brushed them off as a madman's ravings. He said things to Holder, but nothing in private."

"What else did he do?"

"He provided bandages and salve for Holder's leg wound and provided us with the locations of abandoned cabins and huts so we would be out of the weather on our journey back."

"Are you certain you have never seen or heard anything traitorous?"

"Yes, sir." *Liar.*

Why? Why did he cover for his friend? By doing so, he almost committed treason. If Holder was innocent, surely there would be proof.

"One final question, Specialist. How can you reconcile your answers to the evidence? Captain Geros found *Verum* in Lygor's saddlebag, along with a treasonous letter."

By the stars. Was this a simple questioning or one of the interrogations Officer Torgord was known for? "I do not know how the book got in Holder's saddlebag, sir, only that I believe Holder. I've known him for a long time. I know when he is hiding something. He truly does not recognize the book. And I know nothing about the letter. I do know, though, that Holder has no one to write to."

Officer Torgord's mustache twitched. "Thank you, Specialist Cetrin. You may go."

The need to know Holder's fate burned Rogan's tongue, but asking would be disrespectful. He bowed again and left. His heart hammered. The slight bit of optimism he possessed said Holder would be cleared of wrongdoing and released to the job he loved so much.

But something else warned him things would not go so smoothly.

Rogan cringed as he changed direction and walked the path to the stables. Did they suspect he snuck in and took Holder's saddlebags? Did they know anything about the journal?

The scents of fresh straw and horse took Rogan back to the days of autumn horseback rides with Holder. How simple life seemed back then. He knew with certainty what he wanted to be. Training went well, and he could escape the Cetrin cabin, which so often felt like a prison.

"Hello?" Stable master Slowman trundled into the room. His craggy face bunched in surprise. "You're Holder's friend, aren't you? You're the one who took his saddlebags."

"Yes, sir. I came to ensure Holder's horse was taken care of." Blackie too, but Holder would be beyond irritated if his precious mount was ignored.

Stable master Slowman scoffed. His chest puffed out like pride inflated his torso. "Of course it was taken care of. I leave no horse uncared for under my watch, even if they are snappish devils."

"Right," Rogan muttered. The past forty-eight hours crashed down on him, tightening his lungs and suppressing his ability to breathe. "I'm just going to saddle my horse and go for a ride."

"With this melting snow? You'll not be able to see where holes or ruts are. That is a fine mare. She is of supreme stock and breeding. Don't go ruining her."

"Don't worry, Slowman. I know what I am doing."

But did he? Did he really know? Before reading Holder's father's journal, meeting Argus, and Holder's arrest, life felt secure despite his parents. Things looked promising and it felt possible to obtain his captaincy and fifth dagger within the year.

Now life felt as jumbled as a skein of yarn left in the hands of children and kittens.

Rogan led Blackie into the crisp air and mounted. The mare's gentle walk lulled the tension from his shoulders as he reined her toward the forest. Out here he did not have to think, or feel emotions, or consider his future or recent events. Out here he could forget who he was and just enjoy the fresh air and his horse's silent companionship.

⬩⬩⬩⬩⬩⬩

"Where were you?"

Rogan grit his teeth and paused. "Riding."

"Riding." Disdain filled Father's words. "You sure about that?"

Any peace gained from the soothing, sylvan ride disappeared. Rogan swallowed to keep the rising knot of fear at bay. "Stable master Slowman can confirm."

Footsteps scuffled. "Slowman would say anything since you're that traitor's friend."

"Just because some book was found in Holder's saddlebag does not make him a traitor." Rogan cursed himself as soon as the words left his mouth. He should know better after all these years.

Father's fingers dug into his shoulder and collarbone. "Let me tell you something, boy. If I say he's guilty, he's guilty. His parents were traitor scum, and it is inevitable they passed that down to their son. Best he is taken care of now before he infects others. Eligor's had him under watch for a long time now and Svetlana confirmed Holder is treasonous."

Svetlana? Holder wouldn't harm anything, much less enact treason. He cared too much about the princess to do such a thing.

"Say that again," Father hissed. "Eligor says that brat is guilty. He's guilty. Geros says he's guilty, and he is. Torgord says the same, so it must be. They know what they're talking about. They've convicted before."

Rogan clenched his fists to keep from shying away from the pain throbbing through his left shoulder and collarbone. "Yes, I know. I've seen the executions."

Father's laugh rang out cruel and pleased. "Those are nothing. Worthless sots whose lives held no value or purpose."

Father was crazy, plain and simple. "Then what are you talking about?"

"Sit down." Father shoved Rogan into a chair. He crossed the room to the chest in the corner.

By the stars, what was going on? Father's surprises were rarely good. Pulse racing, Rogan bolted for the door. Thick arms surrounded his legs. He pitched forward.

"Stupid boy," Father snarled.

"What are you doing?" Rogan's voice fractured as cool metal brushed his jugular. The thick, serpentine design King Eligor used for his special daggers, carried only by himself, Captain Geros, and Officer Torgord, filled his right peripheral vision. His breathing quickened. With Father's weight pinning him down, and the blade so close to slicing his throat, there was nothing he could do. "Using a king-issued blade on another soldier is illegal."

Father's cackle sent chills skittering across Rogan's skin. "For you mortals, it is."

"Mortals? What are you talking about? What are you doing?" Would he die before learning if Holder was innocent? Would his father really kill him? He'd come close before, when that rage lit his eyes, his teeth gnashed, red filled his face, and his knuckles cracked.

"Mortals," Father repeated. "You didn't think Eligor is the only immortal one, did you?"

"I...I..." Rogan never thought deeply about his king's age. It just *was*. But for Father to claim immortality?

Just what was going on?

"Stupid boy. You think you know everything, but you know nothing. You and that offspring of traitors were sent to Weedcrag so Holder would meet his end away from the princess."

"What?" He knew it. He knew that assassin was up to no good.

"Aye. My men have yet to return. When they do, I'll show them what happens when they fail an immortal. A *Nolemti*," he hissed.

Rogan fought for breath as the ache in his neck and back grew from Father's fingers gripping his hair to keep his face up. "What...what are you talking about?"

"Your friend"—Father spit out the term—"will be tried and convicted. As he will die, so will his influence over you, and you can become what you are truly meant to be."

This wasn't happening. Rogan had fallen from Blackie and hit his head against a stone. He was ill and experiencing fever dreams. This wasn't real. What Father said was gibberish.

"You." Father's breath tickled Rogan's cheek. "Of all the brats in Orm, your mother bore me you. But you have potential. You have the blood of an immortal, one of the originals, flowing through your veins. Once that spawn of treason is dead, we will mold you into what you were meant to be."

By the stars. Fever dreams. That's all this is. Or from a hard hit to the head.

Father's grip tightened before the floor rushed toward Rogan's face.

CHAPTER THIRTY-SIX

IVELLE

"JUST WHAT HAPPENED, exactly? Claudine looked ready to have heart failure."

Ivelle lowered herself to the floor and balanced the newest shipment in her lap. "I'm in here preparing incense satchels for customers when, the next thing I know, a damp cloth is pressed across my nose and mouth."

"Like laudanum?"

"Yes, except you have to ingest laudanum for it to work. When I awoke, I found myself on a wooden floor with two adults and two children hovering over and staring at me." Ivelle undid the lid and handed the first bolt of cloth to Borros.

"Who were they?"

"I don't know the adults' names. The little girls were the ones who were here for a time. The oldest was ill."

Borros slipped the material into a velvet sack. "I remember. Cute little things. Wasn't there an older sister or something?"

Ivelle's throat tightened at the thought of Therese. The woman's pleas, *threats*, to heal the unconscious assassin, combined with Nora and Delli's worried whispers, spurred her to treat Therese's infected wound.

And the look in her eyes when asked about Holder. Part desperation, part defeat. Feelings Ivelle well understood.

"An older sister. Anyway, they wanted me to heal someone." Best not inform him of the man's veiled threat about what would happen should she tell anyone.

"And?"

"She'll be fine if she obeys."

Borros chuckled. "You've led an interesting life, Ivelle Quade."

Not so much interesting as devastating. She withdrew another bolt of satin. "Your hands are clean, right? Claudine would pitch a conniption if you get fingerprints on this cloth. It is not cheap."

"Don't worry. Claudine already lectured me." He lapsed into silence before clearing his throat. His eyes darted to the door. "About the book, Ivelle. What was your decision?"

Words clogged Ivelle's throat. What could she say? If she lied they would eventually discover it. If she told the truth they could cast her out.

"Hey." Borros leaned forward. "We meant it when I said it is your decision. I'm just wondering why."

Why. Such a small word with such a large meaning.

"That older sister you asked about. Her job allows her access to Rex Dorcha's archives. She repaid me—us—by investigating what happened to my home village." Ivelle picked at the crate. "She told me she found a record stating Mort was destroyed because they housed two traitors. When they did not hand them over, King Eligor ordered Mort razed and destroyed with no survivors."

Borros' jaw worked, and he leaned back. "No survivors? Did that include women and children?"

"It means what it sounds like." Ivelle's voice thickened with the bitterness raging in her heart. "No one was to live. I hid myself beneath a rock ledge after watching my family be slain by men in blue capes. There was more blood than the water in the nearby stream. More smoke than air as everything burned."

The remembered sound of screams and panicked animals replayed in her memory, and the pain and stench of burning flesh drew nausea.

"I can understand how that would alter your opinion of the king, but to read treason? What were you thinking?"

"I was thinking about my past. How close I was to death." The old scars marring the underside of her forearms ached. "I almost died from burn complications, Borros. When I found that book and began reading, it was like…like light in the darkness, fresh air amidst the stench of decay. It was something *more.*"

"Do you believe it?" Borros' question was soft, quiet. Genuine.

It struck Ivelle in the heart. Did she? Did she believe the dangerous claims? The story of an innocent life sacrificed for no apparent reason? "I don't know if I believe it, but I know I no longer believe in the stars and their supposed role in our lives."

"Ivelle, King Eligor is the one who encourages that."

"I'm just surprised he doesn't encourage worship of himself," Ivelle muttered.

Borros growled. "I understand you are hurt and scarred from our king's actions. I even understand you reading that book. But you cannot speak treason. I would be arrested at the very least if the king ever discovered I withheld this information. You could be labeled treasonous. A traitor. Do you want that?"

Since when did truth become marked as treason?

Ivelle shoved the crate aside and stood. "He may be your king, but he is not mine."

⸺◇◀⸺ • ⸱⸱⸱ • ⸺▶◇⸺

'He may be your king, but he is not mine.'

Ivelle ground her teeth and slammed her fist into the pile of folded cloth. She'd been stupid before, but this was unlike anything she had ever said and done.

Stupid, stupid, stupid.

"Ivelle?" Emmi appeared at her elbow, hair awry and eyes wide. "Can we go riding today?"

"I don't know if that is a good idea, sweetie." Ivelle forced down the emotional maelstrom. "Don't you remember what happened last time?"

"I know, but I want to. Claudine said it is not too cold out today and I want to be good at riding when my family comes back."

The impending lie choked Ivelle. How could she tell this sweet little soul her family would never return from their new home in the graveyard's criminal section?

"Please? Claudine said yes and Borros offered to fetch the horses. He even said he would carry me to the stable to see them."

Ivelle smoothed Emmi's hair. "Then why ask me?"

"Because you and Claudine are who really take care of me, like my family did before they left."

Tears stung Ivelle's eyes at the simple statement. She'd given up hope for a sister after the attack, but Emmi helped fill that space in her heart. "Go change into pants and a heavy shirt. Don't forget your cloak, ear muffs, mittens, and scarf."

"I'll look like a bundle of wool instead of a human."

"Better a bundle of wool than a frozen human. Those are my conditions. Go. I will meet you out here."

Emmi chirped her thanks.

"Is she your sister?"

Ivelle turned at the voice. A matronly woman stood before the counter like she thought she was the queen of Orm. A red velvet gown draped over her wide frame and made the rouge dotting fleshy cheeks look pale.

"No."

"Good." The woman sniffed. "To have a sister in that condition would mar your marital prospects."

"Excuse me?"

"Just look at her, dear. Afflicted with stars know what, covered in that unsightly rash, and her fingers are just repulsive. Our king would not be pleased if he knew such an unproductive and hideous life existed."

"A good king would base the value of his people's lives on who they are, not what they look like or can and cannot do. Emmi is a sweet girl whose personality makes yours look repulsive and smell like a decaying deer." Ivelle could not keep the snarl from her voice. "Before you step into our store, ma'am, I suggest you reconsider insulting those who live here."

She turned her back on the woman's spluttering and brushed past Claudine. Once in her room, she slammed the door. The gall of that...that bloated fish.

Ivelle yanked on her riding clothes and snapped her cloak around the base of her throat. Emmi and Borros were waiting as she stepped into the hallway.

Emmi grinned. "I'm ready."

"I see that." Ivelle braided Emmi's unruly curls. "Let's go."

The bloated fish stood in the same spot when they emerged. The overabundance of flesh dangling beneath her chin jiggled as she waved her arms, spouting something about disrespect.

Ivelle huffed. The woman was right in one regard. King Eligor would be most displeased if he knew Emmi existed, though not for the reason the woman presumed.

So help him if he tried taking Emmi.

The sun shone pale against the ice blue sky. People bustled along the street, acclimated to the constant breeze. Voices rose in barter, greeting, and laughter.

How could they act so cheery when a tyrant, a murderer, ruled them?

"Here we are." Borros opened the two double doors of a wooden building at the end of the business sector. "My friend runs this place. Has some of the best horses in Varway. Out back opens to a corral and pasture. That door over there leads to the tack room, and up on that loft is where his office and the grain supply are."

"I like that horse." Emmi pointed to a red roan tethered between a sorrel and dun. "It's pretty."

"He's a good looking one, but temperamental. I purchased him from Rex Dorcha's stable master. Man was eager to rid himself of the beast. Said he can be ridden but is selective."

"Does Claudine know you bought a horse you cannot ride?" Ivelle patted a palomino mare's muzzle. "She won't be happy if you endanger yourself."

"Ivelle, my *job* endangers me."

"How does helping Claudine put you in danger?" Emmi patted Borros' arm to be let down. She limped toward the red roan gelding. "Hi, boy. Borros says you're grumpy."

Ivelle followed Borros three stalls down. She attuned her ears to his voice and her eyes to Emmi as the little girl carried a one-sided conversation with the gelding.

"She will have to ride with one of us."

"I know." There was no way Emmi could stay in the saddle and hold the reins. "I assume she will be with me. Which horse will we ride?"

"The palomino. Emmi should get a thrill out of the coat and mane colors." Borros dragged a hand down his face. "I know that horse."

"What do you mean?"

"I have seen that horse before. Remember that royal bodyguard you dug a bolt from? That's the horse I pulled him and the princess off of."

Ivelle eyed the horse. Its color wasn't common, but it wasn't rare. "There are other red roans in Varway. Even more in Orm."

"I think I know the same horse when I see it," Borros dryly replied. "Darn thing tried the same method to bite me. Wait until I'm close enough before pinning his ears back and lunging with those big teeth. Plus, that's the only red roan I've seen with a pastern marking on its right foreleg. That gelding is healthy, young, and fast. There is no reason it should be sold."

A pit formed in Ivelle's stomach. Had the one soldier she didn't hate died?

Had Therese changed her mind and completed her mission?

"A little stiff?" Claudine grinned over the teacup's rim. "You haven't ridden in a while."

"I'm being reminded of that." Ivelle hobbled to the table and sighed as she sat. "Is this how you feel? Old and worn down and sore?"

"I'm getting there." Claudine pressed her lips and joined Ivelle. "Borros told me of your conversation about Mort and the king. I don't know what to say except be careful. Even though you disagree with King Eligor, you must still present a façade of honor. What you pulled yesterday with that customer almost pushed the line."

"You mean the decaying fish?" The hovering worry increased its attack. This was how Claudine would begin a conversation telling her one more mess up meant removal.

Claudine laughed. "Only you, Ivelle. All I ask is that you take heed and care. Borros and I are concerned about you. Emmi's family did nothing wrong, and look what happened to them."

Ivelle sagged into her chair. "I know."

Something flashed in Claudine's eyes that set a premonition growing in the back of Ivelle's mind. "If this continues, and the king suspects you, you will not be able to stay here."

Throat thickening, Ivelle swallowed. So here it was. "I—"

"What I mean, Ivelle, is that if this grows worse and suspicion turns to you, you will have to leave Orm."

CHAPTER THIRTY-SEVEN

HOLDER

"WAKE UP."

The feminine voice floated around Holder like it was made of smoke. He fought the darkness filling his vision and cracked an eye open. The assassin who had haunted his steps for weeks gripped the door's bars.

Dressed in her usual dark gray with a cloth obscuring from the bridge of her nose down, she appeared little more than a shadow.

The first time she arrived, she meant to kill him. To keep him from experiencing the awaiting punishment, she had said. That visit ended with her silently slipping away. Later, the guards had raised a ruckus about the missing key to his cell.

Holder kept his expression still to keep from irritating the fresh bruise still stinging his cheek. He'd been locked up for stars knew how long. It was obvious he couldn't steal the key.

Innocent. He had protested his innocence to Rogan and Officer Torgord. Would either believe him?

He clenched his fist to keep that familiar, sharp pang at bay. He'd known Rogan for years. Was his friend truly so blinded by his aspirations that he refused to see the truth?

The assassin unlocked the door and entered. "Keep silent and stand up."

Holder struggled to his feet. His leg protested, stiff at sitting for so long. He hissed a breath as he placed full weight on it. If she intended harm, he possessed little defensive ability.

She glided to his side. "You can walk?"

"Yes."

"Good. Say nothing and follow me." She turned and led him from the cell and down the aisle.

The hairs on Holder's neck prickled as the other prisoners stared at him. He recoiled as he entered the small foyer. The two guards slumped over the table, bodies still. "Did you—"

"They still live. Be quiet."

Holder risked grabbing her arm. He spun her around and stared into calculating blue eyes. "What are you doing?"

Her eyes narrowed. "Helping you escape. Now, please keep quiet. We haven't much time before someone comes down."

How had she slipped through security? Usually King Eligor doubled the guards when he perceived a threat.

The assassin led him up the stairs and into the hallway before turning down a dark corridor. "Do you know where this leads?"

"To a side door."

"Yes." Her fingers dug into his bicep. "A horse is waiting for you outside the door. Mount it and ride."

"They'll see me." As much as he appreciated her attempt, she clearly knew little if she thought he could slip away without notice.

"Yes, they will, which is why you have the horse. I'll go before you and try to take down one or two, but it is unlikely I'll be able to neutralize any more than that."

Holder's skin crawled at the knowledge that she could slit his throat where he stood and he'd never see it coming. "Why are you doing this? You've tried to kill me at least two other times."

"If you continue asking questions they will catch us. Let's go."

Despite the premonition in the back of his mind, Holder followed. His heartbeat quickened as the door approached. He really was escaping. Really was destroying any chance of clearing his name and proving his innocence.

Was it worth it?

"Come on," the assassin hissed.

He limped forward. Good thing she didn't expect him to run.

She worked the door open and pulled him outside.

Bright sunlight stung his eyes, but the fresh air helped ease the nagging hint of a cough in his lungs and chest. A saddled chestnut mare stood paces away. Average height, sturdy legs made for short distance sprints, and in good shape.

A dependable horse as far as quality and breeding went.

"Come on."

He held his breath as he approached the mare. Anyone could see them at any time. What would happen if that occurred before they reached the bridge?

And how would they get across the bridge?

Holder mounted. "There's no way your plan will work. Archers are at a shout's notice. You'll be shot down before you have a chance. Get on." She might still be planning to kill him, but she aided his escape from the dungeon. He owed her this, at least.

She hesitated before mounting behind him, one arm around his waist while the other hand gripped a knife. "Ride at a trot. When we reach the bridge, change to a canter. She's not the fastest, but she'll get us to Varway or the forest's edge. Your choice."

Holder signaled the mare to trot. Each bounce sent pain through his leg. He swallowed as his stomach lurched and his fingers chilled. If they caught the guards by surprise they might have a chance. It would take them time to prepare horses and, if they were too busy shouting at them, the archers wouldn't be signaled.

"Hey!"

The mare lurched into a canter. Holder adjusted his grip and balance and shifted forward. So much for waiting.

The bridge guards stepped into the mare's path, spears angled.

"Keep riding," the assassin ordered.

The guards faltered as the mare neared. Holder grit his teeth at the private insignias on their cheeks. They'd likely lose their positions after this.

If the mare made it through.

"Hold your breath." The assassin flung pale yellow powder at the first guard. He doubled over, wailing. The second guard did the same as the powder poofed around her face.

"We need to go faster." Both arms wrapped around Holder. "I see them."

Holder patted the mare's neck and nudged her to a gallop. "She won't last long at this pace." Especially while carrying double weight.

When Rex Dorcha disappeared from sight, Holder maneuvered the mare into the forest and slowed her to a trot. The league passed too slowly. His skin crawled. King Eligor wouldn't just let him escape. How many soldiers was the king assembling to hunt him down?

He drew a breath to steady his pounding heart. It chaffed, his life being in the hands of an assassin, but right now, she was his best chance at survival.

When the path disappeared, Holder risked reining the mare back onto the road. Sweat flecked the mare's coat as Varway's gate loomed less than one hundred paces away, and her steady trot faltered.

The assassin gasped. "Archers!"

So soon? Doom spread through Holder. There was no way they could outmaneuver archers. He again urged the mare to a gallop.

The mare screamed as she stumbled and crashed.

Holder kicked himself free of the stirrups and rolled off the downed animal's back. Breath fled his lungs as his shoulder collided with a stone.

"Come on. *Run.*" The assassin grabbed his hand and helped him up.

Holder fought away the pain throbbing through his leg and bolted. Blood pounding and heart crashing against his chest, his boots hammered the dirt road. *Run*, his mind commanded. *Flee*, his body urged.

Arrows peppered the road around them as the gate approached. Holder gasped for breath. He could make it. He had to.

So much for proving my innocence.

If anything, running solidified it in King Eligor's mind.

"In the name of King Eligor, stop!"

By the stars. Holder borrowed one of Rogan's favorite curses. If the soldiers were close enough to call the command, they'd be on them in minutes. At least no soldiers milled around the gate.

"This way." The assassin sprinted ahead, the short, dark gray dress flapping about her knees.

"Stop! Stop them!"

Townsfolk stared past Holder like the command confused them. Some startled while others darted away.

"Come on," the assassin snapped. She turned more corners until the business district's hustle and bustle dimmed the shouts.

Fire flared through Holder's side. A knife embedded next to his foot, the red hilt flashing.

Go, go.

A hand caught his shirt and yanked him into an alleyway. "That brick building two alleys down. That's where we're going."

Holder stumbled as the assassin led him behind a tarped mound. Firewood protruded from the bottom. He pressed a hand to his side as warmth spread along his shirt and dampened his palm.

"I think we lost them." The assassin panted as she braced her hands on her knees and gulped for breath. Strands of dark auburn hair danced about her face, puffing up with each heavy exhale. Sweat glistened on her forehead.

Shouts and screams filled the air.

"But not for long," she muttered. She adjusted her face cloth and stared at Holder. Her eyes widened. "You were hit."

Holder fought for breath and sagged against the building. His surroundings dipped and blurred.

"Here's a fresh footprint," a familiar voice called.

Nausea rose in Holder's throat. He had considered Juan a friendly acquaintance. Now he was an enemy.

Would Rogan be the same?

"We need to get inside. Put more pressure on the injury." The assassin slung his right arm across her shoulders.

Holder stumbled. His body resisted movement, fighting it like he swam through a substance much thicker than water.

The sharp scent of herbs and fragrances snapped him into a higher level of awareness. He stood before a table covered in crates and filled pouches. Bookcases and cabinets lined the walls.

The assassin jammed a chair under the door latch. "Stay here. I'm going to—"

Holder staggered back as the other door burst open. He should have known hiding would backfire. His hand fumbled for a sword not there as a swell of energy fueled him.

"What is going on? What are you doing? You should be recovering," a dark-haired young woman barked.

Ivelle. That was her name. The girl who helped him with the bolt injury.

"He's hurt. They're after him."

Ivelle stared at Holder for what felt like days, eyes sweeping to his side, then his leg, then back to his face. "Keep pressure on the injury. And stay silent, both of you." She moved the largest bookcase aside to reveal an opening in the wall. "This leads you to the attic. Don't move around too much, and walk softly. Too loud and they will hear you below. I'll be up in a few."

The assassin peered into the hole. "The stairs are not wide enough. We cannot fit side-by-side."

"I can make it." Holder forced the words. Ivelle showed him kindness before, but why would she risk her life for a man now surely labeled traitor and wanted?

Only the dim light streaming through the miniscule entrance provided a way to see the stairs' dim outlines. Smooth wood brushed under Holder's hand as he gripped the railing. These were used often.

Sweat dripped down his face and his lungs struggled for breath when he reached the top stair. Rafters, a sloped ceiling, and stacks of crates, items, and trunks marked the room a storage space. Hopefully his pursuers would not find the building's schematics and locate the stairs.

"Sit." The assassin tugged off her gloves and readjusted Holder's hand over his wound. "You do not feel like you will pass out, do you?"

"Not yet." His words dragged and slurred. It required too much energy to speak. Too much effort to plan what to say.

"How is he?" Ivelle stepped into the room.

"Weak. The bleeding will not stop. It's not even slowing down."

Holder forced his eyes open. Ivelle spread a blanket on the floor before kneeling beside him. She removed his hand and scowled.

"I'm going to cut off your shirt. You smell like you've been in a dungeon."

Holder stared at the knife in Ivelle's hand. Where had it come from? Didn't she know the assassin could take it and still kill him? His back arched as a new throb of pain spasmed through his side. The assassin placed her hands on his shoulders, pinning him down.

Ivelle cut through his shirt and slowly removed it. "Did you see what hit you?"

"A knife," he gasped. The pain continued, relentless. Worsening.

"What did it look like?"

"I think…the hilt was red. Looked…looked like snakes."

The assassin's intake of air matched Ivelle's. The brunette scowled and grabbed a cloth. "Press this to his side. I'll be right back." When she returned, she placed a cup to Holder's lips. "Drink. Now."

Water filled his mouth. Holder choked at the heat as he swallowed. It burned his tongue and throat. Was this a quick way of killing him so he didn't suffer?

"Cayenne powder." Ivelle sprinkled red-brown powder onto Holder's injury. "It is the only thing what will stop such severe bleeding. You were hit by an eligor blade, the deadliest weapon in existence. It tears open the flesh and everything beneath and creates continual bleeding. This should help the blood clot. Once it does, I'll clean the wound and stitch it."

Holder writhed beneath the assassin's hold as agony consumed him. A simple cut shouldn't hurt this bad. He struggled for breath as cold filled his body.

A distant voice said something about fever and infection. Pressure tugged at the grimy bandages around his thigh injury.

A cry lodged in his throat. Why couldn't he draw enough air? Why did everything tilt toward the consuming darkness invading his vision?

Fingertips brushed his forehead, a woman soothing him with gentle shushes and reassurances he would be okay.

Everything faded.

CHAPTER THIRTY-EIGHT

"HE WILL NEED time to heal." Ivelle held the needle used to stitch Holder's wound. Blood dripped from the pointy end. "Just what is going on, Therese? First I'm all but kidnapped and threatened to heal you, then you sneak in the back with the princess' bodyguard, who's covered in blood and has been in the dungeon."

Therese flipped off her hood and removed the cloth over her nose and mouth. How much should she tell Ivelle? She sighed. The majority, probably, since she was risking her life. But still, she had her sisters to think about. What Ivelle didn't know wouldn't hurt her. "He is wanted for treason because a book, *Verum*, was found in his saddlebag. He's innocent."

Ivelle continued cleanup, intermittently checking Holder to see if his fever worsened. "Go on."

How could she be so calm? Therese rubbed her stomach. If this continued, eating breakfast would be for naught. "I broke him out."

"How did you get in?"

"I threw some old, fancy dress over my normal clothes and said I was there to visit on of the soldiers." The hideous pink thing was still at Rex Dorcha where she left it stuffed behind a door.

"And the guards?"

"A special sleeping powder. You're taking this well."

Ivelle answered with a dry laugh. "Trust me. This fits in with the past few days. Why did you bring him here?"

Therese stared at Holder. He lay on his side, one hand clutching the blanket between him and the floor. He had slumped into unconsciousness when Ivelle was halfway through cleaning his wound, knocked out by pain and weakness.

"I knew you could help his leg wound. I didn't know he'd been hit until we stopped. They traced our footprints down the alley."

"You mean they know he's here?"

"I didn't see a blood trail when I looked, but they might conduct a search." Therese rubbed her eyes. The implications of what she had done were beginning to crash on her. "You can keep him safe?"

Ivelle studied her as though doing so would open Therese's mind and reveal everything. With a sigh, she nodded.

"Ivelle? Visitors," a man called.

"No," Ivelle whispered. "They're here. Follow me. He'll be out for a while. You need to change."

Therese swallowed the new swell of fear as she followed Ivelle down the stairs. Ivelle shoved the bookcase over the entry and beckoned Therese to come. She crept down the same hallway she'd led Therese through when Holder had been shot. Deep voices mixed with Claudine's to create chaos.

"Soldiers," Ivelle ground out. "They'll know something is up. I can't look through our premade clothing without being seen. You'll have to wear one of my dresses." She opened a door and dragged Therese inside.

A bed was shoved against the wall, with a dresser, nightstand, and chair being the only other furniture items. Dresses hung from hooks in a small alcove.

Ivelle tossed a blue dress to Therese. "Change. I'm going to see what's going on."

"Be careful." Therese clutched the dress. What would happen if Ivelle was discovered?

"Don't worry. This isn't the first time."

Therese yanked off her dress as soon as the door closed and pulled on Ivelle's. The material bunched around her feet, illustrating the four inches difference in their height. She froze as shoes pounded the floor before kicking her dress under the bed.

"And what's in here?" The door flew open. A man in simple armor stared at her, blinking.

Therese scowled at him over her shoulder as she laced up the bodice. Best play the part of an affronted young lady and not an assassin in disguise.

"My apologies, miss." The man's narrow eyes thinned and the emblem on his cheek shifted. "I am Officer Torgord, miss. I hate to intrude on your privacy, but I am obligated to ask why you are changing."

Therese fumbled the ties. "I went riding with my friend. My horse stumbled and threw me into the mud. 'Tis a long way home, so my friend offered to loan me a change of clothes so I wouldn't catch ill."

Officer Torgord stared at her like he suspected she hid something. "And where are these dirtied clothes, miss?"

"Nora, I—oh, I beg your pardon, sir. Is something wrong?" Ivelle peered over the officer's shoulder.

"Not at all, miss. I was merely validating your friend's— Nora, is it?—Miss Nora's story."

Ivelle tsked. Her expression, though a smile, was stiff. "Such a shame, it was. Why, you should have seen her fly over her mare's head. I never knew I could pray so fast. Nora doesn't feel any injuries, but her riding suit was torn and covered in mud. Mother's cleaners will have a time of it scrubbing that filthy thing clean."

"Your mother is Claudine DeGrim?"

"Why, Officer, do you not think I look like her? People say I do. 'Twould be better than looking like my father. Mother oft compares him to an oversized, utterly cantankerous black bear."

"Is that so?"

Panic bloomed in Therese's chest. He didn't believe them. "Did Claudine think it could be cleaned?"

"Eventually, though it may never be the same color. Such a fine garment, too, with that beautiful stitching. And such a beautiful pale pink. A true shame."

Officer Torgord backed from the room. "I apologize for intruding on your privacy, Miss Nora. Ladies, it sounds like you both are independent and know your way around Varway. A dangerous criminal suspected of treason has escaped, aided by a female assassin, and we believe they are in the vicinity. Please be cautious and let us know if you see them."

"An assassin?" Therese's voice squeaked. "There are assassins in Varway?"

Officer Torgord's mustache lifted with his thin smile. "Of course, Miss Nora. They are certified by the king. Keeps the population down and people in check."

"I had no idea. Do they harm normal citizens?"

"They never have in the past. Listen, ladies. I must continue my search. Good day and, again, please alert the nearest soldier if you see the criminals. Announcements will be going up this afternoon."

Announcements? Therese gripped the dresser's edge as the room tilted in a dangerous slant. She was a criminal. Wanted. Hunted by the most powerful man in the world.

"He's gone." Ivelle shut the door and placed a hand on Therese's shoulder. "You alright? You're almost as pale as Holder. Is it your injury?"

"I'm a wanted criminal," Therese whispered. True, no one knew it was her, but Jolie and Lucian were smart enough to fill in the missing information and, if Scholl caught wind, Therese would be clapped in chains and thrown into the dungeon.

"Therese…"

"What will happen to my sisters? The guards have a general sense of what I look like, my size, and what I wear."

"Therese." Ivelle guided her to the bed. "Breathe. Everything will work out. I am going to go check on Claudine and Borros and Holder. After that, we must tell them."

"They will turn him over." Despite being her target, she felt a connection with Holder. Perhaps it was the fact they'd both lost their parents, or the way he treated her when she snuck into Argus', or how he protected the princess with such gentleness and courage.

"No, they will not." Ivelle withdrew a book from her dresser and handed it to Therese. "A few days ago they discovered I was reading this. They did not evict me or turn me in as they could have—as they are obligated to do. They told me they trusted me. That trust will carry over into this. Stay here. When I return, they will be with me."

⬦⬦ • • • • ⬦⬦

A floorboard creaked.

Therese stiffened and readjusted her weight. No lights shone in the windows or rooms. No one stirred. She swallowed and continued into the office. Closing the door, she lit a candle and set it on the desk. The desk was where she'd seen him store the money, but was that just to throw everyone off?

A quick search led her to the right-hand drawers. The bottom drawer revealed velvet bags filled with coins. Therese withdrew the smallest one and squinted at the label.

Her name, written in Scholl's quick scrawl. She slipped it into her pouch and extinguished the candle.

Nothing moved as she snuck upstairs and into the room right next to her sisters'. The fresh bandage protecting her injury hindered her movements as she slipped off the simple black dress Claudine had procured.

Surely the search party wouldn't investigate Scholl's this late in the night. Scholl once mentioned there were other businesses in competition with theirs; hopefully, that was where they would look first.

Hope. Therese bit back a bitter laugh. Everything rested on hope. She *hoped* they wouldn't come to Scholl's. She *hoped* Jolie and Lucian wouldn't uncover her identity as the mystery assassin. She *hoped* she could protect her sisters from her foolish and idiotic actions. What had possessed her?

He's innocent.

Therese curled under the heavy blankets. Come sunrise, she wouldn't have time to even sit and take a breather.

"Nora, Delli. Come on." Therese shook the two bodies swathed in blankets. "Time to get up."

Nora grumbled as she shifted away. "Jolie lets us sleep in."

"You are not sleeping in today. Come on, Nora. Up you go. You too, Delli. I know you're listening."

Delli's little giggle struck Therese's heart like a knife. If only there was a place they'd be safe. If only there was a different way. If only she'd considered the ramifications of helping her target.

The Westa girls stuck together. That was what she promised Mother all those years ago, staring at the gaunt, pale face through a curtain of tears.

And sticking together meant taking them with her.

If only she needn't choose who survived between her innocent sisters and her innocent target.

"Come on, sillies." She kept her tone light. No need to burden their sweet little hearts with what happened.

"'M up, 'm up." Nora staggered out of bed. "Why? What are we doing today?"

"I'm taking you home." The lie weighed on her soul.

"Don't wanna go home." Delli pooched her bottom lip out and stared at Therese with wide eyes, an expression only Lucian could have taught her. He employed the expression more than once, usually in attempts to wheedle Jolie into going on walks with him. "Hungwy at home."

Another way she failed them. "Not anymore, sweetie. Come on. Let's see if you can get dressed faster than Nora."

Sneaking down the stairs proved much more difficult with two children under age ten. Therese grabbed them some slices of bread from the breadbox and ushered them out.

"We riding?" Delli pointed at two of the three horses Therese had brought back to Varway.

"Yes." Therese shushed her with a finger to the lips. "Nora, you will ride on the smaller horse. Delli will ride with me."

The silent streets fed the silent anxiety holding Therese in its clutches. Something was not right. The normal amount of guards stood in their usual places. Where were the extra soldiers? Was the king no longer concerned? Or—*stars forbid*—had he traced Holder to Ivelle's?

"Why're we going home?" Nora sat upon her horse stiff as a sword's blade, arms crossed and face scrunched in a scowl.

"Hold on to the reins, Nora."

"Still doesn't answer my question."

"Trust me."

Trust. A word that could make or destroy a person.

A word that could be their undoing.

CHAPTER THIRTY-NINE

ROGAN

THERE WERE DAYS where Rogan questioned if he possessed any luck

When a thin, reedy fellow in swishing orange robes nearly accosted him as he entered the throne room, he decided the day was definitely a luckless day.

"I am interim herald while my predecessor recovers from being bitten to smithereens by that devilish red horse." Secretary Lanso tutted and tapped his quill against the pad of vellum in his other hand. "That is what happens when one is hasty and attempts to saddle a horse—the wrong horse—without assistance. I digress. King Eligor will now see you." He stared down his narrow nose. A pathetic attempt at a handlebar mustache limply framed the aggravating man's mouth.

If anything, Secretary Lanso more resembled a waterlogged rat than a man.

Rogan scoffed at the supercilious tone. He really wasn't in the mood to deal with an arrogant rodent, and if he wasn't in the castle, he'd give Secretary Lanso his thoughts on the matter.

"Specialist Cetrin."

"My king." Rogan bowed. Spots crowded his vision at the action. Ever since waking up with a bleeding nose and a headache larger than Orm, simple movements threw him off balance and altered his vision.

King Eligor's gaze focused on Rogan's face. "What happened?"

Rogan swallowed the thick lump in his throat. Father's unnatural words replayed through his mind. "I ran into something. I wasn't looking where I walked."

"That happens to the best of us. Tell me, Specialist, did you know Holder Lygor escaped?"

"What?" This was a test. It had to be. No one had ever before escaped the dungeon and its dark cells.

"Two days ago. Where have you been?"

Recovering at home. Sleeping so he couldn't suffer through the headache throbbing through his skull and behind his eyes. "At home, my king. Father—First Lieutenant Cetrin—said nothing about this."

King Eligor rested his chin on his fist. Officer Torgord stood to the left and Captain Geros to the right. "Yes. He was seen escaping into Varway with a female assassin who somehow incapacitated two dungeon guards and the soldiers stationed at the bridge and the left wall. Captain Geros nicked him with an eligor blade, but they still disappeared."

What was an eligor blade? Why would Holder run? If he was innocent the truth would emerge. "Why would he do that?"

"We were hoping you could tell us, Specialist, seeing how you two are such close friends."

The statement almost sounded like a threat.

Rogan rubbed his forehead, careful to avoid his sore nose and the area surrounding it. *Why, Holder, why?* Why must his friend make everything more difficult? "The only reason I think he would run is if he didn't believe he would get a fair investigation."

"You believe him innocent?"

"Yes, my king, I do. Holder doesn't think half the time, but when he does, he is smart. He knows better than to read treasonous material."

King Eligor sighed. "That is most unfortunate. Do you think you could find Holder? A fair trial is of utmost importance. If I could, I would release him, but my duty prohibits me. Find him and assure him he will have that fair trial. It is what I give everyone. Holder is a good lad and Anastasia is most upset. Once this fiasco passes, Holder will once again reclaim his bodyguard role."

"Yes, my king."

"Thank you. He was last seen heading down an alley near that ridiculously ostentatious place...what is it called, Torgord?"

"Claudine DeGrim's Emporium, my king."

"Yes, that place." King Eligor grimaced. "Sells worthless items, but that is beside the point. He and the assassin were last seen in that area. Find Holder and bring him back. Wear civilian clothing so you do not scare the townsfolk and alert the assassin."

"Yes, my king." Rogan bowed at Officer Torgord's nod of dismissal. As he reached for the doorway, King Eligor stopped him.

"Specialist?"

"Yes, my king?"

"If you find the assassin, capture her. She will face trial for breaking the law."

"Yes, my king."

Claudine DeGrim's Emporium.

Rogan growled at the women streaming into the place. With the stars' help, he could avoid the steely-eyed Ivelle. He gripped his sword and entered.

Eyes turned to him and hands shielded mouths as whispers and giggles flew.

Great.

"How can I help you?" A mountain of a man approached the counter. The lines between his eyes deepened. "Specialist."

"I need to speak with your proprietress." Rogan held the man's gaze. The man's sheer size and bushy beard likely cowed most, but he was nothing compared to Father.

"Of course." The man's teeth bared in more a snarl than smile, but he couldn't legally refuse the request of a king's guard. "Stay here."

Yeah, right. Stay in almost the middle of the doorway where he could be run over. Stay still so the ladies could begin rumors about the *scandal* of a second king's guard in normal clothing visiting the store.

No.

Rogan perused the displayed axes and daggers. Sharp. Deadly. If anything happened, this emporium had potential for superb defense if anyone knew how to use the weapons.

"Can I help you?" A woman's brisk tone grated his ears. Claudine DeGrim sailed into the room, bright green dress contributing to King Eligor's accurate description. "Specialist."

"This needs to be a private conversation."

"Of course." Lips pursed, she beckoned him to follow. Once within a narrow hallway, she halted and surveyed him with a cold demeanor. "What do you need to say?"

"I am searching for—"

A scuffle sounded from above.

An attic. Of course a place like this had an attic. The ceiling was too low and the rooftop too high for there not to be. Why hadn't he thought of it before?

"You will show me your attic."

"So you are searching for crates and trunks?"

Captain Geros had said confidence and severity were how to persuade people to comply. Rogan drew his sword and leveled it at the woman. "Ms. DeGrim, on the authority of King Eligor, I command you to show me your attic. If you resist, you will be reported and subsequently arrested for hindering an investigation."

Claudine DeGrim swallowed. Though the light dimmed as it filtered into the hallway, it did little to obscure her paling skin. "Borros?"

"This way, *Specialist.*" The man spit the title like it tasted poisonous.

Perhaps it did. These people definitely hid something.

Borros led Rogan into a tiny back room filled with cabinets, bookshelves, and crates. With another glower Rogan's way, Borros moved a bookcase and pushed at the wall, revealing the beginnings of a staircase.

Rogan flicked his sword. "Go on."

Candle in hand, Borros led the way.

Rogan shouldered the man aside when they reached the attic. His heart ceased beating. Holder lay on a pile of blankets, with the dark-haired, sharp-tongued Ivelle kneeling above him. "Get away." He charged her. So help him, if she harmed Holder in any way...

"Rogan, no." Holder's strained voice ceased with a cough. "She's helping."

"Helping? What do you mean, helping? Look at you, you look awful." Thick bandages covered the space between Holder's ribs and waist. Another bandage protected his leg injury. Even in the dim light, Rogan could see the sweat beading along Holder's forehead.

"Rogan…"

"What happened to you? Who did this?" Was that what King Eligor meant when he said Holder had been hit? Why would they nail him in the side when the leg or shoulder made more sense?

"Will you shut up and listen?" Ivelle hefted a knife in her hand. "Why are you here? To spy on and report us?"

"Ivelle," Holder whispered. "Could you give us some space? We need to talk."

"Can you guarantee he won't try anything?"

"Yes."

Rogan ignored the slight pause before Holder's answer. When Ivelle's footsteps faded, he knelt beside his friend. "What happened to you?"

"I was hit. Would have bled out if Ivelle hadn't cared for the wound." Holder slumped down. His hair matted with sweat to his forehead. "You can't tell Eligor."

"King Eligor. By the stars, Holder. What's going on? How did you end up here?"

Holder kept his eyes shut as he relayed his story. "How'd you…find me?"

Curse Holder. Curse that assassin.

Rogan grit his teeth to withhold the sharp words begging for release. "That was stupid, Holder. Just stupid. You made yourself look guilty."

"Do you believe I am?"

"Do I believe you are what?"

"Guilty?"

Rogan rolled his eyes. Of all the things to ask when time ran short. "I believe the evidence will provide the answer. Why'd you run? You would have had a fair trial. You know that." He rubbed his forehead and sighed. "Look. Before I came here, King Eligor assured me you would receive a fair trial, even after running. What are you so afraid of? The king is a man of his word."

Holder stared at Rogan, a hard glint replacing his fatigue. "You really believe that."

"Yes."

"Even after what Argus told us?"

"You heard their reason for sending him away."

"Even after what you read in my father's journal?"

A journal tucked beneath Rogan's mattress. "That's one man's opinion and view. Running always means you're guilty. I know you miss them, but, Holder, your parents were running."

"Running always means guilty, Rogan? Always?" Holder's glare pierced like a blade.

"Almost always."

Holder's jaw worked. "Whatever you believe, please do not report Ivelle and her family."

"They broke the law. Ivelle, twice."

"Ivelle saved my life, Rogan. Kept me from bleeding out. If she hadn't stepped in, I would be dead."

And the lies Holder required of Rogan kept growing. Was the friendship worth it? Lying to the most powerful man in the world? Lying to the king? Lying to one of few who believed Rogan was worthwhile?

"I'll think about it." Rogan ignored Holder's inhale and stood. "Are you able to travel?"

"I'm not going back, Rogan. The assassin was right. I'll never have a fair trial."

"You for sure would if you hadn't been stupid and run," Rogan snapped. What was Holder's problem? Why did he insist on digging himself deeper into a pit easily escaped by simply returning?

"I'm not going, Rogan."

"He would not make it far." Ivelle's sharp tone startled Rogan. "He lost a lot of blood and is unable to walk to the stairs, much less let you drag him to that death trap."

Rogan's grip tightened around his sword's hilt. When had she snuck up? "You are one wrong word away from that *death trap*, as you call it. I would watch what you say."

"Ivelle." The man lumbered into the attic. "Go help Claudine." He turned to Rogan. "You need to leave."

"And you need to keep your daughter in line." Rogan passed the man. When he was halfway to Rex Dorcha he reined Blackie to the road's edge and rested against the mare's neck. What happened to Holder? What would he tell King Eligor?

And if Father heard about his failure… Rogan cringed at the thought.

Why, Holder? By the stars, why?

⟡

"Well?"

Rogan forced himself to meet King Eligor's eyes. "He is weak and unable to travel."

"I gave you an order, Specialist."

Rogan's blood chilled. If he weren't careful, he could end up demoted or with a dagger being revoked. "I know, my king, and I would have hauled Holder back if he were in even a bit better condition. He could hardly hold a conversation, let alone ride. He would be no use dead."

King Eligor leaned back before whispering to Officer Torgord. The man nodded and exited the throne room. King Eligor then spoke with Captain Geros, who shook his head.

"Rogan, I understand your reasoning, but do not do such a thing again. I will let it pass this time, since I see the wisdom in your choice. As a future captain, you must learn that I make the decisions and you see them through. Understood?"

"Yes, my king." Rogan's tongue felt thrice as thick, and he almost stumbled over his reply.

"Very well. Do not let it happen again. I see great things in your future. Do not ruin that by assuming. You are dismissed."

"Yes, my king." Rogan bowed and left. The cold breeze dried his sweat as he stepped outside. The king's words did nothing to quell the burst of panic running its course through his veins. How close he had come.

King Eligor's disappointment was punishment enough for lying for Holder. The warning of almost jeopardizing his future hit like an anvil on the chest.

Rogan fisted his hand. No longer would he allow Holder to jeopardize his future.

CHAPTER FORTY

IVELLE

BREATHE.

Air tainted with blood, sweat, and struggle entered her nose.

Beware your surroundings.

Wood beneath her. Dim voices around her. Crying. Blood lingering on her tongue. Throbbing in the back of her head.

Awaken.

"...wake up."

Open your eyes.

"Come on, Ivelle. Wake up."

Cold hands framed Ivelle's face. She sucked in another breath and forced her eyes open. Colors swirled until merging into Claudine's face. A dark bruise covered her cheek and hair escaped her elaborate bun.

"There you are." Claudine's shoulders lurched with a sob. "You didn't respond."

"Did they take him?" Ivelle commanded her arm to move. Glass cut into her skin.

"Yes. We couldn't stop them." Borros knelt beside Claudine. "He convinced them, though."

"He lied for us?" *To protect us.*

Borros dragged a hand over his face. "Yes, and they didn't find Emmi."

"Careful, Ivelle. Those animals left glass all over. Here, Borros, help me."

Ivelle winced as they drew her into a sitting position. Her head ached where the soldier had hit her. "What is the damage?"

"Enough to force us to close for today and tomorrow. They broke the door and the front window, upset the shelves in the sewing room, and completely destroyed this area. Borros will be busy fixing holes and putting up new mounts for the weapons."

The room swayed as Ivelle stood. Her stomach churned and twisted at the dark spots splattered on the floor.

Blood.

His blood.

Borros took her elbow. "Easy. Don't want you collapsing into a pile of glass shards."

"We failed him," she murmured. The scene replayed with vicious accuracy, highlighting how someone innocent had presumably been taken to his death. "He did nothing wrong."

"We know that, Ivelle."

"Did you hear something?"

Claudine cradled her wrist. Rips marred the stunning pale yellow taffeta dress and dirt dulled the color. "No, but if you trust him, a soldier, then we trust you."

Ivelle's shoulders slumped. After betraying their trust and reading treasonous content, they still trusted her? "Thank you," she whispered.

Glass crunched under footsteps. "What happened?"

Ivelle swayed as she turned. How hard had that soldier hit her?

Therese stood in the doorway, Delli on her hip and Nora partially tucked behind her. The assassin's gaze swept the room before darting between Ivelle and Claudine. "Who did this?"

"King's guards," Borros growled. When Delli whimpered, he sighed. "I didn't mean to scare you, little one. They came in, found what they sought, and left after incurring destruction."

Therese's mouth opened then closed as her face paled. "They took him?"

"Yes."

"We did all we could." For the first time in ten years, Claudine's voice wavered. "We tried."

The room spun again and Ivelle stumbled for the counter. If she could hold on to something, perhaps she wouldn't fall.

"Nora, Delli, do you remember the way to Emmi's room? Yes? Then would you go keep her company and tell her everything is alright? Us grownups are going to play cleanup."

"Good thing I'm not a grownup," Nora muttered as she tugged Delli into the hallway. "I hate cleaning up."

After they disappeared from view, Claudine turned to Therese. "Is everything alright?"

Therese hesitated, but nodded. "They hurt you."

"Aye. One whacked Ivelle on the back of her head. Knocked her out for a bit. Would you help her get to her room? She needs to change before those glass shards cause harm."

Therese glided across the floor without stepping on the scattered glass and tugged Ivelle's arm around her shoulders. "How close to fainting are you?"

Ivelle grunted. Her head throbbed and her body ached, but her spirit raged. "I've never fainted."

"Perhaps not, but you are close to it."

"What are you doing here?" Claudine may have missed the dark circles under Therese's eyes, and her pale face and weary eyes, but Ivelle hadn't.

"I... We just need supplies." Therese opened Ivelle's door. "Go change. Do you need me to check on Emmi?"

"If you wouldn't mind. I'm sure she is terrified after all the shouting and commotion."

Glass clattered to the floor as Ivelle eased out of her dress. Of all the places to land, why did it have to be in glass?

Her hands trembled as she pulled on a shirt and skirt and dug through her dresser's top drawer. Thus far, the book offered little in the way of encouragement, but perhaps she could locate something in its back pages.

"'Golden light pierces the darkness, pushing it away and bringing forth a new day. My brothers and I stand on Uri's highest mountaintop, watching the land slowly awaken. I still cannot believe the glory and power and victory over evil. Only He could do that. Mihai said it reminded him that, just because we are Assistants, doesn't mean we know everything. We certainly did not foresee the incredible display of power witnessed forty days ago. People were always sinful, and mercy and grace were granted through their sacrifices—the sign they truly repented. Now, an equal mix of love and justice combined so all may be saved through One's sacrifice. Sheer glory and awe and majesty fill the kingdom.

"'Behind us lays a land darkened by evil. Eligor and his followers, the Nolemti, have tainted good with their pure hatred. A darkness not visible to the human eye cloaks the land, though our sight pierces the deception weaved into layers of lies. What will become of it? What will become of those whose

minds were warped? Whose hearts were darkened? We asked the King, and He answered with mention of a plan. Whatever it is, His glory can dissipate the darkness, though the darkness will put up a fight.

"'The Prince has said a day will come when, in the darkest dark, light will be seen. What could be darker than the betrayal? Gabreel and Mihai both serve near the King, and they say His plans span every century there ever will be. Wherever those plans place us, may we never forget the glory, mercy, power, and justice of the King, Prince, and Counselor.'"

Ivelle jerked as knuckles rapped against wood. "Come in."

Therese paused mid-step as she entered. Her mouth formed an *o* and her eyes rounded. "Where did you get that book?"

"It was in one of Claudine's orders. Why?"

"I...I..." Therese released a shaky exhale. "That is the book that got Holder in trouble."

The whisper of a warning breathed in the back of Ivelle's mind. "How do you know that?"

Therese cringed. "My job."

⸭

"That's the last of it." Claudine leaned against the counter and exhaled. "For this room, anyway. Therese, thank you for helping us."

The assassin nodded her answer.

Ivelle deposited her muddy rag in the bucket and crossed her arms. Ever since arriving, Therese had acted twitchy. She'd glance at the door ever so often, jerked at sudden sounds, and kept her back to the front window.

"Your cleaning demands ruined my calluses," Borros groused as he dried his hands. Hair wild and beard unkempt, he looked more like a disgruntled cub dressed in soaked garments rather than the mountain of a man he really was.

Claudine rolled her eyes. "We were almost skewered by soldiers and you're worried about your calluses? Come along, you big baby. Grab some buckets and let's go dump them."

When the back door closed, Ivelle faced Therese. The assassin refused to meet her gaze. "What brought you here?"

"Supplies."

"For what? You've come here once for supplies, and I don't think those were even for you."

Therese's shoulders slumped. "Helping Holder escape cost me my job. The girls and I are leaving Varway."

Something was missing, but at the deep weariness dulling Therese's eyes, Ivelle didn't prod. "You want to leave right now? At the beginning of spring? This is hardly the time to travel. Therese, it's a five day journey to the nearest substantial village. Your sisters can't handle that."

"That was the only true job I could find in Varway, Ivelle." Therese's soft voice thinned as her gaze turned icy. "If I don't have a job, I cannot provide for them."

"Still, traveling in early spring? Is there not a temporary job available?"

"Girls." Claudine swept into the room, followed by Borros, who hauled the buckets. "Do keep your voices down. The young ones are napping." She drew the curtains before beckoning. "Come. We need to talk."

Once in the break room, Claudine motioned Therese to the table. "I know your business is your own, but I have been to every village within twenty leagues' distance. None of them save DorFord are suitable for a young woman with even younger sisters."

"Then we will travel to DorFord." Therese brushed stray hair from her face. "Claudine, I came to purchase supplies. My apologies if my sisters and I intruded."

Ivelle stared at her hands. Dirt and dried soap caked her skin. Had she and Therese set off a dangerous chain of events by helping a disgraced soldier? What price would she pay? What if the king decided he did not believe Holder's lie?

"Here." Borros removed a framed map from the wall and placed it on the tabletop. "If you plan on travelling, there are things you need to know. Ivelle, pay attention. This will affect you as well."

"Where did you get this?" Ivelle leaned over the map. Rough edges lined yellowed animal skin covered in dark ink. "This is ancient."

"Borros recently acquired it." Claudine leaned into Borros, gracing him with a tender smile.

Ivelle's throat thickened.

Borros' thick finger rested near DorFord. "Whenever you see the prefix 'Dor' it means the village primarily trades goods and supplies. Villages without it produce most of what they need, and only trade with neighboring villages for the necessities they themselves cannot make. Villages with a line under their name indicate they are on the main trading route. For those without, you must take paths often difficult to find."

Therese hugged herself as she peered at the map. She always acted nervous, but this was almost ridiculous. "How do you know this? My employer knows almost everything, and he knows nothing about this."

Borros smirked. "Part of the job."

Why would he hint to Therese what they truly did? Ivelle rubbed her arms. The morning's fiasco, combined with the blow to the head, incessant scrubbing, and trying to figure out Therese created a headache.

"You import things?"

"Yes."

Therese's eyes widened. "You...oh. *Oh.* You're smugglers?" Her shoulders hunched as she shrank into the chair. "Ah, how—how many of you are there?"

"We smuggle in illegal goods that will bring us profit. We don't know for sure how many of us there are and that is how it needs to be," Claudine murmured. "Secrecy and discretion are necessary. We keep a tight rein on who knows what and who does what. Borros has his group of men, but they aren't exactly King Eligor's idea of model citizens."

If possible, Therese looked even warier. More vulnerable. Almost like a mouse attempting to hide from the cat cornering it. "Then why are you telling me?"

"Because of what you did for Holder. And because we will help you leave Varway."

✦ ⋯ ✦

"Take the girls. Please."

Ivelle curled under her duvet as Therese's begging infiltrated the walls. Her heart ached. That the sisters might be separated was upsetting, but for the best. Taking Nora and Delli was only slightly better than taking Emmi. Travel in the summer proved no easy task, let alone during the cold, rainy springtime.

"We can't, Therese. We can't break up your family like that, even if it is for their own good."

"If there is any option I can take besides dragging them into the mountains, I will take it. Please, please. I will pay and—and repay and—and I'll return for them as soon as I have a job."

"Oh, Therese."

Ivelle could imagine Claudine placing her hands on the assassin's shoulders.

"Borros and I are under suspicion due to them finding Holder here. We already have one young one to take care of. We cannot, in good conscience, put two more children in such a predicament. I am sorry we cannot help that way, but we will provide anything you need. Food, clothing, cooking and camping supplies, horses—whatever you need. For free."

A chair scraped on wood. "Thank you for hearing me out." Therese's voice sounded hollow. "We have horses stabled nearby."

"Stay for the night. Like Claudine said, we will provide you whatever you need. I can even arrange for someone I trust to escort you the first two leagues."

"We will be fine. Again, thank you."

Ivelle crept into the break room after Claudine bid Borros good night. Therese hid something, something important, but the desperation in her eyes, voice, and demeanor was genuine. There had to be a way the girls could stay behind until Therese was ready.

"I wondered when you would show." One lone candle cast equal shadow and light across Claudine's face. "You overheard the conversation?"

"Yes." Ivelle sank into a chair. The day's events crashed down on her. The soldiers barging into the emporium. Holder being all but dragged out, his hands bound behind his back. The trail of blood. Therese and her sisters.

"And?" In the candlelight, Claudine looked like a spectral entity lingering in the shadows.

"I heard your reasoning for not taking the girls, but I think they will be alright. Nora has enough fire in her to help me in the store and Delli would be a good companion for

Emmi. I know she gets lonely, and I am unable to spend as much time with her as she deserves."

"Ivelle…"

"Please? I know I would feel the same way if I were in Therese's place. She loves her sisters, and for them to travel in early springtime, with snow, frigid winds, multiple rainstorms, and no shelter for the night could prove fatal."

Claudine took Ivelle's hand. The way the candlelight glimmered made it look like tears gathered in her eyes. "Ivelle, trust me, please. We will speak of this tomorrow, after I speak with Borros. We told Therese to stay here for a few days so we can ensure we have the supplies they need."

Ivelle withdrew. "What is the difference between a few days and a few months? If we can keep them safe, shouldn't we? Is that not our obligation?"

"Ivelle, there are things at work you know nothing about. I understand you, and I agree. But you do not, cannot, fully comprehend our reasoning. I promise it will all work out. Perhaps not in the way you think best, but it will work out."

Knuckles rapped against wood before the door swooshed open.

Ivelle forced herself to fully awaken. A distorted, dark blur moved toward her, emitting the perfume Claudine claimed smelled like her favorite flower.

"Are you awake, Ivelle?"

Ivelle burrowed into her mattress. "No."

Claudine chuckled before brushing hair from the side of Ivelle's face. Her hand trembled and, ever so often, her breath would hitch. "Ivelle, I need you to wake up. Right now. No, hear me out. I need you to follow my instructions to the word.

Get up and change into the outfit on your dresser then meet me in the break room.”

Full awareness rushed into Ivelle, and she sat. “Why? What’s going on?”

“Just obey, Ivelle. Please?”

After blindly struggling into an outfit that felt similar to how Therese’s assassin uniform looked, Ivelle stumbled into the break room. She grumbled under her breath as she peeked past a curtain. Darkness spread across the sky.

By the stars, why was Claudine getting her up so early?

“Come along, Ivelle. We haven’t much time.”

“What are you doing?” Ivelle blinked the break room into focus. Therese sat at the table, a cup in her hands and a plate of toast and eggs before her. Claudine stood near the window, arms crossed and forehead pinched.

“The girls are getting dressed. Sit and eat.”

“Claudine?”

Therese stood. “I will check on the girls.” She padded from the room, no expression on a face still marked by exhaustion.

“Ivelle.” Claudine crossed the room. “Dear, I need you to obey everything Borros and I tell you.” She cupped Ivelle’s cheek. “Dear girl, you filled a void I never knew I had.”

Ivelle’s stomach dropped. Foreboding churned within like a storm. She clutched Claudine’s wrist.

“You’ve been a greater help than you realize, Ivelle. I imagined losing you to some young man who swept you off your feet.” Claudine sniffled a watery chuckle. “Not this way. No, listen for a bit more. You’ve been a joy in mine and Borros’ lives, but it is time for you to move on.”

“Claudine…”

"Your opinions about the king, you reading that book, and your involvement with Holder are putting you in danger."

Ivelle's mouth dried and her lungs struggled for breath. Claudine wanted her gone? Where would she go? What would she do? How would she survive?

Claudine exhaled and stroked Ivelle's hair. "My dear, dear girl, you are going with Therese."

CHAPTER FORTY-ONE

HOLDER

COLD AIR BLEW through the small, barred window just above Holder's head. Chains clanked with his shiver and he grit his teeth as pain throbbed through his thigh and side. Fatigue ragged at his senses, but if he dared close his eyes, all his weight would be transferred to his arms and shoulders.

How long?

He had tracked the shadows until Officer Torgord entered, but time eluded him.

Rogan. Holder grit his teeth as his knees threatened to buckle. He saw the struggle in Rogan's eyes. The battle between their friendship and Rogan's loyalty to the king. Heaviness filled his chest. No one was taken but himself, but what damage had been inflicted?

'You know what they do to traitors. Do you want to face that? They will not believe you. Not if Captain Geros and Lieutenant Cetrin speak against you.' The assassin's words revisited once again.

Ivelle said something similar, an odd, almost dark glare in her eyes. *'There is no such thing as true justice. Eligor will do anything to eliminate perceived threats. And you are a threat.'*

A threat? How? What had he done to threaten the king? No word had been said about his father's journal or mother's letter, so they must not have found those. What grievous thing had he done so that they would target and falsely accuse him?

Metal clanked as a guard opened the cell door. First Lieutenant Cetrin and Juan entered the cell.

Holder's blood turned to ice at the grin spreading across the first lieutenant's bearded face. Officer Torgord's interrogation consisted of questions and multiple punches. The first lieutenant...he thrived by inflicting pain.

Would Holder be a bloody mess for his trial?

"Time to answer to your crimes, traitor," First Lieutenant Cetrin rumbled. He unlocked Holder's wrists and secured them behind his back. Thick, rough rope bit into the tender flesh rubbed raw by the shackles.

With the first lieutenant's grip crushing his collarbone and Juan's sword hovering near his side, Holder limped from the cell. With every lurching step his leg threatened to give, and without his arms it was difficult keeping his balance. His side sent shards of hot agony throughout his torso with every breath.

Death, death, death. The word repeated in his mind, in sync with his pulse. This was the end. He was going to die.

The thought left him oddly numb.

Holder's heart thudded as First Lieutenant Cetrin pushed him into the main hall. Soldiers filled the back half in neat, precise rows. King Eligor sat on his throne, flanked by Captain Geros and Officer Torgord. Both groups of king's guards joined them.

He scanned the faces. Where was Rogan?

"On your knees, traitor." First Lieutenant Cetrin shoved Holder down.

King Eligor laced his fingers, but it was Officer Torgord who spoke. "Holder Lygor, the first charge against you is treason upon discovery of traitorous materials in your possession. After being detained and put in holding until further discourse could be had, you escaped and were subsequently found at Claudine DeGrim's Emporium. You claim you forced them to help you. Is this true?"

"Yes, sir." Holder's voice rasped. Lack of water made it feel like sand lined his throat. Why did Officer Torgord ask the questions? They were the same ones he asked during the interrogation. Was this not King Eligor's decision? The king's duty to interrogate?

"How? You were injured. They could have killed you."

"I lied. I told them I was injured by a criminal, that they were the closest medical help I could get." His head and torso rocked forward as metal slammed the back of his head.

"Address him with respect, traitor."

"So you made them help you by appealing to their pity?"

"Yes, sir."

Captain Geros stepped forward, hand on sword and cape swishing. "Who is the female assassin who helped you escape?"

"I don't know." Holder grit his teeth as First Lieutenant Cetrin delivered another blow. Why did he demand the same level of respect given to the king?

"Who gave you the book?"

"No one. I've never heard of it."

Another smack.

The floor blurred as his eyes watered and dark spots gathered around his vision.

King Eligor leaned forward. His robe's wide sleeves slid down his arm, revealing black tattoos. "Do you take us as foolish?" Danger lurked in his voice like a rattlesnake hiding behind a rock.

"No, my king." Holder blinked the room into focus as warmth dribbled down the back of his neck. The ache in his leg and side worsened to where he tensed his jaw while speaking to keep his accusers from hearing his pain.

"Then cease acting like it," the king snarled. "I did not become king by being a blind fool, nor did Torgord and Geros become like advisor and son to me by accepting the words of the accused. We are not dumb sheep who tolerate a wolf in our midst."

Holder's gaze locked with the king's. *The journal.* Had his father's writings been correct? Had Eligor murdered the son of the land on the other side of the mountains? Did Eligor think Holder a wolf because he suspected he knew the truth?

Movement shifted in the shadows, and murmurs grew as a couple emerged into the light.

Holder choked. How? They were dead. He had stood over their coffins with their daughter sobbing in his arms. He had glimpsed the mangled bodies. Seen the king's guards' corpses. Had interrupted the funeral.

"Lord Frigdor, Lady Ancelle." King Eligor greeted the couple who looked like they'd never met any danger. "Men, calm down."

As the room quieted, Officer Torgord stepped forward. "Holder Lygor, the second charge against you is conspiracy in the attempted murder of Lord Frigdor Harris and Lady Ancelle Harris." His words dimmed to a distant haze, brief clauses striking Holder like they were hot iron. "...witnessed...the guards sacrificed...proved...draw out traitors...determine where loyalties lie..."

When everything cleared, King Eligor was speaking. "I had hope for you, that you would refrain from following in your parents' treacherous footsteps. You reacted rightly to the planted threats on the princess' bedroom wall. I don't know where you fanned your flames of insubordination, or why you targeted the ones I call family, but that ends here. I will not allow threats to my successors and kingdom. Bring in the witness."

Witness? What next? Holder held his breath to keep from dry heaving. His stomach felt like it was being hung from a noose. What more would they do? Would they give him a chance to show his innocence?

Whoever listens, whoever cares, please. King of Uri, if You are real, please.

The prayer ripped from his heart and soul. If there was a deity, if there was some higher power, perhaps it would listen to his plea.

"Specialist," King Eligor greeted.

"My king."

Holder's heart sank into the dread slowly enveloping him.

"Specialist Cetrin, in private questioning, you denied knowing about this criminal's treasonous actions. You have also expressed desire in obtaining your fifth dagger, which would begin your training as a captain."

"Yes, my king." Rogan sounded genuinely shocked. Surely, if he had known, he would have warned Holder.

Then again, perhaps not.

Holder swallowed the rising bile. What could he say and do to convince them of his innocence?

"Lygor has been questioned and found guilty." Knives formed King Eligor's voice. "You have been selected to assist in the implementation of former Specialist and bodyguard Holder Lygor's execution. This is the fifth and final step of loyalty. Completion will earn you your captaincy and fifth dagger."

Holder closed his eyes. How could his life compete with Rogan's dream? Another dry heave rose at the thought of his *death* carried out by someone he thought was his best friend.

He couldn't bring himself to look at Rogan. If the specialist couldn't even keep Ivelle and her family a secret, he would do nothing about Holder's sentence.

Holder couldn't hear Rogan's response through the roaring in his ears. Was his former friend grappling for words to express his acquiescence? Was he vigorously nodding his head? Anticipating the title of captain?

The noise settled just before King Eligor spoke.

"Very well." King Eligor sounded too calm, like something happened he'd long expected. "If you are unwilling to do your duty, you will share your friend's punishment. By my law and decree and power, this is my final word: Holder Lygor and Rogan Cetrin are sentenced to death by hanging tomorrow at dawn."

ACKNOWLEDGMENTS

To my family, both immediate and extended: thank you so much for supporting me in my crazy, insanity-inducing endeavor to write and publish. I couldn't do this without you.

To Mom, for helping me with the final polish, and to Dad and Lil' Sis, for reading, rereading, and re-rereading this story and helping me catch those pesky typos and plot holes.

To Lynette Bonner, for taking my scattered ideas and, from them, creating a stunning cover.

To my beta readers: K.R. Mattson, Brooklyn O'Brennen, Olivia G., Cat, and Katherine. Ladies, you helped me so much in strengthening the story and characters. You five are the reason there are humorous scenes in this tale.

Another round of gratitude goes to K.R. Mattson, who patiently answered my multitude of equine-related questions.

Most importantly, thank You, Lord. May these words bring honor and glory to You. *Soli Deo gloria.*

ABOUT THE AUTHOR

Madisyn Carlin is a Christian, homeschool graduate, blogger, voracious bookdragon, and author. When not spending time with her family or trekking through the mountains, she weaves tales of redemption, faith, and action.

OTHER BOOKS BY MADISYN

Enforcing justice comes with a price.

Detective Redwyn "Red" Deathan will stop at nothing to uncover those behind the ruthless kidnappings of multiple children. But things are not as they seem, and Red's efforts are thwarted at every turn. With each discovery the danger grows, putting Red and the lives of those she cares about at risk. Can she reveal the mastermind's identity before she herself becomes a target?

COMING SOON:

Shattered Reflection
A Snow Queen Retelling

A Past to Bear
featured in
Whitstead Harvestide

ABOUT *A Past to Bear*

The town of Whitstead may change, but not so Eltaen MacGredd, a recluse with a secret to keep, a curse to bear, and a community to protect.

www.ingramcontent.com/pod-product-compliance
Lightning Source LLC
Chambersburg PA
CBHW070238200726
48293CB00005B/1674